The Rolling Stones

A Beyond Good and Evil Novel

Michael Hannan

TiPS Technical Publishing
Chapel Hill, NC

First Printing: August 2013

ISBN (print): 978-1-890586-27-0
ISBN (ebook): 978-1-890586-28-7

Printed in the United States of America. 10 9 8 7 6 5 4 3 2 1

Library of Congress Cataloging-in-Publication Data
Hannan, Michael, 1944-
    The Rolling Stones : a Beyond Good and Evil novel / Michael Hannan.
    1 online resource.
    Description based on print version record and CIP data provided by publisher; resource not viewed.
    ISBN 978-1-890586-28-7 () -- ISBN 978-1-890586-27-0
    1. Undercover operations--Iraq--Fiction. 2. Undercover operations--Iran--Fiction. 3. Iraq--Antiquities--Fiction. 4. Iran--Antiquities--Fiction. I. Title.
    PS3608.A715745
    813'.6--dc23
                        2013028804

The text of this book is composed in Warnock Pro using Adobe InDesign®.
Cover image is Achaemenid Cylinder Seal courtesy of CAIS.
Production services by TIPS Technical Publishing, Inc.
Copy edit by Dale Koontz.

To Gloria

Mathematician,
Jane Austen devotee,
Cackler at Janet Evanovich's Plum series,
Sudoku solver,
New York Times crossword worker,
NYC born and bred,
Adirondacker,
Scourge of exotic vegetation,
Daughter of Neptune,
and
My cutie.

Table of Contents

Acknowledgements

While some details of this book are historically accurate, on the whole it is a work of fiction. Any similarities between the characters of this story and real people (with the exception of those whose actual names I've used) are either coincidence or an unusual need for recognition on the suspect person's part. *Beyond Good and Evil* is a creation of the author's imagination as well as the title of a philosophical work by Friedrich Nietzsche. The inn's setting, however, was the site of another Adirondack inn that had a marvelous restaurant many years ago.

The National Museum of Iraq in Baghdad was looted for three days beginning on April 10th, 2003, and fifteen thousand pieces of art and antiquity, including Sumerian cylinder seals dating back to 3,500 B.C., were stolen from it. About half of those pieces have been tracked down and returned to the museum, mostly through the efforts of the Coalition Task Force. Since Roth, Jassim, Kennedy, Wade, and Socko Lollard are products of my imagination, they were not part of that effort. Matthew Bogdanos, however, was. His qualifications and duties were at least minimally as I've described them.

After the historical verities of the cylinder seals themselves, the looting of the National Museum, and the Coalition's efforts to recover as many pieces as they could, the story becomes fiction, and the sole product of my imagination. I do know that some of the cylinder seals have been returned, however, I have no idea how many were returned or even how many were stolen.

I have taken literary license with the Miami Showband Massacre – which actually took place in 1975 – in the scene where Keagan's father rescues Niles.

Obviously, because Keagan is a fictional character he never fought Eamon McGee, a real Irish boxer.

Many thanks to Don Mellor, author, *Rock Climbing Guide* (WW Norton) and *American Rock* (The Countryman Press) for his help with the technical-climbing terms. Any remaining errors are my fault.

I am also indebted to Gordon Edwards' *A Climber's Guide to Glacier National Park*, for the general description of the route up Mount Cleveland, though I have taken liberties with it for the purposes of my story. I am also indebted to M3 (wherever he is), the wolverine that climbed Mount Cleveland in the winter in under 90 minutes, for a glimpse into the heart and soul of the wild, and to Douglas H. Chadwick for both his research of these magnificent animals and also for his writing of *The Wolverine Way*.

Finally, I wish to thank Robert Kern, Publisher; Dale Koontz, Copy Editor; of TIPS Technical Publishing Inc. for their keen eyes in spotting my many typos, curious constructions, and various other creative forms of literary errata.

While no fiction is purely imaginative, my characters – especially Mick Keagan, Kelly O'Neill, Niles, and Teal – are my creations. Alas, I sometimes wish they were real because I'm very fond of them. I wonder if other writers, especially writers of a series, are also adults who haven't been able to discard their childhood imaginary friends.

Prologue

April 10th, 2003:

In the aftermath of the Coalition invasion of Iraq in 2003, widespread looting occurred amid the chaos of Iraq's authority vacuum. On April 8th, three weeks after the invasion began, the last of the staff at the National Museum of Iraq in Baghdad – barely able to fend off the initial attempts of looters – left the museum fearing for their safety. Two days later, looters broke into the museum. Much of what was stolen was a factor of opportunity, but not all. Saeed ibn Musaiyib and Abdul Awwal, while not master criminals by any stretch of the imagination, knew exactly what they wanted. When the doors were broken through, they were among the first of those to take advantage of their nation's unprotected cultural repository, leading off the three days of unchallenged looting that followed.

While others around them grabbed what could be gotten easily on the first floor, Musaiyib and Awwal made their way downstairs to the underground storage rooms. Bypassing the first three, they entered the fourth and went directly to the cabinets in the far northwest corner, to the most valuable collection in the museum's holdings; 103 cylinder seals, which conveniently for them, if not for the museum, were also the most transportable collection. The seals were thimble size *intaglios* – ranging from less than an inch in length to slightly over two inches – that were used to roll over wet clay to sign official documents thousands of years ago. They were priceless, not

ix

only because of their age, some dating to 3,500 BC, but also because they formed a link between Cuneiform and Sumerian, the latter of which many scholars credit as the first written language.

Musaiyib and Awwal gathered up the seals, still in their trayed boxes, put them into a day pack, and walked out the museum's front door as new looters streamed in. Meanwhile, some of the early arrivals struggled out with weighty sculptures, unwieldy vases, and cumbersome reliefs.

In just three days, slightly more than 15,000 pieces were stolen. When the museum finally re-opened in February of 2009, approximately 8,500 pieces had been returned, the result of an intense international effort. However, only three of the cylinder seals had been recovered by the museum's re-opening.

One

April 28th, 2011:

This time, Kelly called first. She never had before. She just showed up, which was fine with Keagan. He didn't care how she came to him, only that she did. This time was different, though, and her reason for calling made all the difference in the world to Keagan and later would to Niles and Teal as well, because now people were trying to kill her. At least the Iranians were. The Americans would be as well if they knew who or where she was.

Usually, when Kelly visited Keagan she flew into Montreal from Dublin or sometimes from London, drove south, crossed the U.S./Canada border crossing at Champlain and continued south for another eighty miles to Lake Placid where Keagan owned an inn with the unusual name of *Beyond Good and Evil.*

Those tracking Kelly were professionals, but their task wasn't easy because so was she. Kelly had several sets of credentials: identification documents – including a number of passports – and matching credit cards. She rotated her sets of financials, photo ID's, and citizenship credentials regularly. Currently, she had two passports issued by Ireland; one by England; one by Australia; and two by the U.S. All were authentic, but only one was legal. They were easy for her to get as long as the issuing country had a substantial Irish population. On this visit, she was using the Australian passport – a recent acquisition – a matching driver's license, and even a Canberra library card that matched her address on the other two documents. Her credit cards were brand new to her but had been issued two years earlier and used by others, which created an irregular purchasing history and made the holder difficult to pattern. They currently carried zero balances; they were covered by a branch of the organization for which she worked.

The new credentials should have been all the cover she needed, but Kelly didn't stay alive doing what she did by taking chances. In fact, she took many chances, but they were always calculated and coverable ones. This time she flew from Belfast to Paris and then into JFK in New York, and took a cab into the city to the Loews Regency, where she had a reservation under the odd name of Finn Ni Cool. Shortly after checking in, she took a shower, redid her hair, ruffled the bed, and was picked up by two contacts who put her up in a protected house in Yonkers. In addition to access to official documents, Kelly also had contacts around the world, or at least wherever the Irish diaspora had taken the children of Erin. The next morning they saw her safely onto the Amtrak Adirondack. After checking out the train's other cars for suspicious persons, they felt confident there were none even though three of the passengers were Muslim and two were U.S. military. Despite their confidence, her escorts stayed with her in the same car – both facing Kelly, one in front, the other in the back, all the way to Albany. They left her there to continue alone, certain she hadn't been followed.

The work Kelly did provided her many perquisites; however, it also brought not a few dangers. She raised money for the unification of Ireland – a lot of money – usually by liberating artwork that someone else had already stolen. The Iranians couldn't care less about her political activities, but they did care about her search for the cylinder seals. They wanted them for themselves because they believed, and they weren't alone, that they originated in what is today southwest Iran, meaning they were rightfully the property of Iran and not of Iraq. The Iraqis, of course, had other ideas. The Americans' – two Americans and one Canadian actually – antinomy toward Kelly stemmed from her temerity for trying to co-opt the $25 million payday they anticipated for finding and selling the seals.

The Iranians were following her as their best hope of finding the seals. However, once she located them, they would have no further use for her and she would become a liability. Kelly wasn't sure about the Iraqis. They had the most obvious legal claim to the cylinder seals and wanted them returned without having their provenance being settled by an international court, a ruling that could take even longer than the Iran-Iraq War (1980-88) and probably end in a similar fashion. What she wasn't sure of was the Iraqis' participation. If they were in this mix, their motivation was obvious.

The Coalition Forces that had invaded Iraq had been embarrassed by the looting of the National Museum, and had even been accused of letting it happen, so when their embarrassment became international, they formed a task force of their own, charged with returning Iraq's antiquities. They had the resources of a network of countries to aid in their recovery and had been responsible for the return of almost all of the 8,500 pieces to date, so perhaps the Iraqis would defer to them. Still, Kelly wasn't sure, but when you have group of former U.S. Special Forces and an Iranian Takavaran unit trying to kill you or torture out of you the whereabouts of the cylinder seals, whether the inept Iraqis were in the mix or not was of little additional consequence. So, while on different timetables and with different motivations – financial, jingoistic, legal – at least two groups would like to see Kelly dead. Two that she was sure of, in any event.

* * *

It had been a cold winter in New York. While the daffodils were in bloom and the trees were budding in Yonkers, the morning sky was gray with pink streaks. By Albany, it was raining and the landscape looked like Belfast's in winter. At the Westport Amtrak station on an open Lake Champlain, where Keagan met Kelly's train, it was still raining and holdover patches of snow mottled the hillsides. By the time they had gotten to Elizabethtown – only nine miles and five hundred feet higher than the train station – the rain had turned to wet, fat flakes of snow. At *Beyond Good and Evil* – over the still frozen Lake Placid – the snowflakes swirled small and hard.

There were no guests at the inn. While the bar was open year round, the rest of the property was closed during April. Keagan kept the bar open for those locals who either didn't have the wherewithal or the inclination to travel south to assure themselves that winter had indeed ended in other parts of the country.

Keagan took Kelly to his private office on the lake. He had a business office in the inn's main building and a lodge on the property where he usually lived, but his lakeside office was where he went when he wanted to be alone. Only Niles, who had a key to it, and Kelly when she came to visit, were allowed in. Not even Teal was permitted there; Teal, who was part of the team. But Teal had his own secrets from Keagan, though fewer and fewer as the years passed. So did Niles for that matter. Kelly was the only one from whom he kept no secrets, nor she from him.

'Office' was a bit of a misnomer. The cedar-log structure built on the lakeshore contained four large rooms; a bedroom with a full bath, a spacious and well-appointed kitchen, a gun and equipment room, and a combination living room/dining room/library/den/office that took up half of the floor plan. The gun and equipment room was essentially a walk-in gun vault where he stored his weapons, outdoor gear, project equipment, and emergency cash. Keagan put Kelly's bags in the bedroom. When he came out, he lit a fire in the fireplace that had been prepared with two sheets of crinkled newspaper and split cherry wood, stacked log-cabin style.

"We're having an appeasement party at five," said Keagan. "We were supposed to have it this morning. It was going to be a brunch at ten o'clock, but then you called. Also, it was five degrees at ten o'clock, so we postponed it until this afternoon. Would you like a drink before we go down?"

"Please, it's been a few hectic days. Make it neat, will you. Whom do you have to appease? You haven't fired Cassie or Jimmy the Gimp or Teal have you? Or any of the other curious characters for whom you provide a refuge?"

Keagan poured Kelly two ounces of Jameson 12 into a Waterford crystal tumbler and a similar amount of Jack Daniel's for himself.

"No, nothing so drastic, though this winter has got a number of the refugees on edge. No, we're hoping to appease the gods of winter, convince them to take a break for a few months, and also to cheer up Cassie and Ky."

"What's wrong with them?"

"Cassie just back from Grand Cayman, where she's been visiting friends for the last three weeks. And, of course, Ky, who has made a good go of dealing with her move here, knows that in south Louisiana she'd be wearing shorts and a T-shirt by now, not a parka and snow pacs."

"So, what have you gotten yourself into, Kelly?"

"Oh, this is a grand cockup, Mick, but let's just sit here by the fire and warm ourselves with our drinks and each other, and we'll talk after your Druidic appeasement."

Two

Keagan and Kelly met Jimmy the Gimp and Cassie on their way to the greenhouse. The Gimp was trying to offer an arm to Cassie so she wouldn't fall on the ice. While Teal had sanded the steps that led from the main house to the greenhouse, there were still some icy patches where the wind had blown the sand away and burnished the ice to a polished translucence. Cassie was having none of it. She thought of the Gimp as a bigot and a misogynist. While she had great respect for him as a *maître d'*, she couldn't get passed his strange behaviors, which were several and varied. Jimmy loved Cassie platonically and knew his persona drove her crazy, and while he thought the world of her, he took some pleasure in that knowledge.

"Leave me alone, you bigot," Cassie said as she swatted at the Gimp.

"Cassie, you dark-skinned people aren't as agile on ice and snow as we Belarusians are; let me give you my arm."

Anyone else would have said 'a hand', but part of the Gimp's quirky persona dwelt in the early twentieth century.

Cassie swatted at him again, "Get away from me you bigot."

Cassie was naturally more coordinated than the Gimp. In fact, when Keagan first saw her in Jamaica, she was in mid-pirouette of a roundhouse kick that planted her left foot just above the right ear of her two-hundred pound, male boss, knocking him unconscious. He had given her an ultimatum – *fuck or forget promotion*. While

Cassie had been conditioned by the early circumstances of her life to appear diffident, she didn't lack confidence; but ice was not her element and 'different' is the greatest test of confidence.

"Jimmy, Cassie, everything all right here?" Keagan asked.

"Fine, Mr. Keagan, oh, hello Miss Kelly, nice to see you again, just that this bigot doesn't think we dark-skinned people can take care of ourselves."

"Hey Kelly, good to have you back," acknowledged Jimmy the Gimp. "That's not what I said, Mick. I was just trying to help her over the icy patches."

Keagan knew that Solomon would have a tough time sorting out their differences, and he knew he wasn't Solomon.

"Well, if you have things under control, we'll see you down there."

Keagan and Kelly went ahead. The Gimp gave up his Sir Walter Raleigh routine and left Cassie to fend for herself. She took one step and uncharacteristically slipped and dumped herself on her backside, albeit a very shapely backside currently covered by a long down coat. Teal and Anjali, his daughter, came along behind her after she picked herself up and was brushing off her said shapely, but-now-bruised, backside. Pretending they hadn't seen Cassie's flop – although she knew they had – Anjali and Teal could barely contain their laughter as they asked her to join them.

Ky had come to the inn just before the team's last project. She and Teal had been high school sweethearts but had married other spouses for reasons that made sense at the time. Both of their spouses were dead now. When Teal had fled south Louisiana after the death of his wife, Ky had no idea where he had gone. They talked occasionally, but otherwise had no contact. Then things came to a head last year. Buck, Ky's husband who had been a state trooper, died of injuries sustained three years earlier in a shoot-out with drug smugglers in the Atchafalaya Swamp near Morgan City. When Teal's nemesis Cleo Aucoin tried using Ky to get to him, she called Teal, and he told her how to get to where he was. They were married now. Anjali was

Ky's goddaughter, so the marriage hadn't created any stepmother-stepdaughter strains. But Ky was a Chitimacha Indian from south Louisiana and she had never experienced a winter as she had in the last six months. Now in late April, it didn't look like it would ever quit. It stayed just cold enough so that the lake ice hadn't melted, and the rain, while promising spring, instead alternated with snow.

Ky, looking for a way to be a part of *Beyond Good and Evil* rather than just Teal's wife, gave Keagan the idea of building a greenhouse to provide fresh flowers for the inn. He had been thinking along the same lines for a while but didn't want to undertake the project himself. He had enough to do. If it would make the winter more bearable for her that would be an added bonus. The inn had been successful before Ky, but if she were happy, Teal would be happy, and Keagan didn't want to lose Teal, who was his head of buildings and grounds and who could fix anything. More importantly, he was a part of the team. Losing him would be a big loss.

Outside, lower portions of the greenhouse were still hoared in frost, but the electric heaters warmed the interior up nicely. The flowers were all in pots, arranged on plats that sat upon potting tables. There wasn't much color yet, but they were budding, and next year the greenhouse would be lush and full of petunias, geraniums, orchids, and herbs and spices for Cassie's kitchen, with the latter two sproutings being Keagan's suggestions.

"Jimmy, isn't that the waiter from the closing party two autumns ago, the one you told to take off his earring or leave?" asked Keagan, indicating a young, handsome black man, serving drinks.

"Yeah, Mick, I've hired him for the season."

"Why the change in attitude?"

"Easy; the kid's good. I've seen him at a couple of places in town. He works three different houses putting together his week. Besides, he agreed to leave the earring home. I thought the party would be a good place for him to start. Afterward, I can show him the dining room, bar, and kitchen. Then I have him follow me around for the first week after the dining room opens. He's smart enough to catch on; it's just a matter of whether he's willing to go with the program." The Gimp's prejudices – feigned and real – didn't cloud his judgment about competency. If he found someone who was smart and willing to work, he found a way to work him in.

The appeasement group included Ky, Teal, and Anjali; Jimmy the Gimp and Reverend, the Gimp's best waiter; Tippler O'Neill, the inn's alcoholic fill-in bartender; Cowboy, the dishwasher; and a few other full-time staff who lived on the grounds. Niles brought a lady friend.

Some of the plats had been moved to free up one of the potting tables. The table was draped in white linen, on which sat platters of cold hors d'oeuvres; crudités, cheeses from Montreal, and melons and grapes from South America. There were also chaffing dishes of hot hors d'oeuvres; jerked chicken from Cassie, a Ro-Tel dip from Ky, the Gimp's quiche, Teal's crawfish beignets, and Keagan's *Blue Highways* shrimp with warm French bread.

The chief libation was champagne, a respectable Tattinger. There was also a single-malt Scotch, Jameson 12 for Kelly, Jack Daniel's, and Absolut vodka for Bloody Marys. There was also special-ordered beer; Bass for Niles and Dixie Voodoo for Teal.

Everyone knew everyone, so it was unlike the usual cocktail parties where guests arrive, are greeted by the host, circulate among friends, introduce themselves to unfamiliar guests, and then go to the bar. The staff hit the bar without fanfare. Keagan watched the bartender that the Gimp had hired as a waiter. He handled the orders efficiently and congenially. He was good. Keagan knew he would be if the Gimp hired him, but he always liked to follow up on things.

Kelly was over talking with Cassie, and Ky was with her.

"So, Ky, how have you adjusted to this great frozen wilderness?" asked Kelly.

"It sure is different. Teal tried to warn me, but his words didn't match the experience. He told me how long the winters were and that it snowed and that it was cold. I can't deny that he said the winters lasted eight months. But in south Louisiana, it hardly ever snows and if it does it melts the next day. It doesn't snow two feet at a time or worse, two inches a day for thirty days in a row. Shit. Oh sorry Cassie, I got to clean up my act a little. I'm used to talking to shrimpers, roustabouts, and other roughnecks. Anyway, and cold! How do you explain fifty-four below zero to someone who's a Chitimacha Indian? We don't have thermometers that go that low in south Louisiana. Fifty-four below zero – no wind chill, actual temperature!"

"Or lack thereof," said Kelly. Cassie shivered and nodded.

"But the worst was the gray. I never saw the sun in January. I sh... kid you not. We had more sun during Katrina than we had here last winter in Lake Placid, which was none."

"I've gotta stop complaining. I've got Teal and I've got Anjali. I didn't have either in Jeanerette. So, all in all, the winter was fine. I'll get used to it. Teal has."

"What about you, Cassie?" Kelly said. "Mick tells me you just got back from visiting friends in Grand Cayman."

"Friends and family, yes. You know, I can't go back to Jamaica, so some of my family come over to Grand Cayman. We visit and catch up on everything that has happened in the last year. You know, who died, who got married, who has a new child. Family things."

"That must have been nice, but tough when you came back here and saw everything still frozen."

"It was – both a nice visit and a little depressing seeing the ice still on the lake – but as soon as the inn opens up, I'll get back into the swing. I'll be busy and I'll be fine."

"What's the weather like in Ireland, Kelly?" asked Ky.

"Awful! Our plague is rain, not snow, but still it's awful. And Belfast, where Mick and I grew up, is the worst. It's amazing that over a half million people live there. But circumstances like birth or marriage put you somewhere and you get used to it. You'd think that when the Irish leave Ireland for the States, they'd go to Florida or California, some place that's sunny. No, they go to New York and Boston – more cold and wet. Even the ones who went to Australia, at least the original ones, they went in chains so they didn't have much of a choice.

"Ky, tell me about this greenhouse. How did you come up with such an idea?"

"Well, in spite of my complaining about the winter here, I'm not much for whining, so I decided if I'm going to live in this ice box, I had better do something about it. I watched Cassie and Anjali in the kitchen, and Cassie comes from even farther south than I do, so I figured if those two southern girls could adjust, so can I. And not just us girls; if you don't pay attention to Teal's accent and skin color, he looks and acts like he was born here. He actually gave me the idea. He told me, 'Cassie brought her cooking with her, what can you bring from south Louisiana? She and Anjali already have the kitchen staked out, so it has to be something else.'"

Cassie laughed at her possessiveness of the kitchen, but didn't deny it.

"Well, I'm pretty good at raising hell, but so is everyone else around here – too much competition, and I got to set a better example for Anjali."

Cassie said, "amen to that" and laughed again.

"I got a pretty good voice and I'm real good at two-steppin', but I don't want to be a lounge singer and that's not what the inn is about anyway. So I asked myself, what could I bring from home that would fit in here? What would brighten up this bleak place? And then it came to me; flowers. I didn't think Mick would go for the idea because of the cost, but Teal said, 'you won't know until you ask him'. So I did. And what do you know, he had been thinking along the same lines for some time but didn't have anyone here he thought could pull it off. So that's how it started. What you see budding here is my first crop, and over there on those back tables I have herbs and some spices sprouting. I don't expect it will be a roaring success the first year, but I'll continue to make adjustments and I'll get it right after a while. Mick seems patient enough."

"Yes, he is, isn't he?" answered Kelly wistfully. "Aye, I see my glass is down. Can I get either of you something?"

"No, thank you," said Cassie.

"I'll walk over with you, at least as far as Teal and Anjali," said Ky. "Cassie, come join us."

"So what have you been plotting over there with the women?" asked Keagan.

"More like reconnaissance work for you, Mick. Ky's very happy with the greenhouse, and she's smart enough to know that it's a multi-year project. In spite of your awful winters here, I think the flowers and herbs will help her with the adjustment. And she has Teal and Anjali, but of course they are portable. She seems fine, but you had better find a man for Cassie. It's not just the winter. She goes down to Grand Cayman, where her friends' and family's news is largely about family – who's married, who's had a baby. She's lonely, Mick. And while she didn't say anything, now that Ky's here, Anjali will be less her daughter even if she continues to work in the kitchen. It's only natural."

"Aye, Did I ever tell you about Jimmy the Gimp and *Lester the Molester*?"

"Oh, Mick, and who is Lester the Molester? I hope he's not a new addition here."

"Quite the contrary. The problem with finding a suitable man for Cassie is that there are so few Blacks among the locals, and there aren't too many suitable white men who are so liberal as to be attracted to Cassie, in spite of her beauty and her cooking. Let me rephrase that. There may be more than enough, but few who believe that their friends would accept her."

"Lester the Molester was a black reprobate, who lived in Lake Placid. He didn't get his nickname from Jimmy the Gimp or any of the other Whites in town, rather, the Blacks who live here gave it to him. He was attracted to Cassie and used to come to the inn, asking questions about her. He'd try to time his visits to when she was just finishing up for the evening and would flirt with her when she came out to the bar for her closing Ting."

"The Gimp figured out what he was doing. So, one night he goes down to the Grill, a locals' bar in town – you've been there – where Lester is shooting pool. He challenges him to a game. Lester's good, and he knows that the Gimp is good, but he wanted to make a racial pride thing out of the challenge. You know, beat *whitey*. They started playing for $20 a game. The Gimp is telling him, it's just a friendly game, but Lester says, 'cut the shit, this be about who be the best pool shooter in town.' The Gimp strings him along, drinking a beer between every game offering to buy Lester a drink. Lester stays with Cokes. The Gimp's winning most of the games but only by a ball or two, and Lester figures he's got to crash soon, all the beer the Gimp's drinking. Lester does manage to win a few games and make some nice shots. He gets cocky and raises the ante every time he wins the table back. He raises it to $50 a game, then $100, then $500. Still, Lester is into the Gimp for over $1,000, so he raises the stakes to $2,000 a game. The Gimp questions whether he can cover that kind of bet. He says he can and that it doesn't matter because he's going to win, so they play for $2,000. Jimmy can cover it."

"Lester's in bad position for the nine ball shot, the game winner, so he buries the Gimp behind his one remaining ball, leaving him with what looks like an impossible shot; the cue and Jimmy's ball are kissing. The Gimp looks the shot over, looks at Lester, barely strokes his cue stick, and *massés* his ball into the corner pocket making the shot look like child's play. Not only does he make the trick shot, but he leaves himself in beautiful position for the nine, which, of course, he makes.

"The Gimp tells Lester to pony up. Lester says he's a little light – like about $3,000 light. The Gimp takes his IOU and explains reality to Lester. He says, 'Lester, as you said earlier, let's cut the shit. You don't have the $3,000 to cover this IOU, and this wasn't just a pool game. You've been hanging around *Beyond Good and Evil*, trying to have your way with Cassie O'Sullivan. Everyone I know, even your own people, call you 'Lester the Molester,' so I don't want you near her. There aren't many of your people in town, so I probably couldn't convince her that you are the lowlife scum that you are. Instead, I'm going to tell Niles to collect this for me. I'll give him a couple of C's as a collection fee. You know Niles don't you, the bartender at the inn who put those three G-balls in the hospital last year. He's not nearly as understanding as I am, Lester. He's out of town for a day or two, but the minute he gets back I'm going to give him this note. I suggest you take the Dog south before he returns.'"

"Jayus, Mick, does Cassie know any of this?"

"No. The Gimp told me and Niles, and you're the only one I've ever told."

"Who would have thought, Mick."

"The Gimp's a complicated guy. What you see isn't what you get, unless you're around him all the time the way I am. He thinks the world of Cassie. He's a professional, she's a professional, and that's his metric, at least in this case. He has many metrics."

"But what about all the racial slurs, the jokes, the bigotry?"

"What bigotry? Did you ever see him discourage customers because of their race? Do you remember the bartender? The black one, I might add. He worked the season-end party two years ago."

"Is he the one who Jimmy wanted to send packing because he was wearing an earring?"

"The very same. The Gimp has hired him for the season. The kid's good, I've been watching him. Anybody can come here as long as they're civil. Anybody can work here, as long as they're professional according to the Gimp's personal professional code."

"But what about his code?"

"Have you ever seen a better run dining room?"

"No, Mick, I can't say I have, but I don't know how you keep all these colorful characters in line."

"I don't, I just establish a standard. Why don't you get us a couple a drinks? I've got to get ready to put some polish on this affair."

Keagan read seasonal passages from Yeats, Behan, Wilde, and Joyce, finishing off with a reading of *Liadan of Corcu Duibhne* in Irish, then lying about the translation. Everyone thought the Seventh Century poem was beautiful, because Keagan's revisionist translation made them feel wistful about winter slipping away. Kelly looked at him queerly but didn't say anything.

In little more than an hour, the group had had their full of *hors d'oeuvres* and most of them even of alcohol. Cassie was sitting with Teal and Anjali and Ky or as Cassie referred to them, 'Teal's family'. She didn't feel jealous of them – a bit pensive perhaps, but not jealous. Ky told the Gimp to just clean up the party stuff and she would get the greenhouse back in order tomorrow. The new waiter, whose name turned out to be Dylan, although the Gimp had already come up with a moniker for him, had begun breaking down the bar, showing that he knew that the fastest way to close down a party was to pack up the booze.

Niles asked Keagan if he needed him right away. Keagan told him, no, he'd fill him in tomorrow after he got the specifics from Kelly.

"Enjoy the rest of the evening. From what I know so far, nothing is so immediate that it has to be dealt with tonight."

Three

Keagan and Kelly were in Keagan's lakeside office. "Are you still hungry?" Keagan asked.

"No, I ate my fill at the party. That was a wonderful spread, Mick. What were those puff pastry things that Teal made?"

"Oh...the crawfish beignets. Those are good. I could eat a dozen of those."

"I think I did."

"Another drink?"

"Aye, just a wee one. I think I've settled in now."

Keagan made the drinks and rekindled the fire, adding a new stack of split cherry to it. They caught and flamed blue and red.

"So, tell me about this grand cockup you've gotten yourself into," said Keagan as he handed Kelly a small, neat Jameson 12 and settled in next to her.

"Aye, it is that. Where to start?"

"The beginning is usually a good place," said Keagan.

"Aye, but which one? All right, hmm...all right. Since most of my previous visits here have been tied to the projects we've worked on, I'll use the project as a starting point."

"When the Coalition Forces invaded Iraq in 2003, chaos erupted in the way it always does with war, especially in repressive regimes. Saddam Hussein was trying to fight off the Coalition Forces, and the Coalition Forces hadn't yet taken control. Iraqis long subjugated under Saddam's oppression, suddenly found themselves *sui juris*. As you know, one of the common manifestations of anarchy is looting. And since most citizens profited little under Saddam's regime, they were more interested in what they could do for themselves rather than what they could do for their country. So when the looting began, many Iraqis took full advantage of the situation, especially in Baghdad. If it wasn't nailed down all around, they took it."

"Excuse me, Kelly, is all of this necessary?" asked Keagan. "We both have too much experience with war."

"Yes, Mick, I think so. Bear with me, please. Grand cockups get that way because they are so very complicated, and this is the most complicated project I've ever brought you."

"Remember that Iraq is a British creation and a crucible of ethnic and religious enmities, rather than a conflation of common interests. The Kurds aren't Arabs, and while the Sunnis and the Shiites are both Muslims and get along in some countries, they don't in Iraq. Sort of like the Catholics and Protestants in Ireland, as opposed to America, for example, where religion doesn't seem to factor into employment or housing, at least not nowadays."

"So, in Iraq before the invasion, you have a repressive regime, populated with people who are more concerned with their own needs than with those of their country. Add to that mess some religious contention with its attendant political and economic conflicts, throw in a stock of chaos, and you're well on your way to a grand cockup."

"OK, but what about the project? How is all this background linked to it and our immediate problems?"

"You mean my immediate problems, Mick?"

"If they are yours, then they are mine, Kelly. Moreover, if they are mine – even tangentially – they are Niles' and I suspect Teal's as well. So, how does all of this - Iraq's history, culture, religion, and invasion - affect us?"

"Because in that post-invasion vacuum of authority, looters broke into Iraq's National Museum in Baghdad and stripped it of more than 15,000 pieces of art and antiquity, the most important of which was a collection of 103 cylinder seals."

"Cylinder seals?" Keagan dredged up the memory after a second. "They're the thimble-like rings that officials used to sign documents, aren't they? Some of them are more than 5,000 years old."

"Correct as usual, Mick. Anything else?"

"Yes, they're a link between Cuneiform and Sumerian, the latter of which is credited as being the first written language that has morphemes – the basic unit of language – a syntax of sorts, and even a rudimentary grammar."

"Right again," said Kelly. "But why should that surprise me given your linguistic background and proclivities."

"They must be worth a fortune. I mean, I know we never do low-end recovery, what with the Picassos, the Fabergé Imperial Eggs, and the Mazarin Diamonds. Still, their collective worth must pale in comparison to the cultural importance – if that's the right term, *species importance*, really – of 5,000-year-old links to the world's first written language."

"Exactly! But there is still more. The Sumerians settled in Mesopotamia, in the Fertile Crescent. Remember, the land between the Tigris and Euphrates Rivers. Actually, their territory wasn't limited by those rivers, especially on the Tigris side; It even extended into what is modern day southwest Iran. Moreover, scholars believe it was there in approximately what is modern-day Susa, Iran that the cylinder seals originated."

"So, if I may be so pedantic as to fill in the obvious," said Keagan, "the cylinder seals are out there in the hands of looters, without national protection; the Iraqis want them back as part of their cultural heritage; their recalcitrant neighbors (in a part of the world where there is a lot of competition for that title), the Iranians, see their chance now to regain what they and some academics believe is rightfully theirs; the looters want to sell them; and I'll bet there's an iniquitous, rich guy trying to buy them."

"Almost the complete picture."

"Almost? Well, of course the American cops are involved, or do we have to go overseas?"

"Not overseas, but given that the Iraqi invasion was the hobby-horse of your former President or one of his puppet masters, the Coalition Forces – led by the Yanks, of course – are doing their best to recover all of Iraq's treasures, especially the cylinder seals. I guess they're the substitute for the cops who usually get involved one way or another in our projects."

"Finished?" asked Keagan.

"Not quite. There doesn't seem to be a – what did you call him – *iniquitous, rich guy* trying to buy them, or at least, not one that I'm aware of."

"Finished now?"

"Yes," said Kelly.

"I've lost count. How many groups are trying to kill you?"

"At this point, I think only one. There would be at least one other if they knew I existed and was trying to do what they're doing, albeit for different reasons," answered Kelly.

"Who are they?"

"Of the original 103 cylinder seals that were stolen from the National Museum, only three have been returned. The seals hadn't surfaced for five years. Nothing. Then in 2008, three of them re-appeared. I believe that one of the original looters, Abdul Awwal, pinched three of the seals from his partner and tried to sell them to a Coalition soldier. Awwal was subsequently tortured and killed, but not before giving up his partner, who, if I am correct, is Saeed ibn Musaiyib. The soldier must have been spooked by Awwal's death or had run out of time or patience because he missed the three seals Awwal had with him. They were later discovered by the Baghdad police when they investigated the murder."

"I believe that several soldiers, at least two, probably three, and almost certainly American, although there is a slim possibility that they were Canadian, are now searching for Musaiyib. I say possibly Canadian because while Canada refused to send troops to Iraq the second time around, there were some exchange officers there who were temporarily attached to British units. Not many, but a few, so they could have been Canadian."

"How did you learn about this? I mean, the specifics of the robbery? There isn't an Irish presence in Iraq."

Kelly ran an intelligence service, which she designed for Sinn Féin, the political arm of the IRA, but almost all of her intelligence came from countries that had significant Irish populations.

"No *significant presence*, but there are two regiments of Irish troops, *The Irish Guards* and *The Royal Irish Regiment*, also serving with the British Army. While both of those regiments recruit in Northern Ireland, some of our *boyos* also serve in them. They tipped me off about the cylinder seals, but that's not where I got most of my information."

"When I heard about the looting of the National Museum, I searched for any information I could find on it. Generally, the news stories were overviews. There were no inventories given until I came across one *Times* article – *London Times,* not your *New York Times* – that mentioned the cylinder seals. That piqued my interest. Then I read about Awwal's murder. I ran across a picture documenting the initial looting of the Museum and, who's in the vanguard, but Awwal and another man."

"How did you know it was Awwal?"

"There was also a picture of him with the murder story. I suspect the torture altered his appearance significantly, so *Reuters* used a picture from Awwal's national identity card. The photos matched."

"Why did you say his torturers could have been Canadian with so few Canadian troops in Iraq?"

"A flattened can of Molson Export was found at the scene. Well, in front of the machine shop where Awwal was murdered. There was only one can, as though one of them had dropped it when they were cleaning up inside and they missed it," said Kelly.

"Maybe it rolled out of a vehicle," said Keagan. "Of course, it could have been there for months. Besides, we sell that at the inn."

"Police didn't think it was litter; the sun hadn't faded the can much, and this was definitely Canadian. You sell the American version that has a lower alcohol percentage. The can listed its *alcohol by volume* on it. Too high for America," answered Kelly.

"How do you know that there was more than one torturer?"

"Had to be at least two because Awwal was apparently held fast to a chair. There were strap marks on him; three, in fact. The bruising was slight, so they must have been removed right after he was shot, or maybe even just before. Anyway, I'd say probably three. Two to hold him down, one to fasten the straps."

"So, a group of either American or Canadian soldiers – could even be private contractors or a combination of both – are also trying to locate the seals."

"Yes, and of course, that makes me a competitor."

"How do they know who you are?"

"I don't know. I'm not even sure they know my identity, but somebody who's interested in the seals seems to know that there is a Finn Ni Cool," Keagan recognized one of Kelly's aliases, "who, with the help of a very capable team, has made some high-end art recoveries in the last few years. My contacts who scurried me out of New York and hid me in Yonkers told me that my room at the Loews Regency was broken into later that night. Also, I know that there have been several attempts from North America to hack into my computer system. Unsuccessful attempts, mind you. The Brits have attempted it several times, but they seem to have tired of taking world tours around the Internet, so I don't think it's them. Could be the Iranians, although I wouldn't have thought they were that organized yet."

"Anything else?"

"Well, there's a task force, a spin-off of the Coalition Forces' recovery effort, charged specifically with finding and returning the cylinder seals."

"Is that it?"

"We have to consider the possibility that the Iraqis aren't going to sit back and wait for the Yanks to return their treasure. However, I believe they lack the necessary talent. And, even if they could drum up a team with sufficient genius, without Saddam Hussein threatening to wipe out their families if they don't locate the seals, they probably lack sufficient incentive. The Republican Guard was capable enough, but this new batch is a bunch of bungling idiots. I don't think I have to worry about them, or not yet anyhow. Still, it's something to consider."

"OK, so a grand total of four groups; the presumptive thieves, the Iranians, the Coalition's Task Force, and possibly the Iraqis, all of whom wish you ill, and at least one or two groups terminally so?"

"Right now, just the presumptive thieves and the Iranians, yes. As we get closer, maybe even the Iraqis. The Yanks may want to arrest me, but I doubt they'll be trying to kill me."

"You're lucky I've got Niles and Teal, although Teal's participation in this one is at best problematic now that he is married. Without them this would be a bitch to recruit for; I'd have to go up to the *Big O* for troops," said Keagan, referring to the regional mental health lock up.

It was still early, not yet ten o'clock, when Keagan dampened the fire and he and Kelly went to bed. It had been months since they had been together, but Keagan realized that Kelly needed to be held right now more than she needed love-making. So they held each other fiercely until they fell asleep. The morning found them in the same position.

Four

March-May, 2011:

Major General Firouz Bandari had just left the office of the Supreme Leader, Grand Ayatollah Sayyid Ali Hosseine Khamenei, in the holy city of Qom. The meeting had been very brief. The Supreme Leader told the General that he had a special mission for him and that he was to report directly to President Ahmadinejad from whom he would get specific instructions. The Supreme Leader added that the General should follow Ahmadinejad's instructions as though they were his own. Not waiting for confirmation, the Supreme Leader dismissed him.

An hour later, the General was shown into the Iranian President's office in Tehran. Ahmadinejad greeted him warmly and asked him if he'd like some refreshments. The General knew his being there was not a social meeting, but rather a serious matter of state, so he wisely declined the President's offer.

"General, have a seat, please," said Ahmadinejad. "I assume you've already met with the Supreme Leader."

"Yes, I have, Mr. President. But all he told me was that you had a special mission for me which you would explain when we met. He also said that I was to report directly to you and only to you."

"Correct on both counts, General. Let me start at the beginning. Almost eight years ago, when the Coalition Forces invaded Iraq, the National Museum in Baghdad was looted. Among the antiquities that were stolen were 103 Mesopotamian cylinder seals. However, since they originated in what is present-day southwest Iran, they rightfully belong to the citizens of our country. The government of Iraq stole them from Iran and now their citizens – having strayed from the tenets of Islam and been corrupted by western ways – have demonstrated their unworthiness to possess them by looting the seals from their own national museum for their personal benefit."

"The seals have been missing for eight years now, but recently our agents have uncovered evidence that suggests they have been taken to the West, presumably to be sold. Not to be sold back to the Iraqi government, but worse – to the meretricious infidels."

Ahmadinejad paused, allowing time for the import of his words to register with the General.

"Your mission, General, is to ensure that such a travesty does not take place. I want you to hand-pick a small, elite unit, charged with locating the cylinder seals, taking possession of those seals, and returning them to their rightful place, specifically, the *Muze-ye Irân-e Bâstân*, the archaeological holdings of the National Museum of Iran here in Tehran."

"I'll leave the details to you, General, but I want to be perfectly clear; I am holding you personally responsible for the success of this mission. Moreover, I expect you to keep me informed as to your progress. All is in your hands, *Fi Amanullah*."

"I will see to it, Mr. President," said General Bandari.

The following morning, Major General Bandari met with Colonel Atashe Zare, the head of Takavar. Takavar was a naval commando force made up of approximately two hundred soldiers. While technically a naval unit, it fell under the direct command of the regular Iranian Army, or *Artesh*. *Tak* in Persian meant attack, and thus, a Takavar was an attacker, specifically, a covert attacker. Takavar candidates were hand-picked and trained for a variety of missions, including dry-land actions far from the sea. In addition to traditional naval special operations, such as hydrological reconnaissance and beach head demolitions, Takavar commandos were charged with small-unit raids that involved sabotage, demolitions, or assassinations, as well as kidnappings or hostage rescues. This was why the General chose this unit to carry out Ahmadinejad's mission. If full responsibility for finding the cylinder seals was to fall on him, Major General Bandari was going to do everything in his considerable power to ensure the successful return of the cylinder seals to Iran, their place of origin. While the mission was an unusual one for a military unit, he fully believed that his best chance for success was with Takavar.

Since it was Iran's elite military unit, Takavar's selection process was rigorous. To be eligible for selection, a candidate must have at least two years of regular service in the Iranian Armed Forces and only males could apply. If an individual was selected, he underwent a strenuous training regimen, much of which was created by members of the former Soviet Union *Spetznas* units and the German KSK naval commandos. The KSK *Kommando Spezialkräfte* (Special Forces Command), itself an elite military unit, was modeled on the British Army's SBS (Special Boat Service) and the U.S. Navy SEALS.

Training for Takavar was a twelve-month process. First, the trainee must meet the minimum physical requirements specified. If the candidate met these requirements, he was sent to various schools. The first eight weeks involved general physical training, then dive school, jump school, weapons school, unarmed combat school, land-warfare school, and finally, close-quarter-combat school. After completing his training, the prospective Takavar joined a team and served out a six-month probationary period before becoming a full-fledged commando.

General Bandari explained the mission to Colonel Zare, adding that it had been delegated to him by both the Supreme Leader and the President.

"Given the importance of this mission," said Bandari, "I believe that its best chance for success lies with your commandos."

Takavar was usually broken down into eight smaller units, but, after a short discussion, the two agreed that the men chosen for this mission should come from the Lashgare 23 Commando Unit, which was the smallest and most elite unit in Takavar. For the next two hours, the two went over the unit's roster. All of the men's files were reviewed, not only for their training, but also for their education, skills, and even personal attributes.

While the mission strategy was still vague, requirements for selection were specific. They looked for fluency in English, the ability to improvise, a rather common appearance, by which the general meant the ability to blend in with the civilian population, and no obvious military bearing. They needed to be athletic, but not obviously a soldier, to have no physical irregularities such as scars, big ears, unusual dentition, or a conspicuous skin condition, and, if possible, to not be obviously southwest Asian. They looked for soldiers with some Jasz, Digor, or Iron ancestry, which usually resulted in lighter skin, less facial hair, and even blue eyes.

The General knew that there was only so much he could hope for, especially with a pool of candidates as small as the Lashgare 23 Commando Unit. Finally, he settled on four men; Corporal Hadi Karimi, Sergeant Aram Sharifi, Sergeant First Class Farid Shaker-Doust, and Sergeant Major First Class Hooshmand Akbari.

General Bandari told Colonel Zare to summon the men to him for his personal review. The Colonel made two phone calls, which brought the four men to the general in ten minutes. The General and the Colonel met each candidate individually, speaking only English to them and engaging each in conversation, even using colloquialisms to ensure their fluency. The General himself was fluent in English and accent-free if one discounted his British pronunciation. He had each candidate walk casually toward him, away from him, left-to-right, and right-to-left. He quizzed each candidate on his strengths and his weaknesses. He graded them all. He had slight misgivings about two of them and expressed his concerns to the Colonel.

"I am impressed by both Corporal Karimi and Sergeant Major First Class Akbari. However, I have some concerns with Sergeant Sharifi and Sergeant First Class Shaker-Doust."

"Yes, General, I can see where you might. Sharifi seems to lack confidence and is almost timid, and Shaker-Doust appears undisciplined."

"Exactly, Colonel."

"Let me assure you, General, I had the same concerns with them when they joined the unit, but after working with these men I came to realize that Sharifi doesn't lack confidence, but he is very quiet in everything that he does. He only speaks when he has something important to say. He rarely raises his voice, even when he is angry; but if he does voice an objection, there are very few men in the whole of Lashgare 23 who would dare to go up against him. He's ruthless. As for Sergeant First Class Shaker-Doust, what he lacks in discipline, he more than makes up for in creativity. Many unit leaders would not put up with him. In fact, he transferred to Lashgare 23 from *Andimeshk Ahvaz* where he was deemed too headstrong. However, when the sergeant plays to his strengths, he is very useful. I will suggest replacements if the General still feels uneasy with these choices, but in my opinion, these four are the best."

"No, I'll keep that in mind, but for now I'll stay with your recommendations. If you feel these are best for this mission, then they are fine with me. After all, you will be commanding these men."

The Colonel was afraid of that. While he knew that successful completion of this mission might very well lead to his promotion to Brigadier General with its two wheat staffs, he also knew that, while both the Supreme Leader and the President were holding the General responsible for the success of the mission, if it were bungled, the General would not suffer alone the full weight of its failure. He would take the colonel with him, and the colonel knew he would be lucky to keep his head, let alone his three *qobbes*.

For the next hour, Major General Bandari laid out an initial training routine. It was a necessarily short regimen, as President Ahmadinejad believed that, since that cylinder seals were stolen eight years ago and were almost definitely already in the West, their sale, if not imminent, was not far off. The training regimen included watching American movies and news shows, taking note of how Americans carried themselves, what clothes they wore, their hair styles, their mannerisms, and their affectations. For six hours a day, the team listened to American music, watched American sports, and perused a raft of publications ranging from news to celebrity gossip, sports, the outdoors, culture, science, and many others. They familiarized themselves with American culture. For the first time in their lives, they were given free rein on the Internet; they were encouraged to look at everything from HealthCare to porn. They memorized American cars, celebrities, political figures, and other details that the average American would know. In short their job was to absorb as much American culture as they could in the four weeks allotted to their training. The remainder of their day was spent in rigorous physical activity.

Finally, the Colonel – bowing to pressure from the General, who in turn acquiesced to orders from the President – flew off to America with his team. Zare did not travel with his men. In fact, his men didn't travel together. They all flew on separate flights, each bearing different credentials documenting their various assumed nationalities. Colonel Zare carried a Turkish passport as did Sergeant Major First Class Akbari; Sergeant Shaker-Doust carried an Israeli one; Sergeant Sharifi, Russian; and Corporal Karimi, French. They rendezvoused in New York.

Five

Saeed ibn Musaiyib had been living in Montreal for the last three years. Not in Aldarbouneh, the Baghdadi neighborhood, but among the Lebanese and Syrians in Saint-Laurent. He had relatives in Montreal, but that's not why he chose to come to Canada. His relatives didn't even know he was in the country. He chose Montreal because he wanted out of the Arab world, at least for a while. It was becoming too chaotic. There were signs everywhere that, despite despotic regimes and ruling fundamentalist religious sects, civil unrest was growing. He could not stay in Iraq after learning of Awwal's murder, and he didn't want to be a refugee in some neighboring country, living in the squalor of an overcrowded camp. Nor did he want to go to America because he originally believed that it was the Americans who had tortured and killed his friend. Moreover, he suspected that Awwal had given him up under torture. Awwal was his friend, but Musaiyib had no misgivings about him. Awwal was a fool – a likeable fool, but still a fool. Besides, Musaiyib knew that everyone breaks under torture. He learned that from living almost his entire life under Saddam Hussein.

He considered England, but didn't like that the Americans and the Brits always seemed to be political bedfellows, nor was he sure who actually killed Awwal; Americans, other Coalition troops, Iraqis? Besides, England was where Arabs emigrated to if they wanted to leave the Arab world, after September 11th, that is. England would be a likely place to look for him. Canada was less obvious. Canada made sense to him. It had had a very limited role in Iraq. A sufficient number of Arabs lived there so he could blend in, it had a strong economy, and it was a big country with a small population. Its only real drawback was the cold, but if he were successful in selling the cylinder seals, maybe he could move back to the Arab world when the unrest settled down, If not to Iraq, then perhaps to Kuwait, Qatar, or some other comfortable Arab country. He knew he'd have to wait until the Americans pulled out of Iraq; most of the Coalition Forces had already. The American President had said they would before the end of 2011. The civil unrest would take longer to resolve, so maybe returning was a fantasy. He liked Canada so far. If the cold got to him, he could always go to Australia, where the Muslim population was similar to Canada's, about 2.5 percent of the total population. Besides, he still had to sell the cylinder seals. Musaiyib's plan had always been to sit on them for several years. He was a patient man and Canada was a good place for him to be patient. The cold wasn't really that bad, and Canada had lots of water, unlike his native country. Musaiyib found he very much liked water.

Musaiyib had majored in computer science at the University of Technology in Iraq, so he easily found work in Canada's growing economy. Unlike the United States and Europe, Canada hadn't been hit as hard by the recession that had plagued both the U.S. and the Euro Zone for the last five years. Its tightly-controlled banking system precluded the scale of mortgage foreclosures that the too-easy credit policies of the U.S. inspired. Consequently, Canada's foreclosure rate was only one-tenth of that of the United States'. So Musaiyib made good money. Moreover, he was a frugal person, wrought by custom and by necessity.

* * *

Musaiyib had been the planner of the theft. He wasn't dishonest by nature, and, in fact, he felt more than a little troubled about stealing his country's cultural antiquities. Yet, despite his religious practice and his civil concern, he reasoned that the seals were his ticket out of a culture where religion and government had imprisoned him. Mental gymnastics or not, those were the thoughts that led an until-then law-abiding Muslim to act counter to the dictates of his upbringing.

He rightly anticipated the wide-scale looting that came with the Coalition invasion. He knew that looters didn't plan; they were like impulse shoppers, only they were impulse thieves. Curiously, he thought, *the poorer the looter, the larger the object will be that he will steal.* While Musaiyib didn't take much time on April 10th, 2003, observing whether his theory was correct, his random observations that day suggested it was. Value, not size, was Musaiyib's criterion. Musaiyib was a planner.

His only reason for including Awwal in the theft was that he knew a young woman who worked at the National Museum. He would have given Awwal a portion of his proceeds, because *he* was his friend and in need, but he never would have included him in the actual robbery if Awwal hadn't known a museum employee.

Sabeen Rahman was more an acquaintance of Awwal's than a friend or a lover, but when Musaiyib learned of the connection, he asked his friend to step up the relationship. Then, Musaiyib laid out his plan to him. Awwal's part was to find out just where the seals were located in the museum. Musaiyib knew that they were not currently on display and hadn't been for more than two years. They had been moved as part of a joint, multi-discipline program so that archaeologists, anthropologists, and linguists from both Oxford and Cambridge Universities could study them. But now the scholars had gone home and the seals were stored away somewhere.

Musaiyib was fairly confident that if he limited his friend's initial responsibilities to stepping up his relationship with this woman, Awwal was within his realm of competency. After all, he was a likeable fellow. His sole purpose in dating Rahman was to learn the precise location of the seals in the museum. Under Musaiyib's coaching, Awwal chatted her up about her work and how interesting it must be to deal with all that antiquity and culture. He did so gradually; first, taking her to cafés where they had coffee and sweets, funded by Musaiyib. They walked among the markets, through Al Jazeera Park, and even through Baghdad Island. Interspersed with these outings were tours of the museum where Awwal asked clumsy questions about the various displays. Rahman thought the questions were cute, and, what is more important, she thought they were sincere. He was indeed a likeable fellow. Over the course of two months, with Musaiyib guiding him all the way, Awwal finally asked Rahman what had happened to the cylinder seals, although, he called them the *rolling stones*. Rahman was confused; surely he couldn't mean the decadent western band. How would she know about that? Awwal saw the confusion on her face.

"You know, those little stone things that they used long ago to sign documents. I used to love to come here to look at the funny carvings on them; I haven't seen them for some time. Are they on loan? The Museum hasn't sold them, has it?"

Rahman's face brightened. "Oh, you mean the cylinder seals."

"Yes, yes. What did I say?"

"You said, the "rolling stones." I thought you meant that immoral western band. I was wondering what kind of woman you thought I was, listening to western music."

"Oh, Sabeen, please forgive me. I never would have possessed such thoughts."

"It was only that I was confused, Abdul. No, we had moved them so the scholars from England could study them. With the threat of an invasion, however, the scholars have all gone home, more than a year ago now. We haven't put them back on display because who knows what will happen with the invasion."

"Could we see them?"

"You would really like to see them?" questioned Rahman.

"Yes, I would like to hold one and have you explain to me just how they were used," said Awwal.

Rahman knew she shouldn't take him into the basement to see the seals because it was strictly against museum policy to take visitors into unauthorized areas, but also because she would be alone with a man in a locked room. But he looked so sincere and he had taken her to so many places, even if they were just for coffee and sweets, and for walks. He was nice to her. She liked him.

"All right," she said. "But you have to be very quiet and do as I ask." She felt brazen saying such things to a man.

Awwal answered, "Yes, yes, of course."

He met her the next morning as soon as the museum opened. She reasoned that few visitors would be in at that hour, and employees would either still be socializing with their colleagues or starting in on their day's work. Rahman herself wasn't scheduled to start work for another hour.

She led Awwal down to the basement, back through the storage rooms, and into the last one. Only the first door was locked, but as an employee, she knew the code to open it. The other storage rooms and even the cabinets that housed the seals were unsecured.

Rahman removed one of the boxes, opened it, and selected one of the cylinder seals. She put it on her finger and showed Awwal how an official would roll it over a tablet of wet clay to publicly document the text inscribed on the tablet, be it a law or a decree; or, in more common use, to record a marriage or a deed. The particular seal the Rahman had chosen was made of lapis lazuli as were quite a few of the others in the box. Only a few were made of stone; others were made of opal, carnelian, glass, or ceramic. All were in excellent condition, considering their age. These were not the only cylinder seals there, but they were the best of the oldest ones. Rahman explained that these seals – 103 in all – were more valuable than all the other five thousand the museum had in its collection. Their value had to do with their age, the material used to make them, their condition, and something to do with the language inscribed on them; it was something to do with the kinds of words. She did not know, for she had not gone to college or even as far in school as Iraqi boys did.

Awwal asked her what the writing meant.

Rahman answered that she didn't know. They were in an ancient language, but it was probably the name of the office or the station that the official held.

She offered, "The lapis lazuli, carnelian, and opal ones were most likely to be those of high officials or very rich people because they would have been expensive to make."

"The writing is more important, though, than who owned them," she continued, "because it is a link between very old writing and modern writing. That is why the scholars were here."

As per Musaiyib's instructions, Awwal had continued to see Rahman even after the theft. He would have anyway; he liked her. Rahman never made the connection between Awwal's interest in the cylinder seals and their theft. She just thought the seals disappeared as part of the general looting of the museum. Rahman wasn't a particularly bright woman. After all, she was attracted to Awwal. Of course, when she learned of Awwal's murder and the discovery of the three seals that had been found at the crime scene, she finally understood. She never said anything, though, because the police never came to her to inquire about her connection to Awwal, and she knew that she would be in trouble if she admitted that she had shown him where the seals were kept.

* * *

Musaiyib had been enjoying life in Canada. Certainly, there were drawbacks. One was always connected to the land of one's birth, however poor, barren, or corrupt it might be. He missed his relatives and his friends, but many of them had been killed even before he left. Who knew how many more were gone now? He missed being among his own kind. Regardless what the intellectuals claimed, people enjoyed being among others like themselves. He lived in an Arab community – albeit an enclave, and not even an Iraqi one – and the French lived among the French-speakers, and the English lived among the English-speakers. People had always been suspicious of outsiders; this had helped them to survive.

Perhaps, thought Musaiyib, *social integration was a better system, and that when peoples' differences were reconciled the world would be a more peaceful place. But only fools would think that successful survival measures that had evolved over eons could be changed easily because reason dictated it was the better way. What bosh!*

In the winter, it was cold in Canada, but it was cold in Iraq, too. People think deserts are always hot, but in January in Iraq, the temperature is frequently below freezing. And, as the Inuit in Canada say, *there is no bad weather, only bad clothing*. His apartment was warm. That was not always the case in Iraq, in spite of all its oil. He liked that he could listen to whatever he wanted to hear, read what he chose, watch what piqued his interest. He could say what was on his mind, even if others thought him a fool. At least they wouldn't shoot him. He especially liked the water.

Musaiyib had lately entertained thoughts of returning the cylinder seals. He knew about the amnesty program, but he also knew that if he were successful, selling the seals would bring him a great deal of money, even if it exposed him to a great deal of danger. Even if he escaped the danger, money – especially large amounts of it – brought its own problems. He saw where all his plans could go wrong. *No*, he thought, *that wasn't correct.*

While perhaps not in the way he had envisioned it, his plan had already worked for him. He was free, he was employed at a good wage, and he was making new friends, some of whom were even Christians.

He analyzed the problem of the cylinder seals the way he analyzed a computer project. He thought of it as a problem, perhaps because of his mathematical training. He liked the word, *problem*, for it inherently suggested a solution. He didn't understand why people his age called problems, *issues*. He thought it a silly word. What did it mean? His command of English was good, and had been since childhood; he took to it naturally in school. That silly word, *issue*, hid what the person wanted to say, but was afraid to.

Stealing the seals had been a problem, but it was one with a solution. Now that he had them, the cylinder seals were a different kind of problem. He analyzed it slowly, looking at it from many perspectives. He could return them; he could sell them; he could leave them buried and return them to the earth where they had been found originally, albeit thousands of miles away; or he could forget them. He could even decide not to act, putting off the decision until a time when other solutions might occur to him. He was free to think, to act, or not to act. He liked the idea of being free. Of course, no one was really free. All decisions resulted in future constraints and new problems. Musaiyid wondered if decisions were like matter in that nothing was ever created or destroyed, its form only shifted.

Returning to his choices, he reviewed the complications of each. He had recently grown fond of watching TV – the news, some sports like football, although the Canadians called it *soccer*, the History Channel, and especially cop shows. Even the reruns were all new to him. Sometimes the thief or the murderer got too smart and instead of just going about life as he had before the crime, he decided to do or say something that would get the police to look elsewhere, but, instead, made them focus more on him. Returning the cylinder seals might work out the same way. Maybe it would infuriate the others, the ones who killed Awwal. The cop shows suggested that cover-ups often exposed more felons than they concealed.

Leaving them buried and forgetting about them seemed to be an awful waste; nobody would ever enjoy them again and all of his effort would have been in vain. Awwal would have died for nothing.

If he sold them, then at least he would profit and the buyer would get to enjoy them. Selling them was not without serious risks, however. Although Musaiyib knew a great deal about computers, the

Internet, and how to manipulate both, he also knew that others did as well, and that if he attracted the attention of the wrong people, there was always the possibility that they could track him down.

Musaiyib decided that, at least for now, he would hold off on making a decision about the cylinder seals.

Six

May 4th, 2011:

Keagan had woken up early and gone for a run with Niles and Teal. Back now, he had made coffee and was standing in front of his living room's east-facing window, looking over the lake at the Sentinel Range. The forest on its slopes was thick with black and red spruce, eastern hemlock, and balsam fir. The snow looked like it had melted. There was none visible on any of the Sentinels' slides nor on the tree boughs of their slopes, but Keagan knew that given the thickness of the slopes' forest there would be snow under those branches for at least two more weeks. It took a while for the sun's rays to get down in there and it took even longer to melt away the winter. The lake was still ice clogged, but the ice was rotten. Keagan knew that all it needed was a couple of warm nights with a good wind and it would be gone until November. The sky was the color of lead, but bright, early-morning blue skies were rare in the Adirondacks. If you had one, you had better get out and take advantage of it, because it would be gone by ten o'clock.

Keagan heard Kelly stirring in the bedroom. He popped his head in the door.

"Tea?"

"I'd love some, Mick."

He generally kept a tin or two of Lyon's Gold Label loose tea on hand for when Kelly visited. He had already heated the water, so all he had to do was bring it back up to a boil and add the tea.

"Do you want it in there or are you coming out?"

"No, I'll be right out."

Kelly poured her tea from an Irish Belleek Limpet.

"Aye, Mick Keagan, you run a quality house. A Belleek Limpet for the pot, and what's this? Lyons Breakfast Tea?"

"Yes, and it's just one of the many reasons we're called *Beyond Good and Evil*," said Keagan.

Kelly looked out the window and then at the indoor-outdoor thermometer.

"Is it ever going to warm up here, Mick? It's the fourth of May."

"I think today, Kelly. It had better soon, because we open in two days."

"Are you going to be busy all day with that?"

"Yes, I should be."

"Good. That will give me time to get with my contacts and find out where we are with the seals and with the *boyras* who would wish me ill."

"By 'wish me ill', don't you mean, kill you?"

"Ah, well, the Irish usually aren't so crass as to say such a thing. It must be your American side showing, but, yes, that would be the gist of it, Mick."

"Oh, by all means, let's change the subject to more pleasant things. what can I get you for breakfast?"

He knew that the Irish didn't like to face up to the dark side of something, and if they did, they usually made light of it.

* * *

Keagan met with the staff in the dining room.

"Everybody here?"

It was a rhetorical question; he had already scanned the room and knew that one of the busboys and one of the maintenance men were missing. He made a mental note to check with the Gimp and Teal after the meeting.

"Welcome back! I'm not going to waste time giving you a pep talk about how important the new season is to all of us, because you already know that. You're professionals, so you know that the solvency of this inn and your very incomes depend on how well you do your jobs. The one thing I do want to re-iterate is that, contrary to what your teachers told you in school, there are plenty of dumb questions, but I'd rather have you ask a dumb question than not ask at all, if only to find out that it was really an important question. So, if you don't know something about your job, ask! And don't ask someone who's as confused as you are; ask your department head."

"Enough of that. Now, it's time for a couple of announcements. First, I'd like to introduce two new employees – Mary Wilson, from Saranac Lake, who will be working in housekeeping, and Dylan Cooper, from Boston, who will join the wait staff. You may remember Dylan from the closing party two autumns ago, if, indeed, you remember the closing party. Take my word for it, we had one. He graciously and efficiently served you. Please welcome them."

Most of the audience clapped, but a couple of waiters yelled out variations of, "Poor guy. If he's working under the Gimp, he better not forget to take out his earring!"

"That's right. He better not," rejoined the Gimp, "just the same as the rest of my staff better remember to show up properly groomed."

The Gimp didn't crack a smile but even Cassie knew that for all his bluster with his staff, he was a good boss. Now, if she could just get around his other, more colorful behaviors.

"Right then," Keagan said, "on that happy note, I'll let you get with your department heads. We'll break at 12:30 for sandwiches, salads, and soft drinks. Otherwise, the inn opens for its sixth season for lunch on Friday."

Keagan gestured to the Gimp, Teal, and Niles that he needed to speak to them.

"Jimmy, are you missing a busboy?"

"Yeah, the dumb bastard got pinched last night. DWI."

"That going to be trouble? More to the point, is he going to be trouble?"

"I don't know yet; I got enough staff for the first week. Push comes to shove, I'll tell the Marshal to fill in for him."

"Christ, you already hung a moniker on him, Jimmy?"

"The kid's getting off easy," said Niles, grinning his chipmunk smile. "The Gimp didn't go for the really cruel one that he couldn't have, given what he had to work with."

"Aw, I couldn't hang that one on him, Niles. Well, not in the dining room anyway. But thanks for the idea. Besides, he needs a little leveling. I can't let him get too cocky. I let you know how everything works out with the Cuervo-kid busboy as soon as I know."

"Teal, how about your man?"

"He's fine, Mick. You know his wife's pregnant."

Keagan nodded that he did.

"I'm glad you didn't say, 'they're pregnant,' Teal," said the Gimp. "That's got to be the dumbest PC redaction since the TV shrinks began hawking Disney versions of life for reality."

"You might have a point there, Gimp, if I knew what you were talking about," said Teal.

"Jimmy, why don't you go check and see if the Marshal has put his earring back in."

"OK, Mick, I can take a hint."

"Back to Wes, Teal."

"Yeah, he called first thing this morning. She went into false-labor last night. He had to take her to the hospital at 3:00 a.m. He said he'll be in this afternoon, as soon as he gets her comfortable at home."

"Good. Good, that is, that he's not in jail like the Gimp's Cuervo-fool busboy. Have Ky send her some flowers with some soothing woman words that you or I would screw up badly, and bill the inn for them. Listen, Kelly's spending a good part of the day getting updates from her contacts; can we meet in the library at five o'clock?"

Teal said, sure, but Niles reminded Keagan that while the inn was still closed for another two days, the bar remained open all year.

"Of course, what was I thinking? I must have gotten confused by the appeasement party yesterday."

"Let me see what kind of shape Tippler is in when he comes in at four o'clock. With the off season, he hasn't had much work here, and I don't think he's been working anywhere else, so he's been taking it easy. I'm pretty sure he has his first drink of the day here."

"If I don't think he should get behind the stick, I'll catch up with you after the bar closes tonight or early tomorrow when we run."

* * *

Niles was able to make the meeting. Tippler O'Neill showed up at precisely four o'clock, ready for an afternoon and evening devoted to drinking and barroom conversation. He was sober as Niles had predicted and was more than happy to have the work. The beauty of Tippler was that he was absolutely reliable when he worked. He always showed up on time and sober. He always restocked at the end of his shift, and the till showed no more variation than when Niles worked; any overages or shortages were the result of error, not theft. Getting him to work with short notice was problematic though, because, normally, four o'clock was considerably later than his first drink of the day. The season and Tippler's low finances worked in Niles' favor this time.

Kelly led off the meeting with the historical and recent background of the cylinder seals, their theft, their disappearance, their resurfacing, at least for three of them, after five years, and Awwal's torture and murder. Next, she recounted what she had learned about the break-in to her room at the Loews Regency and how she had been spirited away before any unpleasantness occurred, as well as guarded all the way to Albany. Then, she nonchalantly suggested that there might be further attempts to find and kill her because she had the temerity to think that the cylinder seals were fair game.

After Niles and Teal had digested all of that, Kelly began covering the specifics of what she had learned today from her contacts. Kelly had marvelous contacts, partly because of the fundraising she had done, which was for both the IRA (she no longer raised money for them, and hadn't since the Peace Treaty of '98), and now for Sinn Féin, that they hoped would be useful in the reunification of Ireland. The computer system that she had developed gathered information, not only about what the opponents of reunification were up to, but also about art thefts that showed promise for generating funds for political weapons rather than military ones.

"This project is a bit more complicated than the others we've undertaken in several ways. The first, and most obvious, is that this theft took place in Iraq, where, given its very limited Irish demographic, I'm limited to the few direct contacts I have who are serving in either *The Irish Guards* or *The Royal Irish Regiment*. I do have other sources, but they aren't first-hand ones. In addition to that limitation, we have quite a bit of competition – something we've never had to contend with before – among various interested parties who would also like to recover them. As I already mentioned, two of those parties should be considered very skilled and very dangerous. The third one, if it knows about me, would more likely try to arrest me. However, these people are also very skilled. Not just regular cops, but, in all probability, Special Forces personnel. Unlike our previous projects, I haven't found any indication that Musaiyib, the thief, has advertised the seals for sale. The result of all these differentia is that our recovery strategy is going to have to be much more creative than any we have employed in the past."

"I use that confusing clutch of pronouns because I don't think those interested parties know about you three, nor do I believe they know about the inn. However, there have already been attempts to hack into my computer system. Moreover, it seems that the precautions

I took in New York were necessary because my room at the Loews Regency was broken into later on the night I was registered there. It's a good thing I was in Yonkers by then. So much for my new Australian passport and my Finn Ni Cool persona. The miscreants were, however, arrested by hotel security, and NYPD is very interested in why the men were carrying duct tape and Russian handguns, called GH somethings. Niles, ever heard of them?"

"GSh-18 APs," said Niles. "Latest design. Were they Russian?"

"Doesn't appear so. They aren't talking, but my sources in New York believe these two were a second-flight team, cobbled together in the hopes of getting lucky early in the chase. They appear to be Iranian."

"Congratulations, Kelly, you've made the big leagues," said Niles.

"What, you're saying you and your merry men in Northern Ireland were scrubs?"

"Hardly that. But Northern Ireland was a local spat or the order of a family dustup."

"Oh, and those bullets weren't real?"

Kelly was referring to the very curious circumstances that had brought Kelly, Keagan, and Niles together. She and Keagan were raising money for the IRA in the '90s. Niles was a Captain in 14 Int., Unit 22 of the SAS, which was considered the world's best Special Forces unit. Kelly and Keagan's job was to steal expensive artwork and ransom it back to the owners, giving the proceeds to the IRA. Niles was the head of an elite intelligence unit that was charged with identifying and arresting members of the IRA. They were then turned over for questioning to a tactical intelligence unit of soldiers who were trained in coaxing information from the bashful.

Niles didn't know Kelly or Keagan then, just that there were two young, clever art thieves adding to the IRA's coffers. Then, serendipitously, Keagan's father rescued a young English Captain who had been shot by his own troops – at least they were posing as such. It seems that Niles and his unit were to set up a roadblock along the Belfast-to-Dublin corridor, a very routine operation that sometimes produced interesting results. Niles' commanding officer, a major, had come to him and said that he wanted to oversee the operation and that he wanted to bring some new troops with him to give them experience.

At about 2:30 a.m., a van came along carrying a band that had played that night in Banbridge, County Down, Northern Ireland, and were returning to the Republic. The Major's troops flagged down the van, ordered its members out, and lined them up along the roadside, while one of the replacement troops entered the van to search it. Niles became suspicious of the amount of time the trooper spent focusing on one area of the vehicle and went to check on him. The major attempted to stop Niles, ordering him to stand down and move away from the van. Almost immediately, the mis-rigged time bomb that the trooper had been setting, exploded, tearing apart the trooper and the rear of the van . After they recovered, the Major and his remaining two troopers attempted to kill Niles, his men, and the surviving band members.

Keagan's father happened upon the wreckage and stopped to see if anyone was still alive. Aside from the trooper planting the bomb, three of the band members were dead. Niles, the Major, two of his men, and two band members were still alive. Niles was badly wounded, the Major and his two troopers less so, but while one band member was only dazed by the explosion, the other was seriously wounded by a dum-dum bullet fired by one of the troopers who turned out to be a member of the UVF (Ulster Volunteer Force). Keagan's father drove Niles and the band members to the County Down hospital in Bangor.

Later, the Major and his men were mysteriously found bound up, outside a police station across the border in the Republic of Ireland. The constable on duty learned of their presence by an anonymous phone call. Mick's father would tell that part of the story with a glint in his eye, as if to say, "tis our country, after all."

A commission, which was called together because the surviving band members sued the army, later determined that the Major and his three troopers, in addition to being British soldiers, were also members of the UVF, an illegal paramilitary group operating in Northern Ireland. Their plan was that once the van reached Newry, a small town near the border, the bomb would explode, killing all on board. Had it worked out as planned, the loyalists, in an attempt to embarrass the Irish government, would have claimed that the band members were Republican bomb smugglers.

Afterwards, Niles received the Conspicuous Gallantry Cross, was promoted to Major, and was pensioned off. Whitehall wanted Niles out of the army and out of England, if possible, because his presence was embarrassing to the Crown given the circumstances of the night's events and their aftermath. Keagan's Uncle David arranged for Niles to come to the States and work in his bar in Boston, which is where he finally met Keagan and Kelly. It was more than just being thrown together by fate that forged their friendship; it was the combination of Niles' bitterness over effectively being cashiered out of the unit he so loved in spite of the medal, the promotion, and the pension, as well as Niles's and Keagan's mutual respect for each other's skills, that sealed the warriors' bond. When Keagan bought the inn, Niles was his first hire.

"All right, but now you're among the crazies who have God on their side. How did the Iranians get in this mix? I'm sure you said the seals were looted in Baghdad," asked Niles.

"I did, and they were, but the Iranians believe that the seals are rightfully theirs; a claim which isn't so far-fetched given that some credible western scholars agree."

"So, it's unlike the other two projects I've worked with you on, where we only had to track down the stolen artwork and then deal with the bad guy who wanted to buy it. On this one, we're starting off competing against three other teams like ours, and if we're lucky, we'll only get arrested. Is that what I'm hearing?" said Teal.

"Well, don't forget the African hit squad who almost took out Mick and Kelly in the cross fire at Fat Vinnie Picou's place last year.

And what about your friend Cleo Aucoin and his henchmen? And of course there were the New York cops who weren't far behind us in Louisiana, and the museum guy in New Orleans from *Le Louvre*," said Niles.

"Yeah, but the cops and the museum guy weren't trying to kill us, and the Africans weren't after us. They were after that dirt bag, Kadari. Even Cleo Aucoin was only after me because of what I did to him and his brother. Here, we're starting off with fucking Iranians who want to kill Kelly, not because she's recovered the seals, but because she *wants* to recover them," returned Teal.

"Oh, so being accidently caught in a crossfire doesn't make you just as dead as if you were the intended target?" quipped Niles.

"Teal, you need to hear me out. As always, it's your decision. It gets bleaker in parts, but I'm asking that you listen to the entire account before you make a decision, so you'll have an accurate picture," said Kelly.

"Fair enough, Kelly," said Teal.

"My sources didn't have too many details about the Iranians. Most of what they gave me was speculation. Well, more like extrapolation. Here's their collective reasoning: the Iranian government wants the seals as a matter of national pride, not to mention for the propaganda coup of recovering an Iraqi national treasure. In other words, this is a high-priority mission for them, which came right from the Supreme Leader. A mission of that order presupposes an elite commando team being assigned to it."

"Makes sense," said Niles.

"Unlike our other projects, there is a team already in place that is doing what we do. And, unlike the Iranians, they aren't following me around, because they may well be ahead of me. I haven't learned much concerning them. Nonetheless, I think it's safe to assume that they, even more than the Iranians, don't want the competition."

Kelly filled in Niles and Teal with what she had pieced together about them, including who they were, how they got involved, how they tortured and killed Awwal, and that they, in all probability, knew about Musaiyib and were tracking him down now, if they hadn't already.

"My sources confirm that the Iraqis are also considering putting together a team, similar to the one that the Iranians have assembled, but, if they are, they are just getting started and are having difficulty finding competent operatives. And finally, feeling some responsibility for the looting of the National Museum, the Coalition Forces also have a task force dedicated to recovering the seals. At this point, they are focusing on determining the whereabouts of Saeed ibn Musaiyib," said Kelly.

"So, if I may recap for my own clarity, and, I'm guessing for Teal's as well, in addition to our confused and concerned group, a band of nasty, veteran combat soldiers, possibly American or Canadian Special Forces, an elite squad of Iranian Takavaran, a similar squad – although not nearly as elite – of Iraqi commandos, and a Coalition task force are all trying to recover the cylinder seals before we do. Moreover, the first two groups would like you dead and, by extension, us, when they learn of our existence. Although, they might be willing to hold off on execution until we lead them to the seals. Considering our former success and usual cleverness, if we outsmart these two or three brigand units, we still run the risk of being dragged off to The Hague or wherever our jurisdictional contraventions would lead us, for what? Cultural espionage or some other pariah crime? Oh, and don't underestimate the Iraqis; sometimes the stumbling and the bumbling are the most dangerous. Does that about sum up this project, Kelly?" asked Niles.

"Pretty much."

"You call that clarity, Niles?" said Teal.

"Teal, what are your thoughts? asked Keagan.

"It was nice of you, Niles, to recap the high points of Kelly's project, even if they did sound more like low points. I'm not sure how clear it is in my mind, so let me give it a shot:

1.   Real expensive old things were stolen when our idiot, former President invaded Iraq,

2.   Kelly wants to recover them, but three, maybe four, other groups do, too,

3.   Perhaps three, but at least two of them are soldier groups, most likely Special Forces, and the last are kind of like international cops,

4.   The soldiers want to kill you, and the cops want to arrest you."

"Is that what you are saying?" asked Teal.

"Concisely," answered Kelly.

"I may have to sit this one out, Mick."

"Always your choice, Teal," said Keagan.

"All the projects I've worked with you on in the past ended up being dangerous, but most of the danger came from unexpected wrinkles, or when things just didn't fall into place for us. Given what we've done and our pay scale, I guess we have to expect some risk. But with this one, we're starting off with stuff worse than what we ended up with in the other projects. I can't wait to see the wrinkles this one will give us. Actually, I think I can. I'm going to have to cogitate on the possibilities."

"I always had Anjali to think about, but still I went with you on those other projects. I don't think I would have with this one. And now I have Ky. Winter's mostly over. She's got the greenhouse. Things are good; you know I love it here. It's just that the risk on this one seems like too much. I'll sit in for the rest of the briefing, if you don't mind, but I'm leaning toward a *no*. When do you have to know?"

"Two or three days is fine. I've got to follow up some leads on Musaiyib. Might even be a week or more," said Kelly.

"I'll get back to you," said Teal.

Seven

February 2nd, 2008:

Kelly was only fractionally correct when she deduced that the soldiers involved in the killing of Awwal might be Canadian. One was a Canadian, but the other two were American. Moreover, the Canadian was Nepalese by birth. He was Canadian only by virtue of two emigrations. Regimental Sergeant Major Randy King, a name that had been changed from Ranodip Bahadur Rai, had moved with his parents to England when he was two years old. His father had also been a Regimental Sergeant Major, but in the British Armed Forces. He was killed in Northern Ireland when Ranodip was thirteen. His mother remarried, and she and her son moved to Canada with her new husband. Ranodip did not like his stepfather, whom he considered weak because he was an academic. He wanted to follow in his biological father's footsteps, so he enlisted in the Canadian Armed Forces when he was seventeen. Randy King, né Ranodip Bahadur Rai, a Gurkha by birth, religion, and training, did, however, like Molson Ale. In general, both Hindus and Buddhists discouraged the drinking of alcohol, but Randy King was neither a Hindu nor a Buddhist; he was a Kiranti, which was an ancient religion, not unlike Druidism, whose members worshipped nature and their ancestors. So, while he may not have thought much of his stepfather, Canada very much appealed to Randy, as did being a soldier, not just because his biological father had been one, but because soldiering was what Gurkhas did best.

Living in England and then in Canada had compromised some of his warrior values, if not his fierceness. He liked the discipline of the army, which was less stringent than was his own, if his penchant for Molson Ale be excepted. In England and Canada, unlike in his native Nepal, there was so much that could be had. Nice things cost money, a great deal of money. So when two of the members of the Special Forces unit King was assigned to – Joe Pete Barlow and Howland Bosheers – approached him about joining them in finding the cylinder seals that had been looted from the National Museum of Iraq, it didn't take much to convince him.

Proportionally, the South spawns more Special Force troops than any other geographical area of the U.S. Both Barlow and Bosheers were Southern boys. Barlow hailed from Natchez, Mississippi; and Bosheers, from Sylacauga, Alabama. Curiously though, the Civil War (*The War of Northern Aggression* if you were a Southerner) played a minor, or nonexistent role in their natal towns' histories. Neither town had the strong warrior past that King's native village did. Unlike Vicksburg – Natchez's river neighbor to the north that held out against Union troops for almost two years, much of its population living in caves during the Northern siege – Natchez suffered only one causality during its capture by Union troops. When an ironclad fired on the town from the river below the town's bluff, the noise caused an elderly man to suffer a heart attack. While the rest of the town did raise arms to the invaders, they were welcoming arms rather than firearms.

The leading plantation owners of Natchez at the time had strong ties to the North and were more interested in economics than they were in municipal valor. However, Natchez did become more pro-Confederate after the Civil War, capitalizing on the 'Lost Cause' mythology engendered by its Chamber of Commerce's promotion of both Spring and Fall Pilgrimages, which were tours of many of its sixty-odd antebellum mansions that were extant today by virtue of the fiscal perspicacity of those wise, if not courageous, bellum residents who knew a win-win situation when they saw one, long before the cliché was ever coined.

Sylacauga avoided much of the war by virtue of its location and its lateness in development. The town was well east of where Alabama's major battles were fought; moreover, it was a Creek Indian village until 1836. White settlement followed slowly, so that, according to the latest census, less than thirteen thousand citizens lived there. Sylacauga is best known for its marble, which is considered to be the hardest and whitest in the world. The town lies atop the Murphy Marble Belt, a 32-mile-long, mile-and-a-half wide, 400-foot thick deposit of calcium carbonate, making it the world's largest commercial deposit of *madre cream* marble.

While Barlow and Bosheers may have lacked the ancestral *bona fides* of Randy King, both had advanced training in unconventional warfare, reconnaissance, and counter-terrorism (*read here as terrorism*). In terms of training, Barlow and Bosheers were just a notch below Delta Force and Navy SEALS, the second most elite Special Forces in the world. Barlow and Bosheers were the real deal.

Randy King was on his second tour in Iraq when he met Barlow and Bosheers; they were on their third. The military had pleasant names for very unpleasant places and activities. 'Tour' made soldiers sound like vacationers, happily out seeing the sights and broadening their experience, which in a grim way Randy was. He was learning more effective ways to kill Iraqis. Much of what the unit did was to go from one hot spot in the Sunni Triangle to the next, clearing out insurgents.

Barlow had heard of the looting of the National Museum in Baghdad but didn't think much about it, until one day an Iraqi national working with his unit approached him about buying some Iraqi artifacts, some things to take home with him as souvenirs of the war. It wasn't cheap stuff though, the man told him. They were very old, very important cultural artifacts. Being a Natchez native, living in the past was familiar to Barlow. Being a true Natchezean, he immediately saw the potential of scoring big on the deal. That they were stolen and had great historical importance bothered him not at all.

He didn't know anything about Iraqi artifacts; hell, he didn't know much about American artifacts. Barlow wasn't stupid, though. Moreover, he possessed an innate cunning and charm that led most people to trust him. He told Awwal that he might be interested, but that he needed to know more about what exactly Awwal had to sell. They arranged a meeting to see the merchandise. In the meantime, Barlow – sensing he might be onto something very lucrative – enlisted Bosheers. It was the obvious choice; Bosheers was the one he trusted most in his unit. He was a fellow Southerner and a skilled, intuitive killer.

Barlow's first meeting with Awwal took place early in 2008, when his unit returned to Baghdad. He signed out a Humvee from the motor pool at Camp Victory and met Awwal in town. They drove to Baghdad Island, which coincidently was where Awwal learned about the cylinder seals from Rahman. He parked in a quiet spot, away from both vehicular and pedestrian traffic.

"Well, Abdul, what do ya got fer me?" asked Barlow.

Awwal reached into his trouser pocket and extracted a small box. When he lifted the lid, Barlow saw that the box held one of the lapis lazuli cylinder seals. While Awwal wasn't clever, he knew a little about salesmanship. The seal shone brightly. Awwal explained that some of the seals were made of different material, but that all were worth a great deal of money because they were very old and were connected to the first known alphabet.

Barlow didn't know why anything connected to an alphabet would be valuable, regardless of how old it was, but he could sense that what Awwal held in his hand was indeed worth a great deal of money. It was probably worth much more than Awwal ever dreamed of having. Barlow knew how much the Army paid Awwal, and he knew Awwal was grateful to have the job.

"How many of these do ya have, Abdul?"

Awwal didn't know how to answer Barlow. He just wanted to sell this one that he had brought to the American. He wasn't supposed to know where Musaiyib had hidden the seals. Musaiyib hadn't planned to cheat him, but he knew that Awwal would get impatient waiting to sell them, so he hid the seals to ensure that he couldn't impulsively do something stupid. Musaiyib had told Awwal, even before they had stolen the seals, that they would hold onto them, perhaps for as long as a couple of years, before they began looking for a buyer. *The longer they waited*, he had said, *the safer we will be and the more money we will realize when we do sell them.*

But then the war dragged on and there was no chance to sell them because the looting had become a national disgrace. While Awwal had agreed with Musaiyib, he never thought he would have to wait this long. All he wanted now was to sell just this one. Maybe he would buy Rahman something nice, or maybe a bicycle for himself and some new shoes. It had been almost five years.

"Listen," said Barlow, "I want ya ta bring me as many of these as y'all have. Do ya understand?"

Awwal nodded that he did.

"I'll give ya $100 fer each seal that ya bring me," he said.

Barlow held up a hundred-dollar bill for Awwal to see. Awwal stared at it, licking his upper lip. He nodded again, trying to calculate at the same time how many he could sell Barlow without his friend Musaiyib missing them. He thought three would be a good number. With $300, he could not only get Rahman something nice, but he could also buy a new bike and a new pair of shoes for himself.

Yes, three would be a good number. Not this one, though. It would be three of the stone ones. Maybe Musaiyib hadn't counted the seals. One hundred was a good, round number, Awwal foolishly thought.

Barlow knew what Awwal was thinking, but it didn't matter, because he also knew that once he got Awwal alone with a few seals, he could get him to reveal where the others were hidden. He had no intention of paying Awwal any money. He knew that if he did, Awwal would go out and buy something new and showy. Everyone would know that he had come into some money and would wonder where he had gotten it. Once Barlow knew where the rest of the seals were, Awwal was expendable. Iraqis who worked for any of the Coalition troops were always getting killed by those who wanted the infidels out of their country, or, more often than not, by those who just wanted a job with the infidels.

Barlow accessed the meeting as he would a mission, and he quickly decided that he needed a third partner. He asked Bosheers what he thought. Bosheers agreed that they did, and that King was the obvious choice.

"That boy may not be a Southerner, but he's as good as us, and he's a hungry boy."

Barlow had told Awwal to meet him in a part of Baghdad that had little traffic. The address he gave him was a small machine shop that had long ago been stripped of its tools. All it contained were some work tables, a barrel of oily rags, and a couple of rickety chairs.

While Awwal was foolish, he wasn't altogether stupid. He arrived at the address an hour before the appointed time. He didn't see a Humvee anywhere nearby. He wanted to arrive first to see if Barlow brought others with him. He had decided that if Barlow brought Bosheers with him, he would not show himself, and he would return the seals to their hiding place. While Awwal knew that Barlow was dangerous, he had an easy way about him. Bosheers, on the other hand, scared him.

Awwal's plan, such as it was, was to first determine if Barlow was alone. If he was, Awaal would ask to see the money. If Barlow did bring $300 with him, he would give him the three seals. His dates with Rahman had given him some idea of what the seals were worth, but he knew he'd never get that much. The soldiers had much more money than he did, but they still weren't rich men. They were richer than many Iraqis now, but not truly rich men. Nonetheless, if he could get $100 for each seal, 103 stones at $100 each was more than $10,000. Five thousand dollars for him and five thousand dollars for Musaiyib. Maybe he could marry Rahman if he had $5,000. Also, maybe he could get more than $100 for the pretty blue ones or the red ones or the iridescent ones with the many colors. He could probably get as much as $200 for those.

Awwal knew that he was no match for Barlow, who was stronger, a trained killer, and had weapons, but he saw the greed in Barlow's eyes when he showed him the blue seal. He wanted the American's money, but he wanted it for things he needed. Americans were much greedier; they wanted many more things than they needed. Awwal thought he could make Barlow's greed work in his favor, and take advantage of his weakness for his own benefit.

He believed that the only way he could trust Barlow was if he strung him along with the hope of buying even more seals. He was prepared to sell the three seals he had brought with him today and then offer Barlow five more or so in another month. At ten seals, he planned to let Musaiyib know what he was doing. As long as he didn't offer to sell all of the seals at once to Barlow, Awwal believed he would be safe. He hid the three seals in some rags in a barrel behind the shop.

Barlow arrived at the appointed time, but Bosheers and King were with him. Awwal knew now that he had been a fool. King was even scarier than Bosheers: the big knife he always carried made him so. Awwal tried to duck behind a stack of pallets, but King had already spotted him. Barlow opened the shop door while Bosheers and King cut off Awwal's escape. They led him back to the shop. Barlow stood before a metal chair with a shredded fabric cushion. A shop table stood behind him, and on it was a military duffle.

"Why were ya tryin' ta run away, Abdul? I thought we were gonna do some business today. Where were ya goin'?"

Bosheers and King were lightly gripping Awwal at the elbows, but he knew that their grips would tighten quickly if he even flinched.

"I did too, but when I saw the three of you I got scared."

"Why'd ya get scared, Abdul? Don't ya trust us? Y'all know us; we all work together in the same unit."

"I don't see why you brought two others, and why they are now restraining me."

Barlow ignored him.

"Well, we kin still do some business. Where are the seals?"

"Is the money in the bag?" asked Awwal. "Let me see it."

"Well, no, Abdul," he said, answering Awwal's question about the money. He turned to the duffel, unzipped it, and extracted three cargo straps. Turning back to Awwal, he motioned to Bosheers and King to lower him onto the chair that was near where they stood. Bosheers held Awwal from behind and rocked the chair back on its two rear legs. King looped one of the cargo straps over Awwal's lap and under the chair's seat, tightening it. Next, he dropped a strap over Awwal's head and lashed his chest and arms to the chair's back. He placed the last strap around Awwal's ankles and the front two legs of the chair.

"Randy, why don't ya go on outside and make sure nobody bothers us," said Barlow.

Awwal was terrified. He was not a brave man.

Barlow turned back to the duffle, taking out a small propane blowtorch, a flint striker, and his army-issue Beretta (M9) 9mm pistol. He turned back to Awwal, holding the blowtorch in his left hand and the Beretta in his right.

"Now, Abdul, here's the deal. Ya were right ta be scared because I'm one scary *sumbitch*. Here's what's gonna happen. I'm gonna ask ya some questions. Yer answers are gonna determine whether I use the blowtorch on ya or the gun. Make no mistake; I'm gonna kill ya."

Barlow said the last sentence with all the casualness of saying he thought a cold beer would be nice.

"The only choice y'all have here is whether I use the blowtorch on ya and how many times I do before I kill ya. Yer choices are a shitload of pain and death or a quick death. What we call bein' 'tween a rock and a hard place. No good outcome here, pal. Do ya understand me, Abdul?"

Awwal nodded, terrified.

"Good, because we're not gonna be fuckin' around here today. No skinnin' my knuckles, beatin' ya to pulp, tryin' to get ya ta understand that only the truth will set you free. No dunkin' yer head in the toilet and then pullin' ya up just when ya think your lungs are gonna burst. None of that TV shit. I'm not even gonna let Randy out there work on ya with his Khukuri. What I'm gonna inflict on ya is honest-to-god, down-home torture."

Barlow didn't care whether Awwal understood his Southern colloquialisms; he knew the insouciance of his speech was far more terrifying than screaming at him, even if he didn't know the meaning of *insouciance*.

"I'm gonna ask ya a question, and yer answer is gonna be truthful."

Barlow nodded to Bosheers to light the blowtorch for him.

"Answer each of my questions truthfully and I'll turn off this torch and shoot ya in the head. No unnecessary pain. Ya won't feel a thing. We'll be finished here in less than five minutes and y'all will be with Allah."

"Let's be absolutely clear — ya will tell me the truth. If ya try ta hold out or lie ta me, I'm gonna burn ya. I'm gonna burn ya bad. And I'm gonna start with yer right eye. Believe me, ya will tell me everythin' I wanta know well before I get ta y'all's left eye. We clear?"

Barlow didn't wait for an answer.

"Now, how many seals do ya have?" Barlow said, already lowering the torch.

Awwal's bladder released and he yelled out, "Three! No, 103!"

"Well which is it?"

Barlow ignored the acrid odor of fear. He was used to it. The torch got closer to Awwal's eye. Awwal was so scared he couldn't think. Finally, he said, "103."

Barlow withdrew the torch.

"That's better. Now fer the all-important question; where are they?"

Again, Barlow began lowering the torch almost immediately. Awwal's mind went blank. His sphincter muscle let loose...*what was the question?* Then it came to him. He cried out in Arabic, *Musaiyib forgive me.*

The flame tip melted his eye, just as he revealed the seals' location.

"Shit," said Barlow, "what happened?" He turned off the torch.

Bosheers was straddling Awwal, slapping him.

"I think the fucker croaked, Joe Pete. Pissed hisself, shit hisself, and then died a fright."

"He said somethin' in Arabic. Shit, what was it?"

"Get the straps off him," said Barlow.

When Bosheers had the straps off Awwal and packed away in the duffle, Barlow said, "What the fuck did he say? It sounded something like 'Allah, forgive me', but it wasn't Allah."

"I don't know Joe Pete, three tours in this shithole and I still don't understand that lingo they speak. But then, I was never much interested in talkin' ta 'em, only in killin' 'em," said Bosheers.

"It wasn't Allah," said Barlow, "but it might a been a name. Not Muhammad, but somethin' like it. I'm pretty sure it began with a *M.*"

Barlow checked the brass cone on the blowtorch to see if it had cooled. When he was certain it had, he put it into the duffle and told Bosheers to take the bag out to the Humvee and check with King to make sure nobody had come around. After a few minutes, King stuck his head inside and told Barlow there were no intruders. Barlow then picked up the Beretta and shot Awwal through the right eye. He went out and joined the others in the Humvee but didn't notice the empty can of Molson that had rolled out of the vehicle and onto the street when Bosheers put the duffle inside the Humvee. He did wonder, though, what he had rolled over when he pulled away, but a quick look in the rear-view mirror didn't reveal anything to be concerned about.

Eight

April, 2011:

T he initial international reaction to the looting of Iraq's National Museum was very critical of the U.S. and Britain for not anticipating the cultural plundering. Given the recent vacuum of authority, particularly in a nation that had so long been repressed, it shouldn't have taken a quantum leap in logic to predict that looting was a distinct possibility. Some cynical critics even went so far as to suggest that U.S. and British forces were under orders to secure the oil industry, and when that was accomplished, to secure the less valuable assets of the country, according to a pre-planned priority of which antiquities were on a very low rung. It wasn't really a surprise when one considers that the American President, whose brainchild was the Iraq invasion, once quipped that, where his fellow Eli, William F. Buckley, Jr., had written a book while he was an undergraduate at Yale, he had once read one.

Following initial criticism, the International Police Organization (Interpol) convened a commission consisting of seventy-five experts from eighteen countries and nine international organizations to track down Iraq's stolen artifacts and cultural antiquities. Unfortunately, not one of these experts was directly involved in the investigation of the looting. As a result, Interpol began forming recovery strategies based on faulty information and a ready-shoot-aim approach, so common in problem solving. As might be expected, early efforts bore few fruits, and as with many commissions, when all is said and done, more got said than done. The commission members lamented the cultural travesty, and the media continued to demand *account-ability*, which was one of their tool-box words that was as nugatory as a campaign promise. In spite of all the high-toned phrases uttered and all the ink that had been expended, little was accomplished.

Whether the criticism for the lack of foresight, or worse, for the priority given to Iraq's oil assets, was valid, there was, and had been, a task force operating in Afghanistan since 2001 that consisted of investigators from a dozen different law enforcement agencies, including the CIA, DEA, FBI, ICE, and ATF, that had been charged with, if not anticipating looting, at least recovering the stolen art-work and antiquities there.

Matthew Bogdanos, a colonel in the Marine Reserves, was part of that task force in Afghanistan. In 2003, he was in Basra, Iraq when he learned of the looting of Iraq's national treasures. He immediately requested permission from General Tommy Franks to head up the investigation. Since Colonel Bogdanos held a law degree, a master's degree in Classical Studies from Columbia University, and another master's degree in Strategic Studies from the Army War College, and since he had been an assistant district attorney in Manhattan with extensive criminal investigation experience, General Franks quickly appointed him to head up the task force.

The task force was given wide latitude as to what to do and how to do it. In short order, its members designed an approach to recovering the stolen holdings. First, they needed to identify what was missing. Once the items were identified, they needed to send photographs of them to the various international law-enforcement agencies and art communities who could assist them in intercepting the stolen objects in transit. Next, they reached out to religious and community leaders, and established an amnesty program so that anyone could return the stolen objects, no questions asked. Finally, they conducted raids within Iraq, based on information developed during their on-going investigation.

While the approach was sound, it wasn't without problems. There were various levels of cooperation among the museum staff, meaning that some staff were resistant to working with the invading force. Many of the holdings had never been photographed, much of the inventory documentation was destroyed during the looting, and there were conflicting accounts as to what the actual museum holdings were. Moreover, there was evidence that museum staff had removed pieces, either for their own benefit or at the orders of the Hussein Administration. Finally, without exact documentation of the museum's inventory, there was always the problem of just how many pieces had been stolen. And this problem was exacerbated by media hyperbole.

Matthew Bogdanos returned to the New York District Attorney's Office after being released from active duty in October 2005. When the three cylinder seals had been discovered at the site where Awwal was tortured and murdered in 2008, no special effort was made for their recovery, even though the three seals were the first evidence of the collection's existence in Iraq in the five years since they had been stolen. A new task force dedicated to recovering the remaining one hundred seals was formed when the CIA learned that an Iranian commando unit had been charged with recovering the seals and bringing them to Iran. The Coalition Task Force was led by Zach Roth, a Commander in the U.S. Navy's Judge Advocate General Corps (JAG).

Given that the Iraqi Army had limited combat successes in the last sixty years, winning only three of its ten wars, and that two of those wins were internal ones against their own people, and given that whatever limited success the Iraqi Army did experience was strategic rather than tactical, which was another way of saying that while its generals had been marginal, its troops had been dreadful, Premier Nuri al-Maliki was loath to put together a commando force similar to the Iranian one. Most of the current Iraqi forces were still being trained by American military. The exception to Iraqi troop incompetence was the Republican Guard, but since they had all been members of the Ba'athist Party, mostly Sunnis, and because their allegiance had been to Saddam Hussein, they were disbanded in 2003. While Maliki briefly considered forming a special unit with the best of the former Republican Guard, they had been inactive for nine years and he was certain they would defect if the investigation took them out of Iraq. The Prime Minister was happy to turn the problem over to the newly formed Coalition Task Force.

Kelly didn't know it, but the number of groups that were potentially gunning for her had been reduced by one even before it had been formed.

The Coalition Task Force wasn't charged with further investigation of the looting, although they would do some investigative work; it was charged with recovering the cylinder seals. Accordingly, its composition was similar to the Iranian commando unit. That is, it was made up of four members, which, in this case, were three Americans and one Brit, serving under a commander. The Americans were Gunnery Sergeant, Bo Wade; Sergeant Major, Wesley Kennedy; and First Lieutenant, Ali Jassim who was a naturalized American. The Brit was Staff Sergeant Ian (Socko) Lollard. Wade was the only marine and his specialty was reconnaissance. Kennedy's was finding people. He had been an MP. Jassim spoke fluent Arabic and was the computer specialist. Lollard specialized in covert operations in both urban and primitive environments.

Like the Iranians, the Task Force members were newly assigned to this mission. Unlike the Iranians, they didn't have to spend time learning about North American culture to try to fit in. As it turned out, the one foreign member of the team, Lollard, the Brit, was more comfortable in the surroundings than were two of his mates. And unlike the Iranian Colonel Zare, Commander Roth didn't have to worry about his life or his livelihood if the mission failed. While he may have suffered some angst about his next promotion, his anxiety wouldn't be existential.

Still, he and his unit had a lot of catching up to do, as none of them had any experience investigating stolen antiquities. They met at the Office of the Judge Advocate General at the Washington Navy Yard, where they were assigned an office and living accommodations.

Commander Roth was quick to explain the mission, why it was important, and why they were coming to it eight years after the fact. He assigned specific tasks. Jassim was the pivotal member, at least in the beginning, as he not only spoke Arabic, but was also the computer expert. Kennedy worked with Jassim, showing him how to find someone who didn't want to be found. Like Kelly, the Coalition team knew about Musaiyib's involvement in the theft of the cylinder seals. It had taken them a lot more leg work than it had taken Kelly, but they finally ran across the same newspaper photo that she had found early in her search.

They also knew that Musaiyib had emigrated from Iraq. Unlike Kelly, however, they hadn't narrowed their search for Musaiyib to North America, so they went down some time-wasting paths. None of the other Arab countries seemed right to them because they felt that those countries presented too many obstacles to selling the seals, such as freedom of movement, and other political and cultural obstacles. Still, they made a cursory check of their Iraqi refugees. Having ruled out the Arab countries, they were lured to England by its obviousness and wasted more time looking for him there until Commander Roth realized that England's obviousness was, ironically, the flaw in his logic. They were left with America. Still, it didn't seem right.

While waiting for Jassim and Kennedy to provide them leads to follow up, Wade and Lollard cross-trained each other. Wade was no stranger to covert ops, having served in a Marines Direct Action platoon, RECON. Lollard's real specialty, however, was infiltration – urban, rural, and primitive. The thinking was that if Musaiyib still had the cylinder seals, getting him to reveal their location would be fairly simple. However, if he had sold them, they could assume that the buyer, knowing they were stolen, had underworld or hostile government connections and recovery would be more problematic.

Also, the seminal reason the unit had been formed and the reason the cylinder seals hadn't been left to other international efforts, was that the CIA had learned of the formation of the Iranian recovery team. While the CIA had informed the FBI about the Iranians, as a result of September 11th, the FBI, which had pioneered stolen art recovery, had experienced a major focus shift away from white-collar crime to counterterrorism. Since the CIA was prohibited by law to operate on U.S. soil, which was usually only a minor obstacle, and since the FBI would rightly rank investigations involving terrorism on American soil higher than locating old, document seals, Lollard's skills would prove invaluable if the task force met the Iranian commando unit. At least, that was the initial thinking.

Nine

May 4th, 2011:

Musaiyib had entered Canada under a *Skilled-Worker Visa*. Had he tried to enter under a *Humanitarian Visa*, he would have been much easier to find. Refugee programs, by their very nature, are chaotic. However, computer access for locating refugees was commonplace. Family and friends were always looking for lost loved ones, so governments and non-profits made the search, if not easy, at least easier than a random search for an individual visa rather than an ethnic one.

He had changed his name, but not in one of the two more common ways – legally or illegally. He had changed it mistakenly, albeit intentionally. While, on the surface, a name change might be the obvious first move in roiling one's personal history, doing so puts the person in another special category that facilitates locating him. All the searcher has to do is run a computer check with the Vital Statistics Office. Illegal name changes also open the person to detection, especially by security agencies, both governmental and those that perform background checks, which frequently led to deportation. What Musaiyib had done, though, was to make some subtle changes to his identity. The first was to enter his country of origin on the hand-written application form in such a way as to make the reader more likely to read it as Iran rather than Iraq. This was a calculated risk because Iran was fast working itself up to the top of the list of the world's most dangerous pariah states, in spite of North Korea's unwillingness to relinquish the title. Still, being an educated person from a pariah state frequently brought sympathy, as well as risk, to the application. Additionally, if detected, he could always maintain that the error must have been a clerical one. After all, there was only one letter difference in the countries' names. If undetected, he added another obstacle to those searching for him. Under 'First Name', he entered his name, Saeed, but wrote it in such a way that it looked more like *Salar*, which, when questioned by the clerk, is what he answered. Certainly the clerk wouldn't remember asking for clarification in a month or so, and probably not even by the end of the day. In the 'Last Name' box, he wrote Musaiyib so that it appeared to be *Wusaivid*, again clarifying the clerk's confusion. The result was, at least as far as Canadian officials and his employer were concerned, that Shia Iraqi Saeed ibn Musaiyib was now Salar Wusaivid, an Iranian. To someone bent on finding an Iraqi named Musaiyib, the changes might not seem like much. Given the way computer searches were done, however, they were significant enough so that Musaiyib did not show up in any of the many attempts made by Colonel Zare or any of his team. Since Barlow, Bosheers, and King were even less computer savvy than Colonel Zare, their searches also failed to locate him.

Kelly, however, was much more computer savvy, intelligent, and resourceful than either the Colonel or Barlow and his associates. Her original search turned up sixty-four finds. Only thirty-four were male, with twenty living in the U.K., nine in the U.S., and five in Canada. Kelly didn't think a good Islamic boy would go so far as to have a sex change, even if it would ensure his safety. Unless he changed his name to *Wilgefortis*, his beard would be too hard to hide, at least until the hormone shots kicked in. Still, none of those she found looked right. In most cases, the age was off. When Awwal was killed, the police listed his age as twenty-six, and the photo Kelly had of him taken during the looting of the National Museum squared with that age. While the photo was a cell phone shot, so not the best definition, Awwal did indeed look like he was in his early twenties, and so did Musaiyib beside him. The search results whose ages were consistent with the photo were living in rural places. Logically, a good place for someone to hide. But what the hell would Musaiyib be doing living in Alnwick, Northumberland; Harrogate, North Yorkshire; Sayre, Oklahoma; Hanna, Wyoming; or Churchill, Manitoba? He'd stick out like plaid on stripes.

When Kelly's people were finally able to locate Musaiyib's Iraqi records, they sent a copy of those records to her. Her Musaiyib had gone to the University of Technology in Baghdad, where he majored in computer science. Kelly didn't think there were many jobs in computer science in Churchill, Manitoba, even for those working at home. She added the education parameter to the Musaiyib search and told her people to look for similar names. When Kelly was working for the IRA, most of the undercover people she met had picked names that were close to their own, so they could remember the new name easily, even under extreme duress. Kelly told her analysts to look for pseudonyms with the same initials, although it was much harder with Arab names than Anglo-Saxon ones, as well as homonyms, eponyms, anagrams, and other cipher attempts.

Her new search returned four names. Two were in the U.K., one was in the U.S., and one was in Canada. The only one in his twenties was a Salar Wusaivid. Despite Wusaivid being listed as an Iranian, Kelly felt confident that this was indeed Saeed Ibn Musaiyib, looter of the National Museum of Iraq, former friend of the late Abdul Awwal, and current possessor of one hundred Sumerian cylinder seals.

* * *

Keagan hadn't seen Kelly all day. She was busy on the computer and on the phone, and he was busy opening the inn. There had been a good crowd for lunch. Five couples had checked in by five o'clock, which was his best opening day. Keagan had gone down to his lake cottage shortly after four o'clock to shower, change, and be ready to welcome the dinner crowd. Kelly was still on the phone when he came out of the bedroom, dressed for the opening in a blue silk blazer, French blue shirt, tan linen slacks, and a pair of Tutty's handmade loafers. He briefly interrupted Kelly, who was on the phone, to tell her to come up to the bar whenever she was ready.

The bar was starting to fill up. Even though it remained open all year, opening day for the inn was special, so there was an array of warm bar food to remind the locals, not so subtly, that the restaurant was now open. At Keagan's entrance to the bar, he received a number of catcalls from the locals who were used to seeing him in more casual dress. Usually, he wore blue jeans and a Woolrich shirt or an Arc'teryx turtleneck.

The bar was full with locals, and the tables were almost full with guests and walk-ins. Moon O'Brien, a big, florid Irishman who did PR work for the Lake Placid Tourist Bureau, was at the bar, quoting Ezra Pound to Mike Hannan, an English teacher at the private school that Anjali attended. Moon must have repaired to the bar after his late lunch at the inn and stayed the entire afternoon, chatting up Niles. Moon had a photographic memory that rarely betrayed him, even after a night of drinking. He must have been in his cups though, because he didn't usually quote Pound this early in the day. Hannan was rapt with attention. Jim Adams, the town's equivalent of Atticus Fitch, was asking Matt Devlin, a local bar owner, what the hell he said to the couple that came to his office around two o'clock.

"Well, you had the whole place draped in plastic, and old Jacques must have been off takin' a leak because he wasn't on the roof tearing off your old shingles; and this couple drives up in a big Cadillac. I'm over at Harky's, fillin' up my truck, and the couple gets out of their car. The guy's scratching his head and he looks over at his wife. She shrugs her shoulders – good looking woman too, I might add – and, finally, the guy yells over to me, 'Hey, how do I get in to see the lawyer?' So, me being the helpful sorta fella that I am, I yells back at him, 'Punch your wife."

"Jesus, Matt, why did you say that?"

"Well, it was the first thing that come to me."

Tippler O'Neill, the inn's alcoholic fill-in bartender, was talking to Madeline Spears, who was drinking a club soda with lime. Two young women, who Keagan knew worked at the Research Center, were sitting at the near end of the bar by the waitress' station, drinking white wine and trying to flirt with Niles. Niles asked Keagan if he wanted a beer, being pretty sure he wouldn't have whiskey with opening night before him.

"No, I'll wait to see if Kelly comes up," Keagan told him.

"Well, I had better get you one then, because here she is now."

Keagan, who usually had a keen sense of presence, which was especially acute where Kelly was concerned, turned to look around the room, surprised, but didn't see her. Then he saw what Niles had seen from his two inch height advantage and the stage of his duckboard flooring behind the bar. It was a Scally cap. The door opened and, sure enough, there was Kelly in green silk pants, a cream silk blouse, and a green silk vest. The Scally cap made her look like an adorable gamin, but there was no mistaking her feminine beauty. Kelly had a thing for hats and hats had a thing for Kelly. The complement, which would fall flat with many women, on her was a makeweight to the sublime.

First, Moon stopped talking and turned from his audience of one to Kelly, gasping. Then, he paraphrased Pound:

The apparition of [this face] in the crowd;
Petals on a wet, black bough.

The rest of the bar turned toward Kelly, including the two female researchers vying for Niles' attention.

"Mick Keagan, who is this vision?" asked Moon.

"Why, do you think I'd introduce you to this poor innocent street urchin, you silver-tongue divil, you," Keagan teased him in brogue.

"Street urchin! Mick Keagan."

"Well, you look like you should be hawking newspapers in Brooklyn in 1920. On second thought, with all that silk, maybe a jockey out to watch the morning field trials."

"Street gamin or point-to-pointer? Is that the best you can do, Mick Keagan? In that case, you had better buy me a drink."

"Dear lady, allow me," said Moon.

"No need for that. This flatterer here, as inept as he is, is my one true love, and he owns the place, so let him pay," replied Kelly.

"A small price to pay to talk to a beautiful lady," said Moon. "Niles, put her drink on my tab and put the uncouth owner's beer on it as well. So, tell me, dear lady, how did you end up with the likes of Mick Keagan? There must be some aspect of his personality that I have missed. Oh, I know he's a charming hotelier, but that's just a front to hide the brawling, hard drinking, decadent progeny of horse thieves and apostates I know him to be."

Just then Keagan returned with Kelly's drink and his Budweiser.

"Moon, you can drop the twinkle-in-the-eye, witty Hibernian act. Kelly's from the old country, and she could see through you before she opened the bar door."

"Aye, but could I do the same, I would have rushed to open it for her."

Keagan rolled his eyes.

"Have I been found out, dear Kelly?"

Kelly, leaned forward and kissed his cheek.

"Yes, you have, Moon, but don't change. There are a lot worse personas you could affect than a charming Irish wag."

"Aye, my fair lady, there are, and I have taken on any number of them."

Keagan went around to the diners and either introduced himself or welcomed the regulars back. To the newcomers he inquired as to where they were from and invited them to talk about themselves, which he knew was a much better entrée than telling them about the inn. People would have their own experience, and telling them what it was supposed to be wouldn't change their assessment. To the regulars, he asked about their vacations south, if they had indeed left town. To each came the offer of a complimentary cordial, though not the Louis XIII. Keagan wasn't cheap; he just understood human nature.

Keagan and Kelly were seated at his table in the private area toward the back of the dining room. It wasn't an enclosed room, but it was a dining area separated from the rest of the room by being two steps up and being surrounded by a balustrade.

"You've been a busy *boyo* today, Mick."

"I have, and you?"

"Aye, I think I've located our Iraqi looter."

"And where on the planet is he currently residing? I ask with some trepidation," said Keagan.

"Not to worry, Mick. If I'm correct, he's right up the road in Montreal. And even if I'm wrong, I'll leave the number four suspect for last. He too resides in Canada, but in Churchill, Manitoba."

"How far up is that?"

"Too far, Mick."

"Where's number three?" asked Keagan.

Before Kelly could answer, Reverend brought out the wine. It was a fine, fruity Washington State Pinot Noir, which would be a nice complement to the Oysters Rockefeller that would soon follow. Reverend went through the red-wine tasting ritual, allowing Keagan to sniff the cork for signs of the wine having turned. Then came the taste pour, including a white napkin under the neck of the bottle to absorb drippage and remove any residue that had formed under the neck seal of the bottle. When Keagan nodded to Reverend that he was pleased with his choice, Reverend poured Kelly a normal glass and topped off Keagan's. Reverend wasn't called Reverend because he was a former priest, or even a former theological student, but rather for his deep, booming voice that would make him a well-respected preacher in the Deep South. That is, if he could keep a straight face through all the *hallelujahs* and *amens*.

"The oysters will be out in a minute, Mick."

"Oh, yes," continued Kelly, "you were asking about number three. He's in Hanna, Wyoming. We'll leave him unmolested as well. At least for the time being."

"Too bad. I like Wyoming. It's a beautiful state, lonely too."

"You are a dark Irishman, Mick Keagan."

Kelly had started to tell him about candidate number one, when Reverend re-appeared at the table with the Oysters Rockefeller. The dish was named after John D. Rockefeller, who was the richest man in America at the time. Actually, he was the richest man in history, if you allow for inflation. It was named for him because, like John D., the sauce was very rich. While the exact recipe was a secret, the recipe for the beauties before them called for oysters on the half shell, which were covered with a puree of a number of green vegetables, topped with bread crumbs, and then baked. As with most inventions, or creations, if you will, necessity was its mother. It was created at Antoine's in New Orleans in 1899 by the chef, Jules Alciatore. He modified the original French recipe, substituting oysters, which were plentiful in New Orleans, for French snails, which were scarce there at the time.

"Maybe we should wait until we finish these lovelies," said Kelly.

"Aye," said Keagan.

Reverend cleared the dinner service and brought them coffee. They finished the last of the wine, and then Kelly took up her narrative again.

"If I'm right, Saeed ibn Musaiyib has changed his name, though not officially, to Salar Wusaivid."

"Seems like a stretch, Kelly. Are you sure this is the same guy? Given, it's not a legal name change."

Kelly took him through the search process.

"To answer your question, I'm about as sure as I can be without seeing him. The age is right, the location semi-fits, and both Musaiyib and Wusaivid are computer scientists."

"So, what are you proposing?"

"That we go up to Montreal and have a peek at him."

"Then what?"

"I haven't the vaguest idea. You're the lateral thinker; I'm just the slow, plodding data miner."

"Slow, right! It took you part of a day to find a guy who stole the most valuable collection in what must be the world's largest art and antiquities theft ever. This is the guy who has gone undetected for over eight years, even though a picture of him and his partner was in the paper, as well as the guy who probably has two different nations' commando units, one black ops group, and a Coalition Task Force looking for him, some of them for as long as eight years. Poky, Kelly, really poky."

"Do you think any of those other groups have located him too, or maybe even snatched him?"

"Good question. Maybe we should go up to Montreal for the day on Sunday and check."

May 8th, 2011:

Kelly had spent Saturday tracking down Musaiyib's address and workplace address. Working with Keagan, at least in the morning when he felt his presence wasn't required at the inn, she checked out Musaiyib's neighborhood. They looked around, projecting where he might worship, shop, take public transportation, exercise, or do anything connected with living his daily life. For the simple locations, like Musaiyib's neighborhood and workplace, they used Google Earth. For the more complex aspects of his life, they turned to ArcInfo, a very powerful software system used by city planners, transportation dispatchers, cartographers, and astute thieves familiarizing themselves with unfamiliar territory.

Sunday, except in high season, was usually a quiet day. Most guests checked out after breakfast, or after lunch, if home wasn't too far away, so Keagan told Kelly that he thought he could get away after one o'clock.

"I don't know why you fret so," said Kelly. "You trust your staff and from what I've seen on many occasions, with good reason."

"It's just that it's the beginning of the season. I keep thinking we haven't done something that's absolutely necessary."

"What? Like turn on the hot water? Do you even know how to do that?"

"Of course I do. And where the emergency gas shut off is and how to restart the boilers or turn on the emergency generators. I know this whole place. Attention to detail is what makes the inn so good."

"Aye, and do Cassie, the Gimp, Niles, and Teal pay attention to details? Speaking of whom, has Teal told you if he's in or out?"

"Not yet. I haven't needed to pressure him yet, since we're just starting out. Maybe, we'll go up to Montreal, have a little chat with Musaiyib or Wusaivid or whatever the hell he's calling himself now, and he'll be so relieved to get rid of the damn seals that he'll hand them over to us, we'll collect the $25 million reward, and we won't even need his expertise."

"You know that never happens to us."

"To be sure, I do, but I can't imagine why Teal would want to get involved with cops, killers, and terrorist governments, all of whom aren't above setting off their own bombs."

Here, Keagan was referring to Teal's history of setting bombs to dispatch drug traffickers the team encountered during two of their projects with Kelly. Teal once told Keagan why he hated drug traffickers so much. Kelly had a thing for hats; Teal, for drug traffickers, but for much different reasons and with much different outcomes.

"I don't want him to commit to something out of sheer loyalty. These guys have long memories," said Keagan.

"And what about you?" said Kelly. "You don't need the money anymore. Don't you commit to these projects out of sheer loyalty to me, and doesn't Niles do the same for you?"

"I suppose Niles does, but no, Kelly, I commit to them out of love for you, not loyalty."

They were sitting side by side in front of the computer. Kelly reached over and took Keagan's big right hand, held it in her two hands, and then placed it on her breast. She didn't say anything at first, just looked into Keagan's eyes. It was just the two of them, reading each other's souls, communicating silently. Finally, Kelly spoke.

"Oh, Mick Keagan, why do you put up with me? You're fighting a battle that isn't yours anymore, and that will probably never be won in our lifetimes, if at all. And this time, I've brought danger to you and all the wonderful misfits you've collected at this inn of yours with the silly name. Why do you love me so?"

"What else can I do, Kelly? Tell me."

The ride up to Montreal was pleasant. It was a warm, sunny day, and warmer still once they got out of the mountains. Montreal was about three hours to the north, depending on how long the Customs stop took. They got to Saint-Laurent, Musaiyib's neighborhood, and crossed Pont Champlain at about 4:30. According to Kelly's searches, Musaiyib lived in an apartment on Rue Décarie, which is what Boulevard Décarie became when it narrowed on its way north. Rue Décarie was a two-lane road with parking on both sides. The apartment buildings along it were four-story – three if you were French and included the *rez-de-chaussée* in your calculation – rectangular, brick structures that lined the street on both sides for several blocks. The street verges were lined with trees, mostly mature maples, which both helped and hindered surveillance. The neighborhood, notwithstanding its French appellation and the French street names, was solidly Arabic. It was almost wholly Lebanese and Syrian, if Kelly's research was accurate. Neither Keagan nor Kelly could tell for sure. What they both knew in short order, however, was that anyone sentient enough to be able to walk down the street could tell that they were neither Lebanese nor Syrian, and not even one of their Arab cousins. Kelly might have passed for Gallic with her auburn hair, but as Keagan's hair was brown, his nose straight, and his visage not imperious, he couldn't even pass for Gallic.

Two Micks inquiring about an Iraqi in an Arab neighborhood was going to be about as fruitful as trickle-down economics, Keagan thought.

Keagan had reserved a room in St. Jacques, which was about six miles from where Musaiyib lived, but not far from where he worked. He and Kelly checked in and went out into the neighborhood to a small restaurant where he sometimes ate if he had to spend the night in Montreal. He had a reservation there, as well.

They ordered drinks but told the waiter they'd like to sit for a while before ordering dinner. The old waiter recognized Keagan because he was such a good tipper, so he already knew what was expected of him.

"How are we going to handle this, Mick? You saw that neighborhood. We might as well be a couple of Micks in Damascus."

"You have his cell phone number, right?"

"Yes, I do."

"You have a photo of him from the newspaper, right?" said Keagan.

"Yes, but it's poor quality. I could mistake another man for him if the age were right," answered Kelly.

"Well, in that case, you have his cell number and his apartment address, so why don't we go out to his apartment at about 6:30 a.m., situate ourselves so we can see every man who comes out of the building and who looks like he's off to work, and then give him a call. We'll see who answers. And just to be safe, I'll take a picture of any off-to-work male resident who comes close to looking like the one in your photo. How's that?"

"Mick Keagan, how did a publican, rich kids' English teacher, sailboat transporter, and innkeeper become so devious?" Kelly said, referring to the various jobs Keagan had held in the States before he bought the inn.

"It's easy, Kelly. I'm Irish. We lure you in with the smile and the gab, and then we trick you. We learned it from the leprechauns."

"Mick, you don't smile much."

"I do when I'm with you, Kelly."

***

A little before 6:30 a.m., they were parked across the street in a Guest slot in the parking lot for the building that faced Musaiyib's. Keagan had already driven around the block and knew that the building had only one way in and out, unless Musaiyib used the fire escape. Kelly had already determined that, while Musaiyib had a driver's license, he didn't have a car, or at least none registered to him.

"There are eight apartments in his building, according to the mail boxes."

"Whoa, wait this is a little confusing," Kelly interrupted Keagan as six to eight men went up the stairs and into Musaiyib's apartment.

"What's going on?"

"Ah, yes. I should have made allowance for that," answered Keagan.

"For what?

"Morning prayers. The men are probably returning from their mosque after morning prayers. The women will say them at home. Depending on the mosque, women may or may not be allowed in."

"Where was I? Oh, yeah, there are eight apartments in his building, according to the mail boxes and apartment buzzers. So there are probably no more than ten to twelve men living there, assuming that a couple of the apartments may be bachelors."

"Mick, I've been thinking about what you said last night about calling Musaiyib. There's a serious flaw to that logic."

"Oh, and what's that?"

"Suppose you are right that there are ten to twelve men in that apartment house, and Musaiyib's the last one out. In which case, he'll have ten to twelve dropped calls, but not for poor service. Don't you think that many dropped calls will make him a mite suspicious? Especially since his friend Awwal was murdered three years ago."

"It would indeed, if I thought he might have that many, but I know he won't. He'll have two or three at the most, because as soon as a man exits, I'll take his picture, but you're not to call Musaiyib's number unless I tell you. You're right, we don't want to spook him. But we have a rough idea of what he looks like, how old he is, and that he works as a systems analyst, so we can rule out the blue-collar workers and anyone who looks older than thirty. You do have his number on speed dial, don't you?"

"Aye, I do," said Kelly.

They didn't have to wait long. The first man came out at 6:40 a.m. He looked more like a tradesman than a systems analyst. Keagan took his picture, but told Kelly not to call Musaiyib's number. Two women with children came out next, and then three men together. Keagan told Kelly to hit the number. Nobody reached for his phone.

"Disconnect, Kelly. He's not in that group."

One dropped call.

An older man came out just at seven o'clock. Keagan took his picture anyway, but told Kelly to hold off trying Musaiyib's number. Two men, about the same age and height, came out at 7:20. Keagan didn't think they were roommates, but they were possibly neighbors. Keagan took their pictures and told Kelly to try the number. One of the men already had his cell phone out and was talking to someone. The other man didn't reach for his phone, but Kelly got a busy signal. She disconnected.

"I think that's him, Mick. The one talking on his phone. I got a busy signal. But maybe not. He could still be upstairs on the phone."

Questionable dropped call.

"That's OK. Let's give it a few minutes. By my count, someone from six of the eight apartments has come out. We know where

Musaiyib works, so if we don't get a hit in another few minutes, let's go down there and see which one of our candidates shows up. We should be able to get there before he does if we don't spend too much more time here."

No one else came out of Musaiyib's building in the next seven minutes, so Keagan took off. He already knew the quickest route to Gentec, Inc., where Musaiyib worked. Taking Autoroute Décarie to Autoroute Ville Marie, and ignoring the right angle approach to downtown, which only looked faster, he skirted Parc Mont Royal, which actually was faster. Parking would be a bitch, though.

Keagan briefly pulled into a no-parking zone near Gentec, Inc., and told Kelly to take the wheel, park wherever she could, wait for twenty minutes, and then swing by and pick him up. Keagan stationed himself at the only place he could that was out of the flow of pedestrian traffic. He stood with the smokers that had gathered and were having their last hit until their morning break. It had been a long time since Keagan had smoked, and he found that the longer he was away from it, the less tolerance he had for the smell of burning tobacco. It was a wretched habit. Still, he needed to be where he had a clear view of Musaiyib. Waiting in the lobby would probably attract the attention of the security guards, though security wasn't as pronounced in Canada's major cities as it was in America's. You have to be a pretty fucked up extremist group to be pissed off at the Canadians.

Keagan patted himself down as though looking for his cigarettes, then, feigning disappointment, bummed a smoke and a light from the woman standing next to him. She was a good looking woman, but smoking was a major turn-off for Keagan, and besides, he had Kelly. He remembered how to hold a cigarette and didn't try to fake the inhaling. He only hoped he wouldn't start coughing. The woman had red hair, so he had used his brogue when he asked for the cigarette. He heard he was right to do that when she responded to his request. There were a lot of Irish in Canada, even in Montreal, although not as many as in Toronto, but still the third largest ethnic group after the French and the Italians.

Christ, the buggers breed like bunnies. Why wouldn't they have a presence here? Keagan thought.

Keagan wanted to quickly run through the pictures he had taken at Musaiyib's apartment building, but the woman took Keagan's cigarette request as an entrée, and started to converse with the *damn fine looking fella*. She asked him where he worked and Keagan answered, Gentec.

"Funny," she said, "I work there too, but I don't think I've ever seen you before. You're not shinning me on, are you? I would have noticed you," she added smiling. Keagan smiled back.

"You probably wouldn't have. I work in Boston and am only here to give a training seminar, 'Expanding the Uses of Tupple Calculus in Database Structures'."

"Aye," she said, dropping her cigarette into the sand can. "Good luck to you with that one."

Keagan started to run through the digital pictures of Musaiyib candidates, but before he got to the picture he was pretty sure was Musaiyib's, there he was, incarnate, entering the building right in front of him.

Kelly picked Keagan up five minutes later.

"What now, Mick?"

"Find some place where we can get coffee and maybe a brioche or a croissant, and I'll tell you what I think."

Kelly found the *Pâtissierie Belge* on Avenue du Parc. They had come by it on their way to Musaiyib's office. Kelly preferred tea in the morning, but she didn't think she could get a good Irish tea at a *pâtissierie*, and certainly not Lyon's Gold Label, so she ordered coffee with Keagan. The two shared a plate of croissants with honey.

"We've found our man. There's no doubt the guy I saw walk into Gentec is Musaiyib. The newspaper photo was poor, even having been through Photoshop, but I was within ten feet of him. I'm sure it was him, given all the other information we have on him."

"We need to get a read on Musaiyib. So far, we know he lives in a modest apartment in a predominately Arab neighborhood and works downtown at, what appears to be, a good job. So, at first glimpse, I'd say he is living well below his means, which I take to indicate that a) he's keeping a low profile, and b) he hasn't sold the seals. Or, if he has, he's showing a prudence rare among those who come into sudden wealth."

"I think we need to keep a close eye on him for a week to ten days," added Keagan.

"I agree, but short of approaching him and telling him that we know about his part in the theft of the cylinder seals, what could we do? Not only do we know, but three other groups, two of which are much less finicky about their methods of extracting information than we are, which would be a graphic reminder of how his mate, Awwal, met his maker, also know. They also know about his part in the theft and can't be too far behind us. And the best he can hope for from any one of those three groups is a very long imprisonment."

I wonder if he knows about the amnesty program? Keagan queried to himself.

"What about you snatching him and convincing him to hand over the seals to us?" asked Kelly.

"Mostly a frivolous thought. He's got no real reason. We can threaten to torture him, and even pretend we're the ones who killed Awwal, but you know we're not going to and so will he. I doubt he keeps them in that cracker box of an apartment building, but I can take a look later. The National Museum hasn't reported their return, but, in a pinch, he could always take advantage of the amnesty program. No, I think the best strategy is the one we have always used, which is to follow him until he leads us to the seals."

"He hasn't done anything in eight years, Mick. Maybe he left them in Iraq. Maybe he's hidden them, and with the good job he has now, he figures he doesn't have to sell them, but should keep them for security's sake. My point is, we can't afford to spend years looking for them. Especially not with the others searching for him as well," said Kelly.

"You haven't seen anything recently that suggests he's been looking for a buyer, have you?"

"No, nothing. It's very frustrating."

"So, here we are, looking at what could, potentially, be our biggest payday and our most dangerous project, without the benefit of a bad-guy buyer whom we can track when he moves. Bad-guy buyers are, unlike our farsighted Iraqi here, usually very greedy and very impatient."

"You're right though. Musaiyib hasn't made a move in eight years. Maybe he never will. He has a good life here that's well beyond anything he could have imagined back in Iraq. What does he need all that money for? A good Muslim boy like him, he probably doesn't smoke, drink, or do drugs. Hard to tell yet if there is a Fatima in the offing. So what does he need a lot of money for? He's not going back to the old country, to visit mom and dad. Are his parents still alive?"

"No, both are dead."

"Doesn't need to build them a house then. Yeah, he could just leave the seals where they are and hope he remains hidden as well. Of course, the flaw in that logic is that we have already found him, which probably means what I said about the other parties not being too far back is likely more accurate than I thought."

"Mick, you're not suggesting, are you, that these other fellows are on par with me and my organization?"

"Well, not exactly on par, Kelly. That's why we're here and they aren't. At least, I haven't seen anybody else so far. Only suggesting that they might not be too far behind, because, you see, these fellows are starting where we normally do. Namely, tracking both the thief and the avaricious criminal buyer. Substitute 'good-natured, shrewd recovery team' for 'avaricious criminal buyer', and they're at our usual starting point. In short, they have two avenues to the seals; we have one. I want to know all I can about that one. Who his friends are, what his interests are, where he banks, how religious he is, and what his vices are, if any. Everything we can learn in, let's say, two weeks."

"How are we going to do that, Mick? You've seen his neighborhood; we can't just hang around. We're too obviously Irish, which is an ethnic group that is very rarely Muslim."

"You need to contact your analysts to find out whatever they can about Musaiyib. He's a computer geek, so he probably banks on-line. Find out where."

"Mick, I work with computers; am I a geek?"

"Of course not, Kelly. You're a political activist trying to subvert the British government by providing information, which you extract from computer systems you hack into via a system that is financed by stealing artwork, and, in this case, cultural antiquities. Moreover, you're much too pretty to be a geek.

"Where was I? Oh, yes, responding to your groan. You and I will stay in Montreal and learn what we can, given our ethnic limitations. I'll call Niles and see if he can relieve us after a couple of days. Maybe we can even get Teal to help us over the weekend. That shouldn't be too dangerous. If necessary, I'll come back for a few more days."

"Why don't you go back to the inn and send Niles up in three days. I'll rent a car and watch Musaiyib."

"Because, Kelly, you are never to be alone until this thing is finished. I want you to be with me or Niles or both of us at all times. We clear on that?"

"Clear," said Kelly.

"Good. In the meantime, after we finish here, I need to pick up a few things. Then I think I'll check out Musaiyib's apartment."

"In broad daylight?"

"Best time."

Ten

May 11th, 2008:

When things calmed down after Awwal's death, Barlow and Bosheers began posing as military investigators, asking questions about Awwal's associates. The dodge was easy; Awwal had worked for their company. If any of the brass questioned what they were doing, they could claim that they liked him and that they were just trying to find his murderer. No one ever questioned them, though.

First, they asked around the company, specifically among the Iraqis that held various jobs, like Awwal, and then among the troops. No one seemed to know much about his life off base. Next, they canvassed the neighborhood where he lived, but no one there wanted to talk to them. It wasn't healthy to be seen collaborating with the infidels. The only people who would talk to them were the ones they managed to get alone and strong-armed, but even they only gave up vague leads or deliberately false ones.

Then, in February, 2009, Barlow heard over the radio that the National Museum in Baghdad was re-opening. He thought to himself, *Awwal didn't appear all that bright, so how did he end up scoring the most valuable stuff out of all those raghead looters? Sure, he had help; That's who I'm looking for. But maybe, just maybe, he had some inside help too.*

He and Bosheers decided to ask around the museum. They started with the Director. This time, though, they pretended to be investigating the theft of the cylinder seals rather than Awwal's murder.

They showed their credentials to the Director, which were simply their military picture IDs, explaining that they were with a special coalition task force. The Director wanted to know why, since he had already talked to several investigators, he was being questioned again. Barlow showed the Director a photo of Abdul Awwal and explained that he had been linked to the theft of the seals and, while he had been murdered, Barlow suggested it was in a falling out of thieves, they wondered if any of the staff might recognize him or, perhaps describe any associates he may have come into the museum with while they were casing the building. The Director had a justifiably difficult time understanding the idiom 'casing', in spite of his fluency in English. Notwithstanding, he told Barlow and Bosheers they could show their photo to the staff, if they did so discreetly. He gave them a list of employees who worked back in 2003 when the Museum was looted and another list of the current employees.

The museum complex was enormous, so it took them several visits to question the people who were on both lists. Many of the employees spoke English, as it had been Iraq's leading museum, frequently visited by English-speaking scholars and tourists. For those who didn't speak English, Bosheers had lined up a translator from the battalion pool of nationals. They questioned the English-speaking employees first.

Many of the employees, especially those working in low-level positions, were women, because, like nursing and lower-school teaching, it was a job that was culturally acceptable for them. Instead of dividing the list in half, both Barlow and Bosheers questioned each employee. While it took twice as long, they believed the approach produced more accurate results. Finally, on their eighth visit to the museum, they found Sabeen Rahman in the break room.

Rahman had never been a strong personality, and she had become even less so after Awwal's murder. Now, here were two large, armed men – invaders of her country – showing her a picture of Abdul and asking her questions. At first, she denied having ever seen the man, but Barlow and Bosheers had earlier questioned a woman who said she had seen Awwal in Rahman's company on at least two occasions. Even without that information, they knew immediately that she was lying. Anyone would. Rahman had no experience with dissimulation.

Barlow asked her about Awwal's friends and associates. She was reluctant to give them the names they wanted. He told Bosheers to go out by the door into the break room and make sure no one disturbed them.

Barlow took special pains to leave off his Southern pronunciation, so she would understand him.

"Listen to me, Sabeen. I know where you live. Do you want me questioning you at your home and involving your parents? Did they even know you were seeing Awwal? What will they think about you not telling them about him? About where you met? About what you two did when you were off alone? Hmm? Do you want them to know about him or would you rather just tell me about his friends? Which will it be, Sabeen?"

Rahman couldn't face the shame. She gave Barlow three names – the only three she knew – but they were enough for him because the first name began with an M, and then he understood what Awwal was saying through the torture and his terror. Not *Allah, forgive me*, but *Musaiyib, forgive me*. He got the addresses of the three men on the list Rahman gave him, or at least they were their addresses as of early 2008, after which she no longer saw them because of Awwal's death.

* * *

Barlow and Bosheers eventually tracked down two men who knew Musaiyib, and with just a little pressure, which was certainly nothing like Barlow exerted on Awwal, one of the men told them that he had heard that Musaiyib had gone to North America. He added that he didn't think Musaiyib went to America because he said he was afraid of going there, although he didn't know why specifically.

Next, they tracked down the source of this information. That man had been a student with Musaiyib. He said he had seen him at the University on a computer doing searches for visa regulations for North America and was focusing, at least at the time, on Canada. Other than that, he knew nothing. He, too, agreed that Musaiyib was afraid of going to America, but didn't know why, other than because he was an Iraqi Muslim. Whatever Musaiyib's reasoning, Canada seemed to be the consensus.

* * *

King hadn't been a part of the source checking because he had been rotated back home. Barlow believed King had served his purpose and, being in Canada and still in the army, he wasn't going to have much free time to help them search for Musaiyib. King agreed. He still wanted to tap into some big money, but he wasn't going to leave the Army, give up his income, the money he had vested in his pension, and his room and board for the thin promise of a big payday. Barlow and Bosheers re-assessed King's value to them when they found out about Canada. A quick phone call and Randy King was back on the team.

Barlow and Bosheers returned stateside in December of 2010. They decided to leave the Army and spend up to a year looking for Musaiyib and the cylinder seals. If, after a year, they still hadn't found them, they would re-enlist, picking up a hefty bonus for re-upping. Soldiers with their skills were rare. They didn't have enough savings to spend all their time looking for Musaiyib, and, in fact, they soon realized they'd need professional help finding him, so they took security jobs at the Beau Rivage casino in Biloxi, Mississippi.

They could have gotten highly paid jobs with a firm doing security work overseas, but they had just come back from three tours overseas. Biloxi suited both of them fine, as it was less than five hours from both their home towns. More important, their work allowed them ample time to continue looking for Musaiyib.

While King was happy to be back on the team, he still wasn't going to give up the Army, but, as Barlow had explained to him, as long as he could get some leave time, never more than thirty days, that would be enough.

King knew Canada, even though he hadn't moved there until he was fifteen. Neither Barlow nor Bosheers had even been to Canada, and since neither was a voracious reader or overly computer savvy, King had now become a major asset.

He had been in the Army for seventeen years. He had spent two of those years in Iraq, an aggregate of almost four more years in Kosovo, in the caves of Tora Bora, and in Northern Ireland. He had been stationed in Canada for eleven of his Army years and had lived there two years as a civilian, albeit a teenage civilian.

During his Army years, he had been stationed at Suffield, Alberta; Leitrim, Ontario; Petawawa, Ontario; and Inuvik, Northwest Territories. He had been around the country, living in urban, rural, and remote parts of it. For the last fifteen years, that is, after serving the minimum requirement of two years, he had become a member of Joint Task Force 2, Canada's elite Special Forces team that was formed in 1993 to affect counterterrorism operations. King was in the Assaulter branch of the Force, which was what other services called Direct Action, meaning they took the fight to the enemy. In spite of his training and skills, King's role being back on the team was mostly to wait for Barlow and Bosheers to discover new leads to Musaiyib.

Joe Pete Barlow was smart enough to know that he didn't know much about computers. He knew how to open and send e-mail; he knew how to find things on the Internet, at least those things that wanted to be found, like where to get the best ribs in Memphis; he knew how to place a bid or sell something on eBay; he knew who was the all-time best pitcher for the Braves since they have been in Atlanta that is; but he didn't know how to find people who didn't want to be found. He didn't even know how to perform simple searches like how to get around unlisted phone numbers or find an e-mail address. However, when Joe Pete Barlow wanted to know something that he didn't know how to find, he found someone who did.

There were a couple of guys in his former unit who were pretty good with computers, but the ones he knew personally would want to know why he wanted the information. And then, he'd have to cut them in for a share, and it would have to be a full share because Barlow knew that he'd need more than one search done. He hadn't ever taken a psychology course, had never even been to college, but he had a firm grasp of human nature. Human nature being what it was, Barlow knew that a man wouldn't sit at a table eating a smaller piece of pie than his mess mates, no matter how big his piece was.

If he needed someone to find Musaiyib for him, he knew that person would have to be a professional who wouldn't ask questions, but would do the job he was being paid for. He knew what he had to do, but it required money, so he put the problem to Bosheers and King.

"Here's the deal, guys. We know who's got them seals and we have a pretty good idea he's in Canada, but we don't know how ta find 'im. So, I'm proposin' that we hire a private investigator ta find this fucker. It shouldn't be too hard fer someone who has access ta all them databases and such. Private investigators cost money, though, so if y'all still interested in findin' them seals, we're gonna have ta pony up."

"How much is that going to cost?" asked King.

"I don't know. I'll have ta make some calls, but ya gotta know this ain't gonna be a one-shot deal. It's not like we're gonna hire a guy, tell him ta find this sand nigger named Saeed ibn Musaiyib from Iraq, and wait a couple of days fer him ta call us with the address."

"He's going to check whatever databases he subscribes to, probably come up empty, and then have ta get creative. The real question,

I guess, is not how much this is gonna cost us, but how committed are we ta findin' them seals. How big our balls are without bein' stupid about it."

"We fell inta this thing when Awwal approached me with that pretty blue ring. So far, this deal hasn't cost us a cent, but, if we wanta continue, it's commitment time. I'm willin' ta commit $10,000, and maybe more later, but right now my ceilin' is 10K. Ya don't have ta match that, because maybe it'll cost less, but let's say you're only in fer 5K, and we haven't found him yet. If y'all are not willin' to pony up some more cash, then you're out. No refunds. Same goes fer me. If ya guys wanta keep goin', and I can't see the why – I'm out. How do we stand?"

Bosheers thought about what he had saved, what he thought he could afford, and what he thought was the possibility of success.

"I'm in fer 10K."

King was less sure. These guys knew each other well, were both American and Southerners, and understood money in a way no other nation did. He was a Gurkha, a Rai, and a warrior. But these men were warriors too; he had served with them and he knew that to be true. And while he was a Gurkha, living in England and Canada had changed him somewhat. He wasn't changed to the point of having American values, but he wanted things – a house, a better car, and maybe even a wife.

"I'm in for $5,000. Let's see how far that goes and maybe I'll give more later, but let's see how long that lasts."

Barlow had been worried about King, because without him, things would be a lot more difficult.

"Good," he said. "Let me make some calls, see what a PI will cost, then I'll get back ta y'all."

"Joe Pete," said King, "I don't know how these things work, but maybe you should look for someone who not only gets results, but also doesn't care why we're looking for this guy. You know better than me that America isn't Iraq, and Canada's not either. Remember what happened with Awwal. We don't want some private investigator hearing that a Mr. Musaiyib, who three of his clients were looking for, turned up dead in a not-so-nice way. He might have a sudden urge to become a responsible citizen, or maybe even want a part of the deal."

"I hear what yer sayin', Randy. I'll keep that in mind."

Eleven

K eagan, Kelly, Niles, and Teal were back at the inn, in the library, piecing together Musaiyib's activities' composite and trying to get a picture of what he was like, what his interests were, and how he spent his time. They wanted to learn as much as they could about him with the purpose of being able to anticipate his moves, or, failing that, at least being able to play catch-up.

"OK," started Keagan, "what I'd like to accomplish here is, not only the pattern of Musaiyib's life, but also what we can extrapolate from that pattern. First off, it would appear that he practices his religion, or at least goes through the motions for the sake of his neighbors. The first time we saw him, he was coming back from having said morning prayers at the local mosque, and we've seen him go there for other prayers as well. He's gone in the late afternoon and even after sunset, so I'm assuming he adheres to the rest of *Salah*."

"What's *Salah*, Mick?" asked Teal.

"That's the term for the practice of formal worship in Islam. Not exactly prayer as Christians understand it, but more like a reminder of the worshipper's relation to his creator. A reminder that he should be in awe of his creator, meaning 'awe' as in fear, reverence, and wonder; not the catch-all meaning that the vocabulary-challenged use as a synonym for 'wow'. The practice is very ritualistic in that the preparations, the words, the times, and the frequency are prescribed. The

97

prayers are rooted in the Qur'an and other sacred texts. The times follow the passage of the sun, and the frequency is determined by the sect, but five times a day is the norm. *Fajr* is the first prayer of the day; it is performed before sunrise. *Dhuhr* is performed just after midday; *Asr*, in the late afternoon; *Magbrib*, just after sunset; And *Isha* is the last prayer of the day; it is performed in the late evening, just before turning in for the night. Different sects have different requirements, but they aren't too far afield of each other."

"Jeez, I thought the Baptists had it tough, with going to church twice a week. No wonder the Muslims are so cranky."

"OK, so he practices his religion. I suspect he says his work-hours prayers at his desk since there isn't a mosque near his office."

"His work-day week is routine and quiet. He has prayers, work, more prayers, and then goes home for the night. Oh, yeah, he brown-bags his lunch, I suspect for dietary reasons, but which might also suggest that he's frugal, at least to a greater degree than someone in his pay bracket needs to be. I find that more important. I didn't see any Arabic restaurants near where he works, so that might be the sole reason why he brings his own lunch. Maybe, my suggesting that he is especially frugal might not be accurate, but it's important if it is, because it might indicate that he hasn't sold the seals yet."

"Niles, what did you learn about him?"

"As you know, Teal and I mostly observed him over the weekend. I would agree with what you said about his practicing his religion. We saw him going to the mosque predawn, just after noon, and after sunset. Doesn't leave much time for other things. Not that they take all that long, just that they put holes in the day, so it's not like he can pop up to one of the provincial parks or sanctuaries that fan out to the north of the city for some mountain biking, hiking, or rock climbing."

"Speaking of which, rock climbing seems to be one of his interests. He goes to a gym that's not far from his apartment and works out on a climbing wall. He also seems to have a thing for water."

"What do you mean, Niles?" asked Kelly.

"Well, there are a half dozen parks about ten or twelve miles north of his neighborhood, on the north branch of the St. Lawrence River. The river divides just as it enters Montreal and the biggest branch flows south of the city, while one runs right through the city and another runs to the north of it. He likes to go up to the northern branch. Sometimes he rents a kayak, but other times he just seems to go there to spend time near the water."

"Teal, you have anything to add to what Niles just told us?" asked Keagan.

"Just about his gym workouts. Most of his workout exercises are climbing related – wrists rolls to strengthen his grip, finger-tip pull-ups, high step-ups, and a lot of flexibility and core exercises."

"Core exercises?"

"Yeah, lower back and abdominal work; the kind of exercises that help climbers to develop strength for movement from all kinds of weird angles. You don't always have a nice, straight chimney with convenient hand and foot-holds. More often than not, you've got to stretch way out for your next hold. Think about it. Place a six-foot-long two-by-four between two supports; where's the weakest point? Right in the center. It's the same with people. The lower back and abdomen are at the center of your body, which puts them at the weak point. You can have gorilla arms, but if your core is weak, you're going to be in trouble on Class IV and above climbs."

"Niles, any other ideas on his water attraction? From what you said earlier, I got the sense that he was more interested in the water than he was in kayaking, and you didn't mention swimming," asked Keagan.

"No, I never saw him swim. I'm not sure he knows how. He always wears flotation gear. The paddling seems more like an upper body exercise for him, rather than an enjoyable activity. Near as I can fig-ure, he just seems to like the water. After a life in the sand, who can blame him? Maybe he did the same thing in Baghdad and hung out near the Tigris."

"Mick, what about his apartment?" asked Kelly.

"Yeah, I didn't want to mention that before I heard Niles' and Teal's perspectives. I didn't want to influence their interpretations. Not too much to add, though. The seals aren't there, nor did I find a safety deposit box key, or even a bank record of a security box. The apartment is furnished economically. There are no Eames chairs, no English tufted-leather Chesterfields, no hand knotted, silk Persian carpets, no Baccarat, Murano, or Waterford stemware, and no collectable paintings. Everything there could have been purchased at Wal-Mart."

"No jewelry, expensive suits, or custom shoes. No bank records either, but then, a guy who works with computers would probably bank online. A modest TV; I didn't measure it. It's a flat screen, but I'd guess a 32-incher that could have been bought second-hand. DVD player and a modest sound system – both could have been bought second hand, and possibly on eBay. He had a low-end mountain bike, probably more for transportation than for trail riding or training, which, since he doesn't seem to have a car, I don't know how he would get the bike to the trails."

"I couldn't find any invoices or receipts that would suggest that he had a rented garage where he kept his Bentley Continental. His most extravagant outlay seems to be his rock climbing equipment. Of course, being a programmer and an analyst, he probably keeps his records on his computer, but since I am not in his league, I couldn't get into it. I did, however, manage to bug his land line – the actual line, not the phone. So, while I couldn't get into his computer, I should be able to intercept some of his computer transmissions. I also bugged his apartment and his bike. Except for the land line, the bugs are short range, no more than a half mile reception reach."

"Mick," asked Kelly, "what about what isn't there?"

"Thanks for reminding me. I usually like to consider that, but in this case, I'm at a loss. So much of his life seems to be guided by his religion, yet Muslims, like a lot of people, are frugal from necessity. Musaiyib seems to be living well below his means. His neighbors have cars, and many of them are blue-collar. He's got to be doing better than they are. If pressed, I'd say the conspicuous absence is the conspicuous absence. Maybe he's just a miser, but that doesn't square with him stealing the seals. I don't know. I'll have to think about it."

"Maybe he's nervous," said Niles. "He's got to suspect people are looking for the seals, and for him, too. He's stolen cultural treasures. His people aren't above flogging a bloke for enjoying a pint. It doesn't take too much imagination to picture what they have in mind for him if they catch him. Maybe he's just being bolt-ready."

"So, where does all this leave us?" asked Kelly.

"Well, we have the tap on his phone that we can monitor from here, but if he's using Skype, at least one of us will have to be in his neighborhood to pick up what he's saying. We're going to start having problems with that, given that it's more an enclave than a neighborhood. So, I'd recommend just doing weekend surveillance. Most of his time during the week is taken up with his job and his religion anyway. While that approach leaves us open to missing something important, we're not going to be better informed if his neighbors tip him off about us."

"Also, we need to rent a car for the weekend surveillance. Better yet, let's get two. It's bad enough that Teal's the only one of the four of us who looks remotely Arabic – and that's a stretch – but the frequent presence of a New York registered car among their tight knit group, screams danger."

"Speaking of which, Teal, do you still feel comfortable at this stage?"

"Yeah, Mick, I really can't see myself going through the whole project, but I'm OK so far."

"How about Ky?"

"She'd rather I was just taking care of buildings and grounds, but it's not like she didn't know about these projects when she signed on. And I told her about the attempt on Kelly's life."

"Was that wise, Teal? Doesn't that make her worry more?"

"Ky has lived with threats. First, with Buck and then, when Cleo Aucoin was following her around to get to me. She's one tough Lu-zee-ana girl. Add to that, she's a Chitimacha Indian, so when she's threatened, she doesn't get scared, she gets pissed off. She doesn't know you well, Kelly, but what she's seen, she likes. And she knows I like you, so she equates trying to harm you with trying to harm me. It's only when the Iranians get involved that I may have to back off. Those bastards may be too much, even for a Chitimacha Indian girl. We'll see."

May 14th, 2011:

"Son of a bitch isn't talking to anyone, not even to himself. Either Musaiyib has found one of Mick's bugs or he's paranoid."

Niles and Teal were in a café in Mont-Royal, not far from Musaiy-ib's apartment.

"He comes back from the mosque with his neighbors, but doesn't seem to socialize with any of them."

"Yeah, I've been wondering about that," said Niles. "And what I've noticed is that the shops in Saint-Laurent near where he lives adver-tise Syrian food or Lebanese food, but not Iraqi. It seems that, while it's an Arab neighborhood, it's not an Iraqi one. What do you make of that?"

"I'd say he wants to be among his own kind but not where he'd be recognized. Like how I wanted to go to Michaud's last year when we were in New Orleans. I wanted to listen to the music, do a little two-step, and drink some Dixie Voodoo with my people. I didn't want them to know me in case they were on Cleo Aucoin's payroll, but I wanted to be with Cajuns instead of Brits, Micks, and North Country people for once."

"Teal, I'm hurt...only kidding," said Niles.

"You must feel the same way at times. Mick keeps us in our favor-ite beer, but you must miss pulling a pint instead of opening a bot-tle, and the pubs, darts, and talking football with people who aren't thinking touchdowns."

"Yeah, I guess it's only natural."

"Listen, we better get back. You watch the apartment and I'll be over in the park. Give me a call if something comes up. Otherwise, I'll relieve you in two hours."

"Yeah, OK."

"Niles, Musaiyib got a call from the Trailhead, an outdoor store, telling him the pack and the new rope he ordered are in. I looked up the address; it's on Lucerne on the other side of the 15/40 Autoroute, and a little less than two miles from his apartment. He'll probably take his bike. Yep, here he comes."

"Thanks, Teal. I'll pick him up."

Niles arrived at the Trailhead before Musaiyib and began looking over the backpacks. A clerk, who was also the shop's owner, and whose name was Guy Lévesque, came over and asked if he could help him. Niles told him that he wanted to upgrade his equipment. It had been a long time since he'd done any climbing, he told Lévesque, so for now, he just wanted to see what's available.

"Let me know if you need help."

"Sure thing," Niles assured him.

Musaiyib came in about ten minutes later and went directly to the check-out counter.

"I got a call a little while ago, saying my order was in," Musaiyib told Lévesque.

"Oh, yeah, you got the Arc'teryx pack and the Blue Water rope, and Pete called. I've got them in the back; I'll be just a minute."

Lévesque walked to the back of the shop and disappeared behind a curtain that led to a storeroom, only to emerge a few seconds later. He uncoiled the rope so that Musaiyib could examine it, and when Musaiyib was satisfied, Lévesque fitted the pack to him.

"Very good," said Musaiyib. "These should be better."

Lévesque rang up the purchases, giving Musaiyib a fifteen percent discount. Musaiyib produced an American Express Card, but Lévesque reminded him they didn't take American Express.

"Oh, sorry, I always forget," said Musaiyib, and replaced the AmEx card on the counter with a MasterCard.

Niles had edged closer to the checkout counter and taken out his phone. He spoke a few words into the phone, then realizing he was disturbing the sale, apologized for his behavior and stepped away from the counter. When Lévesque and Musaiyib concluded the transaction and Musaiyib had left, Niles remarked about the cost of the two items, which, even with the discount, amounted to almost C$800.

"Yes, he's come a long way. He takes lessons with us. I think he mostly climbs alone, so he wants only the best equipment, and he's willing to pay for it."

"Is that safe, climbing alone?"

"Well, I wouldn't recommend it, but he's a great student, and very focused."

"Where do you climb around here?"

"We run clinics around Mt. Tremblant, about an hour north of here. There's some great rock there. Some of the best in the world, in fact. If you're getting back to climbing after a long layoff, you might want to consider one of our intermediate courses. Where have you climbed before? In Britain, I suppose? I noticed your accent."

"In the Brecon Beacons in Wales, especially on Pen y Fan."

"I've climbed in Wales. The rock's not all that firm in the Beacons. It's too soft, and mostly sandstones and mudstones of the Senni Beds Formation. The rock is much better in the north of Wales, up near the Ogwen Valley. Besides, that's where those crazy SAS guys go through their mountain selection. It's where the highest percentage of them wash out. They have to cover about forty miles with full equipment, about fifty to seventy pounds, in 24 hours, depending on the weather. Only two to ten percent of them make the cut of this selection. Did you see any of them while you were climbing?"

"Yeah, they were all around. Mostly behind me, though."

"Oh," said Lévesque, blanching.

Twelve

May 12th, 2011:

Akbar Kazmi and Jalil Rezaei had refused to answer any questions that the detectives at Manhattan's 19th Precinct had put to them. They wouldn't talk about the Russian handguns that they carried, about the roll of duct tape Rezaei had in his pocket, about what they were doing in room 316 of the Loews Regency, a room that had been registered to a Finn Ni Cool, about whom Finn Ni Cool was, or even about what their own names were. All either one of them had said, was that he wanted to speak to a representative from an Iranian mission at the United Nations. They had limited choices given that Iran and the United States hadn't had any formal diplomatic ties since 1979. Before granting their request, however, Detectives Anthony Pastori and Kanisha Ellis first called Homeland Security.

Kazmi and Rezaei had already been charged with illegal possession of handguns and criminal trespass so that they could be held over until their court date, but the reality was, unless Homeland Security could implicate them in a terrorist plot, they would eventually be deported to Iran.

Special agents Aidan Ryan and Isaiah (Ike) Ashe responded to Detectives Pastori and Ellis' call. They were a mix of the old and the new. Both had been brought up from the FBI. Ryan was of the old breed; an Irish Catholic and Notre Dame Law School Graduate.

Ashe graduated from Brigham Young with a degree in accounting. Ryan was recruited by the FBI when they favored Irish Catholics, especially Notre Dame Graduates. The theory at that time was that good, Irish Catholic boys were used to toeing the line without questioning why. The Church had changed since then. More correctly, the faithful had changed since then, ironically, in that they were less prone to blind faith. When the shift became obvious to the FBI's upper echelon, it began recruiting Mormons. The practice put a crimp in their gender equity hiring and in their racial quotas, but, hey, they were the FBI.

Special Agents Ryan and Ashe initially didn't get any further than did Detectives Pastori and Ellis, since Kazmi and Rezaei stuck to their defense of refusing to talk to anyone except a representative from Iran's Permanent Mission in the United Nations.

Ryan took another look at the file, this time reading the entirety of the initial report, rather than just skimming the charges. That the two supposed Iranians carried handguns and duct tape clearly suggested that they were in room 316 of the Loews Regency to kidnap someone, and that the room was registered to Finn Ni Cool suggested that she was the obvious intended victim. Nothing in the report suggested why or for what purpose.

"What kind of name is Finn Ni Cool, anyway? It doesn't sound Iranian." said Ashe.

"It isn't," said Ryan. "It's Irish."

"Huh, oh what like Gaelic?"

"No, Ike, like real Irish. Finn McCool, or Fionn mac Cumhaill," Ryan spelled it for Ashe, "was a Irish giant who, according to Irish mythology, built the Giant's Causeway as a pathway to Scotland in order to fight Benandonner, his Scottish counterpart. There are two versions of the myth, but both reflect the cunning of the Irish. One says that when Finn saw Benandonner he was afraid because the Scot was much bigger than Finn. Oonagh, Finn's wife got the idea of wrapping Finn in a blanket and tucking him into a cradle, so that when Benandonner came looking for him and saw the size of his baby, any desire he had of fighting the father left him. Benandonner fled back to Scotland, tearing up the causeway as he went so Finn wouldn't chase him back home. In the other version, Oonagh painted a rock to look like a steak and gave it to Benandonner, while giving the baby, Finn, a real steak. In this version, too, Benandonner bolted back to Scotland when he saw the baby easily tearing into the steak."

"Colorful stories, but what does our Finn, Finn Ni Cool, have to do with a legend about Fionn mac Cumhaill? Isn't our Finn a woman?"

"Myth, actually. Legends have a basis in reality. Yes, she is, but this Finn Ni Cool is an alias. It's also a play on words. Finn McCool means Finn, the son of Cool, or Cumhaill. Our Finn, Finn Ni Cool, is Finn, the daughter of Cool."

"I still don't get it," said Ashe.

"You wouldn't. You'd have to be Irish, an art thief, and a person with a serious sense of humor. You're seriously delinquent in all three, Ike."

It took Special Agent Aidan Ryan several days of making phone calls and positing a few judicial logical leaps before he called ADA Matthew Bogdanos to ask him who was heading up the Iraqi antiquities recovery team.

Ryan and Bogdanos had worked together over the years and, while they weren't drinking buddies, they each respected the work the other did.

"What have you got, Aidan?"

"Well, it may be nothing, but what makes up that nothing is two armed Iranians, one with a roll of duct tape, who broke into a room in the Loews Regency. Also, there's this Irish myth about a giant and a missing woman using the alias Finn Ni Cool. Ever heard of her?"

"I'm still working on the mythical Irish giant."

"I guess there is no reason you should know her, since most of your art recovery has been with antiquities. You Greeks aren't the only ones with a mythology, though. We Micks have a very rich one ourselves. Anyhow, do you remember when the seven lost Fabergé Eggs were returned to an insurance company in New Orleans?"

"Yeah. I do."

"That was Finn Ni Cool who returned them, or at least that was the name she was using at the time. Her specialty seems to be art recovery. No one knows her real name, or no one in law enforcement that is, but she and her team – they're even less well-known – have recovered a number of pieces of high-end art. Paintings, sculptures, and the seven Fabergé Imperial Eggs. There is even a hint that she and her team recovered some diamonds from Louis XIV's court. That one's practically a state secret because the Louvre was involved. We don't know for sure, but we think their pieces were fakes and she recovered the real diamonds, returning them for a hefty finder's fee."

"I'm not sure why, let alone how she would be involved in this thing with the Iranians, or even why they are involved, but Finn Ni Cool is not the first alias your average citizen comes up with, assuming your average citizen needed to have an alias."

"Maybe, I can help fill in a few blanks here before I put you in contact with Commander Zack Roth, the head of the Coalition's task force. Yeah, your Finn was a reach for me because my specialty is antiquities. But if she's working on recovering antiquities stolen from Iraq's National Museum in Baghdad, then I think I can explain the Iranian connection. Of all the 15,000 items looted from Iraq's National Museum, 103 Sumerian cylinder seals were among the most valuable pieces. It's hard to say how much they are worth, but let's just say somewhere in the millions."

"Hold on. What's a cylinder seal?" asked Ryan. "I don't think we had any of those in Hell's Kitchen."

Bogdanos answered Ryan's question by, not only explaining the seals function, but also their cultural and linguistic importance. When he had satisfied Ryan's curiosity, he explained the Iranian claim as the rightful owner of the seals.

"I think you really hit on something here, Aidan. I wish I were still involved; I'd like to be in on it. Anyhow, let me give you Commander

Roth's phone number. He and his team are currently working out of the Washington Naval Yard."

* * *

Colonel Zare had temporarily split his team. He went to Parsippany, New Jersey to a single-family dwelling, where two men were already living. Zare arrived at the house late at night by cab and remained inside the whole time he was in Parsippany. The two men in residence had a decided Arab cast, and, while Zare didn't, he thought that a third male in the household would certainly excite the neighbors. The others remained in New York. He assigned Corporal Karimi and Sergeant Sharifi to find out where Finn Ni Cool had gone after she left the Loews Regency. Sergeant Shaker-Doust and Sergeant Major Akbari were to determine what was to be done about Kazmi and Rezaei.

The two men in the Parsippany house were skilled in computer searches and had access to several databases to aid in those searches. Additionally, they had a file that had been sent to them by one of their agents in Iraq. The file contained the details of a more-than-adequate profile of Saeed ibn Musaiyib.

The men didn't bother trying to locate Musaiyib through his name; Colonel Zare had already done that and had come up dry. It seemed that the Musaiyib family had either been content to stay in Iraq or lacked the wherewithal to immigrate to North America. The two cyber searchers were now focusing on Musaiyib's maternal relatives. His maternal grandfather's name was Al-Qaisi. This search turned up a number of possibilities, not as to where Musaiyib was, but rather where possible relatives lived. The searchers believed that it was logical for Musaiyib to want to live near his relatives, if at all possible.

It appeared that the Al-Qaisi branch of the family had been more adventurous. There were Al-Qaisis living in New York, Chicago, Minneapolis, Toronto, and Montreal, as well as a scattering of others who lived in improbable rural locations. They were improbable, that is, for an urban, educated Iraqi. The urban-dwelling Al-Qaisis were but starter leads that the cyber searchers would need to cross-reference, and then Colonel Zare would prioritize them before he actively pursuing the leads.

* * *

Karimi and Sharifi didn't know what Kelly looked like, but they did know that she was traveling under an Australian passport issued to a Finn Ni Cool. Colonel Zare didn't have the network that Kelly had, nor did he have adequate time to prepare for this project, so the best his men could do with the credentials they had were insurance-investigator inquiries.

They started with the concierge at the Loews Regency, asking him if he remembered a woman with an Australian accent inquiring about directions to train or bus stations, or about any special services like car rentals. The concierge raised an eyebrow on hearing the word 'bus'. Loews Regency guests didn't travel by bus. Kelly had only been at the hotel for an hour, so they could be specific about the day and time, but it was more than two weeks ago. They knew when Kelly had checked in, and they knew when Kazmi and Rezaei had arrived to find the room empty. The concierge, an Irishman named Flynn, told them he didn't remember a woman with an Australian accent. He suggested they ask doormen; perhaps they remembered the woman leaving the hotel with a bag in the evening. None recalled that they did. Karimi and Sharifi checked with the cabbies, but they got nothing. Today's cabbies weren't nearly as interested in their fares as were the noir film cabbies of the '40s and '50s. Karimi and Sharifi kept at it, though, taking several days to cycle through the cabbies because they rotated shifts and worked weekends some weeks and not others.

Karimi and Sharifi knew that without a photo, their chances of success, especially once they left the hotel, were extremely limited.

Next, they checked out the Port Authority Bus Station, Penn Station, and Grand Central Station. Nothing. They went to car rental agencies within a five-block radius. Nothing. They even went out to LaGuardia Airport, but, once there, they knew how futile their task was. Besides, there they'd have to talk to security chiefs, or maybe even Homeland Security. They knew their credentials wouldn't stand up under that kind of professional scrutiny. A twenty might work with a doorman or a fifty with a concierge, which Flynn did take just before he called Yonkers, but all a bribe would buy them at LaGuardia Airport would be cell time.

* * *

Sergeant Major Akbari had a difficult decision to make. He had to decide whether Shaker-Doust should visit Kazmi and Rezaei to determine what they had told the authorities or if he should. The decision vexed him because he knew he was better at debriefing. However, Akbari also knew that the visitors had to show a picture ID to be able to register to visit inmates. Shaker-Doust's passport was Israeli, but Akbari's was Turkish. In America, especially in New York City, an Israeli passport was more productive than a Turkish one. Americans by-and-large liked Israelis and thought of them as allies. More Jews lived in America than in Israel, however, most Americans knew very little about Turkey, or at least didn't know whether they were friends or foes. Regardless, the authorities believed that Kazmi and Rezaei were Iranians. It wasn't much of a logical leap to realize that anyone visiting them might also be Iranian, credentials notwithstanding. The visits would probably draw attention to them; they might even be held for questioning themselves. Akbari finally decided that his overall value to the mission was more important than his debriefing skills. Shaker-Doust would conduct the debriefings.

First, they had to locate Kazmi and Rezaei. The largest segment of New York City's prison population was housed at the complex on Riker's Island, but Kazmi and Rezaei weren't there. Akbari finally found them in the Manhattan House of Detention, better known as the Tombs. The epithet was ascribed to the original structure, which was built in 1838, because its architect, John Haviland, based the design on an engraving he once saw of an ancient Egyptian mausoleum.

Shaker-Doust had used the computers at the Battery Park branch of the New York City Library on North End Avenue to learn the whereabouts of Kazmi and Rezaei, and about the procedures necessary for visiting inmates. Locating the two was more difficult than usual because they had refused to give the police their names. Still, it was far easier than it would have been in Iran. They had been listed as John Iranian1 and John Iranian2. Shaker-Doust had to register for the visit. Registration for the Manhattan Detention Complex was held onsite, Friday through Sunday, between the hours of 7:00 a.m. and 2:00 p.m. It was Thursday.

Akbari and Shaker-Doust arrived at the complex early Friday morning, before it opened. The line for registration had already begun to form. There were no visiting hours on Monday or Tuesday. After that, visits were based on the inmate's surname. The sequence rotated, but this month it was A-L on Sundays and Wednesdays, and M-Z on Thursdays and Saturdays. However, all inmates could be visited on Friday. While Akbari wasn't sure whether they could both be visited on Wednesday, since their last names were Iranian1 and Iranian2, he decided that Shaker-Doust should visit them on Friday, if at all possible, to avoid any confusion. Also, while all inmates could be visited on Friday, no inmate could have more than one visit per day, which is why Akbari suggested they arrive so early on Friday. Shaker-Doust needed to see both Kazmi and Rezaei in one visit to the detention center so as to limit his exposure to authorities.

As it turned out, there wasn't much competition for visiting the men. Akbari didn't think there would be anyone else, with the exception of Iran's representative from the U.N. Still, as it was, they had to wait around for a week before the visit, with little to do since Karimi and Sharifi's search for Finn Ni Cool turned up no leads.

Shaker-Doust filled out the visitor-request form and presented his passport as proof of identification. For 'reason for visit', Shaker-Doust wrote 'relative'. The correction officer at the desk wasn't privy to specific information about Kazmi and Rezaei's arrests, only that they had been charged with unauthorized carrying of a concealed weapon. The Israeli passport didn't raise any red flags. A check would be run on Shaker-Doust to determine if he had any current warrants out for him, but since he held an Israeli passport, they wouldn't check him out with Homeland Security. Before Shaker-Doust left, the correction officer gave him a list of regulations for visits. There were dress prohibitions; He couldn't wear shorts or clothing with rips or holes more than three inches above the knee. Also, underwear was required. They didn't want to excite the inmates who had no idea when their next heterosexual experience would be. Shaker-Doust briefly imagined the duties of the underwear officer and wondered whether the post provided bonus pay.

There were also the obvious prohibitions. He couldn't have guns, knives, or drugs. There were also some less obvious prohibitions. He couldn't chew tobacco or gum, for example. There were even some curious ones, like no tape or bandages. And there was the one that astounded Shaker-Doust; padlocks were not allowed. He couldn't for the life of him think why it would enter a visitor's mind to bring a padlock into a jail. He could see a key, maybe, but a padlock? It was bizarre.

Akbari called Colonel Zare to brief him on his team's status. He outlined the procedure Karimi and Sharifi had followed at the Loews Regency, first, with the concierge, then, with the doormen and the cabbies, and, lastly, with the car rental agencies. Next, he told the Colonel that, while they had also gone to LaGuardia Airport, they quickly realized that without adequate credentials it was futile to try to locate someone without a photo, or at least a description. More importantly, they knew that it would only draw attention to themselves. Colonel Zare agreed and then asked if he had had a chance to debrief Kazmi and Rezaei. Akbari told him about the delay; Zare wasn't happy, but there was nothing that he could do about it if he wanted to talk to the men. Akbari asked the Colonel if he wanted them to check on anything else while they were waiting.

"No, go back to the safe house on Staten Island and wait for Friday or for further instructions," Zare told him.

"Oh, what about the representative from the U.N.? Could you or one of the men there make contact with him? If he's already visited Kazmi and Rezaei, talk with him and get his impression of the men. If he hasn't seen them, perhaps he could do so on Wednesday and Thursday, and then I could meet with him before I go on Friday," said Akbari.

"Good idea. I'll get back to you with that information. Oh, and how is Shaker-Doust behaving?"

"Fine. No problems, whatsoever."

"Good. I'll get back to you after I talk with the U.N. representative."

Akbari didn't tell the Colonel that Shaker-Doust would conduct the debriefing. Sometimes officers, like all bosses, overruled subordinates' decisions for no other reason than that they think they should because they're the boss. Akbari could have been an officer. He knew how to lead men, but he liked where he was. Being an officer paid more, of course, and brought more benefits, but it also brought over and above the additional responsibilities and headaches. Being an officer also brought vulnerability. Akbari had lived his whole life under totalitarian regimes. First there was Mohammad Reza Pahlavi, the Shah of Iran; then in 1979, there was the Ayatollah Khomeini; and now, the Supreme Leader, Grand Ayatollah Sayyid Ali Hosseine Khamene. In more liberal regimes, scapegoats were made to resign. In totalitarian regimes, they were imprisoned or permanently dispatched. Barring out-and-out treason, Sergeant Majors were never imprisoned or permanently dispatched. They were too valuable.

Akbari and Shaker-Doust queued up for visiting hours, which began at 8:00 a.m. on Fridays. There was a closed-circuit camera that took in the queue, but Akbari kept his face shaded or turned away. He wouldn't be going into the facility, but he waited with Shaker-Doust, giving him last-minute reminders and instructions about how to conduct the interrogation. Akbari was to meet Bameen Nariman, the representative from Iran's U.N. Mission, who at Colonel Zare's request had been able to visit both Kazmi and Rezaei the day before, claiming diplomatic privilege to bypass registration. When the door opened, indicating the start of visiting hours, Akbari left Shaker-Doust to meet Nariman at the Nha Trang restaurant for tea.

Iranians are as fond of tea as the British. Tea originally came to Persia, and what is modern-day Iran, via the Silk Road from India, and it soon became the national drink. The tea culture is so much a part of Iranian life that Iran cultivates most of the tea that it consumes. Unlike the Brits, however, the Iranians traditionally drank tea by pouring it into a saucer and putting a lump of sugar, called a *qand*, in their mouth before drinking the tea. If Iran had a national dental association, it would be subject to the tea culture. There were no Iranian tea shops near the Manhattan Detention Complex, so Akbari and Nariman had to settle for a Vietnamese one.

Akbari arrived first. It wasn't hard for Nariman to find him because everyone else in the restaurant was Asian.

Just in case another Caucasian had wandered into the Vietnamese restaurant, Nariman asked Akbari if, in fact, that's who he was. Akbari stood, confirmed Nariman's supposition, greeted him, and invited Nariman to join him. A pot of tea, a cup, and a saucer for Nariman were already on the table.

"So, you've already visited both Kazmi and Rezaei? That was very kind of you to accommodate us like that."

"Your Colonel Zare didn't indicate that delay was a possibility."

"I apologize for my Colonel, but the mission we are on is very important."

"Yes, I know. Colonel Zare suggested the Supreme Leader himself had sanctioned it," said Nariman.

"That is my understanding."

"Regrettably, I'm afraid I don't have much to report about my visits. I spoke to each individually, one immediately after the other, and I had requested that there be no communication between them as the one was led away and the other brought in. Given the exchange time, I can't believe there was. They both said that they provided the authorities with no information. In fact, they maintained that all either said was to request to speak to someone from Iran's Permanent Mission to the U.N."

"How did they seem?" asked Akbari.

"Concerned, not only for their predicament, but also for their families' safety. Neither held himself with the poise of a professional. They were clearly worried, but, if I had to guess, I'd say they were more afraid of what would happen to them and their families if they talked than they were of what the Americans might do to them."

"Was there any hesitation to their answers? Any evasions, nervousness to your questions, looking off to the right or left, or any other telltale signs of lying or evasion?"

"None that I could detect. First, I asked them what the authorities had asked. They were originally questioned by two detectives at Manhattan's 19th Precinct, where they were held before the Tombs."

Akbari seemed confused, "The tombs?"

"Ah! Sorry, that's what the Manhattan Detention Complex is known as locally, or at least the south tower of the complex. I'm not sure why. Anyway, they asked the usual questions. Since neither was carrying any identification, the detectives started with what their names were. When they wouldn't answer, the detectives asked them why they were carrying guns. Then, why Russian guns? Were they Russian? What were you doing in that room when you weren't registered there? Did you know the person who was? What was the duct tape for? Who is Finn Ni Cool? And so on. Kazmi and Rezaei maintained that the only words they spoke were to request a representative from the Permanent Mission."

"You said they were first questioned by detectives. Who questioned them after that?"

"Homeland Security."

"What did they ask?"

"Pretty much the same questions as the detectives. To which Kazmi and Rezaei swore they answered in the same way. However, the Homeland Security agents seemed particularly interested in Finn Ni Cool, the woman who was registered in that room."

"Did the agents have any idea who she was?" asked Akbari.

"They didn't seem to, but the unusualness of the name did pique their attention. Well, one of them anyway. A man named Ryan."

"Any idea why?"

"Other than that it's an unusual name, no. What nationality is it?" asked Nariman.

"Her passport said Australian, but so far we've been unable to locate her to find out."

Akbari didn't bother asking Shaker-Doust what the detectives and the Homeland Security agents had asked Kazmi and Rezaei. He knew that if they lied to Nariman, they would have lied to him as well. Instead, he asked about their demeanor, specifically, what they looked like after more than two weeks in jail, not only physically, but also emotionally and psychologically. Akbari had given Shaker-Doust a crash course on how to double back on questions in ways that the person being interrogated didn't realize, leading him into traps if he was lying. These traps often produced emotional and psychological reactions that manifested themselves physically, which were obvious to the knowledgeable interrogator.

Shaker-Doust's impression was that the men were both very nervous, but that they had been uniformly so throughout his questioning. He, too, believed that they were worried for themselves and their families for having botched the kidnapping, rather than about anything they told the authorities.

Thirteen

May 19th, 2011:

Special Agent Ryan had determined that, whatever it was that Kazmi and Rezaei were doing in room 316 of the Loews Regency, was a criminal act, and not a terrorist act, or at least, not by the legal definition. Had they been successful, Finn Ni Cool might well have been terrified, nonetheless, in terms of jurisdiction, the case belonged where it was, which was with the 19th Precinct. Ike Ashe had to agree. Ryan thanked Detectives Pastori and Ellis for the call, but turned the case over to them.

Later that day, however, Ryan called Commander Roth.

"Commander, my name is Aidan Ryan, Special Agent Aidan Ryan from Homeland Security. I got your name from Matthew Bogdanos of the New York County District Attorney's Office. I may have stumbled onto a case that you and your team are investigating. I'm based in New York City, and I understand you're at the Washington Navy Yard. So, I'm hoping we can work this out over the phone. I'm sure neither one of us wants to jump on a plane to visit the other, if we don't need to."

"You got that right. What do you have for me?"

Ryan gave him a quick synopsis of how he was called in on the case, and then moved directly to the purpose of his call.

"The name of the woman this room was registered to was Finn Ni Cool," Ryan spelled it for him. "Not your everyday Smith or Jones, I think you'll agree."

"No, it isn't."

"Well, as you have probably guessed from my name, I'm a Mick."

"Not exactly Aristotelian induction, is it."

"Yeah, well, Finn McCool is a character in Celtic mythology – bear with me, please – and Finn Ni Cool is also the name of a very successful locator of stolen art."

"Now you've got my interest."

"I'm going to be making some logical leaps here, but indulge me, please. Finn Ni Cool was responsible for the return of seven Fabergé Imperial Eggs and, very likely, some extremely valuable diamonds from the Court of Louis XIV of France. I'm talking about the woman now, not the mythical character. If I had to guess, I'd say she's Irish, but she showed an Australian passport when she registered at the hotel. Now, there are a lot of Micks in Australia, of course, our being drunks and thieves, and our women being loose, but I'm guessing this woman and the woman who recovered the Fabergé Eggs and the Mazarin diamonds are one and the same. She keeps a very low profile, and since the Louvre, where the Mazarin diamonds were supposed to be, doesn't want to admit that for years it had fakes on display, you probably won't get much out of them either."

"Are you with me so far?"

"I think so. This woman, a very good thief in her own right, who has taken on a name of one of the quaint characters in the stories the Irish tell about themselves, is somehow involved with the case I'm working on. That it?"

"Yeah, more or less. I understand that you are heading up a team to recover the Sumerian cylinder seals that were stolen from the National Museum in Baghdad in 2003."

"Yes, that's correct," answered Roth.

"Well, the two guys that were caught in her room at the Loews Regency appear to be Iranian. We don't know for sure because they weren't carrying any identification, but they did request to speak to a representative from Iran's Permanent Mission in the U.N."

"Bogdanos says he thinks there is a link between the Iranians and the seals, even though the seals were stolen from the National Museum of Iraq. Something about their having originated in southwestern Iran, or at least, what is today Iran."

"I don't know where you are in your investigation, but, if I'm right, this may be an angle that you hadn't considered yet. Does any of this make sense to you, Commander?"

"Oddly enough, it does, Agent Ryan. Well, maybe not the Celtic myth, but the rest of it has the ring of possibility. Our team was formed post haste because the CIA learned that the Iranians were trying to make a cultural coup from the looting of Iraq's National Museum, specifically, by recovering the cylinder seals for themselves. So, from what you're saying, I'm assuming that these two men were trying to kidnap this mysterious Finn Ni Cool to learn whether she knew anything about the whereabouts of the seals, and that they were a part of the Iranians' advanced team. That's what I'm hoping, anyway, because if this was their first team, they were ahead of us, the good guys."

"OK, but help me out with this Finn Ni Cool character. I don't know anything about Celtic mythology. I'm a Jewish kid, and all our mythology is well documented in the *Bible* – not the blasphemous *New Testament* you Catholic boys prefer, but *The Word of God*, the *Old Testament*."

Ryan told Roth the story of the giants that he had told his partner.

"I don't see the connection, Agent Ryan. Moreover, my team's made up of an apostate Arab, a cynical MP, a RECON whose only god is the Corps, and a British pagan on loan from the SAS."

"Aye, they are a godless lot, to be sure. As for Finn McCool, I have to admit you've got me there, but let me tell you another part of the myth. Young Finn, whose parents were both warriors, studied under a leprechaun/druid who had spent seven years trying to catch the Salmon of Knowledge. You guys have an apple; we Micks, a fish.

Finally, one day, he caught the fish, and he asked young Finn to cook it for him, but not to eat any of it because the fish contained all the world's knowledge and whoever ate it would then have that knowledge. Anyway, Finn was cooking the fish and turning it to cook it evenly and when he put his thumb on it to see if it was finished, a bubble of fat burned him and a piece of the fish's skin stuck to his finger so that Finn put his thumb into his mouth to ease the burning. When he sucked on his thumb, he ingested the piece of skin and took in with it all of the world's knowledge."

"So you guys have a fish of knowledge and we have a tree of knowledge and a talking snake. How'd the knowledge work out for Finn? Remember, it didn't work out all that well for Adam and Eve, and subsequently, for us. Are you trying to say you Micks are smarter than us Heebs? Agent Ryan, I know you're a colorful people, but come on. A giant, a fish, and a woman a couple of Iranians are trying to kidnap all because of a name is all a little too colorful and imaginative."

"I admit, Commander, this all sounds silly. But the fact remains that there is a very real, intelligent, shadowy woman named Finn Ni Cool, who has recovered some very high-end art. The only solid mention of her involved those Fabergé Eggs I mentioned, but I've also heard rumor of other similar recoveries. There's also a hint, a hint only mind you, that for a while she was hooked up with the IRA, raising money for them by stealing very expensive artwork so that the IRA could sell it back to the owners for a generous finder's fee. So, all I'm saying is, we have an actual woman using the name Finn Ni Cool who does recover high-end artwork, you know there is an Iranian team trying to recover these cylinder seals of yours, and two guys with Russian handguns and a roll of duct tape, who will only speak to an Iranian representative were found in her vacated hotel room."

"When you put it that way, Agent Ryan, it does make a certain amount of sense. Any ideas where she is?"

"Not a clue. The two Iranians were obviously unsuccessful. The two detectives in charge of their case checked with the staff at the Loews Regency, but no one remembers seeing her leave the hotel. The only description we have of her is that she's beautiful. Hell, it's New York. New York's full of beautiful women. She could have gone anywhere, on anything: planes, trains, boats, buses, rental car, limo service, picked up by an accomplice. Let me count the ways."

"You going to do any follow-up?"

"Nope, I'm off the case. I was brought in to determine, given the suspects' nationality, whether this was a criminal offense or an act of terror. In my judgment, it's clearly a criminal offense, so not my jurisdiction. I just thought I'd share my rather curious logic with you because of the cylinder seals."

Roth thanked Ryan and rang off.

Fourteen

May 24th, 2011:

Joe Pete Barlow had a decision to make. He remembered King's warning about picking a private investigator. As he saw it, he had four choices. He could hire a Blackwater-type firm, and he knew a couple of those; he could get one of the national firms, and he'd be able to find those on the Internet; he could hire someone from the casino, and some of the guys he worked with at Beau Rivage had backgrounds similar to his but who also knew about databases, and did some private business on the side; or he could find some sleazy PI, but just how would he do that, he wasn't sure. It wasn't like they were listed under 'S' in the *Yellow Pages*. Hard enough to find normal things in the *Yellow Pages*.

He didn't want a firm without ethics whose tactics might seriously annoy law enforcement and paint him with the same brush, or worse, figure out what he was up to and try to get the seals for itself. He didn't want too scrupulous a firm either, specifically, a company that might turn him into to the cops. Barlow laughed at himself. *It's kinda like a Goldilocks' dilemma – not too bad, not too good.*

If he hired one of the guys at Beau Rivage, he ran the risk of the guy cutting himself in for a full share.

King was right about that, Barlow thought. *I gotta find a sleaze bag, and just how in the fuck do I go about that? I can find all kinds of firms on the Internet. What, do I start callin' and ask 'em, 'are y'all a sleazy firm'? And if the guy says 'yeah,' what next? Ask him, 'how sleazy?'*

Things were a lot easier in Iraq, where ya just stuck a gun in the guy's face and told him ta do what ya wanted and that if he didn't do it, tell 'em you're goin' ta kill his whole family and make him watch before ya killed him very slowly and in such a way that the promised 72 virgins wouldn't be any good fer him, Barlow smiled. *Worked like a charm, every time.*

As it turned out, Joe Pete Barlow didn't have to do anything, because in a few days, the right guy just walked into his office at Beau Rivage. His momma would have called it 'Providence.' Barlow called it 'steppin' in shit'.

"I'm looking for Joe Pete Barlow," the man said. "I hope I'm in the right office."

Barlow was still mulling over his problem when this suited up dude, with what was obviously a 'Great State of Texas' brand of bullshit, came into his office. Clearly, he was Joe Pete Barlow, which this lard bucket knew because of the name plate on the office door. Of course, the man was from Texas, so who knew.

The job paid the bills, though, and Joe Pete had his own brand of bullshit that he liked to call 'Natchez Pure'.

"Yes sir, I am. Have a seat, please. What can I do ta help ya, sir?"

"Well, Mr. Barlow-"

"Call me Joe Pete."

"All right, Joe Pete, my name is Claude C. Dodge, and I'm from Dallas."

At least he hadn't said Dallas, Texas, thought Barlow. The pudge reached into his suit coat pocket, extracted a card case, and presented Barlow with his business card, which read, 'Probity Investigations'.

"Probity Investigations, huh? Just what type of investigations do you do? "

"We do honest ones; that's what *probity* means," Dodge said, pretty sure that Barlow didn't know the word. "Well, Joe Pete, our firm does any number of types of investigations, depending on the needs of my customers."

Barlow noticed that Dodge had switched from 'our firm' to 'my customers' mid-pitch.

"Right now, though, I'm tracking a boy that is trying to avoid his civic responsibilities by purposely missing his court date."

"You're a skip-trace, then, huh."

"That's just one of the services we provide."

Barlow noticed the switch again back to the collective. 'Our firm' probably meant his secretary, who might be his wife, and him. Still, it didn't mean he didn't know his business; his suit looked expensive and his boots were brightly polished.

"Anyway, this boy has a fondness for games of chance. I just missed him at Harrah's in New Orleans." Dodge pronounced the town's name almost like a northerner. He made it two words and four syllables, but at least he put the stress on the first syllable of the second word.

"I'm pretty sure he's headed here. I'm just checking in, letting you know that I'll be here for a few days, unless he's already arrived. Might be, he won a bundle at Harrah's. I won't cause a scene; you can count on that. I'll play it anyway you want, just so I get him. You can steer him out to the parking lot and I'll take it from there, if that's how you want it. It's your house."

"OK, Mr. Dodge..."

"Call me Claude."

"All right, Claude, I noticed you're not carrying a gun. Keep it that way."

"You're good, Joe Pete, real good. How'd you know I don't have a small-of-the-back or an ankle holster?"

"You tugged up your pant legs when ya sat. I don't think ya would of done that if ya were wearin' an ankle holster. And that chair you're settin' on is one of the most uncomfortable chairs in the entire world, maybe even in the universe, and I picked it just fer that reason. Even though I'm a Southern boy, I'm more of a doin' one than a talkin' one. If ya were wearin' a small-of-the-back, you'd be squirmin' in yer seat by now, believe me."

"Let me see y'all's license and the paper on this guy. What's his name by the way?"

"It's Leroy Crowne. The boy's parents had a sense of humor," Dodge said, as he handed Barlow his license and the warrant.

Barlow photocopied the documents and handed them back to Dodge.

"Here's the way we'll work it. First, I'll alert our staff. If yer boy shows up and ya see him before us, call me or one of my men; I'll give ya their names and numbers in a moment. Ya do nothin', understand, nothin'. We escort him to the parking lot, where we'll turn him over to y'all. Is that understood?"

"Yes, sir, Joe Pete. You run a tight ship. I wouldn't have it any other way," said Dodge, rising out of the truly uncomfortable chair, and offering his hand to Barlow.

* * *

Leroy Crowne walked into the Table-Games Room at Beau Rivage at 9:30 that night. Crowne's game of choice was Black Jack. He had tried to get into the High-Limit Lounge, thinking his winnings at Harrah's would qualify him, but he was too impatient to fill out the application necessary for admittance, and he wouldn't have been accepted anyway, given that most of what he owned was in his pockets. The Beau Rivage was serious about its High-Limit Lounge. The credit consultant there called Barlow to report that Crowne had just tried to qualify for the Lounge and, dejected, was now on his way to the Table-Games Room.

Barlow had two of his men meet Crowne there and detain him. Next, he called Dodge.

"Crowne's here. Meet me just outside the main entrance."

Leroy Crowne was not a large man. The two Beau Rivage security men that met him at the entrance of the Table-Games Room were. They didn't have any trouble convincing him of the wisdom in accompanying them. Crowne thought that Harrah's had called the casino to warn them that he was on a roll. Barlow met Crowne and the security men at the front entrance.

"I'll take it from here," Barlow told the men. The men nodded; they had no doubt that Barlow could handle Crowne by himself.

"What's this all about, sir? I just wanted to play some Black Jack. Just 'cause I won some money from Harrah's, shouldn't keep me out. I can pay, I can play, right?"

Leroy Crowne was not a perceptive criminal. He had just been lucky the night before, but that short streak was over.

"Right," said Barlow as he walked him outside, "but it seems you have a friend here waiting to see you."

"Shit," was all Crowne could say when he saw Dodge waiting for him by the valet parking station. Dodge patted him down and hooked him up, with his hands behind his back.

"All he had was a switchblade taped to his ankle. My men took it. Where are ya parked, Claude?"

"Lot Three."

"OK, hold on." Barlow told one of the valets that he'd take this one out. "Bring me around a golf cart."

"There it is, over to the left. It's the white Caddy," said Dodge.

Barlow pulled up to the car. The Cadillac clicked open automatically as Dodge approached it. He opened the back door and motioned Crowne to get in. As Crowne neared the opened door, Dodge pulled out a sap and whacked him across the outside of his right knee. Crowne collapsed sideways into the car.

Crowne grabbed his knee instinctively and howled in pain as he fell into the car. Dodge took advantage of his pain and hooked his ankles up to the shackles connected to the eyebolt in the rear floor of the car.

"He won't run now," said Dodge to Barlow.

"I don't guess he will, Claude. Listen, I'd like ta talk ta ya, if ya got a minute."

"Sure," said Dodge as he closed his car door on Crowne's howling.

"I'm guessin' that if yer a skip-trace, ya must know how ta use the Internet real well, and subscribe ta all them databases fer findin' people, right?"

"Part-time skip-trace, Joe Pete. I do lots a things. Just whatever pays the bills, you know."

"Yeah, well, I'm good at findin' people where I got leads ta follow. Ya know, people ta interrogate and the like, but I got a job that's important ta me, and important ta the guys I served with in Iraq, too. It's a bit over my head, and I need somebody who's real handy with a computer and doesn't mind gettin' his hands dirty, or if other people do."

"Sure, I got you. Why don't you give me a call at my office in Dallas in a couple of days. Give me a chance to get this scum back there and then there's the holiday weekend. How's next Wednesday sound? That's only four days. Can you wait that long?"

"Sure, Claude. I've been waitin' a long time ta deal with this. Four more days ain't gonna matter much."

"Good, then, Joe Pete, call me Wednesday morning. I'll have everything settled by then, and I can give my full attention to your case."

June 1st, 2011:

Dallas was almost 600 miles from Biloxi, but Barlow decided the drive was worth it. What he witnessed in Parking Lot Three of Beau Rivage suggested that Dodge was what he was looking for, but maybe he was just a prick. Barlow wanted to see his office, what his operation was like, and get a read on Dodge's capabilities. He had plenty of comp time. He had been stacking it up just for things like this.

He called Dodge on Wednesday, as Dodge had suggested, but then Barlow told him, he wanted to come out there and have a face-to-face. He told him he didn't like phone calls for something this important.

Barlow was on I-10 a little after 6:00 a.m. on Thursday morning. Two hundred miles later, he was in Lafayette, Louisiana, where he turned north onto I-49 for another two hundred miles. Barlow couldn't see any excuse for I-49 other than linking the parallel Interstates, I-10 and I-20. It went through an empty part of the state, with Alexandria, a town of about 150,000, the most populous town along its route.

He crossed the Red River on I-20 and then turned off when he saw a sign for Blind Willies' Café. Barlow had been driving for a little over six hours, stopping only once for gas. He was hungry. He had resisted all the fast-food restaurants and the ones advertising 'genuine N'aw lins' cooking'. He couldn't understand why a state that had the best cooking in the country would even allow fast-food franchises in it, nor did he understand how a Shreveport restaurant could offer 'genuine N'aw lins' cooking'. If it were genuine, it would be in New Orleans, and if that's what he wanted, he wouldn't be looking for it here in Shreveport; he'd be in the Big Easy. It was a lot closer to Biloxi than Shreveport.

Blind Willie's was in a run-down part of town and looked like a dump, but when you've spent three tours in Iraq, cleaning out shit-holes like Fallujah, Mosul, Basrah, and Tikrit, a run-down neighborhood in Shreveport didn't look all that intimidating. He only hoped Blind Willie put something of Shreveport in his gumbo, but preferably not something from the Red River.

Blind Willie's was a blue-collar bar where men came in at noon for po'boys, dirty rice, and bowls of gumbo with a beer or a glass of *rouge*. Blind Willie made his gumbo with both shrimp and chicken, and, in addition to the usual ingredients, he added some spicy V-8 juice and served it with warm bread. It was just what Barlow wanted, even if he didn't know that when he turned off the Interstate.

Nobody hassled him; it wasn't the type of place where strangers automatically cultivated hostility. Nobody even seemed to pay much attention to him. They were more concerned with their lunch and talking about their jobs in the refineries, or as stage hands in Shreveport's burgeoning movie industry. When he came out, his car was still there. It still had all its tires and nobody shot at him.

Funny, he thought, *how people make up their minds about things without ever having experienced them.* Barlow got gas and was back on the Interstate in forty-five minutes. *Maybe I'll stop here on the way back.*

He reached Dallas at about four o'clock, checked into a Holiday Inn Express, and called Dodge. He told him he was in Dallas and would be right over. Dodge offered to meet him at his motel, explaining that the traffic would be a bitch at this hour, but the whole purpose of Barlow's trip to Dallas was to see Dodge's operation. Besides, he wasn't far from his office.

Dodge's office was located near the heart of Dallas, about a mile south of the Criminal Courts Complex on I-35E, where all the skip-trace offices were. True to form, the bail bonds and skip-trace offices were in strip malls, where they fit in. Dodge's office was not. Located only blocks away from the others, it looked much different. Barlow started to think that maybe he wasn't in competition with the strip mall operations.

Dodge's building had three floors. A forensic accounting office occupied the first floor, and a law firm, the second. Probity Investigations occupied the top floor. His secretary, a very attractive woman, but not so young as to suggest that her only roles were eye-candy for the clients and recreation for Dodge, sat at her desk just inside the office door. When Barlow entered, she seemed to be squaring away her work area to leave for the day. He wondered if Dodge had let her go early so as to guarantee his confidentiality, or this was her regular quitting time. She smiled at him with an equal mix of pleasantness and professionalism.

"Mr. Barlow?" she inquired.

"Yes," acknowledged Barlow.

"Go right in, Mr. Dodge is expecting you. Can I bring you coffee or bottled water?"

"No, thank ya, ma'am. I'm fine."

Barlow took in the reception area. In addition to the secretary's work area, there was a waiting room with comfortable leather couches and chairs that looked the equal to those in the High-Limit Lounge at Beau Rivage. There was also a large flat-screen TV, the latest copies of the most popular magazines, a Rancillo Silvia Espresso machine, whose brand he didn't know, but it looked expensive to him, and a unisex restroom that took up most of the front half of the floor plan. Five offices occupied the back half. Dodge's office was the middle one and the largest, by far. Dodge was standing in his doorway.

"No trouble finding us, I see," Dodge offered his hand and patted Barlow's shoulder when he came through the doorway. "Come in, have a seat," Dodge said good night to his secretary and closed his office door. "Can I get you something to drink?"

"No thanks, your secretary already offered."

"No, I mean something to *drink*."

Barlow understood the tone and followed Dodge's extended hand to the breakfront on the side wall where there was also a conference table that could accommodate at least ten people.

He surveyed the offerings, before answering.

"Jack with a splash of Coke would be great."

Dodge built the drinks while Barlow fixated on the conference table. There was a mill in Natchez that he worked in part-time during high school, so he knew a little about wood. While he didn't recognize all the species that made up the table's parquet design, he recognized the craftsmanship. Barlow could only guess what that table cost, and if he had tried, he would have been too low. He was trying to square with himself how a guy who did his own skip-trace work could afford such a table, let alone have the taste to have it custom made. Even Barlow could tell at a glance that it didn't come from Robb & Stucky.

"How many operatives do ya employ Mr. Dodge?"

"That's a tough question to answer. All depends on what we're working at the time. Usually twelve to fifteen."

"But, it looks like ya only got five offices."

"Seven, actually. Two others are tucked away behind the secretarial area. Besides, they earn the real money on the street. Computers have changed this business a lot, but the edge still comes from working the street. That's where their paychecks are. The offices are for phone calls, computer work, and writing reports. They're usually shared by a team."

Dodge placed a crystal coaster in front of Barlow and handed him his drink, then, rather than sit in his desk chair, he took the seat next to Barlow and turned it to face him.

"Cheers," he said raising his glass. "How can I help you, Joe Pete? I hope you don't mind me calling you by your given name, and I hope you'll do the same. I believe in professionalism, but mostly people come to me because they have personal problems, and if I'm going to fully understand those problems, I can't keep my clients at the arm's length of professionalism. So, tell me, what made you drive six hundred miles to see me?"

Barlow certainly wasn't prepared to tell Dodge about the cylinder seals, but he had to tell him something that was both plausible and extra-legal, so that, once their business was finished, Dodge wouldn't want to cut into it for fear of being indicted for complicity resulting from the unpleasantness that would logically follow. He had rehearsed his story with both Bosheers and King. The three were pretty sure that if Barlow was right about Dodge, it had the proper balance of believability and criminality to lure him in for the fee and then want to get far away from the mess when he had done his job.

"Claude, first I gotta ask ya a question," started Barlow, taking a deep draught of his drink.

"Go right ahead, Joe Pete."

"If I hire ya, is what I tell ya confidential? I mean confidential like with a lawyer or a doctor or a minister?"

"Yes, it is, Joe Pete. As soon as we sign a contract, everything that passes between us as client and investigator is privileged, which means that anything you tell me that has bearing on your case, I can't repeat. If I do, I'm liable for professional censure and criminal charges."

"What about before I sign a contract? I mean," Barlow took another pull on his Jack Daniel's and Coke, "I'm not gonna sign a contract, only ta find out that I can't tell ya what I want and why I want it."

"Of course not, so give me a dollar, Joe Pete"

"What?

"A dollar. You do have a dollar don't you?"

"Of course, I got a dollar," said Barlow, still confused.

"Give it here, then."

Barlow took a dollar out of his left front pocket and handed it over to Dodge, who wrote something on a small pad.

"Here's a receipt for pending services rendered. Now, everything we talk about pertaining to the case is covered by confidentiality."

"OK, just so I'm sure, let me say it in my own words."

"Go right ahead, Joe Pete."

"If I tell ya somethin' I'm plannin' that may be illegal, and ya tell the cops, the State will pull your license and y'all go ta jail."

"That's right."

"Fer how long?"

"Well, that depends on what you're planning on telling me. You're not talking about whacking some guy are you, Joe Pete?"

Barlow purposely paused. This was it. This was where he'd find out if his instincts were right.

"Well, supposin', just fer the sake of argument, that's exactly what I'm plannin'."

"Well, now, Joe Pete," Dodge said, taking a big gulp from his neat, single malt Scotch.

"Let me explain. As ya know, I work as a security director fer a casino, but just a little more than a year ago, I was in Iraq. Did three tours there, Special Forces, punchin' the tickets of raghead cowards who planted roadside IEDs and sat back at a safe distance and watched the chaos."

"Well, a buddy of mine and I got suspicious of one of the Iraqi nationals who worked fer our unit. We started ta notice that when he began gettin' chatty with the LT, the motor pool guys, or the medics, then the ragheads started gettin' more precise about where they planted them IEDs. Taggin' more of our guys, and less nationals on bikes, mule carts, or kids playin' in the streets."

"By the time we put all this together and went lookin' for Mohammed, he disappeared. The guys in my unit really wanted this fuck, so I began trackin' him down. What I found out was that he had booked outta Iraq to North America, probably Canada. I'm good at findin' people when I have a lead or someone ta interrogate, but I don't know my way around a computer well enough ta know where ta look fer someone who doesn't wanta be found. So, bottom line, when I saw the way ya handled Crowne in Biloxi, I thought ya might just be the kinda guy I needed."

"So, what are you going to do to this guy when I find him for you?"

"It's better that ya don't know, Claude. My unit and I will deal with that. For the record, let's just say Uncle Sam would like ta talk ta him about some of his friends. Ya know, in a neutral site, like, say, Poland. And that I came ta ya because he's probably in Canada, and the Army doesn't wanta go through the international red tape of findin' him. But since I'm a private citizen, I can come ta ya ta locate him fer Uncle Sam. I wouldn't worry about any follow up, Claude. Nobody cares about this fuck except me and my unit."

"Well, the good news, is that, unless he's hiding out in an igloo in Eskimoland, I can find him. Hell, even then I probably can. The bad news is, it will cost you $10,000. If I can't find him in thirty days, I'll return $5,000, but I wouldn't count on any refund. I rarely have to give one."

"Deal."

"Give me the particulars, Joe Pete."

Fifteen

June 2nd, 2011:

Barlow didn't stop at Blind Willie's on his way back to Biloxi. At one o'clock, he was in Lafayette, Louisiana, so he stopped at the Olde Tyme Grocery for a shrimp po'boy. He was back in Biloxi a little before five o'clock.

Barlow met Bosheers at the casino that night for dinner. Over drinks, he filled him in on Dodge's operation, his read on him, the $10,000, and the terms of the deal. Bosheers seemed happy with Barlow's handling of the PI, or at least as happy as an ex-soldier can be, having just spent over $3,000 on a maybe. Bosheers asked him if he had contacted King.

"Yeah, I e-mailed him just before comin' down."

"How do you think this will set with him?"

"Well, he ponied up and left it in my hands. What can he say?"

"Just thinkin'. First hire and more than half his money's gone."

"Ya gotta spend money ta make money, isn't that what they tell me? Besides, if Dodge doesn't come through, he gets close to two grand back." Math was never Joe Pete's strong suit. "I don't think we're goin' ta get any money back, though. Dodge seemed pretty confident."

"Ya don't think he'll stiff us, do ya?"

"Nah, then we'd have another person ta kill, and I think ole Claude understands that. I think he'll come through," said Barlow.

"So, the trip was worthwhile? Ya got a good read on'im?" asked Bosheers.

"Yeah, I did. Ya shoulda seen the conference table he had, and his secretary wasn't bad either, and she wasn't even his wife. I may not know shit about rugs and crystal and stuff like that, but I know whiskey and I know wood. The Jack was real; he wasn't fillin' black label bottles with Beam. And I wouldn't wanta guess what that table costs. It sat at least ten and was inlaid with all kinds of exotic woods. I didn't even recognize half of them, but I think I smelled sandalwood. You know how rare that shit is? The good stuff sells for as much as $1,000 per pound. Nah, I got a good read on ole Claude, and I think he's got a good read on me."

Dodge put three teams on finding Musaiyib: two in the U.S. and one in Canada. One U.S. team focused on the East as far west as Minneapolis; the other, on likely ports-of-entry on the West Coast, as unlikely as the West Coast might be. Dodge was pretty sure Musaiyib would steer clear of Texas if he knew anything at all about Texans. He included Minneapolis in the eastern search because, for some unknown reason, Minneapolis seemed to attract war refugees. The easy answer was that do-gooder religious groups sponsored them, but there are do-gooder religious groups everywhere in America, so why Minneapolis? The climate alone defied reason. Why would a Montagnard or a Somali move to Minnesota? And once there, why would he stay? *Curiouser and curiouser*, Dodge thought.

After a full week, all three teams struck out. They had gone through the usual private investigator databases, including background searches, bank accounts, car rentals, deeds, DMV, Homeland Security, marketing rolls, warrants, and the trusty *White Pages*. Nothing.

Early Monday morning, Dodge was sitting at his desk reading about their failures. He couldn't understand it. They rarely failed. Certainly, he never had three teams working on the same search and had them all fail. *Was Barlow's information faulty? That's the last place to look,* he reminded himself. *Don't blame the client for your shortcomings.*

Dodge memo-ed the teams about a name change. Each, of course, had considered that early on in the search. They had searched the usual sources, but with no luck. He told them to get creative and look for other sources that might suggest an unorthodox name change, legal or not.

Three more days passed and they still had no leads. In frustration, Dodge reassigned them to other clients and took over the project himself. First, he eliminated what the teams had done. They were good. If Musaiyib's information was in any of the resources they had searched, one of them would have found him. They hadn't. Why not? Dodge made a list of possible reasons, which included the obvious problems, such as, Barlow got it wrong or Musaiyib never even came to North America. He could have bought street creds, but good ones were expensive and still not foolproof. He might have changed his name in such a way as to get legal credentials for his new identity. After Dodge ran through the fairly obvious possibilities, he tried the unusual. He's dead, or maybe the marshals or the Mounties had him in protective custody. Maybe he had gotten a sex change and was no longer a true son of Allah. When Dodge left the office on Thursday night, much later than was normal for him, he still had nothing.

Cops are fond of quoting Occam's Razor – misquoting it actually. They frame it as, *all things being equal, the simplest and most obvious explanation is usually the right one.* For example, husbands kill wives and wives kill husbands, so they are always the first suspects to be checked out. However, what the razor, a philosophical device used to eliminate unlikely explanations, really says, is that, "when faced with several plausible explanations, one should choose the one that makes the least assumptions."

Dodge's father had been a large-animal veterinarian, and one of the tidbits he picked up in vet school was the same one doctors learned in med school, which was, when you hear hooves, think horses not zebras. Dodge saw a lot of zebras in his list, and only one pony. He started playing with anagrams. M-u-s-a-i-y-i-b didn't offer a lot of possibilities. The extra 'i' was a problem, but Dodge didn't know anything about Iraqi names. *Sumaiyib* was too close, but still a possibility. *Ibaiumy*, was possible, as well. Could it be *Ubaisimy*? How the hell would he know? He tried them all. He found a number of *Sumaiyibs*, but none had a similar profile to the one Barlow gave him on Saeed ibn Musaiyib.

Dodge reflected. To think outside the box, you have to be outside the box. Most people who are familiar with the expression, think that all they have to do is remind themselves to change their mindset, but they can't. Dodge knew why. Most people couldn't think outside the box because they were in a box of their own creation. Sure, parents, teachers, and a lot of others had input, but people allowed them, if not invited them, into the process of their creation. Dodge knew he had to step outside the bounds of his mindset if he were to be effective.

He got up and walked around his office, then out went of his office door, walking past his pretty secretary without saying a word – she was used to it – and then down the stairwell. Dodge rarely took stairs. He generally hated exercise. He went up and down the three flights four times. Back in his office, he wrote the name *Musaiyib* backwards, so it was *Yibiasum*. He considered it. Nothing struck him. Then he wrote the letters upside down, so *M* became *W*; *u* became *n*; *s*, *i*, and *y* either didn't change, or didn't make sense upside down; and *b* became *g*. It was no help.

Wait, Dodge thought. *Wait a minute.*

M to *W* was the change that made the most sense. The *u* to *n* didn't seem to work, so he left it alone. He also left the *b* alone. He ran a search for Wusaiyib through his databases. Nothing. Then a prompt appeared: *Did you mean Wusaivid?* Sure the cursive *d* could also look like an upside down *b* if the loop weren't closed, and, if the tail were shortened, the *y* could look like a *v*. He tried it. There he was, one Salar Wusaivid. It had to be his man! Wusaivid's profile bore out his assumption. Maybe Occam was right, or at least his razor was. Dodge had made only one assumption. Namely, that the transpositions were originally made in cursive, and only typed later.

Dodge printed out the profile and called Barlow. It was five o'clock on Friday afternoon.

"Joe Pete, don't start spending your refund. I think I've found your man."

* * *

Barlow tried to call King in Canada, but he wasn't picking up. He was probably out on maneuvers in some frozen waste up there.

I wonder what he likes better, Barlow thought. *The Iraqi desert or the ice floes.* Barlow e-mailed Wusaivid's profile to King's smart phone with the message to call him when he got back to civilization.

King wasn't on an ice floe. He was currently assigned to teaching advanced hand-to-hand combat at the Canadian Forces Base (CFB) in Petawawa, Ontario, located about 230 miles west of Montreal. It was only about a four-hour drive. None of that would have registered with Barlow, because he, like so many Americans, believed that, except for the very southern fringe, most of Canada was still encased in the last ice age. In the same way that they believed that New York, city or state, was covered by pavement and skyscrapers. When King got back to the barracks at the end of the day, he read Barlow's message. He texted back, saying, "I can't get away till Saturday. I'll check it out then."

The drive to Montreal was a reasonably easy one; most of it was either on the Trans-Canada Highway or an autoroute. King left the base right after inspection at 0800 hours. The Trans-Canada was a major highway in Canada; notwithstanding, the traffic wasn't too heavy. Only when he got near Ottawa and was coming into Montreal, did it pose any problems for him.

He missed his exit when he got to Montreal and, before he realized it, he was in the *Quartier Chinois*. A Nepalese trying to speak French to some Chinese wasn't furthering his cause much. He got back on the autoroute and re-traced his approach until he saw a sign for Saint-Laurent at the junction AUT-740 and AUT-15. The exit took him directly to Boulevard Décarie, which led him to Rue Décarie before he could convince himself that he was lost again. King's sense of direction was much better on foot than in a car, especially in densely populated areas.

Inner-city driving skills excepted, King knew enough about conducting surveillance to recognize in short order that he couldn't just park outside Musaiyib's apartment, waiting for him. Unlike Keagan and Kelly, King was dark complected, swarthy rather than brown or black, and taller than most Gurkhas. Still, he didn't fit in. His car was newer and less beat up than the ones around him, and the neighborhood was clearly ethnic. King didn't know that those around him weren't Iraqis, but he knew that they were Arabs. They could be Syrians, Egyptians, Libyans, or even Lebanese, maybe. Regardless, it was an enclave, and not a place that saw much stranger traffic. As such, it was a neighborhood that knew its residents and was suspicious of outsiders. King moved.

He drove around the neighborhood, paying attention to the shops. Many of the signs were in Arabic, which he didn't know how to speak, let alone read. Gradually, patiently, he started seeing signs in English and French that advertised Syrian and Lebanese staples. He also saw a mosque. It was almost two o'clock and King hadn't eaten since breakfast mess, so he drove out of the area to look for a place to eat lunch and maybe kill some time, though King rarely killed time.

He finished eating by 2:30 p.m. Afterwards, he reconnoitered the area, making sure he knew at least two ways out. When he was confident that he was very familiar with both, at least in daylight, he drove back to Saint-Laurent and parked down the street from the mosque. It wasn't much of a mosque, meaning there were no domes or minarets, and it was nothing like the al-Rahman Mosque in Baghdad; it was just a storefront. It was a place for the believers to roll out their prayer mats and prostrate themselves to Allah. At 4:15 p.m., groups of men started to approach the mosque. Even by narrowing the candidates by the direction they came from, and further eliminating others by virtue of age and physical characteristics, he was still left with six to eight possibles. King wasn't sure how long prayers would last, as the length varied by sect. In Iraq, the usual length was ten to fifteen minutes, so it couldn't be much longer here. He moved the car two blocks down and parked so that he could see the candidates who headed back toward Musaiyib's address. At 4:45 p.m., the men were back on the street.

King wasn't sure if he should try to follow them in his car or on foot. Walking through an Arab community would call attention to him, especially if he had to come back several times, but trying to follow someone who was on foot in a car created its own problems. He decided walking was better. After a couple of blocks, men began to peel off into side streets. A block away from Musaiyib's address, there was only one left. King followed him to the address he had for Musaiyib.

King walked back to his car and called Barlow.

"I got him. That is, if your information is correct." He told Barlow how he had identified Musaiyib. "What do you want me to do?"

"Jesus, that was quick. Can ya hang around there fer another day?" Barlow asked.

"Yeah, one more day. I have to be back on the base by Monday at 0600 hours. But listen, this is a tough place for surveillance; it's a closed neighborhood, so it'd be kind of like you hanging out on Martin Luther King Street in Natchez."

"Yeah, I get yer point. Do what ya can. Try ta get an idea of where he goes, what he does. Ya know the drill. Establish his patterns."

"So you don't want me to snatch him, put my Khukuri to his throat, and make him tell us where the cylinder seals are?"

"No, just establish his patterns as best ya can. I gotta move my schedule around and see how fast I can get up there. You probably should do the same. I don't know how long this will take, but I can't believe it'll go for more than two weeks once we decide ta move. Ya said ya had plenty of leave time. Any problem y'all see takin' that time soon?"

"Well, I got to go through channels and I've got two, maybe three, more weeks of teaching clumsy fuckers how to kill someone quietly. After that, I should be OK."

"All right, do what ya can with him tomorrow. I'll be back in touch with ya as soon as I can put things together on my end."

Barlow trusted King in most things. He had to trust him with his life in Iraq, but he didn't want King finding out where the cylinder seals were and grabbing them for himself.

If that happened, I'd have ta kill the fucker, and that'd be just too bad because he's my friend, thought Barlow.

After *Asr*, Musaiyib went to the Trailhead. He knew he needed to pick up some resin, but when he was doing his final equipment check that morning, he noticed that the toe cover from one of his climbing shoes was beginning to separate, which was not a problem he wanted to face on a Class IV pitch.

Musaiyib usually rode his bike to the Trailhead, but he wanted to sort some things out about his up-coming trip, so he decided to walk. Walking was better than riding for identifying problems. Focusing on problems while riding a bike in the city was much more conducive to injuries than it was to solutions.

Guy Lévesque, the Trailhead owner greeted Musaiyib when he entered the store.

"What can I do for you today, Salar?"

"I need some resin, and I just noticed one of my toe covers is peeling away from my climbing shoes, so I guess I need to get a new pair."

"Yeah, some guys like to tape them down to save money, but it's not a safe solution. Do you know what you want?"

"Not really. My last pair were Evolv Royales, but maybe I need to move up."

"The Royales are a good starter shoe, but you're past them now. If you like the Evolvs, I've got a couple models you can look at, but why don't you take a look at La Sportivas. I carry three different models, and my customers seem very satisfied with them."

"Sure, OK."

"You're a 40.5, right?"

"Right."

Lévesque went into the back room and came out with three boxes of shoes.

"This first model is their Miura; it's probably the best of the three for very technical pitches, especially on edging on tiny chips. Check 'em on the wall."

Musaiyib put them on, went over to the Trailhead's climbing wall, and made several ascents.

"I see what you mean, but I don't think they'd be so great on smears."

"You really are learning. These Katanas here edge almost as well as the Miuras, but they smear better. See what you think."

"Yeah, I see what you mean."

"OK, this last pair, La Sportiva Solutions, heel and toe well, are very durable – platform doesn't flex out in a few months – but notice the closure; it's not just fast. The one string pull allows you to set the tension better and thus, get better control. They're also great for heel and toe holds. Notice how sturdy both are."

"How are they on smears?"

"Great, feel that platform. These would be my choice. Everything I showed you is within $10 of each other."

Musaiyib made several climbs on the wall with the Solutions and came back beaming.

"Yeah, I'll take these."

When Musaiyib returned to his apartment, he noticed a late-model car with Ontario plates pulling away from the curb across from his apartment building. It looked very much like the one he saw down the street from the mosque, but it had already gone when he came out from prayers. There was no empirical evidence to believe both cars were the same; he didn't see the driver on either occasion and hadn't noticed the province or the plate number of the car by the mosque. Still, he didn't like what he was feeling now. Musaiyib mentally filed the observations as something to be aware of in the future.

* * *

Barlow met up with King in Montreal on the following Saturday afternoon in his room at Le Pavilion, not far from Trudeau International Airport.

"I was just gonna order lunch. Have ya eaten yet?"

"No."

"Check out the menu on the credenza over there and I'll call room service. I got some beer. It's over in the mini-fridge."

King got two bottles of Molson Export out of the mini-fridge, popped the caps, and handed one to Barlow.

"What've ya got fer me, Randy?" Barlow asked.

"Not much. I'm only here Saturdays and Sundays, and then only about half of Saturday, so I'm not able to follow him to work. What you sent me says he works for Gentec, Inc., a computer company downtown, but I wouldn't know. Fucker prays a lot. He goes to a mosque about a half mile from here. Not one of them big places we saw in Iraq with the funny towers, just a shitty, little storefront. I guess it's important to him though. He goes to the gym on Sunday afternoons, and maybe during the week too when I'm not here. I've seen him go there twice now, and once was with a buddy. They both look fit enough, but skinny. If you want me to snatch 'em, I'm sure I can handle both of them. That's about it – mosque, gym, home.

He doesn't eat in restaurants, doesn't seem to have a slit. He doesn't even own a car. He either walks or rides a mountain bike wherever he goes. Cheap fuck. I thought computer jobs paid well."

"They do. Maybe he's keepin' a low profile. Ya said the neighborhood isn't much."

"Nah. Don't get me wrong, it's not a slum, but I could do better, and I'm in the military."

"Anythin' else? Hold on, that's room service."

The waiter pushed a service cart in the room when Barlow answered the door. "Where would you like me to set this up, sir?"

"On the coffee table's fine."

The waiter removed the aluminum stacking rings from the tray and placed the sandwich plates, silverware, and cloth napkins on the coffee table before handing Barlow the check. Barlow signed it and added ten percent. The waiter beamed his thanks. Barlow didn't notice that a service charge of twelve percent was already included, as was the norm in Canada. King got two more beers and they ate the sandwiches in silence.

When they were finished, Barlow asked King to continue where he had left off.

"Like I said, these Islamic fuckers don't do much other than pray and stay home. I have cruised the neighborhood quite a few times, getting a good read on it. You know I can't hang out by his apartment; it's a tight-knit neighborhood, so I stand out. Anyhow, I know the area well enough now that I can get out of it fast, day or night. I mean, if we wanted to snatch him and get lost quickly. But we may not even have to do that, because I found a couple of deserted buildings not too far from where he lives. We could take him there, have him tell us where the seals are, and wrap up this thing quickly."

"Show me after we finish eatin'."

King took Barlow out to the abandoned factory, but on the way he drove by Musaiyib's apartment building.

"That's where he lives," said King, as he drove by. "We better not stop. I got a little cover here, but you're a real stand out."

King showed him the factory. There were several buildings on the property, and a chain-link fence ran around it. Razor wire scrolled atop the fence, and a locked chain wound through the gateway.

"I got a pair of bolt cutters in the trunk that'll take care of the chain."

"Drive round the block, Randy. I wanta see what's round here."

After they circled the block, Barlow asked King if there was a night watchman.

"Nah, nothing to steal."

"What about bums, junkies, or teenagers gettin' laid?"

"None that I noticed."

"OK, let's look at this mosque."

"You're right. I guess Allah ain't as rich as Jesus. Ya remember the churches down home in Natchez. Forget the Catholics and the Episcopalians, ya remember the Parkway Baptist Church. Now, those fuckers know how ta raise money. Say hallelujah, brother, and pass the hat."

King had no idea what Barlow was talking about. His English was quite good, having lived in an English-speaking country since he was two, and it was much better than his French, which he had to speak sometimes here. His English was even better than his Kiranti, which he spoke at home when he was growing up. Even his knowledge of the colloquialisms of the day was good, but sometimes understanding Barlow was more like wading through code. He knew what all the words meant, but he had no idea what Barlow was saying.

Once, Barlow had invited him to come home to Natchez with him for a week. King could understand most of what he normally said, but when he got around his people, King had little to no idea what he was saying. It was like he had switched to a language that King had never heard before. What with the regional expressions, the tobacco-chewing, and the swallowed syllables, he spent the whole stay in utter confusion, smiling like an idiot, and listening to Barlow's parents and friends while pretending he even remotely understood what they were saying to him. It was like being surrounded by a town full of mushmouths. Once at dinner, which they referred to as supper, Joe Pete's father asked him to pass the 'all' or maybe it was 'awl'.

All what? pondered King. Covering himself, on the off chance that the old man was even weirder than he seemed, King briefly considered why he would want a leather-sewing tool at the dinner table. After some semi-precise pointing and miming, it finally dawned on him that what the old man wanted was the salad oil.

"Where do ya think we should snatch him?" asked Barlow.

"We don't have a lot of options. He doesn't seem to go out at night, not even here. We can't grab him here; there are too many others around. We can't question him in his apartment, at least not the way we need to. We can't wrap him in a rug and fireman-carry him out the front door or even down the back fire escape. And I got to believe that grabbing him on his way to work isn't likely to be any better."

"So what does that leave us, Randy?"

"How fast can you steal a car, Joe Pete?"

"Well, I didn't bring a slim Jim with me, but get me ta a hardware store and I can make one. Then it's just a matter of seconds, especially if ya don't want anythin' fancy."

"Nothing special. Just one that runs and has a big trunk."

Sixteen

June 3rd, 2011:

"Commander, we checked with INS to see if Musaiyib had applied for a green card or a visa, but we came up blank. We checked with the State Department, but he doesn't have a U.S. passport, which also rules out a DS-5504 used for applying for a name change. He's not in detention anywhere that we've looked. We've checked with Homeland Security, the FBI, ICE, the CIA, even with the cops in the major port cities – Boston, New York, Newark, Philly, D.C., Atlanta, Miami, and even Chicago because it has direct flights from Europe. Nothing. We've checked for credit card accounts, bank accounts, driver's licenses, phone records, both land line and cell, and even Internet accounts. Nothing. Nada. Zilch! If this guy is in the States, he's a phantom," said Jassim.

"I did find three Musaiyibs. There's one in Sayre, Oklahoma; another in Hanna, Wyoming; and even one in Churchill, Manitoba. I followed up with the locals, but even though their ages are consistent with our Musaiyib, the locals told me that all three had been there for a while."

"Jesus, what the fuck does a Muslim do in Sayre, Oklahoma? Let alone Churchill, Manitoba, wherever the fuck that is. Canadians are a lot slower on the trigger, but I'm amazed that some Okie hasn't shot the one in Sayre. Now that I think about it, Muslims aren't real popular in Wyoming either. One notch up from wolves, in fact. Hell,

I'm a Muslim – well, kind of – and I'm pretty sure I wouldn't want to live in Oklahoma or Wyoming, and probably not in Churchill either, but for different reasons."

"Anyway, bottom line is, Kennedy and I are about out of ideas here. You got any, sir?"

"I've got a conference call shortly with Interpol in Lyon, with Bogdanos in New York, and Quinn in Baghdad. Let's get the team together at 1400 hours to see if we can come up with some new ideas," Roth said.

The team met in the conference room at two o'clock. Jassim outlined what he had told Commander Roth earlier in the day. Kennedy already knew the status of the investigation since he had worked with Jassim to develop the leads that had been checked out, which left only Wade and Lollard to be filled in.

"OK, men, you've heard what Jassim and Kennedy have already tried; what haven't they?" asked Commander Roth.

Roth, Jassim, Kennedy, and Wade were thinking about other agencies to contact, other databases to search, and even west coast ports of entry to look at, which they ignored for obvious reasons, when Lollard spoke up.

"Maybe we've been looking in the wrong country."

"Elaborate, Socko," said Commander Roth. "We've already checked out the Arab countries and England. And we can't find him in the States. Where next?"

"Well, you said you found a Musaiyib in Churchill, Manitoba. Did you check further in Canada?" asked Lollard.

"No, that was a mistake. I was too quick on the trigger. I clicked the mouse button before I read where it was leading me," said Jassim.

"Maybe a mistake, maybe not. I don't see why Canada or Australia aren't possibilities. They have Muslim populations, small ones, but big enough to hide in. Actually, I think percentage-wise, Canada has more Muslims than the States. If it does, then so does Australia, if I remember correctly. Plus, both countries might provide a market where Musaiyib could sell the seals. Their economies are doing well. Since Canada is just north of us, I'd suggest we start there, unless you think the west coast is a better choice. Me, I vote for Canada. If nothing pans out, then we can look down under. I'd rather enjoy going there again, so long's it's not to the Great Victoria Desert."

* * *

Jassim and Kennedy began redoing the things they had already done while looking for Musaiyib in America, but this time, they looked in Canada. Only five of Canada's provinces – Ontario, Québec, Alberta, British Columbia, and Nova Scotia – had significant Arab populations. Nunavut, while a territory rather than a province, probably didn't have a single Arab. Jassim doubted there were many in the Yukon Territory either. Ontario and Québec, however, accounted for eighty-two percent of Canada's Arab population, so, after checking out the national databases, like Immigration, National Health, and tax databases, Jassim focused on those two provinces, with special attention to Toronto, Ottawa, and Montreal, which together accounted for almost one third of Canada's total population. Toronto had both a larger overall population and a larger Arab population, but the difference was negligible, so Jassim gave the three cities equal importance. Still, he found nothing.

"Wesley, go find out what Socko is doing. If it isn't critical, bring him over here, will you?"

Kennedy found Wade and Lollard working out on mats in the gym. Lollard was showing Wade the sleeper hold and its variations.

"Sometimes, you'll want to use it just to take the fight out of your opponent. Other times, you'll want to put him under and then take further measures, ranging from restraining him to slitting his throat. You need to know how to read the signs. Experienced fighters might fake a collapse. That's why you ease up on the pressure. You don't remove it until you're sure of your opponent's state."

"Socko, can you take a break?" asked Wesley.

"Sure, Wesley, what's up?"

"Jassim and I need to pick your brain."

"What do you want me to do, Wesley?" asked Wade.

"Ah, shit, you might as well come along. If we're asking for help from a Brit, it can't be much of a stretch to think that one of Uncle Sam's Misguided Children might give us an idea. Although, I always thought Marine was an acronym for *muscles are required; intelligence not essential.*"

"You do know, Wesley, you're going to pay for that. You may be good at finding people, but when I get through with you, you won't be able to find your own ass."

"Nah, I'll just buy you a beer some night and you'll forget about the whole thing."

"I'm holding you to that, Wesley."

"See what I mean, Socko?"

"What've you got for me, Ali?"

"I took your advice and started looking north to Canada, but I'm not having much luck." Jassim filled Lollard in with where he had been looking and why.

"Well, I'd say you pretty much covered the obvious, except for one thing," said Lollard.

"What's that?"

"Fucker changed his name."

"Yeah, that's one of the first things I considered, but if he did, he didn't do it legally. How am I supposed to guess what he changed it to? I figure I can rule out names like O'Leary and Filippini and Rodrigues and Bitucockoff, but where do I go from there?"

"You got a database with Arab names?" asked Lollard.

"Yeah, but they differ according to country," said Jassim.

"Hey, Ali, what are those puzzles that you scramble up all the letters and come up with a different word?" asked Wade.

"You mean anagrams, Bo?"

"Yeah, I guess. You got a program that you can scramble up Musaiyib and then make it look in one of them rag-" Wade caught himself, but not quickly enough that Jassim didn't notice.

"Sorry, Ali. I wasn't thinking. Anyway, look in one of them Arab-name databases."

"Out of the mouths of Gyrenes," said Kennedy.

"You are so dead, Wesley."

"OK, two beers, Bo."

Seventeen

July 2nd, 2011:

King took Barlow to a Home Depot on Boulevard Côte Vertu. When Barlow came back to the car, he had a pair of tinsnips, a roll of duct tape, and a carpenter's saw.

"Take me ta some place where I can work unobserved fer a few minutes."

King drove down Côte Vertu to Boulevard Cavendish, turned right, went down a half mile, and turned into Parc Marcel-Laurin, where he found a nearly empty parking lot. Barlow took the tinsnips and cut the handle off the carpenter's saw. Next, he cut a 2-inch wide lengthwise strip down the straightedge side of the saw blade. Finally, he carefully cut a hook into the bottom of the thin strip. When he was finished, he wrapped the tape around the top of the strip.

"There ya go," said Barlow. "This'll work as good as any I ever used. Drive over ta the trash barrel and let me get rid of the timmin's."

After picking out a car from the long-term parking lot at Trudeau International and having dinner, they went back to Barlow's hotel room. Long-term lots were great for dumping a car, but they were even better for stealing one, especially if you followed the car you wanted into the lot. If the driver was parking in the long-term lot, odds were he'd be gone for at least a couple of days.

Besides, car thefts in major cities held a police priority a rung or two down from hopping over the turnstile in the subway, or the

Métro if you're in Montreal. Barlow found the car he wanted late Saturday afternoon, but left it at the airport until he needed it later the next morning. He figured there was no sense in holding on to a stolen car any longer than he had to. Even given a stolen car's police priority, funny things could happen whenever you did something illegal, at least in civilized countries.

"So, the guy goes ta morning prayers, Randy?"

"He did last weekend."

"OK, we snatch Musaiyib either on his way ta the mosque or on his way back. I vote fer on the way if we can. It'll be darker. Ya should drive because ya know the area better in case we get inta trouble. I'll grab him, we'll drive him ta the factory, and we can ask him some questions."

"What if he holds out? Or what if the seals are in a safety-deposit box in some bank or he's hidden them where we can't get them tomorrow?" asked King.

"He's not gonna have the option of holdin' out."

"What if he tries to hold out? Remember, Awwal did and look how that turned out."

"Yeah, well, I jumped the gun with him, but how long do ya think he's gonna be able to hold out when y'all start cuttin' his fingers off with that blade of yours? Besides, we don't have the luxury ta hang around here until he decides ta sell them. Shit, ya gotta be back on base Monday mornin'. I can spend more time here, but I'm pretty much out of patience. Not ta mention the 10K we spent. Judgin' from what ya've told me of the way he lives, he hasn't sold 'em yet, and he's had 'em now fer over eight years. Maybe he woulda tried to sell 'em by now if I hadn't killed Awwal, but I did, and that's what we have ta deal with. Not *would ofs*, *could ofs*, or *should ofs*. He doesn't seem ta be in a hurry. It's shit or get-off-the-pot time for us, though. If he wants ta go ta his grave and take the seals with him, he loses his life. All we lose is somethin' we never had."

"And the 10K."

"Yeah, well, that's lost any way we go."

"I guess you're right. So we grab him tomorrow morning?"

"Yeah. Let's get some sleep. Ya drop me at the airport at 0400 hours, then go cut the chain on the factory gate, and recon the grounds, makin' sure it's all clear. I'll meet you at the factory, we'll leave your car a couple blocks away, and then we'll get Musaiyib. I already checked sunrise. It's at 0545 tomorrow mornin'. If he goes to the mosque fer that one, we should have him bagged and tagged by 0530 if we get him on the way down."

Musaiyib woke later than usual on Sunday morning. Not so late that he would miss *Fajr* at the mosque, but later than his usual time. He'd have to hurry if he was going to make it before prayers started.

King and Barlow were parked, in the stolen car, on Rue Tassé, just south of Rue Décarie, which was Musaiyib's street. A group of older men came out first, and then, a lone young man.

"There he is," said King.

"You're sure that's him?"

"Yeah, I'm sure. I followed him from the mosque to the address you gave me, and he's the right age. Most of the guys in that building are older, and got fat wives and kids."

"OK, go passed him and make the first right then pull over as soon as ya can."

King drove down Rue Tassé, turned right on Rue Oumet, letting the men from Musaiyib's building cross in front of him, and then pulled over, where he couldn't be seen by anybody walking up Rue Tassé until near the corner.

"Pop the trunk but stay in the car and leave the engine runnin."

Barlow got out. He left the passenger door open, went to the open trunk, ripped off several lengths of duct tape from the roll he had left there, and stuck them, dangling, on the trunk lip. When he was finished, he walked up to the corner. Barlow waited there. The others were focused on the mosque ahead of them. As soon as the young Muslim came into sight, Barlow stepped out, smashed him in the solar plexus, knocking the breath of out of him, and then hit him with a powerful uppercut, snapping his head back, which pinched one of the sympathetic or parasympathetic nerves and rendered him unconscious. Barlow lifted him onto his shoulder, dropped him into the open trunk, took the shortest length of duct tape hanging there and pasted it over his mouth, then wrapped longer lengths around his wrists and ankles. Back in the car, Barlow told King to drive to the factory.

The factory was a good choice. King parked the car between two buildings so that it could not be seen from the street in front of it or the one behind the property. Barlow got the Muslim out of the trunk and carried him into the building through a door that King had prised open earlier that morning. The sun was just above the horizon now, so dawn was beginning to show through the building's broken windows. There was a lot of rubble inside – defunct machinery, broken bottles beer cans, and even a mattress that some kids must have dragged in. There was one metal chair with the back broken out. It didn't matter; they weren't going to be there long. King and Barlow put him in the chair and Barlow ripped the duct tape off his mouth. That brought him around.

His eyes were big with fear and confusion. Barlow asked him if he spoke English. He nodded quickly several times that he did. "All right, let me explain thin's ta ya. I'm gonna ask ya a question. Ya probably won't wanta answer me, but believe me, ya will, because my friend here has a very nasty knife. Show Musaiyib here your knife, Randy."

He started to speak, but when he saw King's Khukuri, he could only shudder.

Barlow continued, "Like I said, I'm gonna ask ya a question; a question that ya probably don't wanta answer, but ya will. Believe me ya will. You will because if ya don't or if ya try ta lie, Randy here is gonna cut off a finger, and he will continue ta cut off y'all's fingers until ya tell me the truth. And if necessary, he'll do the toes too. But I'm sure ya will answer completely and truthfully before then. Oh, yeah. He's gonna start with the thumbs, too. First one thumb, then the other one. You know how important the thumbs are, right? So my advice ta ya, Musaiyib, is not ta try ta hold out. Ya won't be able ta, believe me. This is a tried and true method."

King walked behind the chair.

"OK, here we go. Where are the cylinder seals ya and ya buddy Awwal stole from the museum in Baghdad?"

He started to speak, but found he couldn't.

"OK, Randy, take his right thumb."

The man shouted out, "I am not Musaiyib! You have made a mistake! I don't know any Musaiyib."

"All right, Wusaivid then."

"I am not Wusaivid. He li-"

"Wrong answer. Randy?"

King took the thumb off at the second joint, severing the *princeps pollicis* artery. The cut was quick. The appendage was gone before he realized it, and before the pain came. "Same question, Musaiyib. Where are the seals?"

"No, no, I tell you, you've made a mistake. I am not Musaiyib. I tell you. I am not him, but I know him. He lives in my building."

"What did ya say?" demanded Barlow.

"Wusaivid, Salar, he lives in my building. We sometimes go to prayers together, but he was late this morning. He spent too long on the wall yesterday."

Maloaf, in his fear, had forgotten about his pain. He needed to keep talking before the pain overtook him and he lost too much blood. He couldn't see the blood dripping from the stump where his thumb had been, but he could not raise his arm, so he knew it would continue to bleed. He had to hurry. He had to explain before the pain gripped him or he lost consciousness from blood loss. If he did not explain their mistake, they would surely kill him. He needed to tell them of Wusaivid to survive.

"What wall?"

"The climbing wall at the gym. He is a climber, a rock climber. He bought new shoes yesterday, climbing shoes. He wanted to break them in, and so he was too tired to go to the mosque today. He was to pray at home."

Barlow looked sharply at King. "Randy, check fer a wallet."

King found one in his front pocket; it was a card wallet with a money clip.

"He's got a National Health Card and a MasterCard that both say his name is Asu Maloaf."

"Ah, shit, Randy, what the fuck."

"You gave me the address, Joe Pete, I saw him coming out of that building. He stopped and pulled out his cell phone. I called the number you gave me, and the line was busy. What am I supposed to think? I think he's Musaiyib, that's what. What, I'm supposed to go up to him and ask him his name, like a process server?"

"Yeah, OK, OK." Barlow turned back to Maloaf. "Tell me everything you know about this Wusaivid."

Maloaf's hands were still bound behind him, so he could not raise the one with the missing thumb to slow the bleeding. He was having trouble concentrating. The pain was starting. He looked up at King and the Khukuri and forced himself to think.

"I am in 4B; he is in 4A. We go to the mosque together for *Fajr*, the first prayers of the day. He is very smart. I work in the Post Office. We sometimes go to the gym together, and we go to prayers together. He works with computers. He...he...I don't know what else."

"Where does he climb?"

Maloaf looked at Barlow, his mind muddled over the loss of blood. Barlow repeated the question, miming the movements.

"On the wall."

"Where is this wall."

"Gym."

"I know where it is, Joe Pete," said King

"Where else?"

"I...I...don't know."

"What else do you know?"

Maloaf looked confused.

"Does he have family here? Where does he go at night, on weekends? Does he have a car? Anythin' else ya know."

Maloaf thought hard. "No…no family, no car. He goes to prayers; he goes to work; he does not drin…"

"Ah shit the fucker passed out. Slap him awake, Randy."

King slapped Maloaf moderately hard. Maloaf didn't respond. King hit him again. Nothing. "He done, Joe Pete."

"No, he's still breathin'."

"Yeah, I know, but he's done answering questions. He's passed giving a shit; he's bleeding out."

"Ah, fuck. Do him then, Randy. I don't want some want boy scout comin' along, puttin' a tourniquet on him and savin' his life."

King stood behind Maloaf and drew his Khukuri across his right carotid. Maloaf's blood shot out the way it does from all ruptured arteries but, less far than usual. The thumb excision had lowered his blood pressure significantly.

King wiped the blade of his Khukuri on Maloaf's shirt.

"Let's get outta here, Randy."

* * *

Barlow dropped King off at his car, and King followed Barlow to a Wal-Mart superstore, where he ditched the stolen car.

"What do we do now, Joe Pete?" asked King when Barlow got into his car.

"Nothin' much we can do, short of bustin' into Musaiyib's apartment and draggin' him out in broad daylight. And I haven't had my usual luck interrogatin' prisoners."

"Yeah, well, can't get accurate information if we have the wrong guy. Sorry about that."

"That was a fluke, Randy. All we can do is alternate between watchin' the mosque and his apartment building. What time's the next service?"

"Next one is about 1200 hours, then 1630. One's after sunset, so I guess about 2100 hours, and who knows when the last one is. It's right before bed, so I guess there's no prescribed time. Maloaf didn't go to the 2100 hours one, not last weekend anyway, and I didn't see anybody his age going to it, so I have to guess that Musaiyib doesn't either."

They alternately watched the mosque and Musaiyib's apartment until six o'clock in the evening. He was a no show. King left for his base after Musaiyib missed *Asr*. Barlow called Bosheers in Biloxi and told him the bad news. He said he'd give it one more try tomorrow morning, but if he didn't grab Musaiyib then, he'd be back late tomorrow night.

Eighteen

July 3rd, 2011:

A couple of kids who were looking for a little privacy, stumbled, literally stumbled, onto Maloaf's body. The young lady would probably go through her whole life, regardless of how hormonal she got, without ever again considering having sex in an abandoned factory. She certainly wouldn't ever consider having it with the guy she was with, because when he saw Maloaf's body and the pool of his blood, what the cop shows refer to as exsanguination, the young gentleman bolted, leaving her to deal with the body.

So much for him being my soul mate, she thought. She called 911, told the operator where to find the body, hung up, and got out of there as quickly as she could,

The first police cars arrived at the factory seven minutes after having received the call. They found Maloaf's body right where the girl said it would be. It was no surprise, given his condition. They also found his wallet with his two identification cards in the pool of his blood, and they found Maloaf's right thumb on the floor behind the chair where he was seated.

That Maloaf had been tortured was obvious to the cops, but, with the tortures they were used to seeing, usually drug related ones, they generally saw more damage. Perhaps the loss of three fingers, five fingers, or the victim's face beaten to a bloody pulp. And then there were the ID cards on the floor.

"Maybe he gave them what they wanted," the first cop said. "That would explain why they didn't cut off any more pieces of him."

"Maybe they had the wrong guy," said the sergeant, "which would explain why his wallet and his ID cards are out. Maybe he told them they had the wrong guy, told them to check his wallet. It certainly would explain why they're out and on the floor."

"Wrong guy, huh? That'd be a bitch."

"Yup."

* * *

When Musaiyib got home from Ile Gagnon on the north branch of the St. Lawrence, his neighbors were abuzz with the news of Maloaf's death. The police had been around, asking questions. When he got into his apartment, he noticed a detective's card on the floor that had been slipped under his door. On the back was a hand-written message that said, "call me as soon as you find this."

Musaiyib sat down and considered his options. If he ignored the card's message, the detective would just come back, irritated. He was going on vacation in a week; what if he left early? Surely, they would get suspicious. If they came, what would he say? That he saw a strange car in the neighborhood the last two days?

But why would he notice such a thing? So there was a strange car, so what? Montreal's a big city. He worked both sides of the interrogation. *No, better to tell the police what I know as fact, not what I suppose through fear.* He said *Asr* and called the number on the card.

Detective Inspector Antoine Duclos knocked on Musaiyib's door, nineteen minutes after Musaiyib called him. After Duclos showed Musaiyib his credentials, he let him in. Musaiyib offered the Inspector coffee; Duclos declined. They sat facing each other. Musaiyib was on the couch and Duclos was on the only other chair in the room, a single upholstered chair that didn't match the couch. Duclos took out a notebook from his inside jacket pocket.

"Let me get some particulars first. Can I see some ID, please?"

Musaiyib showed the Detective Inspector his Québec driver's license, which listed his name as Salar Wusaivid and his race as Non-White, which left a lot to interpretation. The demographers in Canada were as confused as those in America as to how to classify Arabs with regards to race, especially since the PC crowd have effectively and curiously lumped everyone living east of the Red Sea, all the way to the Pacific, as Asians. This meant that Arabs living from Egypt to the Atlantic were Africans, those living on the Arabian Peninsula and east to the Pacific were Asians, and, by extension, those living in Spain, especially in Andalusia where they have since the Thirteenth Century, were Europeans. The Canadians at least tried to adhere to the color-coded race designations of Johann Friedrich Blumenbach, which had been used for nearly two centuries until bureaucrats decided to focus on ethnicity rather than on race, but frequently confused the two words.

"What kind of name is Wusaivid?"

"I don't understand the question."

"I mean, what nationality? Is it Syrian like most of the others in this building?"

"No, I am Iranian."

"Were you born here?"

"No, I immigrated to Canada in 2008 from Iran."

"Were you a refugee?"

"No, but I had a university degree in computer science and could not find a job in Iran because I didn't have a bribe sufficient enough for the officials. I came to Canada to work. I possess a *Skilled-Worker Visa*."

"I suppose you know by now about your neighbor."

"Yes, I heard about it when I came home from an outing."

"What can you tell me about him?"

"Not much. We lived in the same building. He lived right across from me. We sometimes went to the mosque together especially for

Fajr, morning prayers. We sometimes went to the gym together. He was a postal worker."

"Nothing else?"

"If you tell me what you are looking for, maybe I can help, but other than going to prayers and the gym, we weren't close."

'Well, he was tortured. Can you think of any reason why someone would do that to him?"

"No, I can't. He was a gentle person," said Musaiyib, doing a very good job of hiding his fear over the similarity with Awwal's death.

"How about anything unusual in the last couple of days. Did it look like something was bothering him?"

"No."

"How about anything in the neighborhood. Anything unusual, even if it didn't involve Maloaf."

Musaiyib thought of the car with the Ontario plates that he had seen down the street from the mosque and pulling away from his apartment building, but answered, "No, I can't. He was just a postal worker, and a quiet person who I went to prayers and the gym with. He came to Canada with his parents when he was sixteen, so I doubt it could have been something that happened back in Syria. Maybe, it was just because he was Muslim."

"Maybe, but why him?"

"I don't know, Inspector. I don't know."

"OK, you still have my card."

"Yes, I do."

"Good. If you think of anything else, give me a call."

"I will, Inspector," Musaiyib lied.

* * *

Finding someone using a computer, especially if you're looking up public domain records, was a lot easier than following up hunches, pounding the pavement, pressuring snitches, bribing bureaucratic clerks, and all the other things that Sam Spade types used to have to do. However, if who you were looking for didn't want to be found and had somehow managed to avoid the public domain databases, then you were left with either hacking into a computer, or somehow acquiring the somebody's username and password.

The movies and TV shows suggested that computer hacking is the stuff of child's play, and sometimes they even showed children doing it. The guru – it was always a guru, regardless of age or ethnicity – sits at his computer, entering backdoor protocols at finger-flashing speed, and *voilà*, he's in – or in the case of Garcia – she's in. In reality, though, while backdoors did exist in firewalls, they required a great deal of trial and error, and the errors usually ended up in an intruder log with all kinds of pertinent information about the would-be hacker. Still, it was done, especially by talented people, gurus or not, who had significant financial and technological resources behind them. Kelly was one of those people.

"So, you were able to blow them up? I wasn't sure if I got anything. I was literally pointing and shooting," said Niles.

"They're beautiful, Niles."

They were in Keagan's lakeshore house. Kelly had just finished running Niles' cell phone pictures through Photoshop. Niles had been up in the inn's bar, setting up for lunch, when Keagan asked him if he could come down for twenty to thirty minutes to discuss their next move. Keagan was taking a shower, also to get ready for the lunch crowd.

"How did you ever get them?"

"Teal tipped me off about a call Musaiyib got from the Trailhead, an outdoor equipment store, specializing in technical climbing gear and instruction, near his apartment. Musaiyib had ordered a couple of high-end items, a pack and a climbing rope, that had come in. I got there before Musaiyib, pretended I was looking to upgrade my equipment because I had been away from climbing for a while, and then, when he was checking over his purchases, I pretended to get a call. He gave the clerk his AmEx card, forgetting the Trailhead didn't take AmEx, but instead of taking his card right back, he left it on the counter while he fished out his MasterCard. I took a picture of the AmEx card on the counter and when he exchanged it for his Master-Card, I took a picture of that one too. Then I excused myself for not walking away when my call came in."

"That was great work, Niles," said Kelly. "You even got the security codes. Mick, come look at these."

Keagan had just stepped out of the bedroom, hair still a bit wet, but otherwise ready for work.

"How'd you get the security codes on the MasterCard? They're on the back. What'd you do, ask him to turn it over so you could get a better shot?"

"No, Musaiyib put it on the counter that way. After the clerk swiped it, he put it down on the counter face side up. That'll teach him to be polite and hand the card to the clerk."

"Always the gentleman, Niles. Now, we can track all his charge purchases," said Kelly.

"Let's hope he doesn't have a reserve with a pile of cash stashed in it."

"Kelly, let's see what Musaiyib has purchased with his credit cards lately other than the backpack and the climbing rope," said Keagan. "Oh, shit, no, you can't do that even though you have his account numbers and security codes. You still need his accounts passwords."

"Yes, I can."

"How? Where did you get those?"

"Remember when you bugged his landline?" asked Kelly.

"Yeah, but he doesn't call anybody. That wasn't much use," said Keagan.

"Yes, it was. Remember you bugged the line, not the phone. You even said at the time that maybe it would pick up some of his Internet transmissions."

"Right, but I didn't know you were able to do anything with that," said Keagan.

"I wasn't until I had the IP addresses of American Express' and MasterCard's payment computer, and now that I have the account numbers and the security codes, I've been able to isolate his passwords – password, actually – he uses the same one for both accounts, a common practice."

"I'll be damned," said Keagan.

"Probably," said Niles.

"Oh, I hope not," said Kelly. "But look on the bright side, Mick; we'll be together for all eternity then."

Nineteen

July 3rd, 2011:

Kelly logged into the MasterCard site first.

"Just the usual: paid his rent and bought some groceries. Not your usual, modern-day conspicuous consumer. From the looks of this and what we've observed, he's unusually frugal, close, and stingy even," said Kelly. Then she logged into the AmEx site.

"Go back ninety days, Kelly," said Keagan.

"Rent, groceries, gym fee, no donations to the mosque. He must do that in cash so he doesn't get traced by your NSA. Pretty much the same pattern. Wait, here's something. He bought an Air Canada ticket from Montreal to Calgary."

"When did he make the reservation?" asked Keagan.

"Over two months ago. Got a good price, I'm guessing. The boy really is tight."

"See if he's gone yet."

Kelly switched sites, clicked the Manage My Bookings tab on Air Canada's site, entered the booking reference from the credit card statement and Salar Wusaivid for the passenger's name. The working symbol rotated for the better part of thirty seconds and then there were the particulars of Musaiyib's ticket.

"Not yet, Mick, but soon; next Saturday in fact."

"Makes sense. He just got a new pack and new rope. I'd say he's off to the Canadian Rockies for a bit of adventure. It is summer, so he's probably taking his vacation."

"Go back as far as you can on his credit card statements. I don't think you can go back more than the beginning of the calendar year without a request, which means – unless you've managed to install a mirror drive somehow, they will send it to him, not us."

"What are you looking for, Mick?"

"Any evidence of similar travel. Seems an unusual expense, in spite of the bargain rate he got, for someone who's as tight-fisted as an English landlord."

"Nothing since January, but then, most of that period has been winter."

"Mick, narrowing Musaiyib's plans down to the Canadian Rockies is an even worse start than we normally have." Niles was referring to some of the other projects they had worked together where Kelly had told them things like: "Florida, I think." "He owns a farmhouse in Woodstock, Vermont, but he's gone to Chicago, to Baton Rouge, well somewhere in south Louisiana." "They were in Cuba, but they are now in Coral Gables, Florida, I think. No, they are on their way to New Orleans. No, we've lost them. Ah, no, here they are."

"At first glance, maybe, Niles," Keagan said, presently, "but Banff can't be more than a two-hour drive from Calgary. Jasper's further north and he'd probably fly to Edmonton if he were going there. There are a couple of lesser known national parks just over the border in British Columbia, and there is also Waterton Lakes National Park, which is an extension of America's Glacier National Park."

"Ah, you've narrowed the search area down nicely, Mick. Can't be more than, what? 8,000 square miles of mountains, lakes and forests? Even the Atchafalaya Swamp in Louisiana was only half the size of that."

Keagan ignored Niles' sarcasm. "Kelly, see if anything matches the time frame of the airline ticket. Hotels and motels usually don't charge you until after your stay, but it being tourist season in an area where the season is short, maybe they require a non-refundable deposit."

"No hotels or motels, no cars. Car rental companies also don't charge until after your trip. I don't see anything. Oh, wait, here's one. There's a $26.80 charge to Parks Canada Campground Reservation service. That doesn't tell us much; we need to know which one. Don't say it, Niles," said Kelly.

"Who me? I wasn't going to say anything, Kelly," said Niles, smiling his most innocent cartoon chipmunk smile.

"No, of course not. You're as cynical as all you spawn of Cromwell."

"Ah, here we go. A $40 charge to the Waterton Shoreline Cruise Company."

"See what an amazing woman our Kelly is Niles? And you were being such a doubting Thomas."

"Kelly, log onto to The Waterton Shoreline Cruise Company and get the specifics of Musaiyib's voyage."

"Here we go. He has a reservation on the 10:00 a.m. sailing of the *International* for July 10th to Goat Haunt, wherever that is. Hum, there's something else; his return ticket is for three days later, on the 13th."

"OK, go back to the Parks Canada Campground site and look up his reservation there."

Kelly was taking longer than usual. "This is definitely not an intuitive site. Ah, got it. Musaiyib has a reservation at the Townsite Campground, located on the south side of Waterton – the town, not the park – for July 9th and July 13th. So, he's got a reservation for a campsite on the same day as he arrives in Calgary. Let's see," Kelly switched to Streets Plus and checked the distance between the airport and the park. "Not impossible. It's a 3-4 hour drive. His plane lands at 12:21 p.m. I'm guessing there isn't a lot of public transportation between Calgary and the Park, which means he'll probably have a rental car."

* * *

The two men working out of the house in Parsippany, New Jersey didn't have much luck tracking down Musaiyib through the Al-Qaisi branch of the family. They found a number of male Al-Qaisis, but only a few were the right age, and those that were, weren't working in a computer science field. Of course, it could be possible that Musaiyib was driving a cab in Manhattan, but the searchers thought that highly unlikely. Somebody who was trying to hide, wouldn't take a job that brought him in contact with the public. You never know when someone who knows you, or worse yet, is looking for you, is liable to get in your cab or sit at your table at a restaurant. Besides, computer jobs went unfilled and the money was good. If Musaiyib hadn't sold the cylinder seals yet, Colonel Zare didn't think he would have immigrated to a foreign country, risking deportation on a daily basis, to take a job just as menial as the one he had in Iraq. No, Musaiyib was ambitious; if he weren't, he wouldn't have stolen the seals in the first place. And ambitious people took risks, or at least calculated ones.

The computer searchers began looking in other areas, one being motor vehicle departments in the U.S., The Ministry of Transportation in Ontario, and the *Société de l'assurance automobile du Québec* in Québec. A lot of people got driver's licenses every year, but not that many got them for the first time when they were twenty-six, and fewer still who were non-white, between 5'6" and 5'8" tall, and between 135 and 150 pounds. And while the searchers knew that Musaiyib had changed his name, they doubted he had replaced it with anything other than an Arab or Arab-sounding name. Thurston Howell III wouldn't work well for someone who was swarthy and had tightly curled hair, lips that would never be taken as English, and a Semitic nose. Given all those parameters, the lists got much smaller.

The searchers next step was to look at tax records. As with the motor vehicle search, they looked for first-time filers. Hacking into the IRS's or the Canada Revenue Agency's computers would have taken significantly longer for obvious reasons, but governments did sell partial lists, wherein the private details of both the government and the person had been omitted. One hundred and fifty-four males, ages 24 to 28, who worked in computer-related industries, remained from the additional parameters of the last search. Still a long list; moreover, there were no Musaiyibs or Al- Qaisis on it.

However, data that neither the U.S. nor the Canadian government regarded as private was Musaiyib's date of birth. Included in the file that agents in Iran had sent to the searchers was Musaiyib's university transcript, which listed Musaiyib's date of birth as November 22nd, 1984. When the searchers ran a query with his date of birth as a parameter, they found only one match: Salar Wusaivid. When Colonel Zare compared Saeed ibn Musaiyib, an Iraqi student at the University of Technology, Iraq, majoring in Computer Science, with Salar Wusaivid, an Iranian émigré, with the same birth date, now working in Montreal as a systems analyst for Gentec, Colonel Zare knew he had found the elusive thief of the cylinder seals.

Colonel Zare left the house in Parsippany, New Jersey at two o'clock in the morning on July 3rd. Before he left, though, he had the searchers construct a detailed report of all the new information that they had found on Musaiyib. When they were finished, he had them send it to a secure mailbox that Ahmadinejad had given him. Later that day, he pulled together his team in New York and left for Montreal on the following day.

Twenty

July 4ᵗʰ, 2011:

Musaiyib had to decide what he should do about leaving. He was scheduled to go on holiday early Saturday morning, but clearly he couldn't wait around and go about his normal activities until then.

Somehow, he thought, *whoever was in the car with the Ontario registration had mistaken Maloaf for me. They must have seen the two of us going to mosque together and, as Maloaf and I were of similar age and build, whoever was in that car mixed us up. What else could it be?*

There was no reason to torture and kill a quiet postal worker. Besides, what Inspector Duclos had described to him about Maloaf's fate was too similar to what he had discovered about Awwal's death. *No, the Americans* – Musaiyib didn't think of the troops that invaded his homeland as Coalition troops – *who just missed me in Baghdad, have now found me in Montreal.*

Musaiyib hated to leave; he had had a good life there – quiet, productive, rewarding – but there was nothing to be done for it now. That life was over. He had to go. Still, there were things he could do to roil the waters, such as things that would suggest that he had only gone on holiday. They would have to wait until tomorrow. Tonight, he would pack as though he were going on a planned climbing trip, which, indeed, he was.

At eight o'clock in the morning, Musaiyib called the HR department at Gentec. He reminded his representative that he was scheduled to go on vacation at the end of the week, but also told her that he had received a call from a cousin that his mother had been involved in a motor accident in England and that he needed to go see her. He had more than enough vacation days accrued, but apologized to the representative for the last-minute request, citing that it was beyond his control. As his request was within the parameters of his contract, she authorized the additional time. He also left a message for his boss to further corroborate the ruse. Next, he called a cab.

Ever since Awwal's death, Musaiyib believed that this day would come. He couldn't leave the seals back in Iraq; he needed them for security, for he had no idea how long it would take him to get established. Once settled in Canada, he toyed with the idea of returning the seals through the amnesty program set up by Colonel Bogdanos. However, he wondered what would happen if the Americans who pursued him didn't know of their return, and then caught up with him. They wouldn't believe that he had simply given them back; they were worth millions. They would torture him until they killed him. They had killed Awwal and Maloaf. There was no reason to let him stay alive now, if he knew who they were. In his heart, he never really believed that he would have the life he had found in Canada. Growing up under a dictatorship stunts the imagination. Even after three years there, he still felt that his peace would be shattered. Such was his lot in life. And so, he made excuses for not returning the seals. It was time for him to retrieve them and sell them.

In spite of his fatalism, Musaiyib had prepared for this day. He had lived frugally, saving a significant percentage of his income. He would have liked to have kept his cache at his immediate disposal, but living in an urban apartment precluded such a convenience. He had rented a safety-deposit box, but at a different bank from where he had his checking and savings accounts. Kelly found no record of this because, unlike his other transactions, he had paid for the box with cash in order to avoid such detection.

The cab first took him to the bank he used for most transactions, where he withdrew about half his savings. Since this account also served as a source for overdraft protection on his checking account, he could always withdraw the remainder of both accounts by writing a check. He just wanted the withdrawal to look as though it were to cover his emergency trip to England to see his mother. The next stop was the bank where he rented his safety-deposit box. Again, he told the driver to wait.

His last stop was the Pierre-Eliot Trudeau International Airport. The cab fare was $54.65, which Musaiyib considered an awful extravagance, especially when he had originally planned to take the Métro to the airport. When he thought about Awwal and Maloaf, though, he realized it was money well spent.

Of course, he incurred a penalty for changing the flight. Additionally, the new ticket cost an extra $100 because, unlike the discounted ticket he bought more than two months ago, for this one, he was paying full fare. Musaiyib hadn't flown enough to work up a proper rage against airlines, nor had he read Alan Hess' essay *If Airlines Sold Paint*. Accordingly, he hadn't been inured to the pricing high jinks airlines employed. Still, he had to leave Montreal today, and he didn't want to cause a scene, which probably wouldn't have resulted in a fare deduction, but would have resulted in the agent remembering him. Being remembered was the last thing Musaiyib wanted, so he stoically handed over his American Express card, hoping the agent wouldn't deduct too much for the changes. Frugality had become a way of life for Musaiyib out of necessity. Paying $54.65 for a cab ride, and a $275 surcharge on a plane ticket he had already paid $389 for meant that this morning was proving to be very expensive. Musaiyib considered the alternative and realized that the additional charges were insignificant.

His plane arrived at Calgary International Airport at 5:38 p.m., more than five hours later than his original flight, so he decided to spend the night in Calgary. Besides, the likelihood of re-arranging his campsite reservations, backcountry permit dates, and cruise date this time of the year was slim to none; he hadn't even tried. He took a cab to an off-site car rental agency for two reasons: it provided one more obstacle to anyone who might be following him, and off-site rentals were far less expensive than airport rentals. Next, he found a cheap hotel. There would be no mosque prayers tonight. Moreover, he would have to find a nearby restaurant that served food that wouldn't be too offensive to Allah. Calgary had a sizeable Muslim population. It was not as large as Montreal's, but still surprisingly considerable, given the overall makeup of the province. Still, he didn't have time to find the food that both Allah and he would have liked.

* * *

Barlow stayed in Montreal for another day. Beginning at 5:00 a.m., he staked out Musaiyib's apartment building. None of the men who came out early to go the mosque were the right age. Later, one whose age looked about right did, but he was clearly a laborer. Dodge had told him Musaiyib was a systems analyst. Barlow didn't know what that was, but he did know it had something to do with computers. This guy clearly didn't do that kind of work.

At 8:50 a.m. a Yellow Cab pulled up to Musaiyib's apartment building and honked its horn. Barlow saw a young man, who was the approximate age and size of Maloaf, come out of the apartment carrying a large backpack. He slid the pack into the cab's back seat and climbed in after it. Barlow followed the cab to a branch office of the Royal Bank of Canada. The cab waited.

Barlow would have liked to grab Musaiyib right when he came out of the bank, and maybe pick up a little extra cash as well, but the street was busy with both foot and vehicle traffic, and the cab was waiting. The driver was watching the bank door for him. It was too risky. He again followed the cab, this time to a branch of the Bank of Nova Scotia. Again, the cab waited. Traffic here was every bit as heavy as at Musaiyib's last stop. He stayed longer at this bank. Barlow wondered if he should go in, see what he was doing, and make sure he hadn't slipped out a side door. He decided not to. Musaiyib came out of the bank after fifteen minutes and got back in the cab. Barlow followed it again. This time it took Musaiyib to the Pierre-Eliot Trudeau International Airport, dropping him off at the Air Canada entrance.

Barlow knew he didn't have enough time to park his car, so he pulled ahead to the next open curb-side slot, grabbed his bag, left the car running, and went in to the Air Canada counter. Musaiyib was in line. Barlow got in line five travelers behind him. Musaiyib stepped up to a just-freed-up online kiosk and began cutting his boarding passes. Barlow was too far back to hear what the agent was saying to him, but he assumed she was asking for his identification. Barlow stepped out of line and moved up closer to the counter. Two of the passengers who were in line in front of him looked over, annoyed because they thought he was cutting ahead of them. Barlow didn't want to draw attention to himself, so he smiled and said, "Just checkin' out the board. Couldn't read it from back there."

"So one bag checked through to Calgary. Is that right, sir?" asked the agent.

"Yes," answered Musaiyib.

The agent wrestled the heavy pack over the conveyor belt, placed it in a large plastic tub, and sent it on its way. Barlow saw that the Calgary flight left at 11:28 a.m. He got outside just in time to find a port authority police tow truck backing up to his rental car.

"Shit."

He ran down to the truck just as the driver was getting ready to hook up Barlow's rental. He approached the tow truck driver smiling.

"My wife took my bag with her by mistake when I dropped her off; I had to run in to get it before she got through security."

The driver looked at Barlow. Barlow put his hand in his pocket. The tow truck driver nodded.

"Step over to the truck with me, sir."

Barlow followed him. The driver turned around when he was abreast of the truck's cab.

"Go back to your car, put your bag in it, take out $50 from your wallet in a way that nobody notices, and get the rental papers. Bring the papers with the money under them to me and I'll drive away. If you don't have 50 bucks cash, bring three 20s or a hundred. Got it? Otherwise, this tow will cost you $250, and you can't run out on it. The rental agency will just put it on your card."

Barlow wanted to crush the tow truck driver's larynx, but instead did what he told him.

He dropped the car off at the rental agency and took the shuttle back to the airport. His flight was scheduled to leave at 2:12 p.m. He didn't see much benefit in trying to get an earlier flight. He checked in and went to find a Starbucks. When he had his coffee, he called Dodge.

"Claude, this is Joe Pete Barlow; I'm in the Montreal airport. Your information was right on, but my guy just got on a plane to Calgary. I need to know exactly where he's headed, and I need to know now. Can you do that?"

"No, I can't find out *exactly* where he's headed now, but if you give me twenty-four hours, I can probably tell you approximately where he's going. But it will cost you $5,000, Joe Pete. I'm going to have to cut some corners on this one."

"$5,000 if you get me near – very near – where he is, but nothin' if you don't. Deal?"

"Deal, Joe Pete."

Barlow got another cup of coffee and sat thinking for a while. Then he called Bosheers in Biloxi. He had already filled him in about Randy's fuckup.

"Howland, it's Joe Pete. Listen carefully. I just saw Musaiyib. He's on a plane headed fer Calgary. That's in Alberta, Canada. It's one of their states. Anyway, I just got off the phone with Dodge. I told 'im we need ta know where's he's goin' in Calgary or where he's headin' after that. I gave him twenty-four hours. If he doesn't find Musaiyib, we don't pay 'im. If'n he does though, it's $5,000. This is it; we either shit or get off the pot. It's worth it if Dodge finds 'im."

"But here's the thing, Howland, are ya ready ta bail on the casino? Because I'll be back tonight. If Dodge gets us the information we need, I'm goin' fer it. We can always go back ta the army if it turns out the prick already sold 'em or he's just goin' on vacation. I gotta believe he bolted when he heard about Maloaf, so, one way or the other, he's not comin' back. Y'all in? Good. I thought about givin' the boss some bullshit story that would cover us fer a week or so, but we both can't say that our mommas just happened ta die on the same day. Maybe he'll cut us some slack, but look, if we find the cylinder seals, there's no reason ta go back ta work. If we don't, we get other security jobs or we re-up, maybe even work fer Dodge doin' special jobs. Fuck, it's what we know. OK, yeah, good. I'm gonna call Randy ta see if he's in. Yeah, I'll see y'all tonight."

Barlow couldn't get through to King, so he left a message for him to call as soon as he could and to be someplace near his phone until Barlow called back. He was on a plane on his way back to Mississippi, so it might be a while.

King called Barlow just as his plane was on approach to Louis Armstrong International Airport in New Orleans. Barlow returned the call as soon as he got to his car.

"Randy, I found 'im, but he's on his way ta Calgary. Stampede? What, they got a fuckin' rodeo goin' out there? He can't be gonna ta that unless they got camels in it. Besides, how big can it be? We can find him there. You're shittin' me. A million fuckin' people? Jesus, I thought I was a redneck; Canadians must be somethin' else."

"OK, listen, I called Dodge; he's on it. Let's just hope he comes up with somethin' else, but the bottom line is we don't move now, he's gone. Howland's in, so, with ya or without ya, we're goin'. I want ya in, but that's the deal. Not until Saturday night? OK, that'll have ta do. We'll see what Dodge comes up with. I'll call ya as soon as I know."

*　*　*

Kelly met Keagan in the bar at six o'clock. He had been working at his office in the inn, so she hadn't seen him since breakfast. He had just come down stairs when Kelly came into the bar from the porch. The lake sparkled in the sun behind her, its surface still crinkled in the late afternoon breeze. It would smooth out in another hour and the fishermen would come with their electric motors, trolling their long Christmas trees, and trying to catch the big lake trout that swam deep below the surface.

The bar was doing a brisk business, and the season was in full swing.

We should go on a climb tomorrow, Keagan thought. *The days have been high blue and dry. We've gotten like an old married couple. I go off to work in the morning, and she stays in the lake office and works on the computer, the fax, and the phone. I miss being on a mountain.*

They had been together now longer than they ever had since he had moved to America. Usually, she would come to the inn for a few days, then they'd go off together and work a project.

She would come back with him for a few days, but would then be off again, back to Ireland, trying to unite a country that had per-sistently resisted reunification for more than four hundred years. She had been here now for a little more than two months. They had taken morning runs and evening swims together, and of course, had dinner together and slept together, but the only days they had spent together – all day long – were when they were staking out Musaiyib in Montreal. They definitely had to go on a climb tomorrow.

"Let's sit out on the porch, Kelly. You want a drink?" asked Keagan.

"Yes, thanks."

"Go get us a couple of seats; I'll get the drinks."

Keagan got a Bud for himself and a Jameson 12 on the rocks for Kelly, and brought them out to the porch. Together, they watched the lake, sipped their drinks, and reviewed their days.

"Disturbing news, Mick. A fellow by the name of Asu Maloaf was found tortured to death in the Saint-Laurent area of Montreal."

"Who's he?"

"As it happens, he's a 25 year-old Muslim lad who lived in Musaiyib's apartment building."

"*Shite*." Keagan caught the implication immediately, thus the use of the more obscene Irish vulgarity.

"*Shite* is right, Mick." Kelly took a long pull on her drink.

"What about Musaiyib? Was he with Maloaf?"

"No. As near as I can figure, the *villains* got the wrong man. I suppose they mixed them up, what with their living in the same building, being about the same age, going to the mosque together, watching football together, and who knows what else. So, the *villains* – probably the ones who tortured and killed Awwal in Baghdad – get a lead on Musaiyib, see Maloaf on the street, thinking he's Musaiyib, pinch him, and it's a repeat of Awwal."

"Blowtorch and a bullet?"

"No, this time they used a very sharp knife. Took off his thumb and the lad bled out. Well, they slit his throat to hasten the process."

"Any idea where Musaiyib is?"

"I hope so. After I read the web version of the *Montreal Gazette*, I checked Musaiyib's credit card accounts. This morning, his American Express account posted a charge of $275 to Air Canada. The transaction was listed as a surcharge. So, it seems our boy has moved his vacation forward by five days."

"What about his other reservations? The campsite, the cruise, and the backcountry permit?" asked Keagan.

"Nothing new there, Mick."

"What time does he get to Calgary?"

Kelly looked at her watch. "Still hasn't; he had to take a later and longer flight than the original. Stops in Vancouver first, and then takes him back where he's been. Curious routing."

"Yeah, I once had to fly from Boston to San Francisco to get to Montana. The funny thing about flying is that about the only thing the airlines get right – and I mean really right – is safety. Statistically, it's right up there with Ivory Soap, but it's still the one thing that concerns people the most. Me, I'd rather drop out of the sky from 35,000 feet than have to sit next to a really fat woman with a weak bladder and a crying kid, whom she is obviously able to tune out, either because she has achieved an abnormally high level of *Samādhi*, or because she is brain dead. I have never sat next to a *Patañjali* follower."

"So, no Calgary charges?" asked Keagan.

"None," answered Kelly.

"Of course, if he's smart – and we know he is – he'll use cash where he can. How much longer before he lands?" asked Keagan.

"I'm still a little fuzzy on your time zones. I assume they're the same in Canada as in the States."

"Pretty much, except in the eastern provinces where it gets confusing. There a couple of half-hour zones, which change summer and winter, but Calgary should be the same as the States' Mountain Time. So, a two-hour difference from here, earlier, that is."

"Let's see, it's 6:20 now, so that makes it 4:20 in Calgary. His plane isn't scheduled to land until 5:38, or 7:38 our time." Kelly looked at her watch again. "An hour and eighteen minutes from now if the flight is on time."

"I suppose you want to get out there as soon as possible. This is the least notice we've ever had."

"I can go tomorrow. Can you meet me in Waterton on Saturday?"

"You're not going out there alone, Kelly. Not with at least three teams hunting Musaiyib," said Keagan.

"I'll be fine, Mick. No one's made a move against me since New York.

"You're not going alone. That's final. I suppose you've already looked at flights."

"Yes, there are three: Musaiyib's original flight, the one that he took today, and a later one that gets into Calgary at 9:54 p.m."

"Get us on Musaiyib's original flight but on Thursday. There's no sense heading out tomorrow. The only way we'd find Musaiyib would be by accident."

"What about Niles and Teal?" asked Kelly.

"I'll have to talk with Teal." Keagan was about to tell Kelly to put two holds on the same flight for them, but then had a better idea.

"Hold off on them for now; I'll need to check some things first. But see if you can get us two campsites in the same campground as Musaiyib for Thursday through Saturday nights. No, wait, there's a wonderful hotel there called the Prince of Wales. Get us a room there for those nights and four tickets for the ten o'clock boat on Sunday. Check out backcountry camping permits in Glacier National Park for the same days as Musaiyib's. They'll be a bear, though."

"*A bear*, Mick?"

"North Country expression. It means difficult."

* * *

Lieutenant Jassim wrote a quick-and-dirty program in C++ to calculate the permutated possibilities of eight letters, the number of letters in Musaiyib's name. It came to 40,320 possibilities, which was obviously too many for Jassim to deal with, so he added some qualifying parameters to filter the output.

The Arabic alphabet was much different from what English used. *Alphabet* was actually an incorrect term, as Arabic used script rather than letters. The Arabic *abjad* was more correct, as an *abjad* was a consonant-cluster based language. There were no vowels in written Arabic; the reader supplied them. Transliterated, there were twenty-eight letters.

The ancient Greeks didn't have an alphabet of their own, so they copied the Phoenicians', an ancient Arab people who lived in, what is today, coastal Lebanon. The Greeks had no need for the Arabic gutturals; however, the phonetic structure of Ancient Greek did require vowels to avoid ambiguities among heterographs and homonyms, so it converted the gutturals to vowels.

While written Arabic was a consonant-cluster language like Serbo-Croatian, Arabic had evolved into an impure *abjad*. Modern Arabic script did imply vowels. Notwithstanding, the language had to be transliterated, where it was used in different alphabets. To reduce his output, all Jassim had to do was include code in his program that precluded certain double-consonant combinations such as *Ms*, *Mb*, *Bm*, as well as multiple-vowel strings, none of which appeared in English. Other letter combinations such as *Ub* were extremely rare in English. Moreover, Jassim knew that, given Arabic's proclivity for consonants, few Arabic names began with *A* or *I* or *Y* or *U*, and none with double or multiple vowels. The exclusions he had included in his code reduced the output to 120 names, which was a workable list.

Then he did a search of the databases for any name that matched. Of the few that did, he found no one whose age, profession, or immigration date matched. He called the team together and gave each of them a list of the 120 names. At first, he thought he'd explain the Arabic naming practice, which was much different from that used in the West, but decided to just give them the list and hear what they came up with. If Musaiyib had changed his name to an anagram of it, it had eluded both Jassim and the computer. He was out of ideas, so he decided he might as well let them have a stab at it.

After a half hour spent in full concentration, the team had no ideas, but Wade did have a question.

"Lieutenant, I know this sounds stupid, but I'm not hearing anything brilliant anyway, so here's what I was thinking. When you passed out the lists, mine was upside down and it took me a second to realize it."

"Only a second," said Kennedy.

Wade was about to further threaten Kennedy's life in more creative ways, when Jassim cut in,

"Let him speak, Wesley. Go ahead, Bo."

"Well, upside down, an *M* is a *W*, but *Wns* is weird, and the *S* would be backwards, but the name was backwards anyway. Then I realized my mistake. I'm just saying what if he changed the *M* to *W*?"

Jassim went to the whiteboard and wrote out Wusaiyib, then he ran that through the databases. Nothing that matched Musaiyib's parameters.

"Good try, Bo, but nothing."

"Lieutenant," said Kennedy, "look how you wrote the *y*; it barely goes below the other letters, so it looks more like a *v*. What if he changed the *y* to a *v*?"

Jassim ran it. No matches.

"Good try Wesley. Wait a minute, there is a Wusaivid." He ran that. "Bingo! Salar Wusaivid is 26 years old, emigrated from Iran in 2008, hum, but not Iraq, works as a systems analyst for Gentec, Inc. in Montreal, and lives in Saint-Laurent, which I believe is a neighborhood in Montreal on Rue Décarie. You're brilliant, Bo!"

"What about me, Lieutenant?"

"You're brilliant too, Wesley."

"What a team, huh, Bo?"

"I still may have to kill you, though, Wesley."

Twenty-One

July 4ᵗʰ, 2011:

*B**eyond Good and Evil* – unless you were on your honeymoon, celebrating a mid-stride wedding anniversary, or having an affair – was an outdoor enthusiast stop. It wasn't for those who favored open bars, all-you-can-eat buffets, or hotels with every imaginable computer connection. Keagan didn't put up any barriers to computers, but, while the inn had Wi-Fi, he did not provide any other connectivity. He catered to guests who worked hard, but who came to the inn to play hard. People who wanted to kayak the lake or one of the other many waterways in the area, climb some of the high peaks, cross-country ski, or slide down Whiteface Mountain in the winter. Fishing was the one activity the inn offered for sedentary types. On rainy days like this one, there was the library with its novels, biographies, jigsaw puzzles, crossword and Sudoku puzzles, cryptograms, and other logic puzzles.

It was after 5:00 p.m. and still raining. It had rained all day, in spite of the clear, dry weather of the day before. Teal's crew had gone home for the day, so the team was meeting in his shop instead of in the library, which, now that the season was in full swing and the weather was bad, was occupied. The team met there because what Keagan had to say wasn't for public consumption.

"The reason for this meeting is that Kelly has learned of some new wrinkles involving Musaiyib. On Sunday, Kelly found an article in the *Montreal Gazette* that detailed the torture and death of a young man by the name of Asu Maloaf, who lived in the same building as Musaiyib. He had bled out after having one of his thumbs sliced off and his throat cut. Different method, but with the same dispassion as the Awwal torture. This probably happened early Sunday morning. We suspect that Musaiyib was questioned by the police about seeing anything or anyone suspicious in the neighborhood, because a later edition of the paper said that neighbors had been questioned by police. Kelly checked Musaiyib's credit card records again and found that he had updated the flight he was scheduled to take this Saturday, so it seems he is now somewhere near Calgary, Alberta."

"Has he changed his camping reservation or any of the other reservations he had?" asked Niles.

"No, it doesn't seem so, but they would be more difficult to change at this late date," answered Keagan.

"Could he have made new reservations?" asked Teal.

"Good question, Teal, but unless he has other credit card accounts that I don't know about, no, he hasn't. And, of course, he couldn't use cash," said Kelly.

"Not unless he did it as soon as he got there," said Niles.

"That's a possibility, Niles, but the backcountry permit would be especially difficult to change at this late date. Particularly because it's a July reservation. Theoretically, backcountry permits are issued from June through the end of September, but, in reality, it's a much shorter season. It's more like July to early September. In June, there is still plenty of snow, and the creeks and rivers are high with winter runoff. If there isn't a high enough bridge across them, getting across a creek that's all but dry in August can be real difficult in June. Four feet deep, thirty-eight degree water, spiked with brush and ice, and roaring off the mountain could be a real serious barrier. My guess, though, is that he hasn't changed that part of his itinerary," said Keagan.

"If he hasn't changed his camping reservations, why don't we just wait for him at his campground in Waterton to do whatever he's doing in the woods, and then pick him out when he gets back?" Niles asked. "I mean, what is he going to do? He's got to take the boat back, right? He can't easily bushwhack to the U.S.?"

"Mick, you want to field that one?" asked Kelly.

"OK. Since we're in the shop instead of the library, I can't put this on the overhead, but if you and Niles come around here, I'll show you on a Montana roadmap."

Keagan unfolded the map, isolating Glacier National Park. "This being a map of Montana, Calgary doesn't show up on it. If it did, it would be approximately here." Keagan tapped a spot of the table about six inches above the map.

"Calgary is about 150 road miles north of the U.S. and Canada border. However, adjoining Canada's Waterton Lakes National Park is the U.S.'s Glacier National Park, with a trail system of over seven hundred miles, and nothing to stop Musaiyib from continuing on south and losing himself somewhere in the States.

The Sunday boat cruise that Musaiyib has a reservation for takes him to the south end of Waterton Lake, which is in the U.S. You get off the boat, walk a couple of hundred yards and sign in with the rangers at a table they've set up there. They don't even ask to see your passport, or at least they didn't ask to see mine when I did it a couple of years ago. And, more importantly, they don't check you back in when you return. It's a real loose operation. The joint parks form a Peace Park, which, by its definition, is supposed to promote concord, not suspicion. I'm not sure how, but regardless of intention, they're a sieve. Real easy to go back and forth. All you need is a good pair of legs."

"Why would he come down to America, Mick? He already has permanent alien status in Canada. He probably wouldn't qualify for that in the U.S.," said Teal.

"He didn't qualify for it in Canada either. We don't know how he got into Canada, but somehow, after he was there, he managed to get a student visa. He had already graduated from the University of Technology in Iraq, and, as near as Kelly could determine – and we know that not much gets by her – he didn't take any courses in Canada. Somehow, though, he managed to get a job because of his computer skills. My read on it is that he implied that he already had a job to the Canadian Immigration to start the process for the *Skilled-Worker Visa*, and then suggested to Gentec that he already held the visa. One implication played on the other and, *voilà*, he had a job and a visa."

"Notwithstanding, Musaiyib's not staying in Montreal. Not after what happened to his neighbor. He didn't stay in Iraq after Awwal. If he left the country of his birth, leaving an adopted country should be much easier for him to do."

"Here, take a look at this." Keagan unfolded a Glacier National Park map, which included its Canadian sister park, Waterton Lakes. Niles and Teal again looked over his shoulder. Keagan located Waterton on the northern edge of Waterton Lake and ran his index finger down to the south end, pointing out the international border about halfway down the lake.

"His backcountry permit is for two nights at Kootenai Lakes, here." Keagan moved his index finger south on the map, stopping at the triangular symbol for a tent. "But follow my finger."

Keagan ran his finger south along a dotted line on the map, jigged east a bit then continued south again to a red line that was tightly crimped where his finger stopped.

"This is the Loop, a very tight turn on the Going-to-the-Sun Road that leads to either the east or west entrances of Glacier National Park. I'm betting Musaiyib will try to come out here. It's his easiest route into the States."

"The most noticeable landmark near Kootenai Lakes is Mount Cleveland, which just happens to be the highest point in both parks. Before this weekend's events, I'd say that it was entirely possible that Musaiyib was just going out there for the rock climbing, but it's also an excellent place to hide something. The summit of Mount Cleveland is eight miles and 6,100 vertical feet from the southern end of Waterton Lake. Only about a mile and a half of this is on a trail. It is not an easy climb. However, the record for climbing it from base to top, which is 4,900 vertical feet, is just under ninety minutes, which – by the way – was done in the winter."

"Wait a minute, Mick, that's not possible. I may not be an expert, but I'm pretty good, and probably as good or even better than Musaiyib, and there's no way I could do that in twice that time," objected Teal.

"That's because you're not a wolverine."

"What the hell is a wolverine?" asked Teal and Kelly and Niles in chorus.

"It's the toughest, meanest, most resolute little fellow in North America."

"I thought, except for the *little* part, that was the grizzly," said Niles.

"These little guys scare grizzlies," said Keagan, as he filled them in on the fact, fiction, and lore of the wolverine.

"This particular wolverine was dubbed M3 by the park researchers because he was the third male they trapped in the study they conducted while attempting to learn more about these rugged creatures. The animal was trapped and implanted with a satellite chip that detailed its wanderings. That's how they know that he scaled Mount Cleveland in winter in less than ninety minutes.

Anyhow, Mount Cleveland is my best guess as to where Musaiyib is headed. I think he's hidden the seals somewhere on the mountain."

"Why way out there, Mick? Why not up in the Laurentians? If he's going to hide them in the mountains, wouldn't they be much closer to home?" asked Niles.

"Good question. And I don't have an answer – at least not a logical one – but my speculation is that he chose Glacier because it is so far away from Montreal, and because of the easy access from Waterton Lakes. If the bad guys tracked him down, he'd have a difficult time trying to explain where exactly he had hidden the seals, especially if he didn't have the coordinates. Even if he did, GPS coordinates aren't exact unless you have a very high-priced device I paid $300 for mine, and it can be as much as seventy feet off, which is usually not a problem for my needs. But you can dig a lot of holes looking for the buried pot of gold in a 70-foot radius.

Musaiyib would have a lot of chances to escape between Montreal and Glacier. Plus, as I've just shown you, Glacier is an easy access to the States. America offers a brand new hiding place for him. We know he's been scrimping for three years now. He probably has enough cash to keep him going until he gets settled again, and, in spite of the slow economy, I have to believe that America is as good or better a market for selling stolen antiquities than Canada."

"So, what's the plan, Mick?" asked Niles.

"Since we have no idea where Musaiyib is now, there is little sense in trying to find him before he shows up at his Townsite Campground in Waterton. He could be hunkered down in Calgary, or in one of the four other national parks in the area. Kelly and I have reservations on the flight that Musaiyib was originally scheduled for, though on Thursday, which will bring us into Calgary at 12:21 p.m., their time. We also have reservations at the Prince of Wales Hotel in Waterton for Thursday through Saturday night. If Musaiyib shows up, we'll take a boat ride with him and see where he goes. It better be where I think it is."

"The next part is up to Teal. If you decide on going, I want you and Niles to approach Kootenai Lakes from the Loop that I showed you on the map. It's about a twenty-mile hike over two mountains, Flattop and Fifty Mountain, and we'll need you both to carry some extra gear for Kelly and me."

"If Teal decides to opt out, and that's your prerogative, Teal, then we'll have to get you on the flight with us, Niles, and figure out a few other things. We don't have much time, and we've got a lot to do," pressured Keagan.

"I'll have to talk with Ky, Mick," said Teal.

"OK, Teal, but I need an answer tonight. We're really pressed for time on this one."

"I'll get back to you in an hour or less."

Teal found Ky at the lodge. Anjali was still working in the kitchen, helping Cassie.

"Ky, I need to talk to you about something."

"So, Kelly wants to take you on one of her projects again?"

"How did you know?"

"Not difficult to figure out, Teal. You told me that whenever she shows up at the inn, it's almost always because she has a project for Mick. And then Mick brings Niles and you in on it. She had me fooled, though. Cassie said she's usually only here for a week or less before she takes you all away with her. This time she's been here for a little over two months, I think. Got here just before the inn opened for the season. Well, what is it this time?"

"They want me to go to Montana. Mick needs me to bring some camping gear in from the south for him and Kelly. They're going in through Canada. It's complicated."

"I'm a smart girl, Teal, tell me."

Teal told Ky as much as he knew about the project, which wasn't much because this one was so different from the others he had worked. He told Ky about Musaiyib, about the cylinder seals, about what he knew, and about what he didn't know. He told her that this one was unlike the past projects where their biggest threats came, not from the thieves who stole the artwork, but from the buyers, who were invariably evil. He also told her that this time there were as many as three other groups after Musaiyib: the Coalition Task Force, three former Coalition soldiers, and an Iranian unit.

"Iranian unit! Teal, are you crazy? Cleo Aucoin wasn't enough for you? Blowing the shit out of him and his men wasn't enough of a challenge for you? You're feeling cocky now. Looking for something a little scarier. You thought now you're ready to take on some fanatics, some crazy bastards who hate all things American. These fucking nut cases who will do anything for Allah and some celestial pussy. Are you fucking insane?"

"Calm down, Ky. Don't go all Indian on me. They may not even know where this guy Musaiyib is. Early on, they tracked Kelly to

New York because they thought she could lead them to Musaiyib, but she lost them there, and there has been no evidence since that they have found either Musaiyib or Kelly."

"It's the same with the soldiers, except they are probably even farther behind. There's no indication they even know about Kelly. I don't even know about the Task Force. For all I know, they're still in Baghdad, looking for clues. What I gave you were the worst case scenarios. I didn't want to suggest that it's a cakewalk. I wasn't going to try to gloss over the danger in the project, hell, the danger in all the projects I've done with them. It only takes one bad guy to kill you, and we've always had more than one. I've been straight from the start about these projects."

"I know you have, Teal, but why do you still want to do them? You're married now; you have a family. Is it the money? You've got enough."

"No, Ky. Maybe the money got me in on the first one, maybe even the second, but that's not what's doing it now. When I showed up here four years ago, I had a ten-year old daughter, a beat to shit pickup truck, and fifty-three dollars and fifteen cents. I had just buried my wife, had no job, was fifteen to eighteen hundred miles from home, and didn't know anybody. Yeah, I had you and Petit Ra and a few others, but you were all in south Louisiana. I was on the run. Mick Keagan gave me a job and a place to stay, and he didn't know anything about me, though it was pretty obvious I was on the lam, and not too hard to figure out from where, especially for a guy as smart as Mick."

"Sure, it was like Butch Cassidy offering work to the Sundance kid."

"Ky!"

"OK, you're right. No need for that."

"No, Ky, what Mick gave me, along with the job and a place to stay, was dignity. You know he still makes out my checks to Teal; he still doesn't even know my last name. Come to think of it, maybe he does; he's a very smart fella. It doesn't matter if he does know because he doesn't let on."

"No, Ky, all Mick has ever asked of me is a good day's work. In return for that, I've gotten a good salary, a lodge for Anjali and me to live in rent free, and four cases of Dixie Voodoo a month. Anjali herself has a good job in the kitchen, where she has learned to be a sous-chef. She goes to a college prep school tuition-free thanks to Mick Keagan. Seems like a one-sided deal to me. The only way I can begin to repay him is to help out on these projects."

Ky ran through what Teal had said. Everything he said was true.

"OK, Teal, it's hard to argue against all that. I guess loyalty is just one of the reasons why I love you. But you better come back or I'll fu-"

Ky cut her threat short because Anjali just came through the front door.

"Better what, Ky?"

"Your father is going off again on another one of Kelly's projects."

"In that case, père, you had better come back safe or we'll both fucking kill you."

Teal was about to admonish Anjali for her language, but instead he just said, "Bad enough I have a foul-mouthed, crazy Indian for a wife, and now she's influenced my innocent, little girl."

Teal called Keagan, "I'm in."

Twenty-Two

July 5th, 2011:

Early that morning, Musaiyib drove to Banff National Park. He had always wanted to see it, especially Lake Louise. His priority, however, was to find a campsite. But, today, Allah was not with him. Banff was a two-hour drive west of Calgary, and, even though he had left at 6:00 a.m., when he arrived at the park, the line for campsites was already considerable. He did get a glimpse of Lake Louise, albeit it was through the trees, when he drove along its northeastern shore.

Musaiyib drove through Banff and entered Yoho National Park thirty minutes later. Yoho was the smallest of the four national parks in the area, which also included Jasper and Kootenai. While contiguous to Banff, it was much smaller, and while beautiful – *Yoho* was a Cree word meaning *awe* and *wonder* – it was much less visited than Banff, and, therefore, a good place to hide. Also, it had plenty of water. Since it didn't have the reputation that Banff enjoyed or suffered from, it didn't take reservations. So, there were no camper lines and he was able to get a secluded campsite in the smallest of the four campgrounds. Musaiyib made camp and then went off to try out his new climbing shoes on the Takakkaw Falls Boulders.

The Takavar team arrived in Montreal, albeit by two different routes. Colonel Zare, Corporal Karimi, and Sergeant Sharifi flew from New York. Meanwhile, Sergeant Major Akbari and Sergeant First Class Shaker-Doust arrived by train, traveling up the Hudson Valley, edging Lake George and Lake Champlain, crossing into Canada at Rousses Point and going on into the St-Lambert Station in St-Denis, just short of the Ile de Montréal. Curiously, it was the same route Kelly, whom the Takavar unit had searched so assiduously for in New York, had taken to get to *Beyond Good and Evil*, although they had no inkling of the coincidence.

Montreal had the second largest Arab population in Canada, most of which was centered in Saint-Laurent. Iran, however, had a very small Arab population; it made up only two percent of the nation's total populace. Notwithstanding, approximately ninety percent of Iranians were Muslims. Accordingly, Montreal's Iranian population centered on the southern edge of Saint-Laurent, where, in spite of ethnic differences, they felt more comfortable than they did in Christian or Jewish neighborhoods. It was here, on Rue Hislop, that the Takavar team re-grouped. They did not all sleep there, but that was where they met when Colonel Zare required them to get together.

As in Parsippany, New Jersey, the house was a computer intelligence nexus. When Colonel Zare was informed by his support network that there was a node in Montreal that might be some use to his team, he called them, directing the two agents there to find out all they could about a Salar Wusaivid living on Rue Décarie. In the day and a half that the two researchers had to investigate the target, they had added significantly to the team's knowledge of Musaiyib. The most important details of which were that his neighbor, Asu Maloaf, had been tortured and then murdered, that Musaiyib had not been seen by his neighbors since the day after Maloaf's body was found, that his boss had said that he had been scheduled for vacation at the end of the week, but had called on Monday informing him that his mother had been involved in an automobile accident, and that he was going to England to be with her.

Normally, law enforcement needs a court order to access a person's credit card accounts. Very little in the CIA's behavior, however, might be construed as normal. And since it was the CIA's knowledge of the Iranian commando unit that had been charged with recovering the cylinder seals that led to his task force being put together, Commander Roth only had to make one phone call to bypass, not only the court order requirement for financial records, but also American Express' and Royal Bank of Canada's MasterCard Division's firewalls.

"Oh, shit, he's on the move," said Jassim.

"Where to?" asked Roth.

"Calgary."

"What's in Calgary, except the Stampede?" asked Roth.

"Commander, I'm an Arab; I have no idea what the Stampede is, unless it involves camels. In fact, I don't even know where Calgary is," answered Jassim.

"Lieutenant, you came to America when you were six years old. Do you even remember ever seeing a camel?"

"It's a cultural archetype. I am one with camels."

"You're going to be one with the non-coms if you don't get a move on and look up the Calgary Stampede for me, Lieutenant."

"Aye, Aye, sir... Ah, here it is. What do you know? It starts July 6th. What is all this, Commander?" asked Jassim.

"It's the granddaddy of all rodeos. It started sometime in the nineteenth century. I don't know if it's the oldest rodeo, but it's the biggest. I hope Musaiyib isn't going there, because it draws more than a million people each year."

"A million people go there to see, what, cowboys?"

"Yeah, cowboys, cowgirls, clowns, even sheep shearers. There are all kinds of ranching events. It's also a mecca, if I can use that holy word in your presence for something so American, for selling and buying stock, and for breeding connections. If it's about ranching, it's there."

"Why in Canada? I thought cowboys were American."

"Interesting question, Jassim. I don't know, except there's plenty of ranchland in Canada, especially in Alberta. Christ, tell me he's not headed there. I don't know how we'd find him. See what else you can find out about his trip."

"I'll get right on it, sir."

Roth hadn't even left Jassim's office when the Lieutenant shouted out, "Commander, I've got something."

Roth returned to Jassim's desk. "What is it?"

"He has several charges, two of them for the same date. Let's see, he has a campsite reservation in Waterton Lakes National Park. I don't know where that is either."

"It's in Alberta. What else?"

"He has a reservation for a boat cruise and a backcountry permit. I don't know what that means."

"OK, Jassim, get the particulars on those reservations, and fill me in as soon as you have that intel."

"Yes, sir."

Twenty-Three

Colonel Zare was about to send Akbari and Shaker-Doust to question Musaiyib's neighbors about his whereabouts, when he had a change of mind. He decided to go himself and take Karimi and Sharifi with him. Ironically, the Takavar unit had been picked so they would appear less Arab and more American. Still, unlike Keagan and Kelly, who obviously didn't fit in in Musaiyib's neighborhood, these three wouldn't raise any suspicions because, in spite of their lighter complexions, Musaiyib's neighbors recognized them as their own, to the detriment of two of them. As it turned out, however, their appearance wasn't a factor in what they did.

Two older men came out of Musaiyib's apartment building, on their way to the mosque for *Magbrib*; they didn't make it to the corner. Zare and Sharifi were waiting in an alley next to the apartment building. As the two men approached, Zare and Sharifi grabbed them from behind, put knives to their throats, and dragged them deeper into the alley's shadows, out of sight of street or pedestrian traffic. They told them not to make a sound. The two men were Syrians and had suffered this experience before. They offered no resistance. Sharifi placed black hoods over the heads of the two Syrian men, then Zare signaled Karimi with his Mini-Mag flashlight. Karimi u-turned their car to the alley mouth, while Zare herded the two into the back seat. Sharifi got into the front seat and Karimi drove off.

Parc Marcel-Lauren was pretty much deserted at that hour. There were a few dog walkers about, but Zare told Karimi to park near a wooded area, knowing the dog walkers would avoid it unless they walked large, aggressive dogs. Zare and Sharifi led the two Syrians out of sight into a small copse. Karimi followed them and kept lookout.

Zare spoke to the first man.

"Listen carefully to me. I'm going to ask you some questions and you will tell me the truth. If you lie to me – and I'm very good at detecting lies – my associate here will cut you. Then, I will ask your friend here the same question and have him cut, too, if he lies. Then, back to you, and another cut if you are still determined to be difficult. Then back to him. If you both persist in lying or being evasive, you will be lifetime cripples. Is that clear?" All this Zare said in Arabic.

Both men nodded.

"Tell me where Musaiyib is. I believe you know him as Wusaivid."

The man who Zare addressed was mute with fear because he did not know Musaiyib, other than someone who lived in the same building. He started to stammer, "I...I...I do not..."

"Cut him!" Sharifi cut one of the man's hamstrings. The man fell to the ground and began to scream, but Zare quickly put his knife to his throat and told him to be quiet. If he continued, Zare told him, he would kill him. His only way to survive was to keep still.

"Now, you. Where is Wusaivid?"

"I do not..."

"Cut him!"

"No, wait, listen! He lives in our building. He goes to our same mosque, but he is much younger. He says he is Iranian, but I can tell from his accent that he is an Iraqi. He is educated; we are not."

"Enough stalling. Cut him."

"No, no, listen! He would to go to the gym with the boy who was killed."

"What boy?" asked Zare, although he knew the answer, having read the story in the *Gazette*.

"Maloaf, Asu Maloaf."

"Where is this gym?"

The man gave Zare the approximate address. Had he given Zare the name and exact address, Zare would have known he was lying and had him cut, just like the other one who was now moaning quietly at Zare's feet.

"What else do you know about him?"

"He is a climber, I think."

Zare was confused. "A climber?"

"Yes, you know, with ropes and bits of metal. I have heard the two young men talking about a climbing wall and going climbing together."

"How would they get there? Wusaivid doesn't have a car. Did the other boy, Maloaf?"

"No. There is a store where they would buy their things, but I don't know what. I am a carpenter. I don't know about such things. But they went to a shop, a store, where they learned. The shop owner took them, I think. I heard them say that."

"Where is this shop?"

"I don't know; I really don't. It is a diversion for young men. If it is not in the neighborhood, it is nearby, because I heard Wusaivid tell Maloaf after *Asr* that he was going there, and he was walking. It is to the east of the mosque."

"What else do you know?"

"Nothing, I have told you all."

"What about your friend here?"

"He knows less than I."

"You are certain?"

"Yes, yes, I am not lying."

"All right, then. Aram, duct tape their mouths, wrists, and ankles, so that it takes them some time before they can crawl out to the road."

When Sharifi had finished with the taping, the three walked away. Ten feet out of the copse, Zare told Karimi to continue to the car but stopped Sharifi, and handed him an H&K P30 9mm pistol with an Evolution suppressor.

"Wait till we get to the car and then shoot them."

Colonel Zare had Karimi drive around the area to the east of the mosque Musaiyib frequented until they found the climbing shop. Of course, it was closed.

"Aram, go find out the shop's hours for tomorrow."

Sharifi came back to the car quickly. "The shop opens at 0900 hours and closes at 2000 hours."

"Good, we will be here at 0800. Shop owners are always the first to arrive."

Zare was correct. Lévesque arrived at 8:15 a.m. When he unlocked the door, Zare and Sharifi stepped into the store right behind him. Karimi stayed in the car.

Zare pushed the H&K P30 into Lévesque's back, and told him to disengage the alarm.

Sharifi locked the door and followed Zare and Lévesque into the back room.

"I understand you teach rock climbing to your customers."

"Yes, we do."

"You like climbing then?" said Colonel Zare.

"Yes, I've been doing it for twenty-five years."

"Do you wish to continue doing it?"

"Of course."

"Then listen to me very carefully. I am going to ask you a series of questions. If you lie to me, I will have my associate, here, shoot you in the right knee. If you lie again; in the left knee. Lie a third time, and the knees will not be a problem, for he will shoot you in the head. Do you understand?"

"Yes, but-"

"No *buts*. Do you know a man named Wusaivid?"

"Yes."

"That's a good start. Where is he?"

"I haven't seen him since…"

Sharifi lowered the P30 to an inch from Lévesque's right knee. "No, wait, he is scheduled to go on vacation at the end of the week, but the last time I saw him was a week ago, when he came in to buy a new pair of climbing shoes and some resin."

Zare raised his hand and Sharifi lowered the pistol. "Where was he to go on vacation?" asked the Colonel.

"Waterton Lakes National Park."

"Where is that?"

"It's one of our national parks in Alberta."

"Where is this, Alberta?"

"It's a province in the West. Like one of America's states. We call them provinces. I don't know exactly where he was climbing, but I know he was camping in the park."

"How would one get there?"

"Flying is the fastest way. That's how he was going, by flying into Calgary."

"Calgary is a town?" The Colonel didn't like admitting in front of one of his men that he didn't know these things. He was familiar with many things American, but, if he had thought about Canada at all, it was only as a place from which to infiltrate America.

"Calgary is one of the largest cities in Alberta," answered Lévesque.

"Where is it located in Alberta?"

"I'm not sure, about 150 miles north of the U.S. and Canada border, but more by road."

"And you think that this is where Mus…Wusaivid is?"

"Yes, he must be, if he's not here. Have you called his office?" asked Lévesque.

"He was not there."

"Well, he must have changed his mind and left early."

With these words, it dawned on Lévesque that, perhaps, these were the men who had tortured and killed Maloaf, and that was why

Wusaivid had left early. Now, Lévesque regretted what he had said, but he was not going to get his knees shot off and then killed just to save a customer.

"Do you have anything else to tell me?" asked the Colonel.

"No. I've told you all I know," begged Lévesque with his eyes.

"Good then. Shoot him, Aram."

* * *

Detective Inspector Duclos was not a stupid man, so when four men were killed, and another was missing from his precinct over the course of a week, it was not likely to escape him. And it didn't. Especially when there were only eighty-four homicides in the entire province the year before.

Accordingly, after doing his preliminary investigation of the three new murders, which he had no doubt all centered around Wusaivid, he called the RCMP (Royal Canadian Mounted Police), colloquially known as the Mounties.

The RCMP was not simply analogous to America's FBI, which was a purely federal law enforcement agency. The Mounties were a federal, provincial, and, even in some cases, municipal law enforcement agency. Usually, they didn't operate in either Ontario or Québec, but when Duclos called an old friend of his, Ewen Mac Ghillie, head of the CIA (Canada's Criminal Investigative Analysis) and explained that three of the four people killed in his precinct in the last week were Arabs, who had a connection with another Arab, who was currently missing, and that the fourth victim was the owner of an outdoor equipment store where the missing Arab had been a customer, Mac Ghillie agreed to send a unit to Montreal.

Twenty-Four

T he Criminal Investigative Analysis unit that Mac Ghillie sent to Montreal was headed by Chief Superintendent Angus Mac Dowell. The other two members of the unit were Inspector Mikaila des Sangs, and Inspector Tom Esterbridge. Des Sangs was a forensic scientist specializing in blood spatter and pattern. Esterbridge's specialty was weapons.

After meeting with Duclos in his office, the unit first went to the Trailhead to view where Lévesque was killed. As this was the freshest site, and because it was in a locked building with climate control, it promised to yield the best residuals. The promise was a false one, however. Lévesque had been shot twice, once in the head and once through the heart. Both shots were fatal. Esterbridge believed that the gun used had a suppressor. Duclos' report stated that his team could find no one who had heard the shots fired, which was highly unlikely given the time of day and the proximity of neighboring stores.

There was plenty of blood, brain, and bone splatter, but all that they suggested was that Lévesque had, indeed, been shot execution style. The shooter had retrieved the casings, and since both bullets had been through-and-through and damaged from colliding with surfaces harder than the human heart or head, ballistic findings were minimal. Esterbridge was fairly certain that the gun used was

215

a 9mm, a certainty that held up after the unit visited the next killing site.

The copse in Parc Marcel-Lauren where two of Musaiyib's neighbors had been killed had been taped off, and a tent-like structure had been erected to protect the site from the elements. Of course, neither the tape nor the enclosure could keep the park's wildlife from removing or contaminating both the blood splatter, and the brain and bone matter, which always resulted when chunks of metal, traveling at over 850 miles per hour, came in contact with human frailty. To compensate, Duclos had provided the unit with photos that had been taken within an hour of the bodies being discovered. There wasn't much to see two days after the murder, but by comparing the actual site with the more recent photos of the murders, Chief Superintendent Mac Dowell and the two forensic scientists had a better understanding of what had happened, which they kept in mind when examining the two bodies in the morgue.

When they had taken notes and additional photos, they examined the abandoned factory where Maloaf had been killed. As in the first case, inspected the photos taken shortly after the body was discovered. There was much more blood pattern here because Maloaf had bled out from the cuts he had received, whereas both Musaiyib's neighbors were shot assassination style and only one of them had been cut, and that was a non-fatal slash.

It was at the morgue that the unit learned the most about the murders. Mac Dowell and his two inspectors examined the bodies and listened to the pathologists' reports about the autopsy findings. When they had heard everything that Duclos had reported about the crime scenes and that the pathologists had discovered postmortem, Mac Dowell asked his inspectors for the observations and conclusions.

Des Sangs said that the differences in the execution methods suggested that Maloaf was not killed by the same persons who killed the two others.

"Why do you assume multiple perpetrators?" asked Mac Dowell.

"Because in both cases the victims were bound. It is very difficult to hold a weapon on someone and bind him at the same time. Too many opportunities for either escape or for overpowering the perpetrator, especially in the case of the two men. No, I would say it took a minimum of two to capture and restrain Maloaf, and three, for the two others," said Des Sangs.

"And, you, Tom?" asked Mac Dowell.

"I agree with Mikaila. From what we've learned from the ballistics report, the park victims were killed by a single shot to the back of the head. The bullets were jacketed hollow points, fired from an H&K 9mm. The one case that the assassin missed in the park, together with the helical land and groove pattern from the bullets found in the soft soil beneath the victims, corroborate that conclusion. Since each victim here was shot once, as opposed to the two shots used to dispatch Lévesque, I believe I can attribute that difference to the realization on the shooter's part that retrieving the spent casings outdoors would be more difficult than it was in Lévesque's back room, a fear that, luckily for us, was born out."

"So, one team of three assassins; is that what I'm hearing?"

Des Sangs was unsure and thus slow to offer an opinion, but, given that weapons were Esterbridge's specialty, he felt more confident. "No, sir, I think two."

"Two people?"

"No, sir, two different teams. Probably three to each team," said Esterbridge.

"And why is that, Tom?" asked Mac Dowell.

"The cuts sir. Look at the hamstring of the one cut victim from the park."

Mac Dowell stepped over to the autopsy table and examined the tendon with a magnifying glass Esterbridge had handed him.

"And?"

"Now look at Maloaf's severed thumb joint." The Chief Superintendent did as requested. "Now, examine the throat." Mac Dowell did. "What do you notice?" asked Esterbridge.

"I'm the boss, Tom. I'm supposed to ask the questions."

"Oh, sorry, sir. I got carried away."

"That's all right. The tendon, while tough and fibrous, should have been an easier cut than slicing through a bone joint, but the thumb cut looks cleaner, like slicing through the proverbial butter. The hamstring, by comparison, looks almost sawed, like a single rip cut, though not from a serrated blade."

"Exactly, sir."

"Mikaila, come look at these wounds and see if you can trip up our smart aleck."

Des Sangs felt like she was the one being tripped up. The greatest reward came from agreeing with Esterbridge if he were right, but if he were wrong, what then? She looked carefully at the wounds through the magnifying glass, then she considered her answer and its ramifications and waffled.

"Weapons aren't my specialty," she said, voicing the obvious and thereby revealing her equivocation, "but I think I have to agree with Tom, sir."

"Good, because I believe he is right. So, what kind of weapons inflicted these wounds?"

"Hard to say about the park victim..."

"Ah, now you're equivocating, Tom."

Des Sangs blanched.

"No, sir, not at all. I believe the hamstring cut was made by a good quality folding knife, something with a thick blade. If forced to offer an opinion, I'd say a Buck Ranger."

"Why that particular brand and model, Tom?" asked Mac Dowell.

"No particular reason, other than the two I gave. Any good quality, sturdy bladed knife would be in the running. I'm just most familiar with the Buck Ranger because I've had one since I was a boy. I always take it on camping trips. A filleting knife wouldn't make that cut, nor would a chef's slicing knife. Not even something like a Henckels carving knife could do that. You'd need something both sharp and sturdy that you could put a lot of pressure on."

"What about Maloaf?" asked Mac Dowell.

"In some ways a more difficult conclusion to draw, but in others, much easier. I'm going to go out on a limb here, but I'd say it was a Khukuri," answered Esterbridge.

Des Sangs felt lost in this conversation.

"A strange choice. Why a Khukuri?" asked Mac Dowell.

"Again, look at the thumb knuckle. It's a very smooth cut. And the throat cut practically decapitated Maloaf," said Esterbridge.

"So, why wasn't Maloaf shot? If the assassins had a suppressor? Why deal with the mess?" This question Mac Dowell directed at both of his assistants.

Esterbridge waited for Des Sangs to offer an opinion because all the focus had been on him. But after a judicious interval, he reiterated, "Because we have two different groups of assassins."

"Elaborate, please."

"If you mean why there are two different assassin teams, I don't know. However, if you mean, how did I arrive at that conclusion? Then I would have to point at the weapons used. The assassins at the Trailhead obviously had at least one gun with them. Lévesque doesn't sell guns, but he does sell knives, including Buck Rangers and others like them. They didn't use a knife though; they shot him. Both guns and knives were used in the park, but not the same knife used on Maloaf. It was a much different cut," said Esterbridge.

"Assuming you're right, Tom, what does the Khukuri tell you?"

"That the assassin is Nepalese and almost certainly a Gurkha, because the Khukuri is the traditional knife used by the Nepalese, both as a tool and as a weapon. Additionally, it is the symbolic weapon of the Gurkhas," answered Esterbridge.

"But how can you be sure it was a Khukuri and not some other surgically sharp knife?"

"Look at the pattern of the throat wound. Unlike most knife blades that taper toward the tip, the Khukuri actually gets wider until the very tip. Notice how wide this gash is, which argues for a thick-bladed knife. And finally, because the blade curves toward the victim, the design adds torque to the cut. In mathematical terms, torque adds leverage to force, which is the measure of effort for a straight push or pull motion, like carving a turkey. Hence, all things being equal, knives that produce torque will yield a deeper cut for the same energy expended than will straight-bladed knives," said Esterbridge.

"So, we have one team with at least one Gurkha, and another team that uses an H&K 9mm with a suppressor. Any idea who they are?"

"If I am correct about the Gurkha, and of course, it could be any-one with a penchant for exotic weapons, the team could be English because the English Army has Gurkhas in it. As for the other team, their weapon also suggests professionals. H&K is a favorite with a lot of Special Forces. Our Special Forces prefer the Browning Hi-Powers and Sig-Sauer P225s and P226s. The U.S. teams also prefer Sigs, but usually chambered for the more powerful rounds, so the .40 caliber or the .357 Sig. They feel the 9mm is a poor replacement for their .45. The Brits use H&Ks, as do the Germans, and most of the other Special Forces that patterned themselves after the SAS or the KSK."

"So, maybe a Gurkha and maybe a Special Forces unit. That's it?"

"Could be two Special Forces units, sir."

"Great!"

Des Sangs had been silent for most of the observations and conclu-sions part of their investigation, and looked like she wished she were someplace else. She was very good at what she did – if her proclivity for trying to discern what her boss wanted to hear was excepted – but on this case she had little to offer. Mac Dowell couldn't help but notice her dejection.

"Don't worry, Mikaila, the next time we're involved in a case where we're up to our ankles in blood, gore, and offal, you'll be the first one I'll turn to."

"Promise, sir," she smiled.

* * *

Mac Dowell met with Duclos, briefing him with what his unit had found and, in turn, asking Duclos if he had anything to add based on what he had just learned. Other than his astonishment that two professional units had seen fit to kill four people in his jurisdiction, he did not.

"The common denominator in all this seems to be Salar Wusaivid," said Mac Dowell. "What do you know about him?"

"Well, on the surface he's an Iranian immigrant, here on a Skilled-Worker Visa. He's a computer programmer and systems analyst who works for Gentec, downtown. A Muslim. Quiet. The neighbors didn't know much about him, because he pretty much kept to himself. The one exception was Maloaf. They both were technical climbers, you know, going up vertical rock walls, and hanging off cliffs by ropes, that sort of thing. His co-workers said he was bright and likeable enough, but he didn't join in many social activities. A loner, but not someone you'd expect to open fire on the métro some morning. More in the sense that he was shy."

"What do you mean, on the surface?" asked Mac Dowell.

"Interestingly, while Wusaivid has a valid *Skilled-Worker Visa*, a valid Québec driver's license, and a valid National Health Card, and while all of his applications for those documents contain the exact date of his entry into Canada, when I checked for any record that he had actually entered the country on that date, I couldn't find any. No flight or ship record, no immigration record, no passport clearance, and no border crossing record. It's as though he either walked in from the south, sledded in over the pole, or parachuted in from God knows where. Nothing."

"Any hint of military training or even service?"

"Iran isn't big on sharing information, period, but they especially wouldn't give out that kind of information. But it has mandatory military service for all male citizens, so he had to have served in the military," answered Duclos.

"No way of telling in what capacity?"

"None. But there is nothing from his history here that suggests anything other than it was just something he had to do. He took rock climbing lessons at the Trailhead and he came to them as a neophyte; he didn't go to the Dojo. I guess he could have been a hacker in Iran, but I could find nothing to suggest that."

"Anything else?"

"His co-workers said he seemed to live well below his means. They thought it was just an immigrant thing, or maybe it was religious. Thought that might be the reason he didn't go out to lunch with them, for instance. The neighbors said the same thing. They were pretty sure he made much more money than they did, the neighbors, that is. Most of them are either blue collar or in a low-paying government or service-industry job. Still, several have families and cars. Wusaivid didn't have a family or a car, though he did have a driver's license. His apartment was clean but frugal, barren even."

"Have you obtained his financial records?" asked Mac Dowell.

"Yes, he has modest checking and savings accounts. Oh, by the way, he withdrew half the funds in his savings account. I don't know if you knew, but on Monday morning, he called his boss to tell him that he was taking extra vacation time because he had received a call from a cousin, I think, saying that his mother, who presumably lives in England, was involved in an automobile accident. He was flying to London to visit her," added Duclos.

"I didn't know that," said Mac Dowell.

"Well, he can find no record that he went to England. What we did find was an American Express charge for changing the date of his flight to Calgary. He was scheduled to go there next Saturday morning, but he changed the flight to Monday. My guess is that Maloaf's death spooked him. However, in addition to calling his boss, he also called his HR Department with the same story about going to England to check on his mother. Both got the impression that he was coming back, just that he was going to England first, and, depending on his mother's condition, was either staying until she was out of the hospital or, if she was just banged up, continuing on with his vacation," said Duclos.

"Tell me he's not going to the Stampede," said Mac Dowell.

"No indication of that. The people at the Trailhead said that he was going climbing in Waterton Lakes National Park, though they didn't know where exactly. And, I did find other charges on his American Express Card for campsite reservations and a round-trip reservation for a cruise on Waterton Lake. The return, however, was not for the same day. Also, the camping reservations were not for two nights in a row, but for July 9th and 13th."

"So, presumably, he's going to camp at Waterton Lakes one night, take a boat cruise on the lake, camp in the area, do three days of climbing, take the boat back, camp again in Waterton, fly back to Montreal, and resume his life."

"Presumably, but Chief Superintendent, you should know that there is only one stop on the cruise and that's at the south end of the lake, which happens to be in the States."

"Ah."

Chief Superintendent Mac Dowell, this time with his team, went to Musaiyib's apartment to see if they could learn anything that Duclos and his forensic team might have missed. Mac Dowell knew it was a long shot, but then, Duclos' forensic team failed to notice the difference in the victim's cuts, a detail that led to the realization that there were two different professional teams involved in the four Saint-Laurent deaths.

Mac Dowell's first impression of the apartment, however, almost convinced him that the effort was a waste of time. He addressed Des Sangs and Esterbridge.

"OK, as you can see, there aren't many hiding places, so this might be a fool's errand. Still, it might be a good learning experience, as neither of you is trained in this area. The first rule is, assume nothing. The second rule is, look at what is there and look for what is missing, meaning what should be there. That's enough for you now."

The search didn't take long, even after removing all the drawers and looking at what was in them, under them, and behind them. They removed seat cushions, searched for pocket fallout in the creases, and moved the heavy pieces, tilting them over. They went through his few clothes, pockets, folds, and linings. The kitchen took the longest. Duclos had taken Musaiyib's computer, but the techies hadn't figured out how to get into it yet.

Des Sangs was the first one finished, so she waited in the living room. Mac Dowell joined her shortly afterwards.

"Anything?"

"No, I just had the bathroom. Even that didn't take long. I could hide a Buick in my bathroom."

"Have you seen Esterbridge?"

"Last I saw him, he was in the study, or at least, I think it was the study. It's where Wusaivid kept his computer."

"Come on, let's take a look."

Esterbridge was standing by an open window, looking out at what seemed to be the building next door.

"What, you see a naked lady over there, Tom?" said Des Sangs.

"No, but Chief Superintendent, would you look at this?"

"What do you see?"

"Well, you said, assume nothing, so I looked outside as well. First, at the sills, then, I stuck my head out to make sure nothing was tacked up on the siding, and I saw that. What is it, sir?"

"Where?"

"On the incoming line, just below the casing."

"I don't know."

Mac Dowell twisted the hex nut on the backside of a thickness in the line that looked like a thin snake had swallowed a .45 caliber cartridge. When he had the back of the device free from the line, he undid the front connection, then reconnected the line. When he was back inside, Mac Dowell examined the device.

"Do you know what this is Mikaila?"

Des Sangs took he device, examining it from all angles.

"No, sir, I don't."

"Tom?"

After Esterbridge did the same, he said he didn't either.

"It's good thinking is what it is. I'd say the exercise that appeared fruitless, ended up teaching us all something, myself included."

"What is it, sir? asked Esterbridge.

"It's a tap."

"What, like a bug?" asked Des Sangs.

"Yes, but it's a land line tap, which means it captures not only phone conversations, but also internet transmissions. Do you know what else it does?"

Both echoed, "No, sir."

"It tells us there's another team involved."

Twenty-Five

Mac Dowell reported his team's findings to Ewen Mac Ghillie, the Head of the Mounties' Criminal Investigative Analysis unit. He informed that, for reasons unknown, two and probably three professional teams – two of which had committed murders in Montreal – were pursuing an Iranian immigrant named Salar Wusaivid, who, Mac Dowell believed, was headed to Calgary, and most likely en route to Waterton Lakes National Park, where Wusaivid had camping and boat-cruise reservations.

Mac Dowell gave Mac Ghillie Wusaivid's profile and a detailed report of his investigation, which included the use of a Khukuri in one of the murders, a silenced H&K 9mm in three of the others, and the land line tap Esterbridge had found at Wusaivid's apartment. Finally, he hypothesized that the only reason he could think of that Wusaivid was of so much interest to these groups, was that he was a computer programmer and a systems analyst, and that maybe he had hacked into – knowingly or unknowingly – a critical Iranian computer address.

Mac Ghillie thanked Mac Dowell for the thoroughness of his investigation and then told him that there may actually be four groups after Musaiyib.

"Four! Who is this guy?" asked Mac Dowell.

"Yes, perhaps four, depending on who tapped the land line. And Saeed ibn Musaiyib is the young man who is at the nexus of all this mayhem."

"Who is Saeed ibn Musaiyib?"

"Salar Wusaivid is his very cleverly contrived alias. Oh, and he's Iraqi not Iranian. One of the teams searching for him is Iranian, though, an Iranian Takavar commando unit, to be more precise. Another is a group of two or three soldiers. Might be Yanks or Canadians, we're not sure which, or both, are trying to locate what Musaiyib and his deceased friend, Abdul Awwal, looted from Iraq's National Museum. The reason I know all this is because I got a call this morning from a Yank Commander named Roth, though not Portnoy's complainer – who is heading up a Coalition Task Force that has been assigned to locate and retrieve 100 Sumerian cylinder seals that were looted from Iraq's National Museum in Baghdad on April 10th, 2003."

"What are Sumerian cylinder seals?"

Mac Ghillie went off for about twenty minutes, detailing their origin, function, and linguistic importance.

"The Iranians are involved because they believe they have a cultural claim to them, and they may well, since they were invented, created, or came into being – I'm not sure of the appropriate predicate here – in what is present-day Iran. While their claim may be valid, they have no authority here and are almost certainly responsible for three of the Montreal murders, which, as you well know, is against the law. Also, undoubtedly, the Coalition soldiers, not to be confused with the Coalition Task Force...this is getting complicated, isn't it?"

"No, no. I'm following you."

He wasn't, or at least not all of it, but he wanted to know what Mac Ghillie had learned.

"How do you know that they are responsible? That's what you were going to say, wasn't it?"

"Yes, Angus, that they are responsible for one or three murders."

"Why not the other group, the one that tapped Musaiyib's land line, is that his name?"

"Yes. Musaiyib, not Wusaivid."

"Right, so maybe there are only three groups?"

"No, Angus, I think you're right. There are four. But getting back to the Yanks and the Canadians. Commander Roth told me about a woman strangely named Finn Ni Cool. It seems she's part of a Celtic myth involving two giants, a magical salmon, and a steak made of rock. A very confusing story, but you know how the Irish are."

Mac Dowell decided he was confused enough, he wasn't going to touch the myth, but he still had one more question for Mac Ghillie. Then, he would conclude his report and let him deal with the Calgary connection.

"But, sir, how do you know that the Coalition unit is responsible for at least one of the Montreal murders?"

"The Task Force or the Yanks and Canadians?"

"The bad guys!"

"Oh, good idea. That'll reduce confusion. Well, they killed Musaiyib's accomplice in Baghdad, an Awwal Abdul, which is a funny first name, even for an Arab. At least, that's what the Coalition commander thinks. Well, not that the name's funny, though he did think Finn Ni Cool had a funny name."

Mac Dowell had had enough. "Well, it seems you're way ahead of me as usual, sir. I'll leave the Calgary and Waterton connection in your capable hands, but please give me a call when you have this all wrapped up. I'd like to hear the full story."

"Yes, of course, I will. We'll have another nice chat then. You've done your usual knocked up job on this. Thank you for your good work. I'll ring off now, Angus."

"Good bye, sir."

Jesus Christ, Mac Dowell thought. *Who's on first? The man is brilliant. He must be, to get the results he gets and to command such an important unit, but I'll be damned if I understand half of what he*

says, and I'm a Scott, too. Maybe it's because he's a highlander. I won-
der how the frogs deal with him.

* * *

Dodge had gotten back to Barlow with the information he needed six hours before the twenty-four hour deadline. Dodge could have given it to him when Barlow called him from Montreal, because he knew that his story was bullshit from start to finish, so, after he found Musaiyib, he had started his own investigation into why Barlow really wanted him.

He thought about telling Barlow he couldn't find anything, or sending him on a snipe hunt, but either tactic might leave loose ends. This way, he could tidy up those loose ends and make an extra $5,000.

Dodge knew that until recently, Barlow had been in the Army. He also knew from informal conversation with him in his office that he was from Natchez, so he started to look for articles about him in his hometown paper, the *Natchez Democrat*. Sure enough, Barlow served in Iraq for three tours. Next, Dodge looked for news in Iraq for the years Barlow was there. Other than articles about the endless skirmishes, burning oil fields, and contractor scandals, all he found noteworthy was the looting of the National Museum, although locals had done that. The troops were too busy overwhelming Saddam's military to be involved. Then he ran across a story about a special task force charged with recovering the 100 Sumerian cylinder seals, and he knew, instinctively, that this was what Barlow and his friends were looking for. Dodge had no idea what they were, so he researched them.

He skimmed the articles. He didn't much care why they were important. He was looking for what they were worth. He couldn't find a definitive value, but when he ran across the word millions, that was enough for Claude C. Dodge. He put together a team of special operatives that he used from time to time, when discretion and abandoned were the qualities he was looking for. Very coincidental when one considers that the team Dodge put together was exactly like what Barlow proposed to Bosheers as a possible career path, if they couldn't find the seals.

* * *

Barlow and Bosheers arrived in Calgary on the 4:18 flight from Houston. King couldn't get away until Saturday: he had to finish his final week of teaching clumsy fuckers how to kill quietly. They couldn't find a room in Calgary because of the Stampede, but they had managed to get one in Lethbridge, which, although it was a three-hour drive away, put them in good position for Waterton. Before they could leave, though, they had two stops to make. The first was at a camping equipment store, and the second was at a *one-percenter* biker bar.

Barlow and Bosheers had all the camping gear they needed from the army, but, while there wasn't much they could do about their physical stature and appearance, they didn't want their equipment screaming out, Special Forces. Barlow thought that finding a camping equipment store in the shadow of the Rockies and by four national parks would be easy, but he underestimated the aleatory nature of the *Yellow Pages*. If he had used the computer, he'd have been more likely to find something in the *Canpages*. He finally found the Out There Adventure store on Eighth Avenue, but that wasn't until he had gone to three RV stores and lots, and two green-living consultants. They got two tents, three sleeping bags and pads, three packs – two large and one medium – cooking equipment, some freeze-dried food, and some other odds and ends, like a water purifier, water bottles, a parachute cord, and a map of Waterton Lakes National Park. He had brought some less visible equipment, like a compass and a GPS, with him. The bill came to over $1,325. Barlow would pay for it out of the fund they had established earlier. King's account was tapped out, but, at this stage, Barlow knew he was good for it.

It was after six, so they decided to get something to eat before they went looking for the *one-percenter* biker bar. The appellation *one-percenter* came from the American Motorcycle Association, which frequently told the press in the early '60s that ninety-nine percent all those who rode motorcycles were law-abiding citizens. It's an oft-repeated quotation, but the original reference was a reaction to a fight that broke out at a motorcycle rally in Hollister, California in 1947, between two rival clubs. Although the damage was minor, the press blew it out of proportion, calling it the Hollister Riot and suggesting that the town had been taken over by the bikers.

The original *one-percenter* tag referred to those bikers who refused to comply to the laws of society, which was a rather vague term – especially given the time period – that could mean anything from not bathing to brigandage. However, according to the Outlaws Motorcycle Club, law-enforcement officials narrowed the meaning of *one-percenter* in the '80s from those bikers who refused to live by the rules of society, to mean members of criminal gangs.

In Canada, a good deal of organized crime, including drugs, prostitution, money laundering, and extortion, was conducted by *one-percenters*. After the 90s motorcycle gang turf wars in Quebec, which were chiefly between the Rock Machine and Hell's Angels, and which left more than 150 dead, Hell's Angels emerged as the most powerful outlaw gang. The Rock Machine still existed and had grown since merging with the Bandidos, a gang originally formed in Texas. While law enforcement in Canada had done a great deal to eradicate Hell's Angels, much in the same way the FBI had all but crushed the Mafia in the States, the gang still operated, reaping the lion share of profits generated by organized crime in Canada. Hell's Angels, however, had been particularly devastated in Alberta. Consequently, the Rock Machine had re-emerged and had a significant presence, albeit a shadowy one, in the province. Barlow and

Bosheers went to one of their bars, the Red and Gold Steel Horse, which was just off Third Avenue, for their next purchases.

Flying from state to state in America didn't present much of an obstacle to transporting firearms. All you had to do was declare the firearm, make sure it was unloaded, and put it in a locked, hard case, in a checked bag. Traveling to Canada with a gun, especially a handgun, was a much bigger problem. Canada didn't like handguns. In fact, there was no legal way to possess a handgun with a barrel length of four inches or shorter. Also, Canada didn't allow concealed carry for the average citizen. You could transport a handgun through Canada in a sealed container if you had the proper paper work, but that took at least three months to affect. It wasn't till three days ago that Barlow knew he would be in Canada. King told him where to go and who to see to get a couple of pieces. He also told him how to act when he got there.

It was still early, so the bar was fairly quiet, but the bikes lined up outside told them that, even if who they were looking for wasn't inside, someone in there could get a message to him. Barlow walked up to the bar and signaled the bartender, while Bosheers stood a few feet behind him and watched the room. The bartender ignored him.

Two men wearing red and gold club colors approached them.

"Incomin'," said Bosheers.

"Deal with them, will ya, Howland."

The two men braced Bosheers, "What the fuck you doin' here? You cops?"

Barlow continued to try to get the bartender's attention, even calling out to him, but the bartender continued to ignore him. Barlow turned around.

"Well, Howland, if the barkeep won't talk ta us, maybe these two fellas can help us."

"Yeah, we'll help ya," said the lead one. "We'll help ya ta the 'mergency room."

"Howland?"

Bosheers piston-kicked the lead one in his right knee, collapsing him, took a lateral step to the right, and put the tip of a black ceramic gravity knife blade into the hollow at the base of the throat of the second biker, causing him to get up on his tiptoes. Barlow stepped over the one writhing on the floor.

"Now listen up, bad asses. I tried ta ask the barkeep a question, but he ignored me, even though I politely asked him fer his attention. This unpleasantness coulda been avoided. Now if y'all are thinkin' of rushin' us, I would advise against it. My friend, Howland, here, will kill this fat fella in front of him, and then me and him will commence ta cause some real trouble. We been killin' ragheads for the last three years, so Canadians might be a nice change."

"Ask your question," said a large, but not overly fat, biker.

"We need ta see Little Mickey."

"What do you want with him?"

"We need ta buy some protection. We heard Canada was a dangerous place."

"How do we know you're not cops."

"You don't, but if we were, I think ya gotta agree that we gotta strange approach ta entrapment."

The big guy didn't move, and he didn't say anything. Barlow guessed he was having trouble processing the information.

"Y'all better make a decision soon. I don't think fatso here can stay on his tiptoes much longer. I think he's fixin' ta impale himself."

"All right. I'm Little Mickey.

"Looks are deceivin'. Let him down, Howland."

Barlow bought two Browning Hi-Powers. All Little Mickey had were 9mms, so the choice was between that and some shitty South American guns, like flashy Tauruses, that only gangbangers would want to buy to look cool, turning the gun on its side. Note to gangbangers: the sights are on top for a reason. Oh, and that finger-flexing shit is also stupid. Calm and deliberate is scary, not physical therapy for arthritis. Besides holding the gun right side up in a steady grip might increase your odds of hitting something and saving ammo. Finally, ever wonder why you keep getting hit in the eye with ejected shells? It's because the ejection port is on the side, so spent shells go out to your right and behind you. Turn an automatic on its side and the spent shells come out the top and back into your face, stupids.

"Pretty heavy freight fer a couple a nines, even if they are Brownin's," said Bosheers.

"Yeah, a thousand a piece is on the steep side, but I didn't feel like wastin' time dickerin' with Little Mickey. And if I had ta kill him, what would we do then? This ain't America where ya can go ta any MLKJ street and get exactly what yer lookin' fer. Besides, they should be more than adequate."

Twenty-Six

July 8th, 2011:

Commander Roth, Sergeant Major Kennedy, and Lieutenant Jassim arrived in Calgary at 9:24 p.m. after having made stops in Orlando and Houston. They had to go south to go north. The airlines had a curious routing system. Still, it was the shortest flight available. His team was met by Sergeant Flynn who drove them to the Sandman Hotel in the Calgary City Center, where the RCMP kept rooms for visiting law enforcement officials. The hotel was just a few blocks from RCMP headquarters on Eighth Street. The Sergeant checked them into the hotel and told Commander Roth that he would pick his team up again at 8:45 a.m. for a nine o'clock meeting with Chief Superintendent Takoda at RCMP Headquarters.

Chief Superintendent Takoda was a striking man. He was six feet, four inches tall with broad shoulders and slim hips, pronounced cheek bones, and copper-colored skin. He was a full-blooded Woodland Cree Indian. The Woodland Cree lived mostly in Northern Alberta and northern Saskatchewan, but, aside from some environment differences, were culturally and linguistically the same as the Cree who lived on the prairies of Alberta, Saskatchewan, Manitoba, Montana, and North Dakota. Canadians called their indigenous people the *First Nations*. That there were 630 recognized bands in

Canada didn't seem to confound their logic of the collective appellation. The term *First Nations*, like America's *Native American*, was, of course, a political one. Cree was a European corruption of the exonym – a name given from outside, in this case by the Ojibwa – *Kirištino'*. Indigenous people on both sides of the border preferred to be called by their tribal name. In the case of Chief Superintendent, he might call himself *O'pimmitish Ininiwuc*, meaning man of the woods, which, like so many tribal names, designated that they were *people* of a particular local site or possessing a particular trait. *O'pimmitish Ininiwuc* was tough on the White Eyes' tongue (forgive the contorted mixed metaphor), so Cree did nicely. It also avoided the confusion of using *Native American* south of the border and *First Nations* north of it for the same people.

Given that Canadian Aboriginals had not fared any better than America's, that Takoda had risen to a Chief Superintendent in the RCMP was an achievement as impressive as his physical stature.

Takoda welcomed Commander Roth and his team, bidding them to be seated and offering them coffee, tea, or bottled water. Roth thanked the Chief Superintendent, but declined, saying that they had just had breakfast and were coffeed out.

"Let's get started then. My understanding from Ewen Mac Ghillie, is that you are pursuing a certain Saeed ibn Musaiyib, who, if I understand Mac Ghillie correctly, which is not always an easy thing, is calling himself Salar Wusaivid. And the reason you are pursuing him is because he is suspected, along with an Abdul Awwal, now deceased, of having stolen a collection of Sumerian cylinder seals from the National Museum in Baghdad."

"Moreover, several people, most probably former Coalition soldiers, have already killed at least one person in Montreal, maybe as many as three, and are also trying to locate this man. I'm going to call him Musaiyib to avoid confusion. Is that correct?"

"Yes, Chief Superintendent. Our intelligence has also identified an Iranian commando unit of Takavar, their elite troops, that is also searching for Musaiyib, and trying to score a cultural coup on the Iraqis."

"They then are probably the ones responsible for the other murders in Montreal," offered Takoda.

"Yes, we're not certain who killed who, but almost certainly these two groups are responsible for the deaths of the four people in Montreal who were associated with Musaiyib," answered Roth.

"So, we have some – for lack of a better name – rogue soldiers, a Takavar unit, and your team. Is there anyone else you're aware of in this confusion?" asked Takoda.

"Well, now the RCMP, and there's a mysterious woman who we only know by the unusual name of Finn Ni Cool. It seems she has a habit of recovering stolen artwork for the finder's fee."

"Well, Commander, you seem to have yourself, what we Canadians call, *a bag of hammers*. It seems you have your work cut out for you. If I understand your purpose in coming here correctly, you believe that this Musaiyib in on his way to our Waterton Lakes National Park to retrieve the cylinder seals, which you believe he has hidden there."

"Yes, Chief Superintendent. Lieutenant Jassim found some American Express charges that Musaiyib made two months ago that suggest he was going to Waterton Lakes. Given the time of the year and his fondness for technical climbing, it seemed obvious that he was going on vacation. However, when he moved his vacation date up, we assumed he did so because of the Montreal murders. It now seems more likely that he's here to get the seals and then, cut and run. So, it's imperative that we find him before he either gets killed or disappears to God knows where."

"Commander, you have your orders, and I have mine. Here are mine. I'm to help you in any way I can, which you can take literally; however, my primary focus has to do with apprehending the murderers of this man's neighbors. So, I can get you lodgings if you need them, either at a commercial establishment or, failing that, at the Waterton RCMP barracks, provisions if you need them, and I can make sure you get to Waterton Lakes whenever you are ready to go. I can also get you firearms or clearances for them if you've brought them with you."

"What I can't do is put any men on the Waterton Lake cruise boat, because, half way down the lake the boat enters American waters. I can have men at the dock, though. So, bearing all that in mind, what do you need?"

Roth's unit was already fed and had brought camping gear and provisions with them. They also arrived in Canada with authorization to carry firearms, which was another door opened quickly by the American CIA. What they did need, however, was lodging in Waterton and good trail maps of the area.

July 8th, 2011:

Colonel Zare, Corporal Karimi, and Sergeant Sharifi arrived in Calgary on Westjet's nonstop Flight 272 from Montreal at 6:04 p.m. Colonel Zare didn't have the connections that Commander Roth enjoyed, but, of course, there was an Iranian cell in Calgary, albeit a small one. The Takavar unit was picked up at the airport by Abdul-Barr Aliaabaadi. Aliaabaadi was a student at the University of Alberta where he lived in student housing. He had arranged with two of his friends to each take in one member of the unit. Aliaabaadi had also arranged for food for the unit that evening and the next morning, and to deliver them to Waterton in the morning after breakfast. He also was able to replace the weapons they had to leave in Montreal.

* * *

Barlow and Bosheers arrived in Waterton National Park late Friday morning. The first thing they checked for was an available campsite. There were none open at the Townsite Campground. They checked out the Crandell Mountain Campground where there were a few sites open because it operated on a first-come, first-served basis. Unlike the Townsite campsites, which were located on open mowed lawns, the Crandell Mountain sites were tucked away among the trees and undergrowth. The two looked over the sites and reserved one, although without paying for it, yet. Then, they drove back the ten miles to Waterton. There were a number of sites at Townsite Campground that were open but had reserved signs on them. One was across the road and two down from the one that was reserved for S. Wusaivid. They staked that one out. About an hour later, an RV with Washington State plates pulled into the site. When the father and mother got out to determine where the best placement of the RV would be in relationship to the utilities, Barlow and Bosheers approached them.

"Hello, are you the Oswalds?"

"Yes, we are. Is there a problem with this site?" asked the father.

"Well, yes, there is," said Barlow. Bosheers flicked the black, ceramic gravity knife open and put the blade tip right under Oswald's wife's sternum.

"Ya see, there have been a number of bears reported in the area – grizzlies mostly – so this area ain't safe fer ya. We suggest y'all will be a lot happier and safer down in Glacier where the American bears are better behaved. Now, we're prepared ta pay ya fer y'all's inconvenience. What'd ya pay fer these four nights here?"

"Ah, ah…" the father said, unable to get his voice. "I got the receipt in the RV."

"Go get it, sir, and remember, we have yer wife out here and my friend has his knife, so no funny stuff, understand?"

"Yes, sir."

"Good."

The husband returned quickly with the receipt. Barlow could see a boy and a girl, peering through the windshield, trying to see what has holding things up.

"Those young'uns of yours sure are curious about what's goin' on out here. I think I'll go over and put their minds ta rest. What are their names?"

"No, no, don't do that," said the wife. "We'll do whatever you ask, just don't hurt them."

"I said, what are their names?"

"Audrey and Rusty, but we'll do what you ask. Just leave them be."

"That's some wise thinkin', ma'am. OK, so Clark – that's your name?"

"Yes, sir."

"Well, Clark, go over ta that table and write what I tell ya ta on the receipt. You got a pen?"

"I do," said the wife. She dug it out of her day pack. "Here."

"Now, Clark, see how obligin' yer wife is. Now I want ya ta assume that same frame of mind, got it?"

"Yes, sir."

"Good, now date it July 1st, 2011. Good. Now write, 'Bein' unable ta make our planned trip, we have given this reservation to our good friend here, Joe Pete.' Make sure ya put the *g*'s in there; I don't tend ta use 'em. Good, now sign it. Thata boy. Now, one last word a caution. We have another friend, whose knife is a lot bigger and a lot scarier than this little thing that my friend here is holdin' on yer sweet wife. It's so sharp that with jest one slash he could cut them young'uns heads right off. Now, I know yer name, Clark, but I don't know yer pretty lady's name?"

"Ellen."

"Helen?" asked Barlow, though he knew that Oswald had said Ellen.

"No, Ellen."

"So, Clark, Ellen, I know y'all's names now and I know where ya live, so don't do anythin' stupid like drivin' down the road a piece and callin' the rangers ta tell them lies about how my friend and me ended up with this campsite, cause if ya do y'all will see us again, and we'll bring our other friend with the big, sharp knife with us. Understand?"

"Yes, sir."

"Good, now ya wanta head out, sos ya can be sure of gettin' a site down in Glacier. We'll walk ya to the RV and say hello ta the young'uns. Here, we go."

"Ya think they'll do somethin' stupid, Joe Pete?"

"I don't think so. Let's set up camp."

* * *

Chief Superintendent Takoda did manage to get a room in the Aspen Village Inn in Waterton for Commander Roth in spite of the season. There was a last minute cancellation of a room with two double beds that was big enough to add a cot. Sergeant Major Kennedy got the cot.

Takoda had also notified the barracks commander in Waterton about Commander Roth, telling him to give his full cooperation to the Commander. The Waterton barracks, because it was located within a national park, came under the jurisdiction of the Mounties. It was also a seasonal substation for the same reason. The barracks was under the command of K Division, headquartered in Edmonton. Commander Roth and his team checked in with the barracks commander at 0900 hours. Roth brought the team along to introduce them, not only to the commander, but also to any of his troops assigned to help his team, and also so that there wouldn't be any potentially lethal misunderstandings concerning their carrying concealed weapons.

After brief introductions and courtesies, the commander, Chief Inspector Wilkinson, asked Commander Roth what exactly he needed from him. Roth gave him a synopsis of the oft-told tale of the cylinder seals and their attendant murders in Montreal.

"Chief Inspector, I'm fully aware of the dicey jurisdictional problems that my team has here in Canada, so I don't intend to step on your toes. All I'm interested in is Musaiyib and the cylinder seals. If things go as they appear to be scheduled, he should be out of your jurisdiction as of Sunday morning. Where our common problems overlap ,though, is with the two groups that are tracking Musaiyib. I'm going to call them units, because, if our intelligence is correct, they are two, separate, highly-trained military units that are responsible for the four murders in Montreal. If they manage to get down to the south end of the lake, then my team's problems increase exponentially."

"Unfortunately, I don't have any pictures of these men to show you. I don't even have a witnesses' description of them. All I can tell you, is that each unit is probably made up of at least three men. I say three because your CIA forensic team thinks that the way the murders happened would require at least two men, but more likely, three. I'm even guessing men. There could be women involved, but I think that is highly unlikely, so let's leave it at three men. We know one unit is comprised of elite Iranian Special Forces, but that doesn't necessarily mean they are going to look the part. Special Forces personnel rarely look like Hollywood stereotypes. Nor will they be especially swarthy. They will be trim and athletic-looking, to be sure, but then I suspect that most of the people who get off the boat to hike off into the mountains will be, as well."

"What they will be, is alert. They'll be very much aware of, not only everything within their immediate ken, but also everything on the perimeter. And, of course, they will be armed and extremely dangerous. These men are murderers. Make sure your men are wearing ballistic vests, but they must not feel confident because the murderers are armed and might be wearing vests themselves. I suspect neither unit will want to cause a commotion, because doing so will compromise their mission. Still, your men need to be on their guard, especially where others are present, like on the dock, in town, or in the campgrounds."

"What we need from you then, in addition to as many men as you can spare, is to discretely check the campgrounds, lodgings, and marinas. Step up the police presence in town, but not so much that the tourists become aware of it."

"How many ways are there to get to the south end of the lake?"

"Basically, two. You could either take a boat or walk the trail along the west shore."

"What about some of the other trails here?" Roth unfolded a map that Takoda had given him.

"Well, theoretically, they could be used, but the West Shore Trail is a little less than eleven kilometers long, so almost seven miles. About four miles are in Canada and three more from the international boundary to the south end of the lake. By comparison, it's twenty kilometers to Summit Lake along the Alderson-Carthew Lakes route, then another, oh, I don't know, about twelve to fifteen kilometers to the West Shore Trail. Then it's yet another five kilometers to the south end. All-in-all, it's about twenty-five miles. Even from Cameron Lake, it's almost fifteen miles. Not a practical approach. Especially the Alderson-Carthew Lakes route. The terrain is very rugged."

"Doable, but not practical. Well, maybe the one from Cameron Lake. How about on the east side of the lake?"

"There is a boat that goes over to the east shore, and hikers use it to access the trail to Crypt Lake." Wilkinson leaned over and traced the route on Roth's map.

"Couldn't someone just follow the shoreline to the south end? I know it would be harder, but remember, these guys are in excellent shape. I wish Socko was here. He'd know."

"Socko?" asked Wilkinson.

"One of our men. His nickname. He's SAS, and the toughest guy in his unit."

"Oh. As to this route, again, it's possible but highly improbable. Crypt Lake drains into Waterton Lake, just south of the boat landing. It does so via Hell Roaring Falls. They don't call it that for its serenity. Look how close the contour lines are together right after the falls, and then again by the border. It doesn't get easy – and by easy, I mean flat – until the last mile and a half of the lake."

"OK, I agree. Mostly. So, in addition to discreet questioning, I'd like you to station men on the West Shore Trail and along the trail from Cameron Lake. There should be three sets on the West Shore trail: one at the trail head, one at – what is it – Upper Bertha Falls, and one at the border. Two sets should be enough on the Cameron Lake trail, with one set about a mile down from the trail head and the other at the border over here."

Roth pointed to a spot on the map about four miles west of the lake.

"For how long, Commander? We don't have a lot of felonies here, but there are some car break-ins, bar fights in town, and there's always some emergency or other. We have to have men to cover our usual small-town mayhem."

"Let's say from 0800 hours on Saturday until the boat sails on Sunday, 1000 hours."

"Around the clock?"

"If you can. Chief Superintendent Takoda is sending down four men. They should arrive by late this afternoon, at, say, 1600 hours."

"Well, that would help, but that will still leave us pretty thin. How about my men make their inquiries today and tomorrow. Then on Saturday, I'll have a team of two men at the West Shore trail head, a team of three on the West Shore trail at Upper Bertha Falls, and one man to join two of Takoda's men the border point. Then, on the Boundary Creek Trail, the one from Cameron Lake, I'll put a two-man team about a mile past the trail head and send a third man to join Takoda's other two men at the border point on that trail. To be able to affect this, I'll need your men to deal with the dock. No, actually, my men will have to take the dock. No offense, but I can't risk a shootout there. That leaves the campgrounds. You're going to have to take those. Most of those in charge there are volunteers who trade their duties for a free stay with utilities. The others, with the exceptions of the rangers, are just maintenance and cleanup people. The rangers generally just cover minor infractions, so only the law enforcement rangers are armed, and there are less than two dozen of them for the entire park. Mostly, they handle backcountry emergencies. We don't get a lot of rogue commando units here, other than bears, that is."

Roth turned to his team. "Any questions while we have the Chief Inspector's attention?"

Kennedy asked if he could see the lake check point.

"Yeah, that would be a good idea. Maybe we all should see them. Do you have a boat and driver available?"

"I can make them available. You can inspect the two check points on the Boundary Creek Trail yourself. There's no way to get you there faster than by hiking the trail. The border on the Boundary Creek Trail is less than six kilometers, no more than three and a half miles."

"Anything else you need?"

"Yes," said Jassim. "Do you have a secure high-speed port I can use for Internet access? In case I think of something that I want to check out."

"That's an easy one, Lieutenant."

One of the Mounties took Roth and his team to the two check-point sites down lake. True to form, the trip down lake was very windy, particularly near Upper Bertha Falls landing where the lake narrowed.

After seeing both sites, Kennedy recommended that the check points should be past the boat moorings and that the launch should be moored out of sight, some distance away down lake from the second checkpoint.

That afternoon, the team checked out the West Shore Tail trail head and afterward, Kennedy ran the Boundary Creek Trail to the border. There was nothing about any of the three sites that recommended anything other than the locations they had spoken about that morning.

Twenty-Seven

July 8th, 2011:

Keagan and Kelly checked into the Prince of Wales Hotel in Waterton at 4:00 p.m. The hotel was a National Historic Site in Canada and with good reason. It sat on a curlicue bluff, so that when you approached it from the prairied north, all you could see was the hotel centered amid two mountain chains. The mountains on both sides of the hotel defined the width of the glacial remnant that was Waterton Lake. From certain vantages, all you could see were the mountains, with the lake and the hotel seemingly floating above water. The impression was that of a surreal gingerbread chateau, suspended above a sward and a narrow, windswept fjord, hemmed in by wild ramparts. The hotel was the only artifact in the tableau; not even the parking lot was visible. The impression was mystical.

The hotel was designed by Luis Hill and built by the Great Northern Railroad between 1926 and 1927. Luis was the son of James J. Hill, the builder of the Great Northern and the person largely responsible for both Glacier and Waterton Lakes becoming national parks. Hill wanted a guaranteed clientele for his railroad, so he convinced Congress in 1910 to make Glacier the nation's tenth national park. Shortly thereafter, he began constructing hotels and stone chalets, high in the mountains. Luis Hill's hotel, the Prince of Wales, was the crown jewel of the parks' hostelries.

Keagan and Kelly had a lakeside king room with a balcony. It was a shared balcony, but the other couple was on their honeymoon so they weren't using it. Keagan had picked up some libations – a bottle of Jameson 12 for Kelly and one of Jack Daniel's for himself. He knew what an outrageous markup most hotels applied to room service alcohol. While not cheap, he saw no reason to waste money. Besides, most minibars didn't stock Jameson, many didn't even stock Jack Daniel's, and the wait for room service could be interminable. So, he almost always brought his own liquor. He built two drinks, opened the balcony doors, and then closed them.

"Better put on a *geansai* and a shell, Kelly, it's really blowing."

The mountains that shouldered the narrow Waterton Valley funneled the wind directly out of the south. Then, it blew unopposed and accelerated by the lake's narrowness northward, until the airstream mingled with the prairie winds. There wasn't even a tree to stop the wind for the last six and a half miles. The effect was wild and romantic, if bracing.

Kelly took a long pull on her drink and before Keagan could comment on how beautiful the view was, she said, "Mick, I hope you don't get mad at me, but I've made an arrangement to get us some help."

Keagan knew that an "I hope you don't get mad at me" preface did not bode well for what was to follow.

"I'm assuming you mean, other than Niles and Teal."

"Yes. Mick. I'm sorry this was last minute, but when Musaiyib left Montreal on Monday, I knew that the Iranians had probably located him, which meant that the *villains* and the Coalition Task Force couldn't be far behind. Usually, we only have the thief, the bad guy buyer and his men, and the police to deal with. But this time, in addition to the thief, we have three commando units and the police, who are maybe even from two different countries. We're over our heads. We need help."

"Who'd you get?" asked Keagan, cautiously.

"You're not going to like this either, Mick."

"Who, Kelly?"

"Coughlin O'Dea and Emmon Mulvahill."

"What, from Belfast?"

"No, they live here in Canada now, in Vancouver. They came over shortly after you did, but for a different reason."

"Let me guess, they're on the scoot."

"In a manner of speaking."

"Which means what, Kelly?"

"Well, there were two bodies found floating in the Lagan, and Coughlin and Emmon were, shall we say, persons of interest. They weren't waiting around to see if they would be promoted to suspects, so they came to Canada. They do some work for us here. British Columbia, as the name might suggest, is a very British-leaning province. They serve a purpose."

"Tell me Sean Byme isn't with them."

"Well, I would, Mick, but that would be a lie."

"Ah, Kelly...you know how I feel about them, especially Byme. How could you involve that troupe of fools?"

"We're in a bind, Mick. Right now, there's you and me against a scared Muslim kid, three commando units, the Mounties, and God knows who else. Maybe even the FBI and the CIA. How are we going to deal with all those people?"

"With stealth and cunning, our usual practice."

"Yeah, well, sometimes there is no substitute for force."

"OK, when do we meet?"

Kelly looked at her watch. "If they were on time, about thirty minutes ago."

"They're late. What a surprise."

Keagan was about to continue in this vein when the phone rang. Kelly answered it. It was the front desk.

"Tell them we'll be down shortly." Kelly hung up.

"They're in the lobby, I thought it would be better if we met them downstairs and walked down to the boat launch. That way we don't have to waste time afterwards, showing them what they have to cover."

Keagan had had run-ins with these three before. On a good day, he could deal with O'Dea and Mulvahill. They were a bit quick on the trigger, but they got things done. Kelly was right, sometimes they did serve a purpose, but Byme was another matter. Keagan had met up with him at the all-Belfast boxing championship just before he came to America. It was a quarter finals match. Byme had better natural attributes than did Keagan, but he was lazy and stupid. Not a combination that often led to success, even in the ring. Byme was very fast, so he threw a lot of punches, hoping to connect with half of them. It was the fourth round and Byme was already getting tired, and his percentage of hits was down by half again, mostly glancing shots on Keagan's forearms and shoulders, but a couple of hard ones had connected. The bookies had them just about evenly matched. Those who favored Byme were betting on his speed; the others, on Keagan's brains. Byme rocked Keagan late in the fourth round but didn't try to finish him off because he was running out of steam. He was sure he'd do it early in the fifth when he was more rested. Keagan understood what Byme was doing and dropped him with three hard hooks and an uppercut that Byme never saw coming. When the hooks came, Byme anticipated an overhand right to follow them, which made sense, so he covered up accordingly. In doing so, he left his chin fully exposed from underneath. Keagan hit him with the uppercut with twelve seconds left in the round. Byme folded onto the canvas and never made the count.

Keagan and Kelly met the three in the lobby that offered a stunning view of the lake and the mountains that framed it. Kelly greeted them and Keagan was civil. He hadn't seen the three since he left Ireland, and he noticed that the Guinness had continued to add to their girths. Byme didn't look like he'd been training much since their fight. Keagan suggested they go outside to see where they would be needed. Right away, Byme started in on Keagan, telling Kelly that a beautiful woman like her could do a lot better than Mick. Kelly suggested he behave and focus on the job at hand.

Keagan walked them to the south edge of the bluff that overlooked the marina and the cruise docks. On the way across the sward, Byme kept hectoring Keagan.

"Have you been lucky in the ring again, Mick? Or did you quit when you were ahead? You know I'd love a rematch. Whenever you grow a set of balls, let me know."

Keagan stopped short of the edge. There was no telling what Byme might try to do. "Coughlin, Emmon, do you think maybe you could muzzle Sean?"

"Why don't you try it, Mick?" said Byme.

"Sean, boy, zip it. We've got a job to do," said O'Dea.

"All right, Coughlin, but afterwards, I want a shot at this *gooter*."

"You're not paying attention, Sean."

O'Dea was a heavyweight, and Byme, a middleweight. Both had gone to seed, but O'Dea was still the heavyweight. Byme shut up.

Keagan pointed out the cruise docks, the launch site, and the parking lot which was across from them.

"Musaiyib's cruise isn't until 10:00 a.m. on Sunday, but come early so you can get a slot in that parking lot. If the Iranians show up, it would be best to intercept them before they get on the boat. That way, you can just load them into a van and dump them at a Mounties barracks with a note explaining their presence in Canada, and suggesting they might warrant a looksee for several murders in Montreal. Taking them out down the lake would be messier."

"Aren't used to getting your hands dirty, are you, Mick?" said Byme.

Keagan ignored him. "Kelly, you have anything to add?"

"No, Mick, other than the obvious. It has to be quick, quiet, and clean. Clearly, with the first sailing of the day, there will be a lot of people around. We know the cruise will be a sellout, or nearly so. We can't bring on a scene and scare Musaiyib off."

"OK, lads, why don't I take you down to the dock and you can see the snatch area up close. Kelly, I'll see you back in the room."

"Aye, Mick," responded Kelly giving him a cautious eye.

The four of them got in O'Dea's van.

"Is this a rental or a street loaner, Coughlin?"

"A rental, Mick. I thought about getting one off the street, but we're in a bit of a cul-de-sac here. Decided it wasn't a good idea."

"Good thinking." *A rarity with O'Dea*, thought Keagan.

The drive was only a couple hundred yards, and they found a parking place in the lot adjacent to the dock. Keagan led them over to the quay. The parking lot, the boat's docking leg, and the pier with the ticket office and shops were compact and didn't need explanation.

"Just don't let them line up along the loading ramp; they'll be much harder to take there."

"Like we didn't know that, Mick. Just because you went to fancy schools doesn't make us stupid," continued Byme.

Byme's idea of a fancy school was passing the eighth grade. Keagan ignored him.

"Where are you *boyos* staying tonight?" said Keagan, trying to lighten the air.

"Kelly got us a place in Cardston, about thirty-five miles east of here. Nothing fancy, but not bad either," answered O'Dea.

They were almost back at the van when Byme asked Keagan how his good friend, the *English ponce*, was. O'Dea and Mulvahill cringed; they foolishly thought Byme could contain himself. Keagan turned on him, hit him with a powerful heart shot, spun him around to the side of the van, side-stepped in front of him, and followed the heart shot with a right cross that broke Byme's jaw.

"Now, maybe you'll shut the fuck up," said Keagan, as Byme crumpled down the side of the van and onto the pavement.

O'Dea and Mulvahill were quick to react. They stepped to both sides of Keagan. He thought he'd have to take them on too, which was fine with him at the moment. But all they wanted to do was to block Byme's prostrate form from public view and get him into the van. When they had, the three of them scanned the parking lot. Unlike at the All-Belfast Championship match, no one other than O'Dea and Mulvahill seemed to have noticed Byme's second loss to Keagan.

"Ah, shit, Mick. I know he's an annoying bastard, and he has a particular hard-on for you, but now I'm going to have to get another driver. How the fuck am I going to do that by tomorrow?" said O'Dea.

"Any problems, Mick?" asked Kelly when Keagan got back to the room.

"I didn't have any."

"Oh, no. What did you do?"

"Byme called Niles an *English ponce*."

"And?"

"I broke his jaw."

"Well, he got half of it right, Mick. Niles is English. You know Byme's not a Mensa man, so couldn't you have been a bit more tolerant?"

"It was the other half I objected to, Kelly."

"Aye, I could see where you would. That far off the mark and all."

* * *

Like Barlow, Colonel Zare didn't find any open campsites at the Townsite Campground. But, unlike Barlow, he was at the campground only to see where Musaiyib's campsite was. Satisfied that he knew the location of the site, and that, if the reserved sign was any indication, Musaiyib hadn't changed his plans, Colonel Zare told Corporal Karimi to drive down to the launch site. When Karimi drove past the campsite two down and across from the one reserved for Musaiyib, Colonel Zare noticed Barlow and Bosheers seated at their campsite table, playing cards. Zare didn't know why, but he took special notice of them, like he was seeing someone from an earlier life, which would be ridiculous for Zare, as he believed only in the here and now. Still, he waved to them, which made no sense.

Karimi pulled into the parking lot by the dock so Sharifi could get tickets for the Sunday 10:00 a.m. cruise. Tickets were in short supply, but he did manage to get three. When he returned to the parking lot, Zare and Karimi were gone. Colonel Zare didn't want to attract attention, so he had told Karimi to drive through town, and then come back when Sharifi was sure to have returned.

After they picked up Sharifi, Colonel Zare told Karimi to drive through town again. He wanted to see if there was an alternate route out of town that didn't show up on his Alberta map. After a short while, he told Karimi to turn around and drive down the Cameron Lake road. It was as he had feared. They were in a cul-de-sac. The only way out was the way they had come, or so it seemed.

About two thirds of the way to Cameron Lake, Zare told Karimi to pull-over at the trail head on the right. The trail led to the Lineham Lakes. There was no camping allowed, either along the trail, or at any of the lakes. Zare had picked it for that reason. Like most of the national parks in America, the Canadian Parks didn't allow random camping. When he had read about that restriction, Zare reflected that they probably frowned on murder as well, which was why he chose not to camp at one of the open Crandell Mountain campsites. Zare didn't want to take the chance that the police might be looking for them for the three murders in Montreal, especially when they were this close to Musaiyib and the seals.

The three waited for a break in the traffic, then, one at a time, they quickly got their packs out of the truck and hustled down the trail, out of view, until all three were together. Karimi had been a guide in his unit, so he had an uncanny sense of direction. For the first two miles, the Lineham Lakes Trail followed a creek, which was the outflow from the lakes. The trail was wooded that far. After that, it wandered through an alpine meadow that ultimately led to a head-wall, from which vantage hikers could view the four Lineham Lakes.

Colonel Zare didn't care about the meadow or the headwall, except that they might offer hikers a view of where they would camp that night. Several hundred yards before the forest gave over to meadow, Karimi left the trail and led the others through the woods toward the southwest. For the last kilometer, the Lineham Lakes Trail had arced at an increasing distance from the creek. Karimi was now leading them to the spot where the creek was the greatest distance from the trail. This was where Colonel Zare thought they should bivouac. They were far enough away from the trail so as not to be heard or seen. Along the trail, pine and spruce dominated, except where there had been fires. There, white birch and aspen took over. Here, the forest was mostly pine and spruce, so as long as they cooked with gas stoves rather than over an open fire, their camp couldn't be seen from above. Karimi and Sharifi cleared two sites among the trees for the tents, which had green flys and lichen-gray tubs. Except for their straight lines, which were duplicated nowhere in nature, the tents were virtually invisible from ten meters distance. When they had set up the camp and eaten, Colonel Zare told Sharifi that he and Karimi were going back to Waterton to see if Musaiyib had arrived yet, and to reconnoiter the campground, dock, and town. Karimi's job in their absence was to guard the camp.

Sharifi parked just outside the Townsite Campground entrance. He and Colonel Zare then walked toward Musaiyib's site. When they were about four hundred meters from it, Zare told Sharifi to scout it from the back side. Rather than stand around looking conspicuous, Zare went into the public toilet, allowing Sharifi extra time to work behind the campsites.

Since the whole campground was open, Sharifi didn't take long reaching Musaiyib's campsite. There was a rental car parked at the site and a tent had been pitched. At his back was Waterton Lake, so quite a few campers were walking by as well, but they were all going to the lake to watch the sun inch over the western bulwark and the day turn dark. The back door of the tent was zipped open, showing the insect mesh behind it and a man sitting in the tent, who appeared to be reading. Sharifi wondered if it were the *Qur'an*.

It would be good for him to prepare to meet Allah, thought Sharifi. He continued walking south and cut over to the road fifty meters passed Musaiyib's campsite. Colonel Zare was walking toward him.

Sharifi told him that he had seen someone sitting in his tent at Musaiyib's campsite, apparently reading.

"His back was to me, so I couldn't identify any specific features."

While Colonel Zare had a front view of the occupant, he didn't have a clear view of him either. The car was a rental, Zare saw, but so were half the cars in the park. However, the reserved sign still read Wusaivid. It seemed clear that he had arrived.

July 9th, 2011:

King had arrived at 2240 hours. Barlow and Bosheers quickly filled him in about Musaiyib, pointing out that his campsite was two down on the other side of the road. They told him about the morning cruise, and about Barlow's plans for hiking to the south end of the lake, rather than taking the boat with them.

"Ya look a good deal different than us, Randy, so it ain't gonna look like yer travelin' with Howland, especially if ya don't board together. Me, I look kinda like Howland, and, shit, we certainly talk the same, so I'm takin' the grunt's way down lake – a seven-mile hump."

Barlow pulled out a Waterton-Glacier map, indicating the West Shore Trail.

"After the Goat Haunt Ranger Station, I'm gonna bushwhack southeast and bivouac along Olsen Creek, about here." Barlow indicated the spot on the map. "I'll meet y'all about a half-mile after the ranger checkpoint. Oh, I almost forgot. Ya need a permit ta camp in Glacier, and ya suppose ta wear it outside y'all's pack. See if ya can snatch one, either before ya get on the boat or as soon as ya can. Otherwise, ya gonna be doin' some bushwhackin', too."

At 2300 hours, Barlow left the tent. Although he was more than 2,000 miles away from the murder scene in Montreal, so was

Musaiyib. And if the police were looking for him, they might also be looking for the three of them. With that in mind, Barlow thought it wise not to travel this last leg together. The last thing he told King was to conceal his Khukuri. If the cops were looking for them, wearing a formidable-looking knife, like a Khukuri, in plain sight would be a dead give-away.

Barlow was wearing army-issue night vision goggles, but even if he weren't, he would have known about the check points, because earlier in the day, he ran the trail to the border. Still, the goggles made bushwhacking a lot easier and on the trail, helped him avoid rocks and roots that wouldn't have been a problem during the day, but could have caused a painful injury at night, especially to someone carrying a pack.

Skirting the checkpoint at Upper Bertha Falls was much more difficult than at the trail head because the area was a very popular site and because there was a long gravel beach there on which to haul a boat out or to anchor one just off shore. Additionally, there was a trail just north of the campground that led to Bertha Lake, and on the east side of the lake there was a trail that led to Crypt Lake. As this was the lake's narrowest point, camping on the west shore wasn't much of an inconvenience for east shore hikers, excluding the wind intensity, which was increased by the mountain shoulders that crimped the lake on both sides. The mountain shoulders that rose just off to the right of the trail, however, were a major inconvenience for Barlow. It took him fifty minutes to get passed the cops at that checkpoint and not wake any campers in his passing.

Like the trail head checkpoint, avoiding the one at the border didn't tax Barlow's skills much. He made camp that night – the next morning actually – at 0330 hours, at a site very similar to the Iranians', in that it was located among the spruce and pines and alongside a creek. Barlow's camp was a bit more primitive, though, as he hadn't pitched a tent – he just rigged a tarp overhang – and he didn't cook. Instead, he ate two protein bars, drank some water, and went to sleep.

9:15 a.m., July 10th, 2011:

Colonel Zare and Sergeant Sharifi were in place near the dock. Zare told Karimi to follow Musaiyib in, and to call him if he seemed to be going anywhere else.

O'Dea and Mulvahill saw the two Iranians arrive.

"OK, Coughlin, les ick up ese two uckers and ge oua a here," mumbled Byme. "My jaw is illing me."

"Take some more Oxy, Sean. Keagan said, he thought there would be at least three of them, maybe as many as five," said O'Dea.

"I don give a fu what that gooer said, my jaw's illing me."

"*Pussy*, huh, Sean boy? Seems to me you're 0 and 2 against that pussy. Now, take some more Oxy and, for the love of Christ, shut the fuck up."

* * *

Bosheers and King arrived in their separate rentals cars and walked singly toward the dock. Synchronically, however, they spotted three campers queued up together, the last of whom had the group's backcountry permit in a plastic sleeve affixed to his pack. Bosheers and King vectored toward the camper from opposite directions. Bosheers bumped him slightly, but just enough that the pack lent momentum and spun him to the right so King could clip the wire twist-tie that held the permit in place, as Bosheers apologized to the camper for his clumsiness. King slipped the sleeved permit under his shirt.

In the men's room stall, King checked out the permit's itinerary: Stoney Indian Pass on Sunday, Glens Lake, foot, on Monday, and Belly River on Tuesday. He found the sites on the Waterton-Glacier map the ranger had given Barlow and Bosheers when they entered the park the day before. He wanted to make sure he'd know where the sites were, in case the ranger at the south end of the lake questioned him about his route.

When Keagan and Kelly arrived, O'Dea and Mulvahill were leaning against their van. Keagan walked over to them, gesturing toward the boat as though he were asking a fellow tourist something about the cruise.

"I thought you needed a replacement for Byme," said Keagan.

"Yeah, I tried to get Paddy Boyle. You remember him, don't you, Mick?"

"Yeah, he's a good man."

"I shoulda brought him to begin with. Ah, well, water over the dam. Paddy couldn't make the flight, so I'm stuck with Sean. If it's any consolation to you, Mick, Sean boy's in a lot of pain this morning.

You know, Mick, we've had our differences in the past, but I got to side with you on this one. Sean just doesn't know enough to keep his *feckin' gob* shut. Anyway, I like what you're doing for the old country. Not my style, mind yah, but this gig you got going with Kelly, it's got to be a hellava lot more productive than topping the odd *Jaffa*."

"Just wrap up these Takavaran *boyras* and keep a tight leash on Sean, and I'll be more than happy, Coughlin."

Keagan saw Sharifi walking toward the dock. "The third one is just now arriving. I thought there'd be two more, but maybe not. I'll leave this to you, Coughlin. Kelly and I'll go over to talk to the Mounties. I've no doubt she'll charm them to distraction while you snatch up those lads."

"Aye, I'm sure she will, Mick. Good luck to ya with the rest of your project."

"Thanks for your help, Coughlin. Say the same to Mulvahill for me, will you?"

The Mounties seemed to be scanning the crowd as though they were looking for someone in particular, rather than making sure there weren't any morning drunks or pickpockets on the dock. In spite of the scrutiny, they had missed the permit snatch that King had pulled off. Now, in Kelly's presence, they were about to miss three Takavaran being snatched, not fifty feet away from them. Keagan couldn't fault them, though; he suspected that Kelly could probably cause Sergeant Bruce to overlook Rose Marie and sing to her, instead.

Mulvahill walked over toward Zare and Sharifi. Karimi was standing near a van, gesturing them over to him, as though he had something important to tell them about Musaiyib. They went over to him. Mulvahill followed them. When they crossed over into the parking lot, O'Dea cut in behind them, as well. Now that they were nearer, Colonel Zare noticed a worried look on Karimi's face and saw that there was a man in the van's open side door, behind him. Colonel Zare started to alert Sharifi, but before he could say anything, Mulvahill placed a .45 Para-Ordnance, Slim Hawg against his spine. O'Dea did the same to Sharifi, although he held a Para PXT 14-45.

"Either one of you utters a word, you'll both spend the rest of your life in a wheelchair, pushed around by people whose limbs still function. Get in the van."

Karimi was already in the van; Byme and his Slim Hawg were keeping him quiet. Byme, himself, was pissing and moaning to Karimi about his jaw, as though he was the one who had just been kidnapped and was waiting to see what his captors had in mind for him.

O'Dea followed Zare into the van; Mulvahill, Sharifi. Byme tugged the door shut and climbed into the driver's seat. O'Dea and Mulvahill searched the three and relieved them of their weapons, which, in addition to their Heckler, Koch P30s, and the suppressors, included three H&K Epidemic out-the-front switch blades.

"You *boyras* seem to favor H&K. Wouldn't be commandos, would you? Not all that skilled, though, judging from your current pickle." Weapons collected, they bound, gagged, and hooded the three. When they were finished, O'Dea threw a tarp over them and told Byme to drive like a normal citizen, not like a banshee.

Musaiyib arrived about ten minutes before a deck hand announced that boarding would begin in a few minutes. Keagan and Kelly queued up behind him. Kelly smiled at him when Musaiyib turned around to see who was there. He returned the greeting.

Twenty-Eight

July, 2011:

While Waterton Lakes National Park was busy hosting – amid the throngs of general tourists – a purloiner of ancient Sumerian cylinder seals; three competing commando units; three Irish former IRA thugs, currently on the lam in Canada; a fey, Irish beauty, who started out this tale sharing the name of an Irish mythological character; and a former IRA art thief come bartender come private school master come sailor come innkeeper; the Loop trail head parking lot off the Going-to-the-Sun Road in Glacier National Park would soon feel the pinch of its own congestion.

Niles and Teal had arrived in Kalispell at 1:40 p.m. After they picked up their rental car, they drove to Lake McDonald Lodge. Kelly had reserved a cabin there for them. They could have made the trailhead in another twenty minutes, but they had been traveling since two o'clock that morning. They drove three hours to Albany, arrived early enough for security clearance on a 6:28 a.m. flight, flew to Minneapolis, went on to Kalispell, across two time zones, then drove another fifty odd miles into Glacier. Why, then, drive another dozen miles, find the trailhead, and hump a pack up a mountain to find a suitable campsite? It was doable, but why do it, when it wasn't necessary? They could enjoy the lake view, have a good dinner – with a few pints – get a good night's sleep, and head out early in the morning. Which is what they did.

Niles and Teal were waiting outside the Lodge's dining room at 6:30 a.m. when one of the waiters opened the door for breakfast. He led them to a table with a lake view, brought them coffee and menus, and returned shortly to take their orders. Service at the lodge dining room was more efficient than personal, which was fine with Niles and Teal. They wanted to order, eat, and be on their way. Had the dining room opened at 5:30 a.m., they still would have been the morning's first customers.

After breakfast, they went back to their cabin, attended to last-minute things, checked out, and drove the eleven and a half miles to the Loop trailhead. There was another party ahead of them – two men and a woman, in their late 20s or early 30s. They were just about ready to take off up the trail, when Niles and Teal arrived. Teal went over to talk to them.

"Sure, leave me with all the work. You want me to carry your pack too?" Niles japed.

"Good morning," Teal greeted the woman. "Is this the trail to Flattop?" he asked her, in a modified Cajun accent.

"Yeah, about five and a half miles. That where you're headed?" asked the woman.

"Yeah, well Waterton, ultimately. I just said Flattop because I wanted to make sure we were taking the right trail. Wouldn't want to end up over in Many Glacier."

"You will if you take the right branch up ahead about a half mile. You could do worse though: it's real pretty there. Where you from?"

"Brooklyn," answered Teal. "The accent give me away?"

"Yeah, we don't get too many New Yorkers here. Oh, plenty in the campgrounds and more than enough driving up and down the Going-to-the-Sun Road in their RVs, but not in the backcountry."

"Where are you from?" asked Teal.

"Columbia Falls, just down the road. I heard what your friend said about carrying both packs. He looks like he could."

"Yeah, he's the brawn. Short on brains, though." Teal tapped his head.

The woman laughed. "Tell him not to forget your backcountry permit. My pack animal almost did. The man she pointed to came over to her and started to open her pack's top flap.

"Here, let me put some more rocks in there," he teased.

Teal saw their permit, in a long plastic sleeve tied to the man's pack.

"Have a good trip," said the woman as the two turned to rejoin the other man and walked off up the trail.

"Enjoy the day," returned Teal.

"You forget you're married already?" said Niles. "Here I am doing all the work and you're over there, flirting with some cutie who's already got two guys. That's just what we need. You getting the shit kicked out of you, then I would have to come to your rescue because Ky, for some strange reason, would be mad at me if I didn't. So then I'd have to clean up your mess, probably have to drive you and the two guys you forced me to kick the shit out of, to the hospital, then I'd have to take care of the woman and go save Mick and Kelly – the way I always have to – all by myself. Not very considerate of you, buddy."

"You finished, now?" asked Teal.

Niles flashed him his innocent, cartoon-character smile that said he was. "What you call *flirting*, I call *information gathering*. I was just double checking that we were at the right trail head. And you know that permit we're supposed to have to camp in the backcountry? Well, not only are we supposed to have one, but we're supposed to attach it to the outside of the pack. What are we going to do if we get stopped by a ranger? You going to kick the shit out of him too?"

"Nah, that wouldn't work, would it? Well, I guess we could steal one, but then again if the ranger is one of those letter-of-the-law guys, he'd probably ask for identification, and then he'd really be pissed off. Not only do we not have one of our own, but he'd have us on theft, then. I guess we better avoid any rangers."

Mick had told them to see if they could get a walk-in permit when they arrived. Niles had stopped at the Ranger Station at Apgar when they arrived at the Park the day before, but all the sites at Kootenai Lakes were taken. There was nothing to do but hope they didn't get stopped by a ranger.

Niles had all the gear out of the trunk, but now didn't seem to be in a hurry. He wanted to let the others build up a lead. Teal wandered over to the trailhead. There was a trash bin there. He looked around, took the top off the bin, and riffled though the black plastic liner. Niles wondered what he was doing, but didn't say anything. After a moment, Teal's hand came out of the bag. He held a long thin plastic sleeve in his right hand.

"It expired yesterday, but unless we run into an actual ranger, we'll look legit to anyone else we meet on the trail. Of course, if we do run into a letter-of-the-law ranger and he wants to inspect it, we're back to being fucked."

"Yeah, but that was still good thinking, Teal."

Another car pulled into the parking lot. "It's getting busy," said Teal. "Let's go; I don't like to be pressed by others. The locals should be far enough ahead of us, so we won't be on their heels, at least not right away."

Two men got out of the car and started pulling gear out of the trunk.

"What are you waiting for, Niles? You don't like to be pressed any more than I do."

"We rarely are, least ways not for long, but walk over with me to that outcropping." Niles got his binoculars and a map out of his pack. He seemed to want to glass the mountains across the way for game, maybe mountain goats or Bighorn Sheep.

"Don't those two look like they're in particularly good shape?" Niles asked Teal.

"Yeah, well, you don't see too many puff balls backpacking in this kind of country."

"How about their complexion?" said Niles

"What, their color?"

"Yeah, not swarthy, but kind of like yours with a different cast."

"So, you think they're part of the Iranian team? Bit of a reach, don't you think, Niles?"

"Yeah, it is, but think about it. Two, very fit, dark, and not obviously Semitic men. Their equipment looks new, no dirt on the bottom of their packs. Neither pack. Mick's not the only smart guy in this mix. And a backdoor approach isn't exactly a novel idea, especially with the problems a border crossing brings into this."

They pretended to glass the far mountain sides for game. Occasionally, Teal would point out something on the map that Niles had handed him. When they had turned back after a few minutes, the two men were gone.

"What do you think, Niles?" said Teal.

"Let me check out one more thing."

Niles unzipped the top flap pocket of his Arc'teryx Bora 80 pack and found the trail description that Keagan had printed for him from the Trails.com site.

"Yeah, here it is. We follow this trail," Niles pointed at the physical trail ahead of them, "for about two miles. Then, we take the left fork." Here, Niles pointed to the Mc Donald Creek Trail on the map and ran his finger along the dotted line.

"The trail has an easy grade for about six miles, then it switchbacks and gains elevation quickly. Let's see, it's about eleven hundred feet in a little over a mile. It continues up over West Flattop Mountain, through the Kootenai Pass, and then it rejoins this trail," Niles again pointed at the trail in front of them, "at the Fifty Mountain Shelter."

"How much longer is the Mc Donald Creek Trail?" asked Teal.

Niles looked at the trail description and then at the map for the original trail. "About three miles farther."

"Elevation?"

Niles looked back at the map. "Almost identical. The Flattop Creek Trail is actually a bit more. The Mc Donald Creek Trail was the original route to Fifty Mountain, but was abandoned in favor of the new trail. The big difference I see, is that one is maintained and the other one is not. The Mc Donald Creek Trail is probably slower, but more private. Probably no rangers."

"So, let's go," said Teal

* * *

Akbari and Shaker-Doust overtook the two men and the woman before the turn-off for the Granite Park Trail.

"Sergeant Major, did you notice the two men at the trailhead who walked over to the outcropping when we arrived?"

"Yes, of course," answered Akbari. "What about them?"

"They looked all ready, then, at the last minute, they took that detour over to the outcropping. I thought maybe they were purposely avoiding us."

"Maybe they just didn't want to be crowded. Americans are strange in many ways, one of which is that they seem to need an inordinate amount of space. People all over the world live in small spaces near each other. Not the Americans, though. Sure, they have their big cities like New York, Los Angeles, and Chicago, but many live in suburbs and have another home in the country, or at the seashore. They live in houses that would keep three or four families in Iran. They drive in private cars, and only in the cities do they ride in mass transit. Only the poor take buses long distance."

"Did you notice the tall one?" pressed Shaker-Doust.

"Of course."

"What did you think of him?" asked Shaker-Doust.

"That he was tall, trim, but rugged-looking."

"Did you notice his eyes?"

"What about his eyes, Farid?"

"They never stopped moving; they scanned all the time. Even when he was looking through the binoculars, he'd pause and check around him."

"That is very observant of you, Farid. I'll have to pay closer attention if we meet up with them again."

The Mc Donald Creek Trail was slower going than the Flattop Creek Trail would have been, but not that much. The biggest obstacle was blowdown from winter storms. They hadn't stopped for lunch. Instead, they stopped for water and snack breaks. The snacks were gorp, an acronym that originally stood for *good ol' raisins and peanuts.* Niles' recipe called for dry-roasted peanuts, Craisins, roasted sunflower kernels, and M&Ms. They had made good time, in spite of the trail. At 3:00 p.m., Niles and Teal were atop West Flattop Mountain, where they could see Fifty Mountain two miles directly east of them. They crested the peak quickly instead of standing in silhouette on the summit and taking in the view. It wouldn't much matter if those over at the Fifty Mountain Shelter saw them, unless of course, there was a ranger over there. Fifty Mountain got its name from the view from its summit, where, on a clear day, which most of them were this time of year, fifty other peaks were visible.

At 4:00 p.m., they made camp off trail about three quarters of a mile below Kootenai Pass, where the old trail skirted Kootenai Creek. They had cleared the pass, but, essentially, they were on a high plateau that was about a half-mile wide. The area where they camped wasn't heavily vegetated, partly because of the winds that blew at that elevation, but also because of the fire of 2003 that burned almost 140,000 acres of Glacier National Park. There was little reason to think they would be visible, though, because their tent's fly was lichen colored, so that it looked very much like many of the boulders that pocked the ridge. While it would be a long time before trees the height of those that were here before the fire accumulated on the plateau, low bushes and shrubs had taken hold in the thin soil. However, wildfires took random tracks, and even in those tracks would sometimes skip areas that wind direction and fuel supply seemed to contradict. Niles and Teal were camped in a depression in one of those areas that still held a dozen or so trees that the fire chose to ignore.

Both would have preferred to have Teal make dinner, but because of time and pack weight, they had to do with a simple high carb dinner of decent whole grain bread they had picked up at the Super 1 Foods in Columbia Falls, and penne covered with Newman's Own sauce. Afterwards, they drank coffee and talked about the next day.

"What do we do tomorrow, other than hike down to Kootenai Lakes?" Teal asked Niles.

"Not much we can do, until we meet up with Mick and Kelly. That is, if they managed to locate Musaiyib. All we know, is that he's supposed to camp at Waterton tomorrow night, take a cruise on Sunday morning, spend two nights camped at Kootenai Lakes, and then return by boat to Waterton on Wednesday, the 13th. If he's here to pick up the seals, there's not much planning we can do. If he shows up, we follow him. When he retrieves the seals, we convince him that he's not cut out for a life of crime.

"I think what I'd like to do is get up early and scout the campsites over on Fifty Mountain, to see if I can learn anything about the campers there. It would be good to know – one way or the other – whether I'm right about those two blokes that struck up the trail ahead of us. Also, see if there's any ranger activity. Can you manage with the tent? I can take the stove and the pots if you don't mind having just fruit and gorp for breakfast."

"No, that's all right. Leave the cooking gear. It's only a little more than a mile over there, isn't it? You going to be all right in the dark? You ever do stuff like this before when you were in the SAS?"

"More times and in more places than you want to know."

"Where will we meet up?" asked Teal.

Niles looked at the map. He pretty much knew where, but he wanted to be sure Teal did. "Here," Niles pointed to a spur trail that led back to the Loop by a very long and circuitous route, or over to Many Glacier by an even longer one.

"Take the left fork and go toward Kootenai Lakes, then, here, turn south for a quarter of a mile. Use your GPS. I'll meet up with you there, unless there's no cover, in which case, I'll meet you at the junction."

In July, very near the 49th Parallel, it remained light until after 10:00 p.m. Neither Niles nor Teal intended to wait until then to go to sleep, however. Niles didn't have to tell Teal to be alert, or that after the junction, he'd be on a travelled trail. He knew from the past two projects that Teal was especially good about keeping out of sight, even when people were actively searching for him.

Teal awoke at 5:00 a.m. It was cold in the dark on the 6,000 foot mountain. While he had lived through four Adirondack winters, he was genetically still a Cajun, whose ancestors had long ago left Nova Scotia for south Louisiana. Once out of his sleeping bag, he felt the Continental Divide's summer-morning nip.

Niles had left some time in the night, so Teal made oatmeal and coffee for one. He put some of Niles' gorp Craisins in the oatmeal because he couldn't get the honey out of the squeeze bottle. He ate the oatmeal fast, before it began to coagulate. He could take more time with the coffee. The sun was now over the horizon. The food, coffee, and sun began to warm him. He heated some more water and washed out the JetBoil stove and cup as well as he could. He'd do a better job before he used them again. Now, his fingers were too stiff to clean them properly. His first winter at the inn, Mick had shown him the warmest hand gear he could have. It was a pair of deerskin mittens with tightly woven wool inserts that could be exchanged if they got wet. They were better that down mittens, better than ski gloves, and better than any of the synthetics. Still, there were a lot of tasks you couldn't perform wearing mittens. He'd clean the cooking gear properly later.

Twenty-Nine

6:00 a.m., July 10th, 2011:

T he trail over to Fifty Mountain was well marked, even though it hadn't had much traffic in the last nine years. At this elevation, there weren't many trees to blow down, especially after the fire of 2003. Unlike the East, where soil was usually a byproduct of decayed vegetable matter, such as grasses, leaves, and trees, in the West, more often than not, soil resulted from the breakdown of minerals, which was a much slower process. So, the soil, especially at high elevations was much thinner. The original trail had worn down to bedrock and thus, was easy to follow. It was a little over one mile from where he and Niles had camped to the junction of the Waterton Valley Trail. The grade was steady at about eleven percent, which was about the steepest grade a motorist would encounter on American highways. Teal was well rested and fed, so he kept up a good pace. He made the junction at a little after seven o'clock. No one was in sight.

The trail continued north along the Fifty Mountain open ridge. Teal stepped up his pace. He met Niles at the next junction on the north-south trail seven minutes later.

"There's less cover on this trail than I thought there would be. No sense wasting time retracing steps if it's just as open a quarter of a mile back. So give me the cooking stuff and let's move out. We need to put some distance between us and whoever's camped at Fifty Mountain."

"There are five sites at that campground. All were occupied. Three were occupied by a group of six, traveling on horseback. Your girl-friend and her two friends were at another one. I recognized one of the blokes she was traveling with when he came out to pee. I'm sorry to have to tell you this, but she was sharing a tent with one of the guys. I guess it was too chilly last night to remain faithful to you."

"You better quit the ball-busting about her before we meet up with Mick and Kelly. And if it ever comes out in front of Ky, expect a grim surprise someday that not even you will be able to anticipate."

Teal was referring to his penchant for blowing up people who seriously pissed him off.

"You got it, buddy. I've had my fun," said Niles. "OK, the fifth site had a squared-away look to it, but it wasn't the Iranians – if, in fact, the two blokes we saw at the trailhead were Iranians."

"OK, no Iranians, unless they rustled up some horses and four friends. They probably did what we did last night and camped off trail. The cowboys and cowgirls were headed south. They put their packs in the bear box. That's also how I know. Your girl…, ah, the three locals from Columbia Falls, have a permit for Kootenai Lakes. If they see us again, they're going to wonder how we got ahead of them when they started out first and we didn't pass them. So, even though they're not a threat to us, we should try to stay ahead of them, if only to not raise their suspicions. And in front of us, we have to watch out for any rangers, and, let's not forget, the Iranians, just in case I was right. Also, there was something funny about that other campsite. There were two men camped there, or maybe a couple of bears, judging from the snoring. Not only was it squared away, but it was rigged against snooping, with monofilament fishing line run-ning around the perimeter and into the tent, probably tied to a fin-ger. We're going to have to be alert today, making sure what's ahead of us and also what's behind us. We're pretty much out in the open for the next four miles until we get down into the valley, so let's step it out, but not so much that we look suspicious."

* * *

Niles was right about the Iranians camping off trail. They had set a fast pace. Akbari grew up in Pataveh, a small village at the foot of Dena Mountain, the highest peak in Iran. He was used to climbing from an early age. Shaker-Doust got used to it through his training in the Zagos Mountains. They had camped along an unnamed stream about two and a half miles passed the Fifty Mountain Campground. They had more shelter than did Niles and Teal – even though their campsite was two hundred feet lower – partly because the fire hadn't reached that side of the Continental Divide, but also because of the natural features of the landscape. Where they camped wasn't heavily vegetated, but it did have more cover than the stand of trees and shrubs that Niles and Teal camped in.

Neither Akbari nor Shaker-Doust knew about backcountry permits; still, they wanted to remain out of sight, so if their mission was compromised in any way, no one would be able to link them to it. They were, after all, commandos, which by definition, meant they were part of a raiding party, meant to hit and run and leave little evidence that they were ever there, other than the casualties of the mission. They had managed to skirt the party from Columbia Falls when they stopped to have a snack and admire a waterfall on Flattop Creek.

While they didn't know about the backcountry camping permit, they suspected that rangers patrolled the area, if only to check for fires and injured or lost hikers. They had struck camp about an hour later than Teal had, but their camp was about four miles ahead of where he and Niles spent the night, so their lead had been cut to only one mile. They were making their way down and around Cathedral Peak, which was all sparsely vegetated; their only cover was provided by the tortuous course the trail took. Periodically, Akbari would drop his pack and jog up about a hundred yards onto the shoulder of Cathedral Peak to recon the area. When they were a half mile from dropping into the vegetated cover of Waterton Valley, he saw Niles and Teal coming down the trail toward Shaker-Doust. Akbari ran-slid down the scree slope.

"We got two men about four hundred meters behind us, closing fast. Move out as fast as you can without running. Perhaps we can make the valley before they see us."

"Do you think they're part of the Coalition Task Force?" said Shaker-Doust.

"I don't know, but if they are, I want to meet them on our terms, not theirs."

Both Niles and Teal saw Akbari. Actually, they heard the scree slide and looked up, thinking it might be a mob of Bighorn Sheep or a mountain goat.

"We may have found the Iranians, Teal. Hard to tell. If they are the Takavaran, that one fellow up on the slope made a mistake that no commando should ever make, moving at a speed that gets you noticed. The way they're moving now, just shy of a trot, certainly suggests that they are trying to avoid us."

"Should we catch up with them?" asked Teal.

"No, but hold the pace we've been setting and keep your eyes open for an ambush once we get into the valley. I don't think they'll risk the noise of shooting us, let alone the bother of having to drag our bodies off the trail, but I don't want to be dead wrong," said Niles.

"How sure are you about them not ambushing us?" asked Teal.

"Certainly not a hundred percent, but then, I'm not a hundred present sure about many things. However, commandos or no commandos, I don't think they can keep their pace up too much longer, so my best guess – subject to minute-by-minute reconsideration – is that they'll cut into the woods when they reach the cover of the valley, wait for us to pass, and get in behind us to follow us for a change."

"That's comforting, Niles."

Bo Wade and Socko Lollard woke up at first light. Usually, the first thing campers did in the morning after climbing out of their tent, was pee, but Lollard was different from the typical camper; he was SAS. What he did first, was peruse their campsite. He hadn't felt a tug during the night, and the alert-lines he had set up were still in place, but neither meant that the site hadn't been visited, only that the visitor had been careful.

He noticed some small stones that seemed to have been rolled out of position. Wade was just coming back from the site's outhouse, having relieved himself like a normal human, when Lollard called him over and pointed toward the displaced stones.

"What do you make of those, Bo?"

Wade looked where Lollard was pointing. "What?" he asked.

"Those small stones seem to have rolled out of position. See, where they had originally set."

"Yeah, well, I guess they might have, but so what. Were the lines in place this morning? Did you feel anything on the tug-line last night?"

"No," said Lollard, "but that just means that whoever was here was careful. I think we had a visitor."

"Socko, this is a national park; there's animals all over the place. What'd we see – fifteen Bighorn Sheep and three goats on the way in? Shit, man, and there are deer, elk, bears, and a whole buncha little fuckers. Coulda been a mouse or a, what are them fat little fuckers? Pikers, peckers, papooses? No, not them..."

"Pikas."

"Yeah, them. I'll bet they did it."

"Could be, but keep your eyes open."

"What, you think the Iranians checked out our site last night?"

"Somebody did, and whoever he was, he was real good, much better than a pika. Unless I'm seriously mistaken, we're about done with the thinking part of this mission, and the action part is just down the trail. I don't mean just catching up with Musaiyib; that part's obvious, if the Commander is right that Musaiyib has come here to retrieve the seals. I mean that we're soon going to meet up with our competition."

"You still mean the Iranians, right?" asked Wade. "That's fine with me. We'll just blow up their shit. Hell, Socko, what did the Commander think – four or five of them? Shit, with just you and me, the odds are still in our favor."

"Yeah, the Iranians, but I got a feeling some others may be involved."

"Like who? The Iraqis? Why would they send a team over? They know we're looking for the seals and that we can do a better job than they can. I mean, why would they? We're on the same team. I'm not sure why, but we are."

"No, those fuckers couldn't find their asses on a bright day, let alone their way through this wilderness. If it ain't open and sandy or in some shithole they call a town, they'd get lost. Nah, they'll leave the work to us because, after all, we allowed their seals to be stolen in the first place, right? Gotta blame somebody; can't admit to the world, you're a bunch of fuckups. Couldn't even protect your own national treasures from your own people. It's not like we stole 'em."

"So, you think those guys who aced Musaiyib's buddy there, Awwal, you think they're following him too? How could they be here? They're just a coupla grunts. Look how long it took us, and we had the Commander and Jassim, and the CIA running interference for us. Buncha grunts wouldn't have those resources," said Wade.

"No, but somebody killed those four guys in Montreal. You think the Iranians did them all?" asked Lollard

"Coulda. Killin' doesn't much bother them fuckers," said Wade.

"Perhaps, but I don't think so. Maybe two or three, but not all four, It doesn't feel right. Speaking about feelings, I got a feeling that there's yet another group," said Lollard

"Jesus, who? This mission is starting to get over booked."

"You weren't there, but the Commander got a call from some Homeland Security guy in New York, a former FBI agent, I think, who was telling him about this woman with an unusual name, something to do with an Irish myth, like Finn Ni Cool. Well, Roth wasn't buying it because he thinks that the link is a real stretch. But this guy in New York says this woman has a habit of locating stolen artwork that others can't. She returns it for the finder's fee, which isn't chump change when what you're giving back is worth millions."

"And it was a stretch; I'll give the Commander that. Story's about some kid who catches a magical salmon that carries the wisdom of the world. Well, this kid catches the salmon, eats it, and knows everything. Anyhow, this woman takes the kid's name. Roth, he doesn't like it because he thinks the Micks are a buncha drunks who love to tell colorful stories about themselves. Besides, the story is too fantastic, he says. But Roth's a Jew, so it's OK that Eve ate an apple and that a talking snake seduced her into doing what fucked up the whole world for the rest of us. That's OK, but an Irish kid can't eat a magical salmon and get smart," said Lollard

"Socko, I think I lost you somewhere around *myth*," said Wade.

"OK, forget the magical salmon. I did a tour in Northern Ireland when I first got in the SAS, and I remember hearing that one of the ways the IRA funded their arms purchases was by stealing art – really expensive art – and selling it back to the owners they stole it from. Or, if the owners wouldn't pay up, they'd sell it to the insurance company that carried the policy. The best of these art thieves were two kids from Belfast, probably a year or two younger than me when I first got my patch. Well, from what I heard, one of those kids was a beautiful girl. I never knew her name, so maybe I'm making too much of it, too, but these kids stole a lot of art and never got caught. And I gotta tell you, Bo, those Micks, while they didn't possess all the world's knowledge, they weren't dumb bastards," said Lollard.

"Is that why Kennedy thinks he so smart?"

"Bo, Kennedy's black."

"Yeah, I know. So, you think they paid us a visit last night?"

"Somebody did. And, think about it, Bo. The Commander didn't send us around to the backdoor because he didn't think anyone else was joining this party. Why don't you heat up some water, while I go and take a leak."

Wade and Lollard ate breakfast and drank coffee while the rest of the campground was just getting up. After coffee, Wade struck camp while Lollard inventoried their neighbors as they climbed out of their tents. The locals with Teal's lady friend were the first out. Then, gradually, the cowboys and cowgirls roused themselves. Lollard walked around the campground, looking for outlaws, or campers without permits. There were none.

"I didn't see any outlaw campsites in my brief tour, but keep your eyes open, Bo. Maybe we'll spot somebody ahead of us. The country's open for about the next four miles, so we should have a good sight line. I'll do rear guard just in case somebody new shows up that shouldn't be there. Only the three locals are going this way. The cowboys and their girlfriends are headed out. And nobody from Flattop should be able to catch us. If they do, let's kill 'em rather than suffer the embarrassment. Shit, if that happened and our mates found out, you'd be drummed out of the Crotch and I'd have my patch pulled."

"Looks like you already did, Socko."

"I just didn't want to advertise, Bo."

They struck camp at 0830. They weren't in any particular hurry because Commander Roth had told them there was no sense in trying to meet the boat as it docked. He and Kennedy would meet up with them at Kootenai Lakes. If Musaiyib didn't stick to his plan, he'd give them a call. Lollard thought that Roth's plan had too many holes in it, but since the Park was more than a million acres and had over seven hundred miles of trails, there were only so many contingencies you could cover, especially with only four men. And there was no reason to believe that Musaiyib would stick to the trails. He certainly wouldn't have hidden the cylinder seals at a campground or anywhere else where some hiker could stumble onto them. At the very least, though, Lollard would have sent another team to cover the Boulder Pass and the Stoney Indian Pass Trails. But Roth was the Commander; he wasn't.

Wade and Lollard moved along at a good clip. A couple of times, they thought they heard someone off trail, but it was just goats sending down scree slides. When they came over the last ridge, the low shoulder of Stoney Indian Peaks, before the trail entered the Waterton Valley, Wade held up. Lollard had been glassing the trail behind them because, after they dropped off this ridge, the two miles of trail behind them would be hidden from their view.

Lollard finished glassing their rear and turned to find Wade digging out his binoculars.

"What have you got Bo?" asked Lollard.

"Give me a minute," answered Wade. "I'm not sure, but I thought I saw two guys hustling – and I do mean *hustling* – down the trail, just where the trees begin again. I don't see anything now. They weren't running. They had a real smooth flow to whatever it was they were doing. Kinda like a lope, I guess you'd call it, but real smooth. I guess it coulda been a couple of bears." Wade held up his range-finder binoculars again.

"Yeah, it's about two miles down there where I saw whatever it was I saw."

"Well, if it was human, Bo, we should be able to catch up to them. Let's see how smooth we can lope on down there ourselves."

* * *

Niles and Teal continued along the trail for another half mile and found a mini-patch of glacier-deposited boulders off on the right side. Niles got behind one and took off his pack. He told Teal to get behind one to the left of his just fifteen feet away. Then, Niles squat walked over to him and checked the line of sight.

"Good, OK. I suspect the Iranians, and I'm going to pretend, until proven wrong, that they're Iranians, saw us pass by. What they'll do, is stay in hiding for a while and then come back onto the trail where they left it. I don't think they'll parallel the trail, not for more than a half mile anyway, and get back on it much further down. It's too difficult and noisy to parallel a trail that isn't straight, especially one you're not familiar with, and harder still wearing a pack."

"So, I say we wait here until they pass, or at least for an hour. We both had an early morning, and we've been moving at a good clip. We can use the rest."

"What I'd like you to do is watch out for rangers, cops, or anybody with a gun or visible ID coming from the south. Signal me whenever you see someone; a slash sign for hikers, right palm up for cops and such, and left palm up if you see the Iranians. I'll do the same for those coming from the north. Anything to add?"

"Yeah, maybe it's time to update Mick and Kelly and find out what they know," said Teal.

"Good idea." Niles looked at his watch. "It's 8:30; let's give it another, say, forty-five minutes. If we call too early, we're likely to miss some important, last-minute news. If I were running a team, I wouldn't show up on the dock too early. I'd want to arrive early enough to get a spot nearby to park, but not so late that I'd stand out. I'd pick a time in the middle when most of the other passengers were queuing up as well."

"You OK with waiting?" asked Niles.

"Sure. They've got an hour and a half before their boat sails, and another hour for the trip and signing in with the rangers to clear customs. Then, at that point, we've got about the same distance they have to where we are supposed to meet up."

"If nothing delays them, we still won't be able to meet up until about noon or a bit before, so we have more than two hours to kill."

At 9:15, Niles called Keagan and explained their situation to him.

"We've found the Iranians or at least we think we have. There are two of them."

"Well, we've got two, no, hold on, three here. Let me call you back in a few minutes, Niles."

"What's Mick have to say?" asked Teal.

"Said he had three Iranians of his own there. They must have had the same idea Mick did. He told me he'd call back in a few minutes; I think he had to take some action. I wonder what he's up to. Can't just walk over to them and shoot them, then get back in line for the boat."

"No, that's what you'd do, Niles."

"Nobody's ever accused me of being brash. Bold, maybe. Creative, frequently, but never brash. Impulsiveness is the hallmark of failure."

No one went by on the trail in either direction in the twenty minutes before Keagan called back.

"She got who?" said Niles in disbelief.

Teal heard Niles and asked, "What happened?"

Niles raised his index finger, indicating he'd tell him later.

"So, they didn't fuck it up? Amazing when you consider that lot, especially Byme. If he were still there, I'd tell you to give him a smack for me...oh you did, good. And he still drove? I'm impressed with the boy. OK, call if things change. Otherwise, we'll meet up at about noon. Yeah, I'll do the same. OK, see you. Tell Kelly she's got some explaining to do. Right. OK."

When Niles had retracted the aerial into the sat phone, Teal duck-walked over to him.

"So what happened?"

Niles told Teal what Kelly had done.

"Why were you angry at her? Seems like a smart thing to do." asked Teal.

"Not angry, Teal. I don't think I could ever be angry with Kelly. It's just, the blokes she chose. Coughlin O'Dea is the best of the lot, and when he's on his best behavior, he's a bully. His partner Emmon Mulvahill isn't any better, and not nearly as smart or as tough. And the third one, Sean Byme, is a psychotic fuckup. I arrested him once in Belfast."

"What happened?" asked Teal.

"Well, I'll stand by what I just said about him, but I have to give the devil his due, Byme had real potential as a middleweight. Mick and him met up in the quarter finals in the All-Belfast Championship."

"Anyway, I arrested him once. I had two other SAS troopers with me, when we found Byme and four of his men who we also wanted to have a conversation with in Paddy O'Regan's, an all-Catholic pub in the Ardoyne area of north Belfast. They were suspected of taking part in the bombing of an Ulster Constabulary station. We knew they wouldn't come quietly, but Byme pulled out some piece of shit Saturday-night special and took a shot at one of my troopers. Missed him, because Byme's a total fuck up. He was trying to clear a jamb when I laid my truncheon across his ear and put him to sleep."

"Nice job you used to have. What happened when Mick met this guy in the quarter finals?"

"Look who's talking, Teal, of the U.S. Air Force's bomb squad," challenged Niles.

"Yeah, well, OK. What happened when Mick fought this fuckup?" asked Teal.

"He knocked him out at the end of the fourth round," answered Niles. "Oh, and I have to add, he fought Mick before I lay my truncheon on him, so maybe he missed my man because his head was still ringing from Mick."

"Mick's one tough fella, isn't he," said Teal, knowing the answer, but wanting to hear another story.

"He is," said Niles with his usual concision, but then added, "There are lots of fighters that have more natural talent than Mick. But Mick's whole package is what makes him tough. The simplest way to put it, is that he works at it. Where others are faster and stronger, Mick is more practiced, and he's creative. And I don't mean just in the work we do with Kelly. I once saw him bust a knuckle on a guy, what they call a boxer's knuckle, a fracture to the ring or pinky metacarpal, the knuckles on the outside of the hand. He was fighting a bloke in Boston, who had a head of granite and liked to block punches with his forehead, which, of course, is the thickest part of the skull.

Anyway, Mick throws a big right cross at him and the bloke, Jefferson I think his name was, turns into the punch and just manages to tuck his head as Mick wangs him with the big hand. You don't want to punch someone with the two outside knuckles because they are the most fragile, but Jefferson turns into the punch and Mick busts the metacarpal. Where most fighters would have backpedaled until the end of the round and hoped the ref would allow his trainer to re-tape the hand, Mick abruptly switched to southpaw and started to throw a lot of rights that were just scraping off Jefferson's head, right above his eyes. Mick's not making the knuckle much worse because he's just scraping Jefferson's face, but not hitting him head on, so kind of like sanding it, but he's doing a lot of scraping and he's using the inside knuckles to do it. Jefferson's perspiring and bleeding, and the perspiration and the blood start getting into his eyes, Next thing you know, Mick unloads a left that Jefferson never saw coming, and that's all she wrote. Mick wins by a knockout."

"Mick is smart, but even that doesn't adequately define him. Again, it's the package. It's easy to say 'he wants it more', and that's what coaches and sports announcers say, but he's creative and flexible. He has an uncanny ability to properly define the situation. But yeah, to answer your question, he's one tough son of a bitch."

Teal thought that Niles may have just broken his personal record for loquaciousness, even though he had no idea what that meant

"What happened this time with Byme? I heard you say 'good', then you were surprised by something," asked Teal.

"Mick busted his jaw. I was surprised Byme could still drive, because he was always a wheelman, you know. Mick said that O'Dea had to load him up with oxycontin."

* * *

One of the curious arguments for cell phones, is that they come in handy if you're stranded or have an emergency in a sparsely populated area. What the argument fails to consider, though, is that they usually didn't work in sparsely populated areas, either for lack of a cell tower, or because there was a mountain between the user and the tower, or the caller and the called. Also, for little understood reasons, they sometimes didn't work between locations with towers, or even without mountains or other obstructions, which was no doubt the work of Murphies.

For those reasons, smart commandos on a raid, or even a member of a brilliant art repo team, carried sat phones. Sat phones were supposed to work anywhere in the world. Well, they did if the technology was the kind you needed. Sat phones worked only within seventy degrees north and south of the Equator. Still, that covered all but the polar regions around the world, where few commandos found themselves on a raid, and it certainly covered areas where any self-respecting member of a brilliant art repo team was likely to find himself, or herself. Other sat phone systems required a cluster of satellites in order to operate continuously. Sat phones that used only one passing satellite had a transitory window of opportunity, which simply meant that sometimes the line was dead.

After Akbari and Shaker-Doust cut off the trail about a half mile into the Waterton Valley and Niles and Teal passed by them, from their hiding place behind a glacier-deposited boulder, Akbari called Colonel Zare from a sat phone that had the proper technology. The call should have gone through, and would have, if Coughlin O'Dea and his patriotic team of thugs hadn't confiscated the Colonel's sat phone and turned it off.

* * *

In the next half hour, only two campers came down the trail in the same direction as Niles and Teal. One was really big. Teal saw them approach and Niles saw them pass. Both heard them. No one else came by Niles and Teal in the next half hour – no other campers, rangers, Mounties, SWAT teams, and not even two Takavaran. Niles was about to suggest to Teal that they should head toward Kootenai

Lakes, their rendezvous site with Keagan and Kelly. He squat-walked over to Teal.

"What did you make of those two, Niles?"

"Hard to say, from the short time I could see them, especially since all I saw were their right sides and their backs. But given that they were only thirty minutes behind us and shouldn't have been, I've got to believe that those are the two blokes whose campsite I inspected last night. Also, the shorter of the two had a clean patch on his shirt, like something had covered it up before and the cloth hadn't yet faded to match the rest of the fabric. I had to guess, I'd say it was a *Who Dares Wins* patch, the slogan of the SAS."

"So, what, we've got the English Special Forces after Musaiyib now, too?" asked Teal.

"My guess would be they're part of the Coalition Task Force. Makes sense when you think about it. The U.S. and England carried most of that load in Iraq. Makes sense that the Yanks and the Brits would make up the task force."

"It's getting busy back here. Maybe we should think about heading out. I've got to believe the Iranians don't know any more about where Musaiyib is heading than we do, and they've got to have sat phones, too. But since O'Dea and company spirited the rest of their mates away, they may try to get to the boat dock or as close as they can to see if they can spot Musaiyib."

"I don't think so, Niles. If I were them, I'd realize I couldn't make the boat by eleven o'clock, especially with two guys looking for them. It would be a mad dash with no thought of caution, and they'd still be late. No, I'd wait a full hour. Most people can't be patient that long."

"I remember once when I was deer hunting, I jumped a big buck that ran into the swamp. I knew the only way out, unless that deer wanted to swim with the gators, was the way he went in. I sat there watching that herd path for a good hour. I was about to say the hell with it, but I decided to stay put for another fifteen minutes. Five minutes later that buck, with his head low, came sneaking out. That was one big buck."

"Did you shoot him?" asked Niles.

"No, I let him go."

"You're a funny guy, Teal."

"Let me ask you something, Niles. Even though you never met up with Mick and Kelly when you were in Belfast, did you appreciate their skill? Or think of them as worthy opponents?"

"Yeah, but I wouldn't have let them go if we had met up."

"Are you sure?"

"OK, we'll do it your way."

One hour and ten minutes later, Akbari and Shaker-Doust came walking by Niles' and Teal's boulder patch.

Niles called Keagan to tell him they had picked up the Iranians and two others he suspected were part of the Coalition Task Force, and that he and Teal were following the Iranians again. He told him that the other two were a good half hour ahead, and maybe more, if they kept up the pace they were setting. Keagan told him how to handle them.

Thirty

10:10 a.m. July 10th, 2011:

"Well, what do you think?" asked Keagan. Kelly replied, "I think it's as windy as Galway Bay."

They were aboard the *M.V. International*, on the open top deck that had just cleared the protected harbor.

"The mountains funneled the wind south-to-north. Today's wind was light, twenty knots," said the cruise docent.

"I meant about the passengers."

"I know you did, Mick. Give me a minute while I try to anchor my hat," said Kelly. Today, she was wearing, or trying to wear, a sun bucket. Kelly had a thing for hats, but this one was threatening to blow away, despite its chin draw string. The cruise docent had already alerted the passengers that the boat would not turn around for overboard head gear, "Unless your head is still in it," he added.

"Maybe, you should brave the sun and stow your hat," offered Keagan. Kelly had very fair skin, but it was milky, rather than pellucid.

"I think you're right. It seems to be a losing battle. I don't want to burn though," said Kelly, looking at the cloudless sky.

"I put some sunscreen in your day pack, in the smaller outside pocket."

Kelly found it and slathered her face, neck, and ears with the SPF 30 lotion. Keagan spread out a glob that she missed on her nose.

"OK, yes, initial impressions. I picked up six possibles. How about you?" asked Kelly.

"Only four. Here's what I would like you to do. When the docent picks up his spiel again, I want you to go forward and take in the view. After a judicious appreciation of this glorious scenery, walk slowly to the stern, noting possibles. Also, take note of their clothes and row and seat positions. Then go down the back stairs and do the same. Use the Ladies and then get some coffee and a tea, if you like. I'll more or less duplicate the process."

Ten minutes later, Kelly returned with two coffees. "What, no tea?" asked Keagan in surprise.

"Oh they had tea all right. Well, they said it was tea, but it could have been rusty water. I would have thought that Canadians could brew a proper cuppa."

"The boat's American registry, Kelly."

"Aye, that explains it. Well, I still have five, six if you count Musaiyib. He's in row twelve, an aisle seat one row back from the gangway. He's put on a dark blue anorak. Downstairs, I've got two more: one right in front of Musaiyib, wearing a green fleece jacket, and another two rows up on the aisle, the black fellow wearing a light green anorak."

"Then I have three up here: two in row three, near the port rail, and one two rows behind us, wearing a Columbia sailing jacket, leaning on the starboard rail."

"Good work, Kelly."

"How many duplicates do we have, Mick?"

"Three. The two sitting together on this deck are gym rats, not Special Forces."

"How can you be sure?" asked Kelly.

"They're watching the scenery, not scanning their compass. Neither one of them has turned around once, not even a phony stretch."

"Who did I miss?"

"The swarthy fellow sitting near the stack."

"He looks fit enough, but he's hardly bigger than Teal. He must be very sneaky."

"He is. Unless I'm way off the mark, he's a Gurkha, which would explain Maloaf's torture. Remember what the *Montreal Gazette* article said? Maloaf's thumb was sliced off at the second joint, which bled enough so he would have bled out without any other damage, but then his throat was cut, almost decapitating him. Your average steak knife can't do that, but a Khukuri can."

"What's a Khukuri?"

"It's the traditional tool and weapon of the Gurkhas. Gurkhas in the British Army are allowed to carry them, not only for ceremonies, but also, instead of the standard issue Ka-BaR."

"So, why did you say, 'good work' when I missed one and misidentified two others?" asked Kelly.

"Because, the only others that I considered were the same two that you chose, but I remembered Niles telling me that Special Forces guys constantly scan their environment. Those two weren't. As for the Gurkha, I remembered what the *Montreal Gazette* article said about how deep Maloaf 's throat cut was. Our minds work differently, Kelly, that's why we make such a good team. You see patterns; I see associations. You hear Special Forces, you think, young, fit, and muscular, as you should. I read 'almost decapitated', I think, knife. I see compact, fit, and dark, I think Gurkha. Gurkha leads me to Khukuri. Moreover, Gurkhas by reputation, are the fiercest troops ever to serve in the British Army."

"Fiercer than Niles?" asked Kelly.

"As a group, fiercer than the English. As individuals...well, we may find out."

"So, Mick Keagan, our complementary minds, is that the only reason why we make such a good team?"

"Well, that and you're so cute."

"Cute? That's it?"

"Aye, that and that you're as randy as a mink."

"Only with you, Mick, only with you."

"So, let's put all this together," said Kelly. "O'Dea and his thugs took care of three Iranians, but Niles says he's got two more. How do you read that?"

"First, tell me that O'Dea is going to drop them off at the Mounties. Not that I have much sympathy for them, given what they did in Montreal, but I don't want him reverting to his usual practice of putting a bullet in each of their heads and leaving them at the side of the road," said Keagan.

"He better not. We don't need those loose ends coming back to tangle us up. My explicit instructions to him were, bind and gag them; take them to some quiet place; alert the Mounties as to their whereabouts, who they are, and their likely part in the Montreal murders; and keep an eye on them until the Mounties come and get their men. I told O'Dea they wouldn't get paid unless I had confirmation that that's exactly what they had done," said Kelly.

"Good, you gave O'Dea the proper motivation. Well, it appears there are two more Iranians that Niles and Teal are following. Teal seems to think that they have the same rendezvous spot we do. He thinks they are too far away to try to meet the boat's docking. Niles agrees. I told Niles to stay out of sight, but to keep close tabs on them."

"I would say the nasty-looking *boyra* sitting in front of Musaiyib down below and the Gurkha over there are two of the *villains* who killed Musaiyib's partner, Awwal, and his neighbor, Maloaf. I think the Iranians killed the other three in Montreal."

"I thought we agreed that the *villains* were three?" said Kelly.
"We did."
"Where's the third one? Did you miss one, too?" asked Kelly.
"Possible, Kelly, but I'm betting he is either coming from the south on the same trail as Niles, Teal, and the Iranians, or, more likely, he hiked the lakeside trail and he's waiting somewhere below the ranger checkpoint, where he'll meet up with his friends."

"If you're right, Mick, then the sailor behind us and the black lad downstairs are members of the Coalition Task Force. Pretty small task force, don't you think?" asked Kelly.

"It would be, if that's all there were, but Niles thinks he's picked up two others who came in the same way as he and Teal did. He thinks they're headed for Kootenai Lakes as well," said Keagan.

"If Niles is right, then the Iranian unit was five strong. Do you think only three for the *villains*?" asked Kelly.

"Seems light doesn't it, given that the Iranians saw fit to send a team of five, and the Coalition Task Force may well be five, if they have a support person at either end of the trail. But think about how Awwal was secured. You thought there were three in the machine shop in Baghdad. I think that Awwal worked for the Coalition Forces in some capacity, and when Musaiyib showed little inclination to sell the seals, he pilfered three of them from the stash and approached one of the troops he worked with to sell him the seals that were found in the barrel behind the machine shop. Of course, Awwal could have met up with them in any number of ways."

"Anyhow, Villain Number One senses that these little things are valuable. He tells Villain Number Two, his closest buddy, that he may be onto a big score. They get ready for the buy, and Villain Number One realizes, for whatever reason, they need another. I'm guessing they picked up a third – the Gurkha – because he's just as greedy and as batshit as they are, so he's next in the trust line. I'm guessing, too, that the first two *villains* are Americans, and the Gurkha is the Canadian Molson drinker. Didn't you say that the Brits had some Canadian troops attached to them in Iraq?"

"Yes, some officers, mostly commissioned but a few non-commissioned."

"When they traced Musaiyib to Montreal, the Gurkha became especially useful. Maybe he's the one who located Musaiyib," offered Keagan.

"So, to recap. You think one of the *villains* hiked to the south end of the lake and will meet up with the two that are on board with us. Two Iranians, apparently unaware that their mates have been removed from the action, are coming up from the south, as are two more Coalition troops, with Niles and Teal in tow. And, you and I and two others from the Coalition Task Force will be heading south, following poor, little – probably terrified – Saeed ibn Musaiyib. And we're all going to meet up at the Kootenai Lakes Campground. Is that correct, Mick?"

"That's the way I read it, Kelly."

"It's going to be, if not a noisy jamboree, certainly a rascally one," said Kelly.

"I'd hate to be in Musaiyib shoes," said Keagan. "Come to think about it, I'm not so crazy about being in my own right now."

Thirty-One

10:45 a.m. July 10th, 2011:

Since the 10:00 a.m. cruise was the first of the day, there were only a handful of backpackers waiting in the pavilion near the dock. They were the ones headed back to civilization, having spent at least one night in the backcountry. The pavilion was an open-air affair that bore many translated tributes to peace, which, of course, was the theme of the International Peace Park, if not of several of the International's passengers.

A macadam path led from the dock, around the pavilion, and along the south shore of the lake for about a quarter of a mile, to where the rangers had set up their checkpoint. Everyone going passed that point had to sign their less-than-official-looking spiral notebook, which was more of a gesture toward conciliation than an adherence to the *Patriot Act*. Also, in keeping with the theme of amity, no passports were required, nor were there any random searches of packs for drugs or weapons.

Musaiyib was one of the first ones off the boat. He didn't pause at the pavilion to read any of the tributes to peace, nor did he stop to use one of the porta-potties set up behind the pavilion. He was the third passenger to sign the rangers' spiral notebook. Bosheers was three campers behind him. King had moved up closer to Bosheers, but they were still maintaining the pretext of being separate.

Keagan and Kelly signed in and, when cleared, moved off to the side near the Boulder Pass trail head, where Keagan pulled out a map as though he were doing some last-minute checking. He knew where he was going; he had looked at the map often enough. He was just waiting for all the principals to pass by.

Most of the passengers from the boat were camping, but a few of them were going to use the five and a half hours until the last boat of the day to hike in the area. The Boulder Pass Trail, near where Keagan and Kelly stood, led to the North Fork Road near the foot of Kintla Lake, about thirty miles away, but there were two lakes on that trail that were viewable by the afternoon boat at 4:30. Goat Haunt, a short steep trail that branched off to the left about a half mile down the Waterton Valley Trail, was doable by the returning 1:00 p.m. boat. Three other trails branched off the Waterton Valley Trail and led to any number of campsites. Given the array of options, Keagan knew that the crowd would soon thin out.

More than half of the campers peeled off onto the Boulder Pass Trail, as did a few day hikers. Keagan knew that most of the remaining hikers would cut off onto the Goat Haunt Trail. Only a few would continue south toward Kootenai Lakes along with Musaiyib's trackers and a few recreational backpackers.

Commander Roth and Sergeant Major Kennedy pulled up the rear. Now that the principals stood out from the herd, the whole scene started to remind Keagan of a bad PI film noir, where a chain of "drop-the-gun" leads to either the dénouement, where the good guy saves the day and loses the girl, or to the anticlimactic cliff hanger that just delays the good guy saving the day and losing the girl. Of course, none of these random associations applied, since there was no PI and Glacier National Park was a poor setting for a film noir. Also, Keagan already had the girl, and with so many armed principals involved, who the hell could predict how this was all going to work out. Still, it lightened Keagan's mood.

Conspicuously absent from this tableau were Joe Pete Barlow and First Lieutenant Ali Jassim. Commander Roth had decided that the unit was better served with Jassim back in Waterton. His value to the Task Force lay in his computer skills and his fluency in Arabic. Since neither was needed in the wilds of Glacier National Park, and since Jassim was not the most physical of military personnel, Roth thought it best that he stay in Waterton and act as a link to the outer world as the need arose. Jassim had joined the military to prove his allegiance to his adopted country, not to perform any feats of heroism. The thought of facing a grizzly bear – even with the rest of the Task Force around him – didn't much appeal to him. He was greatly relieved when Roth assigned him to computer duty in Waterton.

* * *

Barlow watched Musaiyib go by him on the trail. He was making good time, but it didn't seem like Musaiyib was trying to put any real distance between himself and those behind him. Barlow didn't see any reason to grab him now. Let him lead them to the seals, and then he'd get rid of him. There had already been two fuckups; they couldn't afford another one.

Bosheers and King weren't far behind Musaiyib, but they were followed closely by two day hikers who were also headed into the Kootenai Lakes. Barlow let out a mockingbird call, hoping that the two day hikers weren't birders who, if they were, would wonder what the hell a bird never seen north of Wyoming was doing in the Northern Montana Rockies. If they weren't birders, the call wouldn't register with them, but it would with Bosheers.

Bosheers put his right hand out to hold up King.

"What do you got, Howland?"

Barlow mocked the mocking bird again. "It's Joe Pete. Let's step off the trail and wait for him. See what he wants us to do."

Commander Roth and Sergeant Kennedy passed Bosheers and King. Three minutes later Barlow still hadn't appeared.

"You sure that was Joe Pete?" asked King.

"I'm sure." Another mockingbird call. "See. Maybe he's waiting for someone else to pass us."

"I hope you're right, Howland, because Musaiyib just picked up five more minutes on us."

Another call. Bosheers was starting to wonder. He knew it was Joe Pete, but he wasn't sure what he wanted them to do. Then he got it. Barlow was saying wait. Keagan and Kelly came around the bend just behind them. Keagan stopped and said hello to them. King reached behind his head as though he were scratching his neck, but he wasn't. He was wearing a neck scabbard for his Khukuri. Another call. Bosheers rolled his eyes left to right twice. King understood what he meant.

"Hey, where y'all headed?" said Bosheers.

"We're not sure, probably down to the Kootenai Lakes. We'll spend the night there, maybe two, then catch the boat back. This is the trail to the Lakes, isn't it?"

"Yeah, it is, but ya know y'all need a permit fer backcountry campin."

"No, we didn't know that," said Kelly. "Nobody told us."

"Surprised the rangers didn't say somethin' when ya checked in. They musta seen y'all's pack with the tent."

"Well, I put it off to the side when we were checking in. There were others there from the boat, so I guess they missed it in the confusion," said Keagan.

"Maybe, ya better go back. They catch ya, they'll fine y'all. Pretty steep fine, too."

"Well, thanks, but I think we'll take our chances. So, we just continue straight along this trail?"

"Yeah, ya got another two miles or so," said Bosheers.

"Thanks for your help and the warning," said Kelly as both she and Keagan waved Bosheers and King good bye.

"What do you make of that, Mick?"

"If nothing else, there's no longer any doubt that they are traveling together. I'd say they're the *villains*, or two-thirds of them anyway."

"Pretty sure of their numbers aren't you?" said Kelly.

"For good reason, though. I don't know much about birds, but I do know that in the three days we've been here, I've never heard that bird that was calling not far off to the right of the trail. What I am pretty sure of, is that that call was supposed to be a mocking bird. You may remember that we saw and heard plenty of them last year when we were in Louisiana. And, given that our not so friendly trail guide was, if not a good ole Southern boy, at least Southern."

"What about the other one?"

"Now that I got a better look at him, I'm sure he's a Gurkha. I'm also sure that he's carrying his Khukuri in a neck scabbard."

"So you don't think his neck was itchy," asked Kelly.

"Not at all," answered Keagan.

"Neither did I, which is why I was scratching my back," said Kelly.

Keagan looked at her bemused. "I know, Mick; well I know now. I forgot we don't have our guns with us," clarified Kelly.

* * *

"I thought that was ya, but at first I couldn't figure out what ya wanted us ta do. Ya have any trouble gettin' here?"

"Nah. There were check points, as I knew there would be, but they didn't give me much of a problem, especially since I had the night-vision glasses. One check point was a bitch getting around, though, because of the terrain. Other than that, it was cake."

"What did those two ask ya, Howland?"

"If they were on the right trail fer Kootenai Lakes. I told 'em they were, but that they needed a permit ta camp in the backcountry. I wanted ta get rid of them. I suspect it's gonna be crowded enough back there as it is. Don't need a coupla civilians addin' to the commotion."

"Yeah, so you think those two were civilians?" asked Barlow.

"Hard ta say. They looked like they might be just campers, but, at most, they've only got one sleeping bag and definitely only one pad. Somethin' seemed off."

"Randy, you got any ideas?"

"Not much other than what Howland just said. Good looking woman, though. The guy looked fit enough, and there was something about him that he couldn't hide. The way he carried himself. Something about him that doesn't fit with the rest of him."

"Yeah," said Barlow, "He looked like he can handle himself all right. I don't mean just in a fight; I mean out here, too. Did ya 'see his boots? But he was actin' like a dufus – one sleepin' bag, one pad, wasn't sure he was on the right trail, and he didn't know about the permit. The picture ain't the same as the presentation."

"What are you sayin', Joe Pete?" asked Bosheers.

"I'm sayin', I don't like things that don't add up. Didn't like 'em in Iraq either, where when they didn't add up, we almost always walked into some shit. What saved us from being aced was that we heeded those feelin's. I'm sayin' we do the same here."

"Speakin' of which, what did ya think of those two guys who passed just as I first called to ya?"

"They looked military to me," said King.

"OK, so what does that mean?" asked Barlow.

"Means, I'd be more inclined to watch them instead of some guy with a pack that didn't square with you," said King.

"Howland?"

"I don't know, Joe Pete, Randy's got a point, but I been with ya too many times not ta trust yer instincts. I've seen too many times when ya got a feelin' ya didn't like, and the next thing happens is all hell breaks loose. If those feelin's didn't make you pause, we'd be dead ten times over."

"So here's what I think. I think we got Musaiyib in the lead; we got two civilians after him, then we got two military types, and finally we got two questionables," said Barlow.

"So, who do ya think the military types are? Ya think they're MPs lookin' fer us?" asked Bosheers.

"One of them kinda looked like a cop, but the other definitely didn't," said Barlow. "So I'd say no to MPs, but I got to believe that we're not the only ones looking for those seals. Remember when the museum finally opened in '09, the director told us that only about half of their stolen stuff had been found? He said that the Coalition Forces hadn't given up on the rest of their stuff. Maybe those two guys are part of a task force that's still looking fer our seals," said Barlow.

"Just two guys?" questioned Bosheers. "Seems like there should be more."

"Maybe the guy and the woman are with 'em," offered King.

"Well, it appears that things might be more complicated than they first seemed. But that's OK, just as long as we keep that in mind," said Barlow.

Thirty-Two

Musaiyib's backcountry permit was for two nights at Kootenai Lakes, but he had never intended to camp there. Since 2008, when Awwal was murdered, Musaiyib knew those same people would be looking for him. He also knew about the Task Force. Since he didn't know about the Iranians – and since the three Takavaran were taken out before they could board – there was no reason he would have been suspicious of them. Nor did he know about Keagan and Kelly. Still, he had accepted early on that he might be followed. So, if someone had managed to hack into his credit card account, they would find his reservations.

Musaiyib had scanned the dock several times while he was waiting to board the *International,* and he evaluated all the passengers who boarded after him. He was certain that those who killed Awwal were Coalition soldiers. He also assumed that the Task Force would be made up of soldiers, although he couldn't be sure. So, he looked at those passengers whose stature was similar to those who invaded his country. He picked out several possibilities, but had no way of knowing whether any of them posed a threat to him. However, the one who frightened him the most was the man who sat in the row in front of him.

Accordingly, he hurried along the Waterton Valley Trail for about a mile, then, when he was sure that no one could observe him, he left the trail, cutting southeast at about a 110 degree angle. From there, he had about a mile and a half of bushwhacking to the upper reaches of Cleveland Creek.

Bushwhacking in the West was much easier than it was in the East. Not that it was just like trail walking; it wasn't. The forests of the East got more rain than those of the West, so they were much thicker. Musaiyib didn't waste any time putting some distance between himself and any line of sight from the trail where he had left it. Once he was sure he was out of sight, he slowed down. Sound carried in the outdoors. He didn't want to rush getting out of sight, only to find he was not out of hearing.

While bushwhacking in the West may have been easier than in the East, since the Rockies were much younger mountains than the Appalachians, and geological tykes compared to the Adirondacks, what Musaiyib did have to watch out for were sudden drop offs and cliff faces that would cause him to backtrack and lose whatever edge leaving the trail had given him. He knew that the upper reaches of Mount Cleveland were one big cliff face; hence, the new rope and climbing shoes. Another worry he had, was whether he was on the right approach. If he was, he'd be fine once he got to the cliff face. If he wasn't, he'd find himself facing one of several snowfields that flanked Mount Cleveland's western face, like bunkers surrounding a golf course green. He knew he didn't want to have to cross a snowfield alone, especially in July.

Musaiyib carried both a compass and a GPS. The benefit of the compass was that he didn't have to worry about batteries going dead. Musaiyib's compass was a Brunton Eclipse, a model that told him, not only what direction he was going, but allowed the accomplished user – which Musaiyib was – to plot a course, and to calculate distances and elevations. However, on this trip, the compass was backup.

The beauty of the GPS was that it told him exactly where he was, although, exactly was a relative term. It could be within 70 feet or less, depending on the sophistication of the instrument, and it allowed him to pre-set a course at home, out of the rain or snow, away from swarms of insects, day or night, and where fresh batteries were available. Since Musaiyib had pre-set his course, all he had to do now was to move along the waypoints, the first of which was located on Cleveland Creek, where it forked northeast and south. The next waypoint was only a half mile away, on a bend in the northeast fork, which, not only seemed to be the least obvious location for his campsite because it was more than a mile out of the way of his planned route, but it was also in the least likely location that someone looking for him would stumble across his campsite.

The site had water, cover, and protection. Someone looking for him could walk within meters of his hiding place and not notice it. It was in a hanging col. This was where he would spend the first night. He was still a little more than two miles from the summit of Mount Cleveland, but any higher up and he would be exposed on the rock face. He made camp and said *Dhuhr*, asking Allah for his guidance. He had mixed feelings about this, because he was a thief asking Allah to aid and abet him. Still, it was worth a try. Perhaps Ali Baba, too, prayed before a job.

* * *

Because Waterton Valley's elevation was about 4,400 feet, and because the land was relatively flat and much wetter than the mountain slopes that bordered it, the forest was mostly hardwood, rather than conifers. The cover was thick with saplings along the trail, and Keagan had the uncomfortable realization that he was traveling through grizzly country without a firearm. He briefly considered doing what the rangers recommended, that is, talking loudly or, better yet, singing. Keagan hated small talk. At the inn where he was forced to smooze with the customers, he did as little as possible, unless they were regulars. And, in spite of his genealogy, he had a wretched voice, so he sedulously avoided singing, even in the shower.

While the forest around him was unsettling because of its limited line of sight, it was very good for cover. Keagan held up Kelly. He handed her the sat phone and told her to go in about fifty yards and call Niles.

"Tell him the lineup and the order, and ask him to wait for them at the junction where the spur trail leads to the Kootenai Lakes campsites," Keagan said. "We should be there shortly. Tell him to call as soon as he sees Musaiyib, but to call me in twenty minutes if he doesn't show."

Kelly took the sat phone and cut off the trail.

Barlow came into sight within minutes. "Problem?"

"Girlfriend's answering a call of nature," answered Keagan.

"Ah," said Barlow. "Well, if everythin's OK, I'll head out. The campsites are first-come-first-served."

"Good luck," said Keagan.

He wasn't on the boat. Southern boy, and rugged-looking, too. My guess is that villain number three has just introduced himself, thought Keagan.

A minute later, the other two *villains* showed themselves.

"Problem?" asked Bosheers.

"Call of nature. It takes women longer than men."

"Yeah," said Bosheers, "especially in the woods. They gotta check fer snakes. Wouldn't want to get bit in the ass. It really shows whether you love 'em or not."

He and King moved off. Keagan wanted to punch Bosheers, but he reminded himself that these guys were probably armed – certainly the Gurkha was – and he wasn't. Maybe he would later.

Kelly heard Bosheers and King move off, but waited three minutes before coming out to the trail and rejoining Keagan.

"Niles is already at the junction. The two groups he was following made good time. They both took the spur trail, so they're looking more and more like our competition."

"Doesn't seem to be any doubt, does there?"

"I guess not."

Niles and Teal had split up when they got to the spur trail to the Kootenai Lakes. They hid their packs in the woods and reconnoitered the area to locate the four men they had been following. That they hadn't claimed a campsite settled any doubt of their being there for camping.

There were four Kootenai Lakes. The smallest was only about one hundred yards across, while the largest, where the campsites were located, was about a mile and a quarter wide. The lake's two islands shaped it like a figure eight that some giant had sat on. Curiously, it was shaped very much like Lake Placid, except for the giant-squashing part. However, it was much smaller. Teal crossed over the Waterton River and scouted the west side of the largest lake. Niles covered the east side. Teal found the Takavaran first. They seemed confused. They had removed their packs and Akbari had the sat phone raised to his ear. He waited. Again, there was no answer. After about a minute, he lowered the phone. Teal crept closer to hear what Akbari was saying to Shaker-Doust. He wanted to take a picture of them with his cell phone, but he couldn't risk getting that close. Teal saw that both men were wearing side arms.

It took Niles longer to find the other two, but he got even closer to them than Teal did to the Iranians, but more by accident than by design. Wade and Lollard were hidden in a small thicket of Western Red Cedar. The site's lowness and the thickness of the vegetation made for a poor camping place, but a clever hiding place. Niles almost walked right by them, and since he was off the trail and there were no outhouses nearby, his presence would have been difficult to explain. He froze and listened to them. One was clearly American, and the other was English. The English one was relaying the details of a phone conversation he had had with their commander. The American listened at first, then, when the Englishman was finished, the American asked what their ETA was. The Englishman told him approximately forty-five minutes.

Niles and Teal met back where they had hidden their packs and traded information.

"So the Iranians can't figure out what happened to their mates, huh?" asked Niles.

"No. They don't seem to know what to do next. The older guy was focused on how to make contact with his colonel. The younger one was convinced that they had been arrested. It seems the other ones killed three of the four guys in Montreal."

"Teal, how did you know what they were saying? I know you're full of surprises, but I'd be much more than surprised to find out you speak Farsi."

"I don't. They were speaking English, and not very heavily accented English, either. I could understand them better than I can a lot of the old swamp rats in Louisiana."

"Confused or not, they must be very disciplined soldiers to stay in character this deep in the woods."

"How'd you do, Niles?"

"Bloody well almost walked up on them."

"You must be slipping."

"Yeah, well, these guys are good. One Yank, one Brit. The Brit must have picked out their hiding place. It was a tight little clump of trees. Cricky, I couldn't have been more than fifteen to twenty feet from them when I realized where they were."

"Learn anything?"

"Learned I'll have to be more careful around these two. The Yank was a big guy. You wouldn't want to let him tag you," said Niles.

"What about you, Niles? You think he could tag you?"

"I wouldn't want to find out. Besides, there are only two basic rules in fighting, and their order is just as important as the rules themselves: One, don't get hit, and two, hit your opponent, hard and often. Only the foolish ignore rule number one.

"Anyhow, the Brit seemed to be in charge, though much smaller. I was right about the patch though, and, given his accent, I don't think there's any doubt he's SAS. They were waiting for their commander, a bloke by the name of Roth. He was about forty-five minutes away. I think we need to get back to the junction and see if we have any new arrivals."

Commander Roth and Sergeant Kennedy were the first to arrive. Niles followed them to their team members. He didn't dare get as close as he did the last time.

"Any other guests, Teal?"

"Yeah, three uglies. One arrived about ten minutes ahead of the other two, but he waited for them at the junction. They are the ones Kelly calls the *villains*. It was two Southern boys, Joe Pete and Howland."

"That's three, Teal."

"Not in the South, it isn't, where two first names are common. Joe Pete seems to be the leader. Howland is ugly and a mean-looking fucker, to boot."

"What about the third one?"

"That's Randy."

"What's he look like?"

"Different, dark – not black though – and smaller than the other two. Joe Pete once called him what sounded like Ran-o-dip. Does that make sense?" asked Teal.

"Randy is his Anglicized name. I suspect he's a Gurkha," said Niles

"What's a Gurkha?"

"A very fierce fighter. They usually serve in the English Army. I wonder what he's doing with the Yanks? Oh, I guess I can't call them that. Good ole boys doesn't seem to fit either, though, since these boys are far from being good."

"Kelly calls them the *villains*," repeated Teal. "That's good enough for me. Remember when Kelly first told us about this project, she said that she thought the *villains* might be Canadians? Do you think he's in the Canadian Armed Forces and was serving with the Brits as part of the Coalition Forces?" said Teal.

"Makes sense, Teal. Let's fill Mick in."

Niles called Keagan and told him everything that he and Teal had learned. Keagan asked about Musaiyib, and Niles told him he was a no show. Keagan gave Niles the coordinates where he and Kelly were, and he said they'd wait for them there.

* * *

Barlow sent Bosheers and King to scout the area for Musaiyib. Unlike Niles and Teal, they just checked out the campsites at Koo-tenai Lakes. They found exactly what Niles and Teal had found when they checked there. They were all empty, although there was a pitched tent at one site. However, they did meet the three Montana backpackers who were just arriving. Barlow focused on the woman.

"Y'all didn't happen ta see a lone backpacker in the last mile or so?" he asked. "Buddy of ours we were supposed ta meet up with. I was just wonderin' if he missed the turn off. A skinny guy, dark skinned?"

"No, we didn't see anybody at all going in the opposite direction," answered the woman's husband. "Where are you headed?"

"We hadn't settled on a climb yet, but our base camp was supposed to be here. Ah, well, I'm sure he'll turn up. Thanks."

"What'd did you make of that?" asked the woman.

"Could be nothing," said her husband. "But I didn't like the way he focused right on you, like we weren't even there."

"You jealous, Pete?"

"No, but there was something about him that didn't square. He was too sure of himself, too smooth."

"You could do with some smooth, Pete."

"I didn't like the looks of the three of them either," said the woman's brother. "Especially the darker one. Something funny about all of them. Maybe the one who talked to you was just being Southern, but there was an edge to those boys. The one who talked to you, Sally, may have been smooth, but he wasn't all that relaxed either, and the other two were guarded. I noticed how they fanned out, so one wasn't blocking the other. I saw guys like that when I was in the Corps. Besides, they didn't even know where they were going to climb. Technical climbers – if that's what they were – always plan their routes. Even if they were just hiking, you don't come all the way out here without a plan. I agree with Pete. Something doesn't square with those boys."

"Is that why you loosened the strap on your holster, Billy?" asked the woman. "None of them seemed to be armed."

"Well, the dark one kept scratching his neck. He either had a bad case of fleas or he had a knife back there."

"You're just paranoid after Afghanistan, Billy."

"Maybe so, Sal. Maybe so."

"So, where the fuck did he go?" asked Barlow.

"Good question," said King. "Joe Pete, you were in the lead; where did you last see him?"

"'Bout a mile in from the rangers," answered Barlow.

"How far did you stay behind him, Joe Pete?" asked King.

"Hard ta tell, but I tried ta stay just out a sight. I don't think he coulda gotten more than a hundred, two hundred yards out, unless he got spooked and bolted," said Barlow.

"Let me see your map, Joe Pete," said Bosheers.

Bosheers spread the map out on a deadfall. "OK, it's two and a half miles from the ranger station to where we are now. So, the last time Joe Pete saw him was about here." Bosheers tapped a spot on the trail with a twig. "Which means he left the trail between there and here. The question is, where? What's between those two points that would interest Musaiyib?"

"Hold on. Suppose he didn't leave the trail," suggested King.

"What do you mean, Randy?"

"Suppose he went straight. He could have gone right passed here, and while we're looking for him here, he's already a mile down the trail," said King.

"But them three just said they didn't see anybody," said Bosheers.

"I know they did, but what if he stepped off the trail when he heard them coming? If he thought he was being followed, he would have known those three would be asked if they saw him," answered King.

"Randy, drop your pack and run down the trail to about here." Barlow ran his index finger along the trail line where the contour lines were close together. "I suspect y'all be outta the valley by here." He tapped the map again. "And ya kin see if Musaiyib was anywhere on the trail. There aren't any side trails till here." Barlow tapped a dotted line on the map about three miles passed where they were. "You should be able ta see the fucker well before then 'cause it's all open country. If ya see him, call me and we'll catch up with ya and bring yer pack with us. Howland, give Randy your sat phone."

"If ya don't see anything by here, head back double time. We'll take your pack and call you with our coordinates."

* * *

"Where's Musaiyib?" asked Commander Roth.

"I was hoping you were going to tell us, sir," said Lollard. "He hasn't shown here. I even watched the trail ahead of us, in case his reservation here was a ruse. He never passed by."

"Could he have gone into the woods, Socko, and picked up the trail further down?" asked Kennedy.

"I doubt it, Wes. I watched from about fifty yards on the far side of the trail. Unless he took a major detour, I would have heard him."

"What about the Iranians, Socko?" asked Roth.

"They're over on the west side of the lake," answered Lollard.

"How many?"

"Just two," answered Lollard.

"I would have thought there'd be more," said Roth.

"I think there were; they've been on a sat phone trying to raise somebody, but with no luck. Could just mean their sat phone's not working, or it could be the Mounties picked up the others for the

Montreal murders. Commander, did you see anyone on the boat who fit the bill?" asked Lollard.

"I saw two guys who looked like soldiers and some Middle-Eastern types, but nobody who looked both military and Middle-Eastern," said Roth.

"Commander, you want Bo and me to go over and wrap up the Takavaran?" asked Lollard.

"No, then we'll just have to keep them with us, which will compromise our mission. Our number one concern here is to find those cylinder seals. Detaining two Takavaran will seriously compromise our ability to do that."

"We could just shoot them, sir," said Wade.

"Spoken like a true marine, Bo," said Kennedy.

"We don't want to use firearms unless we have to. Nothing is going to spook Musaiyib faster than hearing gunfire," said Roth.

"We could cut their throats; that'd be quiet, Commander," said Wade.

"Thanks, Bo, but I got a better idea." Roth started to call the ranger station by the boat dock when Kennedy raised his hand indicating that he had something to say. Roth lowered the sat phone.

"Commander, if I might make a suggestion..."

"Go ahead, Wes," said Roth.

"If you call the rangers about a couple of Iranian commandos, they're going to call Homeland Security, and they're going to come roaring in here in Ospreys with enough firepower to bring down a division. Can you call the ranger office in Kalispell and ask them to send in their own law enforcement team? No more than four troops. Have them land a couple miles from here. Bo and Socko can deliver the Takavaran to them, all wrapped up, and then meet us, wherever we'll be."

"Socko, what do you think about that?" asked Roth.

"Makes sense, as long as Bo and I don't have to babysit the Takavaran too long. Remember, there may still be more of them somewhere else. Maybe they are just having trouble with their sat phone.

Wes is right about Homeland Security, though. They get involved and we'll never find Musaiyib and the seals."

"OK, let's see what they have to say," said Roth.

Thirty-Three

Niles and Teal hiked back toward the boat dock for about a mile and a quarter and met Keagan and Kelly where they had waited about three hundred yards off the trail.

"Kelly and I looked for some sign of where Musaiyib went off the trail, but we couldn't find any. Since we were behind him, I've got to believe that he didn't double back, but veered off the trail to the east, between us and the Kootenai Lakes spur trail," said Keagan.

"Why east? Why not west?" asked Teal.

Keagan showed him the map. "On the west, you have the Citadel Peaks and not much else. If that's where Musaiyib was headed, I think he would have continued along the trail at least another three-quarters of a mile. Less bushwhacking that way. There's too much of an angle from here. On the east, however, is Mount Cleveland, which, as you'll recall, is the highest peak in the park. Not only is the angle of approach right from here, but he can follow this creek," Keagan ran his finger along the thin blue line on the map, "to up above tree line."

"Anyway, I plotted a course, and Kelly and I – spaced within sight of each other, but about a hundred feet apart – followed that line. Kelly found these tracks, which look fresh to me, but I'm no Daniel Boone, so they could be several days old. They do, however, seem to have been made by a person traveling alone."

"When we first learned of Musaiyib's backcountry permit, I liked Cleveland for his destination. Remember, I pointed it out in your shop. The new climbing rope gives credence to the theory that he was planning on doing some technical climbing. Kelly and I have already tried to find better alternatives and we came up short. Niles, Teal, go ahead and poke holes in it."

Niles and Teal poured over the map. After a while, Niles said, "Everything you've said makes sense to me, but why would Musaiyib hide the seals on the highest peak in the park? If it's the highest, wouldn't it be the most popular with technical climbers?"

"Good point, and I don't have a good response. But maybe he found some place that's off the usual routes. Look at its face; it's almost two miles across. And these rock bands, how many are there? Five or six of them? There are a lot of places up there to hide things that were small enough to fit in his daypack when he and Awwal stole them. It didn't even look like a big daypack from the newspaper photo," answered Keagan.

"Teal?"

"If he hid them on a mountain, it's as good a choice as anywhere, but maybe the new rope is just to make you think that."

Niles reminded Teal that the rope itself cost almost $400.

"A lot of money for a piker to spend on a ruse, don't you think? Besides, why would he think that anybody would learn about the rope?"

"Somebody killed Lévesque," said Teal.

"Point taken," said Niles.

Teal went back to scrutinizing the map. After a few minutes, he said, "OK, let's try it."

"I'd like Kelly and I to follow the trail that she found, while you two provide us with a rear-guard. My reasoning is two-fold; if we're following an old trail or a bear's trail, there's no sense all four of us wasting our time. Also, while three of the Iranians may have been removed from the playlist, there are still two more of them, and there are the *villains* and the Coalition Task Force. So, we can't ignore them. I don't want to recover the cylinder seals just to have them taken away from us by the law or the lawless."

"Niles, you know more about rear-guard action than I, so I'll leave the details to you. Having said that, remember that whatever action you take, we all have to live with it. Use your best judgment."

* * *

Commander Roth had reached the same conclusion as Keagan had. Namely, that Musaiyib was headed for Mount Cleveland. He and Kennedy left the trail not far from where the others had.

When they had gone far enough to be out of sight of anyone on the trail, Roth held up his arm.

"Now might be a good time to break out our side arms," he said.

Roth and Kennedy took off their packs, opened them, and took out their Beretta M9s, the standard U.S. military-issue side arm, which were tucked into pancake-style leather holsters.

"You think these will be any good against a 500-pound grizzly, sir?"

"Probably not, but they will be against the Takavaran if Socko's wrong about the rest of their team, or against anybody else who might be following Musaiyib," said Roth.

* * *

The *villains*, for lack of a better collective, had regrouped and backtracked their route, until Barlow stopped them.

"This is where I last saw him." He dropped his pack and pulled out his map of the area.

"OK," said Barlow, when he had unfolded the map. "We're about here." He indicated a spot on the trail. "Where would the fucker go?"

After a few minutes, King spoke up.

"My guess is, he went up here, to Mount Cleveland. Remember what Maloaf said about the climbing wall?"

"Howland?" asked Barlow.

"A good choice as any, but there's nothin' but mountains here," answered Bosheers.

"Howland, think patrol. We're after a bunch of ragheads who just blew up a bunch of our buddies. Where the fuck would ya look for them?"

"I don't know, Joe Pete. There's a million places out here. He coulda gone anywhere. This ain't no sandbox. And even in them shitholes they call towns over there, we could kick down some doors, blow up the shit of whoever was in there, and move on ta another hovel. It didn't really matter – today's targets, or tomorrow's targets. What the fuck."

"Pick yer best place, Howland."

Bosheers looked at the map again.

"Well, if it's gotta be a mountain, I think Randy's right. That kid on the boat said it was the highest mountain in the park. I don't know if that's a good thing or a bad thing, though."

"How would you get there, Howland?" asked Barlow.

Bosheers, still looking at the map, said, "Straight up this crick, here."

"Randy?"

"That's how I'd go, until proven wrong."

"OK, then, Howland, I want ya to navigate. Randy, I want ya ta sweep across this slope a coupla times; do it in arcs. Go higher each time. Three full passes oughtta be enough. There may be other climbers comin' up there, too. I wanta know about 'em. Then, a course, we still got those two military-lookin' guys and that other guy with the pretty woman."

* * *

Hap Larson, the watch commander of the Kalispell Ranger Office, tried to call in four of the best law enforcement rangers who were either already on duty, or on call, and have them rendezvous at

Simmons Helicopter Rides in Hungry Horse, where the watch commander had already reserved a chopper that could carry six passengers and equipment. It turned out, however, that there were only three officers close by at the time. Two of his choices had already been detailed to the North Fork area of the park, and even if the chopper could land where they were, it would take too long to get them where they were needed. The watch commander prudently realized that if he fucked up an extraction of two Iranian commandos, his next posting would in Gates of the Arctic National Park doing mosquito research, or on litter patrol at the National Mall.

Lollard and Wade made their way over to the west side of the largest of the Kootenai Lakes, where Akbari and Shaker-Doust were bivouacked. Lollard sent Wade just to the west of them with strict instructions: "Don't shoot me."

Lollard gave Wade twenty minutes to circle behind the Takavaran. When Lollard moved forward with his H&K MP5 leveled on Akbari, Akbari was again trying to raise Colonel Zare. Wade literally caught Shaker-Doust with his pants down. Wade let him finish and then marched him over to where Lollard held Akbari at gun point.

"Bo, bring him over here about five yards abreast of this one. Good, now, come over here and give me your MP5. OK, now search this one for weapons first." Lollard motioned toward Akbari. "Always restrain the highest ranking soldier first, unless, of course, it's an officer."

Wade had Akbari leaned into a stout Western Red Cedar while he searched him. He found a Ka-BaR knife in a calf scabbard and removed it. He didn't find anything else. When he was finished, he tied Akbari's wrists behind his back with two lock-tight plastic straps, loosened Akbari's boot laces, and had him sit on the ground.

"Now this one, Bo."

"He's clean, Socko."

"Check him again, Bo. He should have something."

Wade again ran his hands up and down Shaker-Doust's legs and arms, and over his front and back.

"He's clean."

"OK, lock him up, loosen his laces, sit him down, and come over here by me."

"Dumb fuck. I'd have something. Even if it was a ceramic blade. They ain't in our league, are they, Socko."

"Never underestimate the enemy, Bo. You cover them. I'm going to see where that chopper is."

Lollard took the sat phone off his belt and called the number Roth had given him. The call was answered in twenty seconds.

"Where are you? Do you know where you're going to land yet? OK, come north on the Waterton Valley trail and we'll meet up with you.

Good, see you then."

"Where are they, Socko?"

They say there's a clearing down the trail heading south, a bit under two miles. They can't land there, but the rangers can rappel out of the chopper and take custody from us at the halfway point; otherwise, the nearest place they can land is above the tree line on the last flat part of the trail we came down. You know, on that last ridge before the trail drops into the valley, where you thought you saw these two blokes hastily heading for cover. I told the rangers we'd take the closer site. I want to hand these two off and get back to the Commander."

"Sounds good to me. The faster, the better. Up you go, men," said Wade to the Takavaran.

* * *

Barlow and Bosheers were southern boys who had joined the Special Forces, which meant, among other things, that they knew how to hunt. Maybe if they had grown up in Houston or in Atlanta they wouldn't, but in Natchez, Mississippi or in Sylacauga, Alabama, it was a given. Barlow killed his first deer when he was eight; Bosheers, when he was ten. Both below the legal age, but then, not only were they not law abiding, their parents didn't much care for the rules, either, especially when it came to eating.

They followed their instincts and headed for a point on Cleveland Creek where the grade sharply increased. By the time they got to the creek, they still hadn't seen any signs that Musaiyib had gone this way. Bosheers thought they were wasting their time, but didn't have a better idea, so Barlow convinced him to give it another thirty minutes. Ten minutes later, they picked up a trail that appeared to head up to the lower reaches of Mount Cleveland, veering to the northeast. The trail looked fresh enough, but it was hard to tell. The Mountain West was much drier than the Deep South. The one major doubt they had was that there seemed to be three sets of tracks.

"Joe Pete, what if this is a wild goose chase? That skinny sand nigger could be anywhere. I don't like that there look ta be three sets of tracks here."

"Well, I'm not crazy about it either, Howland, but with this crick over there," Barlow pointed vaguely toward the north, "and with this mountain bein' the highest in the whole park, it makes sense ta me. You got a better idea? I'm listenin'."

"I wish I had, Joe Pete, but I don't. I jest don't like that I see what looks to be three set of tracks here."

"Then I say we keep goin'," said Barlow. "We can drive ourselves crazy with 'what if's', but one thing's surer than shit – if we don't act, we ain't ever gonna find Musaiyib and those seals."

"Hold on, that's Randy." Barlow answered the sat phone.

King told him that he had located the two military types that he and Bosheers had seen on the boat, and that Barlow had seen pass by when he was doing his mocking bird imitations.

* * *

The helicopter hovered over a wetland which was equidistant between the trail Akbari and Shaker-Doust had come down getting to Kootenai Lakes and the Waterton River. The side door slid open, someone inside the chopper lowered a rope, and, in short order, three rangers rappelled to the ground and headed north on the valley trail to rendezvous with Lollard and Wade. They met them near the mid-point. Wade told the rangers that the prisoners had already been searched. The rangers thanked them, took custody of Akbari and Shaker-Doust, and marched them down the trail to where Simmons' helicopter hovered over the Waterton River. Lollard noticed that he could faintly hear the wap-wap-wap of the rotor blades in the distance. The sound reminded him of a recent campaign.

Lollard called Roth to tell him the two Takavaran were now in the custody of the rangers, and that he and Wade were on their way back. Roth gave him the coordinates of where he and Kennedy were, but told them that they were heading up Cleveland Creek, following what appeared to be a set of tracks, and that he should call him back when they got to the Creek. He told Lollard he would update him as to their current position. Lollard estimated his time to where they were now and rang off.

* * *

The three rangers followed Akbari and Shaker-Doust several paces behind. Two of the rangers kept their .40 caliber Glocks leveled at the prisoners. The third was calling Simmons to tell him they had taken custody of the prisoners and were about ten minutes away from where he had dropped them off. The rangers were relaxed. They knew they had two Iranian commandos in custody, so they weren't so relaxed as to be stupid, but the prisoners were cuffed – hands behind their backs – and they were at gunpoint three paces ahead. Not much they could do, commandos or not.

Akbari was thinking that their undoing had been his fault. He was caught with his guard down and was now being led off to an

American jail. Not by highly-trained Special Forces like themselves, but by what? Three forest cops. *Huh,* he scoffed inwardly at his hubris.

Shaker-Doust was thinking less self-effacing thoughts. He was wearing a long-sleeve American crewneck shirt, the cuffs of which were two-ply. Taped vertically to the inside of his left cuff was a razor blade. Wade had missed it when he searched him.

There were two sides to training. The positive side was that it taught you how to react in situations where experience had shown that the best way to deal with a problem was to follow proven methods. The English one – most certainly SAS – had known how to take captives. He told the other one, the one he called Bo, to search them, cuff them, loosen their boot laces, and sit them on the ground. All tried and true, proven methods. That's why they were being held captive now. The rangers behind them – at least two of them – had their side arms leveled at them and stayed a prudent distance behind them. Didn't appear that there was much he and Akbari could do.

The negative side of training, however, Shaker-Doust thought, *was that trained people frequently failed to factor in the slightly different circumstances of a situation, because following the manual lead to success, more often than not. But the one called Bo, had run his hands up and down his sleeves but stopped before he reached his cuffs. He did so because he assumed he was looking for a knife, or perhaps a knife blade. Not a thin, single-edged razor blade, which, given that it was taped vertically to the two-ply cuff, he might well have missed, even if he had circled my wrists with his hand instead of following procedure.*

Shaker-Doust freed the razor blade, cupped it, and sliced through his restraints. The two rangers who marched them at gunpoint didn't seem to notice. The third, having finished his call to Simmons, was now trying to raise the Kalispell Ranger Office and update Hap Larson as to their progress. Shaker-Doust suddenly stopped and whirled. It took the two armed rangers a split second to react; it took Akbari less time. He flung himself feet first at one of the armed rangers, scissored his legs in his own, and let his momentum roll him forward. The movement caused the ranger to fall over straight backward and whip his head hard against the ground. Shaker-Doust – hands free now, and within reach of the other armed ranger, grabbed his gun and piston-kicked his knee, then pistol-whipped him while Akbari roundhouse-kicked the third ranger in the temple. All three of them were down and unconscious.

Shaker-Doust sliced through Akbari's restraints, and the two quickly dragged the rangers off the trail, restrained them with their own handcuffs, searched them more efficiently then had Wade, lashed them to separate trees with parachute cord they found in the rangers' packs, and gagged them with their own T-shirts.

When they were finished, Akbari outlined for Shaker-Doust how they were going to proceed, for he believed – just as all the others came to believe – that Musaiyib had hidden the seals on Mount Cleveland. He also believed that was where they would locate their three comrades.

* * *

Barlow and Bosheers met up with King in less than ten minutes. Roth and Kennedy had continued to follow the set of tracks they had found which vectored toward Cleveland Creek. They had just stopped so that the Commander could call Lollard and update him as to their position and learn how far behind them he and Wade were.

The words were faint, but both Barlow and Bosheers could hear them too, once King pointed them in the right direction. They couldn't make out what Roth was saying, but they could pinpoint his location. Slowly, they headed in that direction.

Commander Roth was just ringing off the call when the three caught a glimpse of him and Kennedy. Bosheers and King recognized them from the boat.

"Joe Pete, they were on the boat this morning," said Bosheers.

"Doesn't mean much. I'm probably the only one on this mountain who wasn't on that boat," answered Barlow.

"Yeah, but Randy noticed them right off. He said they looked like military. You said the same thing when they passed by on the trail," said Bosheers.

"OK, fine, let's see if we can get a little closer."

The three moved toward Roth and Kennedy. Kennedy raised his hand to Roth. "What is it, Wes?" whispered Roth.

"I thought I heard a noise," They both listened hard for a full minute. Nothing. Kennedy was doing what most people do when they hear a noise – wait for it to repeat. When they don't hear it repeated in their expected time frame, they assume they were mistaken. Fact is, something made the noise, but, unlike Teal and his buck, they lacked the patience to wait the noisemaker out.

"I guess I just imagined it, Commander. As you know, I grew up in Newark. Put me in a park no bigger than a city block, and I start thinking lions and tigers. Put me in a wilderness known for its grizzly bears, and I'm paranoid. Sorry, sir. What did Socko have to say?"

"They delivered the Iranians to the rangers and are on their way here. He said he could be here in about a half hour. I told them we'd keep moving and update him as to our position. I don't want Musaiyib to disappear, if that's in fact, who we are trailing," answered Commander Roth.

Barlow motioned Bosheers and King to get their weapons out. In his mind, King already had his weapon available, but he knew that Barlow meant his handgun.

"I don't want any shootin'," whispered Barlow. "The guns are for control. We'll move them away from this site, so their friends have trouble findin' them."

Barlow told Bosheers to circle to his right about a hundred and twenty degrees and wait for his move. He told King to go left and do the same.

"When I stand up and come at those two, Howland, you move in on 'em too, quietly. We don't wanta have ta shoot. If Musaiyib is ahead of us and he hears a shot, we'll have ta start all over again, clear? Randy, ya stay back, jest in case these two fuckers are slipperier than I credit 'em ta be."

"Clear, Joe Pete," said Bosheers. King nodded.

Barlow removed his pack and approached Roth and Kennedy. He had his Beretta in his waist band at the small of his back.

"Hey y'all, glad I found somebody."

Neither Roth nor Kennedy had seen Barlow because he wasn't on the boat with them, and Barlow hadn't met up with Bosheers and King until after they had passed by. Still, Kennedy didn't like what he saw. He reached for his side arm, which both he and Roth now carried in power-side holsters. Barlow got to his first, however, and Bosheers walked up behind them.

"Now that wasn't very neighborly of y'all, was it?" Barlow said. "Howland, relieve them of their weapons. Now, I know why I'm carrying, but I'd like to hear why y'all are. M9s. I used to carry one myself. Didn't like it much. Ain't worth a shit against bears. It jest pisses 'em off. Ya must be military too," said Barlow.

Neither Roth nor Kennedy answered.

"Not talkin', huh? OK, I'll have ta fill in the blanks fer ya, then. You're part of the Coalition Task Force that's lookin' for Musaiyib and the cylinder seals. That's too bad, because that's why we're here."

"Where's the other one?" asked Kennedy.

"Yer good. Y'all make Randy on the boat?" Barlow motioned King forward.

"Randy, this hot shot made you and Howland fer bad guys on the boat. I'm gonna have ta get ya two that book about makin' friends and influencin' people," said Barlow.

"I already know how to influence people, Joe Pete," said King.

"Yeah, I know ya do; I've seen ya do it. These fellas here haven't, though, and fer their sake, I hope ta God they never do."

"OK, here's the deal, boys. Howland behind ya is gonna search ya. Y'all better give him any weapons you got before he commences. If'n he finds any, I'm gonna have Randy discipline ya. Randy, come on over here and show these boys your disciplinin' tool."

King walked over to Roth and Kennedy, and when he was about four feet away, he paused and drew out his Khukuri from his neck scabbard. He held the knife in front of them, letting the sun catch on its blade. Kennedy watched the knife. He had seen too many knives in Newark and he was more afraid of them than he was of guns, but he had never seen a knife like this one. He hiked up his pant leg revealing the Walther PPKS he had strapped to his calf.

"Sorry Commander," he said.

Bosheers frisked them, then searched their packs. He found an H&K MP5 in each one. Bosheers left them there but removed their magazines and their chambered rounds.

"Get their sat phone, Randy. Don't want the Commander there doin' anythin' tricky with it. Everythin' OK, Howland?"

"Yeah, they're good boys now," said Bosheers, bringing Roth's and Kennedy's military IDs to Barlow.

"OK, Commander Roth, y'all and Master Sergeant Kennedy are gonna take a little stroll with us. Shoulder your packs and don't forget Randy's Khukuri while yer thinkin' of ways ta get out of this predicament ya got yerself inta."

Roth was hoping he could stall for some time, but he doubted he could drag out any ruse that would fill in the time before Lollard and Wade got to them. They'd just have to go along with these three and watch for an opportunity.

Thirty-Four

2:20 p.m. July 10th, 2011:

Niles and Teal found Roth and Kennedy on their final sweep of the mountainside. Their hamstrings had been cut and they had been seriously concussed. They were lying amid the lower reaches of a glacial drift in a thicket of alders. They were still alive, but unconscious. Niles called Keagan.

"Mick, everything all right where you are?"

"Yeah, what's the matter?"

"Teal and I found two guys with their heads bashed in and their hamstrings cut. It wasn't an accident."

Keagan described the two men he had seen on the boat – a black man and the one Kelly identified as the sailor.

Niles confirmed his descriptions.

"What do the cuts look like?"

Niles examined them more carefully. "Very clean, almost surgical."

"That would the Gurhka's work, then." Keagan described King and Bosheers.

"I haven't seen them yet, but I'm thinking that, even though we've had some eliminations from a couple of teams' rosters, it's still pretty crowded up here. We got two pug uglies, who are probably the ones that killed Musaiyib's friend, and two Takavaran that were part of the team that O'Dea and his boys rounded up. And then we got the two that I saw, probably the remnants of the Task Force."

"I think there's another one, Niles. If I'm right, he's with the *villains*, the ones you referred to as the pug uglies. I suspect he's the brains; a smooth Southern boy."

"Have you found Musaiyib yet?"

"Yeah, I found where he's camped. I suspect he's going for the seals tomorrow, otherwise, there'd be no reason to set up camp. So far, it's quiet up here."

"What do you want me to do with these two? They need medical attention, and they sure as hell aren't going to be walking out on their own."

"See what you can do about their wounds and make them as comfortable as you can. If they wake up, find out what happened. I'll get back to you as soon as I scout around up here."

* * *

Lollard had been trying to reach Commander Roth for five minutes now without success. He and Wade were about where Roth had told them to leave the trail. They cut into the woods and headed east. Lollard stopped when they were about two hundred yards off the trail. He tried Roth one more time to establish the obvious.

"We got a problem, Bo. If the Commander were going dark, he'd have told us. If he got injured, Wes would have let us know. Somebody's gotten to them."

"Can you get a GPS reading on their sat phone?"

"I should be able to, but I'm getting nothing. Time to break out the heavy shit."

Lollard and Wade got their H&K MP5s and four extra magazines from their packs. Lollard checked his GPS.

"Let's leave the packs here and go find Roth and Kennedy."

Lollard took out a small notebook and wrote down N48.94085 W113.88962, the coordinates of where they were.

"Socko, why don't you just establish a waypoint on your GPS?" asked Wade.

"I did, Bo. This is just backup. OK, we can't separate because we have no way of getting in touch with each other."

"Did you try your cell?" asked Wade.

"Yeah, no bars," said Lollard.

"Silly me," said Wade. "How do you want to do this, then?"

"The Commander said he thought Musaiyib was headed for Mount Cleveland, and that he wanted to try this creek here," Lollard pointed to Cleveland Creek on his map, "as their approach. If Musaiyib hid the seals on Mount Cleveland, it would make sense. Let's head over that way, but if we haven't found any sign of them, by the time we get here," Lollard pointed to the first of a tight group of contour lines that told them where Cleveland really became a mountain. "Let's move south and see if we can cross their tracks. Make sure we stay in sight of each other, though, and stay alert. If Roth and Kennedy ran into unfriendlies, they might still be around."

* * *

Keagan had climbed about a half mile above Musaiyib's camp. It was the only place where his site was visible. He had chosen well. *Musaiyib's a city boy*, thought Keagan, *but maybe even city boys who spend their whole lives living under a dictatorship learn survival techniques, or at least, the smart ones might.*

"Musaiyib's still in his camp. He seems to be praying, so, probably *Magbrib*," said Keagan when he made his way back to where Kelly was. "Any movement near you?"

"No, I pretty much did what you did on this side of the first rock band. Not so much as a deer down there. Either that, or whoever is following is awfully good."

"Oh, they're good, Kelly. You can bet on that. I don't know how a bunch of grunts managed to track Musaiyib, not only to Montreal, but also to this mountain. But they must have had professional help, unless they were in the Signal Corps, that is. That they did, speaks to their skill."

"I've got to call Niles. You have any ideas about how we deal with two Task Force casualties?"

"What happened to them?" asked Kelly.

Keagan filled her in.

"Call Niles and get an update on their condition, but if they're alive, he has to call it in. On TV, the hero may suffer a concussion, snap out of it, shake his head, and be good to go out and fight any number of bad guys, but you've delivered enough concussions to know how serious they can be."

"And I remember how Eamon 'Fibber' McGee rang my bell the first time we met."

Keagan was referring to the only fight he ever lost. McGee knocked him out in the fourth round, when his manager had moved him along too fast. In their second meeting, Keagan knocked out McGee in the second round, but he remembered the bell-ringing. He remembered the nausea, blurred vision, and loss of balance that he experienced for the next three days.

"Yeah, that's what I came up with, too, but I was hoping you could invoke the fairies to produce some preternatural solution that was beyond me."

Keagan tapped Niles' number on his contact list. Niles didn't answer.

* * *

Musaiyib had finished with *Magbrib*. Confident that his campsite was all but invisible, except from above, he ventured out of the hanging col. It had been almost two years since he had hidden the seals, and he wanted to re-familiarize himself with the mountain face and locate the approach to the route he had taken then. He didn't dare expose himself on the scree and bare rock above until he had to, but he did need to see what lay before him.

He had hidden the seals at the end of August in 2009. In early July, there was much more snow. He knew there would be, but he wasn't prepared for what he found when the forest thinned out. Actually, he was prepared; he had the equipment to do what he had to do, but this was going to be his first time, alone, climbing on ice and snow, and Mount Cleveland had the longest vertical drop of any mountain in the Lower Forty-Eight. His first obstacle was the waterfall that cascaded down the center of the cliff face. He'd never get across it from where he stood. He followed the run-off down to where it met Cleveland Creek and continued down to a spot where he found a herd path that looked like it led over to the Goat Haunt approach to the mountain. Of course, it could be the approach that grizzlies took to feed on the army moth larvae and ladybugs that thrived in abundance on Cleveland's summit.

Musaiyib followed the herd path for about three-quarters of a mile to a spot that felt familiar. This was the approach; he was sure of it. From there, he'd have a four thousand foot vertical ascent.

* * *

Niles raised his hand. Teal had heard the sound, too. They both faded backwards into the alders and, when they were far enough away from Roth and Kennedy for Niles' liking, they stopped.

"Human?" asked Teal.

"My guess would be their mates. Wouldn't make sense for the thugs who did that to them to revisit. Let's circle behind them, but be very quiet. Our competition are pros," said Niles.

Teal had spent enough time in the Atchafalaya Swamp to know how to be quiet. Niles and Teal met up again, this time about fifty yards behind Lollard and Wade, who had put down their MP5s to attend to Roth and Kennedy, but still had their side arms within reach.

"Step away from the H&Ks and don't even think of reaching for your side arms. Don't think about it. Do it or we'll cut you down," ordered Niles.

Wade began to back up, but Lollard turned to see what he was facing.

"Did you do this?" asked Lollard.

"No, but I need to know who you are. Remove your side arms from their holsters, two fingers only."

Wade looked at Lollard.

"Don't think; do it," repeated Niles. They both did. "Now step toward me five paces. Teal, gather up their weapons."

He brought the guns over to Niles. "Empty them." Teal ejected all four of the magazines and cleared the chambered rounds.

"You want me to search them, Niles?"

"No, I know these two have other weapons, but I'm going to ask them a few questions before I decide whether or not I'm going to shoot them."

Teal looked nervous, Niles gestured for them to sit. "OK, who are you?"

Wade was waiting for Lollard's cue. He had his Ka-BaR in a calf scabbard, but he didn't think he could get to it fast enough to be effective.

"I might ask the same question of you two," said Lollard.

"You might, but you're not holding the guns. We are, and I've got a life and death decision to make, so I'd give serious thought to answering my question," said Niles.

Lollard was pretty sure these two hadn't been the ones to bang up Roth and Kennedy; otherwise, this one wouldn't be asking questions.

"I am Staff Sergeant Ian Lollard. My friend here is Gunnery Sergeant Bo Wade. The two unconscious ones are our mates. We're with a coalition task force on a mission to recover stolen antiquities from the National Museum of Iraq. Now if that satisfies your curiosity, I'd like to attend to them," said Lollard.

"I already have," said Niles. "Their hamstrings have been cut, and they have serious head wounds. I've done as much as I can do, so unless you're a doctor, probably as much as you can do as well. But you're welcome to have a look, after you drop whatever other weapons you're carrying."

"Do it, Bo," said Lollard who was already reaching for his Ka-BaR and his H&K P2000 SK.

Lollard agreed with Niles' assessment of Roth and Kennedy's condition.

"OK, so what do we do now?" asked Lollard.

"Depends on you," answered Niles.

"I need to know who you are and what part you're playing in this," said Lollard.

"You don't need to know who I am, but the second part's easy. My friend and I are after the same thing you are, but for different reasons. We didn't do that to your mates, so that means there's another unit in on this. I suggest that you use your sat phone to call in an emergency medical airlift for them and let us deal with whoever did this."

"And the cylinder seals?"

"They're ours, part of the deal," said Niles.

"You think you two can handle the ones who did this, and find the seals?" asked Lollard.

"Found them and handled you, didn't we? And you're SAS, right? How difficult can the others be?" said Niles.

"Yeah, I thought so. I don't need to have the first question answered. I know who you are. *Who dares wins*, right?"

"Sounds like a good philosophy to me," said Niles.

Lollard smiled. Wade was confused.

"How do you want to handle this?" asked Lollard.

"Call in two injured hikers. See what they say. Then we'll take it from there."

Lollard called in a medical emergency. Told the operator that there were two unconscious hikers on the lower slope of Mount

Cleveland with serious head and leg injuries, who required immediate rescue. He gave the operator the coordinates where the two were located and then rang off.

"They can scramble a helicopter in no time, but it can't land any closer than the ranger station at the south end of Waterton Lake, from there it's going to be ATVs and guys hauling stretchers from the trail up to here. ETA is at least an hour, but more like two."

"Well, they're warm and not in any pain, so as long as they can hold out till they get to the chopper, they should be all right. I'll leave them in your care. We got our own things to take care of."

"Let me come with you; Bo can watch them. I can help," said Lollard.

"I know you can, Socko, but then we might have a disagreement over the possession of the seals. Wouldn't be good. Spend the time thinking up some story that won't sic the rangers on us. We got enough to deal with in this goatfuck."

Lollard smiled.

* * *

"What happened down there, Niles?" asked Keagan.

Niles updated him on Roth and Kennedy's condition and the presence of Lollard and Wade.

"You think they'll make it?"

"Yeah, they won't be running around for a long while, and they'll have killer headaches for, maybe, a couple of weeks, but unless there was internal damage that I couldn't see, I think they'll be all right. Might limp for the rest of their lives, but they're young and in good shape. Physical therapy will probably get them back most of the way," added Niles.

"What about the other two? Will they keep their end of the bargain?" asked Kelly.

"I think so. They won't come after us. Whether they can make the rangers believe their buddies got hurt in an accident or, failing that, keep them from coming after us, is another question. In either event, we'll know shortly," said Niles.

* **

The helicopter had already arrived at the ranger station. The rangers would ride ATVs to the spot where they'd have to start bushwhacking, but that's where the time-consuming part would begin, especially when they had to start carrying two wounded men down Cleveland's slope.

The helicopter had made a pass of the lower slope of Mount Cleveland; however, the pilot was just checking the coordinates Lollard had given him to see if there were any places he could land closer to the injured men. He hadn't come up the mountain looking for others. Once the pilot knew where the injured were and that there were no other landing options closer than the foot of Waterton Lake, he flew back to the ranger station and waited there.

"They won't come, Kelly. One of them, the English one, even saluted Niles," said Teal.

Kelly still had her doubts.

Niles wistfully stared off toward Olson Mountain across the Waterton Valley.

Keagan nodded to himself.

"Any sign of the *villains*, Mick?" asked Niles.

"No, and I don't like that. I found Musaiyib; I should be able to find them. And I'm not so naïve as to think that after three years, they've given up because they've run into some competition. They're still down there somewhere, probably no more than a half mile away," speculated Keagan.

Kelly stayed where she was hidden in a boulder field on the right side of Cleveland Creek. Keagan went to check that Musaiyib hadn't decamped. Teal went to familiarize himself with the climbing route, and Niles scouted the area for unfriendlies. Two hours later, all three had returned.

"Well," asked Kelly, "what did you *boyos* find out there?"

"Musaiyib is still in place, which I have to believe means that, either the cylinder seals are up on the face of Cleveland somewhere, or he really did just come here for the climbing and we're on a wild goose chase," answered Keagan.

"Niles?"

"No sign of the *villains*. I ran across a number of tracks, some of which might well have been theirs, but they aren't camped down there. The good news is, the Coalition guys seem to have kept their word. I didn't find any sign of activity lower down. There were no rangers, no Coalition guys, no left-over Takavaran, and not even any civilians."

"I doubt it," said Keagan.

"You don't like that all our competition has been eliminated?" questioned Kelly.

"I can't believe they have," said Keagan. "Yeah, it makes sense that between O'Dea and company and the rangers, that all of the Taka-varan have been hauled away. And I don't have any problem believing that the Task Force soldiers have retreated owing to injuries. But that the *villains* who went through the trouble of killing Awwal in Iraq, tracking down Musaiyib to Montreal, killing one, or as many as three, of his neighbors, and getting on the boat with us this morning, decided to call it quits because of, what? What could have been so intimidating as to have driven them off?" asked Keagan.

"Maybe, I can answer that," said Teal. "When I was checking out the climbing route for tomorrow, I saw what looked like some disturbance – a kind of mini-slide in the shale. Not much, but it could have made by three or four people walking through it. What if they aren't below us? What if they're above us?"

"Of course, how stupid of me," said Keagan.

"You can't think of everything, Mick," said Kelly.

"I know, but for me to rule out an option, to assume they could only be below us…I'm always raising hell with the inn staff for putting limitations on things, and that's exactly what I did. Shit."

"Yes, well, have any one of the three of you found us a good place to make camp in your travels?" asked Kelly.

"I have," said Teal.

"Where's that, Teal? Bunking with Musaiyib or with the *villains*? I would have thought they might have taken all the good places," said Kelly.

"I found a cave, a fissure actually, just above the scree field, fifty yards or so off the approach to one of the assault routes recommended by Edwards in his *Climber's Guide to Glacier National Park*."

"When did you read that?" asked Keagan.

"Remember when you told us the story of that little fella, the wolverine?"

"M3, yeah," filled in Keagan.

"Well, I was so impressed with the little fella, I wanted to see the route he might have taken, so I looked it up on the Internet. I read the story and I found the reference to Edward's book."

"Assault route? Is that a climber or military expression?" asked Niles.

"Climber. Anyway, unless Musaiyib is going to cut way south to pick up the Camp Creek route Edwards described, which makes no sense, he'll have to come right by there. Not so close that he's going to spot us, but close enough that we should be able to hear him or anybody else that goes by."

"Teal, when you say cave, what exactly do you mean? Remember two years ago in the salt mine? Mick and I aren't at our best in caves or tunnels, or in any underground enclosure really," said Kelly.

Kelly was referring to an earlier project together on the Louisiana coast when they gained access to an armed compound through a defunct tunnel in a salt mine. The experience brought up memories of their both being held prisoner by the Ulster Constabulary in a five-by-five-by-five dark pit. Keagan was there for five days, and Kelly for eight.

"No, nothing like that, Kelly. It's not really a cave. It's a crack in the rock face and, in time, a very long time, Kelly, enough rubble has built up along its sides that anyone who didn't know it was there wouldn't be able to see it. The front is open. It's about twelve to fifteen feet deep. There's plenty of room inside for the four of us."

"OK, let's take a look at it," said Kelly.

The cave was as Teal described it. It overlooked the route that the contours of the mountain pretty much dictated. Kelly felt comfortable with it, and so did Keagan, whose claustrophobia was less acute than Kelly's, perhaps, because he had been held in the pit for three fewer days than she had.

When they made camp, Keagan asked Teal whether he was able to bring it. The 'it' he referred to was his Smith & Wesson 460XVR. Keagan wasn't sure TSA would let it on the plane, even though it allowed guns in checked baggage as long as they were declared, but the 460XVR was equipped with a 2.5x8 variable-power scope, a fourteen inch fluted barrel with a muzzle break, and a bi-pod. It was a scary-looking weapon that looked more like a ray gun than a sporting handgun. The XVR stood for *extreme velocity revolver*, and it was that. The .460 S&W Magnum performed more like a rifle caliber than one fired from a handgun. It was the flattest shooting handgun round ever, which made it accurate out to two hundred yards, and packed fifty percent more stopping power than Dirty Harry's .44 Magnum.

"No problem. Well, the guy who examined it stared at it for a while and called over his shift buddies to look at it, but I told them I was moving to Montana and would be using it for hunting elk in the fall," said Teal.

After a cold supper – they were far enough away from Musaiyib's camp, but Keagan was afraid that if the *villains* were above them, they might just catch a whiff of their cooking – Keagan went down below to stake out Musaiyib's camp. Niles took first watch at the cave.

Thirty-Five

Musaiyib was up at 5:00 a.m. He said *Fajr* and made a quick breakfast. When he was finished, he doubled checked his pack and made sure he had all the equipment he would need for the day. His camp was situated at a little over 6,000 feet above sea level. Mount Cleveland's summit was 10,466 feet high. Musaiyib had hidden the seals in a greenish-gray canister, anchored deeply in a fracture of a rock band at 9,422 feet. He had about four thousand vertical feet to climb to reach the seals because he had to drop down more than five hundred feet to where he could safely cross the cascade of melt that poured off the Cleveland's rock face this time of the year. He could have avoided that redundancy but then he would have compromised his security.

Keagan had bivouacked above him. All he had brought with him was a sleeping bag and pad. He was glad it hadn't rained during the night. He called Niles to tell him Musaiyib was up and would, shortly, be on the move.

Niles and Teal readied their equipment, while Kelly made a quick breakfast of oatmeal – boiling water didn't smell – laced with some of the Niles' Craisons. The honey still wouldn't flow. No coffee or tea, though; they did smell. When they had eaten, Teal went out to check the approach again. He couldn't see any other likely route from this side of the mountain, or not unless Musaiyib was a much better climber than he was.

If I'm right, thought Teal, *Musaiyib will have to pass by here about fifty yards below us.* After scoping the mountainside for a half hour, he went back to the cave to wait. There wasn't much else he could do until Keagan called again.

* * *

Barlow and King were looking at the area map Bartow had bought in Calgary.

"Are you sure this is where we should be, Randy?"

"We're here." King indicated their location on the map. "According to this map there are four possible routes up Cleveland: one from Stoney Indian Pass, one from the Camp Creek access where we are, one from Goat Haunt, and this one from Cleveland Creek. We know roughly where he left the trail, so Cleveland Creek is the only route that makes sense."

"Yeah, if he's up here at all," said Barlow.

"Unless he got cold feet and went back, he's got to be on this mountain."

"Why aren't we over there, then?" asked Bosheers.

"What? With the rangers' helicopter and who knows how many searchers? No, he'll come up here and we'll intersect his route approximately here." King indicated a spot on the map roughly 2,300 feet above them and due north.

"How do we know that he didn't bury them in the woods someplace and he's already dug 'em up?" asked Barlow.

"He had a climbing rope lashed onto his pack, not a shovel."

"How are we going to know when he's startin' out?" asked Bosheers.

"Doesn't matter. We don't want to get there too early because we want to let him get the seals, then take them away from him. Up there, there's no cover. We'll be able to spot him. He can't be in better shape than us. It won't be a problem."

* * *

Musaiyib had left his tent, sleeping bag, and cooking equipment in camp, as though he had every intention of following his schedule of returning to Waterton on one of tomorrow's boats. Keagan found it hard to believe that he was oblivious of everything that was happening around him.

Possible, thought Keagan, *but not probable.*

Musaiyib followed the right fork of Cleveland Creek, passed where it met the left fork, then he crossed over and followed the left fork, which headed almost straight south. This bearing brought him to Cleveland's west bowl at about 6,000 feet, which was about level with his camp, but a half mile south. Ahead, Musaiyib could see Cleveland's cliff face slightly tilted back at less than fifteen degrees off perpendicular.

This was where the real climb began. Keagan had neither seen nor heard anything of the *villains,* which continued to worry him. He knew they had to be out there. They were seasoned troops; it wasn't likely that they were lost. Keagan called Niles again.

"Musaiyib is starting up the face. He should be going by you in twenty to thirty minutes. I'm out of my element here, so I'll let you and Teal pick him up. Probably, it's best not to get too close to him until he retrieves the seals. I'll be coming up behind you. Unless there's anything else, let me talk to Kelly," said Keagan.

"Where are you, Mick?" asked Kelly.

"I'm about three hundred yards behind Musaiyib, who should go by you in less than thirty minutes. You'll be all right by yourself?"

"Sure, I'd rather be with you, but you're right, I'd only be keeping you back. Niles and Teal need you more than I. Well, right now, that is. We're at that point where all that we've done so far means nothing if we can't get this last bit right. Where any number of things could go wrong, and we can't plan for a one of them because they'll all be surprises. I shouldn't be adding to those surprises," said Kelly.

"So, you're all right handling crowd control?" asked Keagan.

"It shouldn't be a problem. I doubt there are any other parties nearer than the Kootenai Lakes campsites, which means you'll have a good lead on any others coming up the mountain today. I don't know what I'll do if some others come along, but I'll think of something to stall them. You just be safe, Mick."

"I'll do my best, Kelly. If Teal's wrong and the *villains* are still below us, let me know when they pass, but keep well out of sight. I don't want you taking any chances. If they come, let them pass. We'll deal with them."

"OK, Mick."

* * *

To Musaiyib's left, was the cataract of glacial melt that cascaded down the center of Cleveland's cliff face. On his right, was the western bowl that led to a scree slope that was partially covered by hard-packed snow. Later in the day, this would be a dicey route because the sun's radiation would have warmed the top half foot or so to mush, or worse, would have created soft spots to the rubble below. Musaiyib made good progress across the hard pack.

Above the snowfield was a shallow run-off trench that hugged a buttress, a steep rock face, that offered access to a chimney. Teal watched him from behind an outcropping in front of the cave mouth. Had Musaiyib had Keagan's proximity sense, he would have realized that he was edging about a hundred and fifty feet below the cave where Kelly and Niles and Teal waited for him to pass by. Of course, if he did have Keagan's proximity sense, he also would have realized that someone was camped just above him last night, and he would have more than likely changed his plans.

The chimney that Musaiyib entered above the team's cave led to the top of the first and tallest rock band. It was partially snow-filled, but Musaiyib was able to negotiate it by kicking footholds into the packed snow and using his swing tool to cut hand holds. He was wearing boots now, not the new climbing shoes he had bought last week. He'd probably need them later, though. He didn't think there would be this much snow still. Snowfields, yes, but he thought the chimneys would be open.

The chimney climb was made easier by a couple of climbers who had preceded him in the last few days. All he had to do was square off what the melt had rounded. Musaiyib briefly wondered if the ones who came before him were the ones who had killed Awwal and Maloaf. It didn't really matter now; there was nothing he could do. He was committed to retrieving the seals. To leave them buried would defile Awwal's and Maloaf's memories. His fate was with Allah.

Chimneys, even snow-filled ones, if they weren't coursing water or weren't *verglassed*, were easier to free-climb than both scree slopes and steep, bare rock faces. They had three sides to them and, because snow and ice filled them in winter, the chimneys provided plenty of hand and foot holds created by eons of frost wedging.

When the chimney became *verglassed*, Musaiyib scrambled out onto a slab of exposed rock, which, though steeper, was clear of ice and snow. He should have changed his boots for his climbing shoes there, but he didn't want to take the time to make the switch. Musaiyib usually didn't take chances, which in climbing, like any potentially lethal sport, would eventually kill you. But in his calculations, there was the feeling that there might be others behind, who would certainly kill him if he let them catch up.

In this second chimney, Musaiyib realized that he must have taken a different route than he had when he hid the seals, because this approach seemed much easier. If this series of chimneys continued, he wouldn't need the new rope he bought until he had to traverse Cleveland's face to the fissure where he had hidden the seals.

The sides of this chimney were snow free, because it got more direct sunlight. He didn't have to kick or cut any holds here. There were plenty of both hand and foot holds on its sides, so that it was like climbing up two slightly separated ladders. Because the chimney was narrow, when he got tired, he just wedged himself against the opposite wall and rested.

* * *

Niles and Teal were one chimney behind Musaiyib. Their chimney ended in a buttress that didn't have an erosion trench or a gully that circumscribed it, so the only way around it was up and over. Teal led the way, pointing out to Niles where the handholds and footholds were. Teal had made it to the top of the buttress and was pointing out the last series of holds to Niles. Niles saw where Teal was pointing, but because of their height difference, he opted for a handhold several inches above it. He was pulling himself up when the choss, rotten rock, broke off in his grip. When the rock broke off, Niles' feet slipped off their holds, as well. The footholds hadn't been secure, but there hadn't been any others. He would have been fine if the rock hadn't crumbled in his hand. The slip had also dislodged his left-hand hold, so that now, he was no longer gripping the outcropping, but his fist was jammed into a small crack to the left of the outcropping that had been supporting him. This was his sole contact with the mountain.

Teal didn't bother asking if he was all right; it was plain that he was in serious trouble, and suspended by one hand off the side of a steep rock face. If his left hand gave out, his next contact with mother earth would be when he bounced 500 feet below.

"Hold on, buddy. I'm coming down."

Niles was now twisted around so that he was facing away from the cliff face. All he could see was the mountain range across the Waterton Valley. As Teal got closer, he realized he couldn't reach him, and, even if he could, he saw that they were no holds secure enough for him to pull up Niles, even if he were strong enough. He couldn't even see where to direct him. The angle of the face was almost perpendicular.

"How's your grip?"

"No fear of falling. I'm not gripping the rock, I'm jammed into it. If I can't find another hold, I'll be here till the eagles find me. Go back up where it's safer. I'm going to try something."

Teal stayed where he was.

"Niles, I can't see enough of the cliff face to tell you where to reach, but if possible, the first thing you need to do is turn yourself around so you're facing the rock. Can you push off with you right foot?"

"I'll give it a go."

Niles made a couple of tentative pushes, gauging the torque he'd need to twist himself around so that he was facing the rock again. Pushing himself straight off the face would just bring him straight back. What he needed to do was extend his right leg with enough angle to turn his arm. He tried it…and his wrist ground in the crack.

He tried it again…and again, the wrist ground against the rock. Niles rested for twenty seconds. The theory was sound, but he wasn't generating enough torque. He slid his right leg across the cliff face, hoping to find something solid to push off. Nothing. He repeated the maneuver, this time, though, he brought his leg up higher. He pushed off hard. *Not quite.* He rested for, maybe, twenty seconds.

His left wrist was pretty raw. Niles raised his right leg again, and slid his foot across the rock. *Got it.* He rocked…one…two…three! He was coming around. *Almost!* Niles rested. He found the brace point again. It was the same as last time, only harder. He piston-kicked off the push, his body twisting and head ducking. *Don't queer it all by bouncing off your left arm. There! Got it!* Niles grabbed hold, with his right hand now, of the outcropping he had been holding onto with his left hand. Now, he had to find a foothold or he would still be stuck. He felt all around him, but his feet found nothing useful. He raised his right leg as high as he could. Nothing. *Now, the left. There's something. No, lost it. Do it again. There it is. Square your foot on it before you test it. Hold, you bastard. There. Push down. Up we go.*

He raised himself enough to dislodge his left wrist from the crack where it had been jammed. Both hands now gripped the outcropping, though Niles couldn't feel much in his left hand.

He took his time and found a more solid foothold, and then another.

"I'm back in solid contact, Teal. I'll be with you in a moment."

"I didn't think you'd be able to get back on the rock," said Teal.

"I hope we aren't too far from Musaiyib and his goddamn seals. This mountain is beginning to use up its amusement potential."

Gradually, he inched up the last few feet of the buttress. When Niles got to where he could stop and rest for a moment, he had Teal get the first aide kit out of his pack, and wash and dress his raw left wrist.

"How's that feel?"

"Better. I felt like a bloody fool, suspended there, and looking very much like one of those orangutans I saw when I was in SAS training in Borneo. I've got more feeling now, though. Starting to burn a little. I guess that's the blood rushing back in. I don't think anything is broken or dislocated. I'll probably need custom-made shirts now, though; my left arm seems stretched out a bit."

"Everything else OK? How about the legs and the lungs?"

"They're fine. Oh, I can tell that I haven't done anything like this in a few years, so I'm discovering muscles I'd forgotten. I'll be sore in the morning, but I'll work it out."

Teal couldn't believe it. He had been with seasoned rock climbers who had found themselves in trouble, but not nearly as dire as the predicament Niles had just extricated himself from. And those people had frozen, and had to be prised off the mountain. He knew about some of Niles' experiences in the SAS, but here he was jammed into a crack, hanging off the side of a very high mountain by one arm. He couldn't see where he's supposed to reach, but he had to trust that there was someplace. *And now he's sitting here, making light of the experience*, Teal thought.

* * *

"This should put us on his route," said King. They had worked their way north from Camp Creek, where the climbing was easier.

"Howland, glass the cliff face above us. Randy, cover below us," said Barlow.

Bosheers spotted Musaiyib after about three minutes of systematically scanning the cliff face, left-to-right and top-to-bottom.

"There he is. At least, I think it is. Somebody's up there."

"Where, Howland?"

"Three-quarters of the way up, just to the left of our position, and movin' right-ta-left."

Bosheers handed Barlow his field glasses. "OK, yeah, I got him. Shit!"

"What?" said King.

"Looks like he's got two others tailin' him," said Barlow.

"Where, Joe Pete?" asked King.

"See where that one climber is?"

"Yeah."

"Go ta the right, and a coupla hundred feet below him. There's a crack there in the mountain. They're in that crack, near the top," said Barlow.

It took King a minute or so to locate Niles and Teal.

"I got 'em."

"You figure they're the rest of that Coalition team?" said Bosheers.

"Shit, I don't know. I didn't figured on the others findin' them. I guess that's what that helicopter was doing up here yesterday afternoon. Still, I would have thought, dead or alive, their buddies woulda gone out with 'em."

"You think they got reinforcements comin' up behind 'em, Joe Pete?" asked Bosheers.

"I don't know, Howland."

"Maybe we oughta pack it in, Joe Pete," said Bosheers.

"Randy, what do you think about that?" asked Barlow, more to see where he stood than whether they should quit.

"I don't know, Joe Pete. This thing has been a clusterfuck from the start," said King.

"Well, y'all and Howland can do what ya want, but I didn't go through all the shit we've been through, just ta quit less than a thousand feet from $25 million dollars. Besides, we handled them other two easily. These boys can't be much tougher," said Barlow.

* * *

Atop the fourth rock band, Musaiyib made a short traverse to his left to get onto the main west-facing precipice. Cleveland's face was scalloped. The route he needed to take was on the western-most curve of the rock face. He had been climbing steadily on the rock for almost three hours, and had gained close to two thousand vertical feet. He rested there, drinking water and snacking on high-energy power bars. It was almost nine o'clock now, and the sun was radiating off the glaciers and the snow fields. The mountain was heating up.

He had been setting a good pace and he needed to rest, but he couldn't stay immobile too long or his legs would stiffen up, which was something he couldn't afford on a pitch like the next one. Musaiyib checked the altitude on his GPS. If it was accurate, he was about seven hundred feet below where he had hidden the seals, although, he'd have to traverse quite a ways off the main route to retrieve them. He was seventeen hundred feet below the summit. He took off his pack and untied his new climbing shoes from the chain loops atop his pack where he had lashed them, exchanging them for the boots he had been wearing. He retrieved his climbing harness from the pack's back pocket and stepped into it. He would be face climbing from here to the seals. There would be no more crack climbing. From here on, he'd be using finger holds and smearing and edging, so nothing solid. He experimented with the shoes' lace tension. When he was satisfied, he removed his fleece jacket, stowed it in his pack, and resumed his ascent.

He was on his final approach now, climbing the last seven hundred feet. He found another shallow, dry trench that hugged a buttress. He edged around it, gaining another three hundred feet. Then, he found a short crevice that led to the top of a rock band that was narrowly ledged at its top. The ledge, about two feet wide, ramped up to the mouth of the fracture, four hundred yards away.

* * *

Teal and Niles watched Musaiyib from near the top of the fourth rock band, where Musaiyib began his traverse. They welcomed the wait. They, like Musaiyib, drank some water and ate some of Niles' high-energy, homemade gorp.

"How's your hand?" asked Teal.

Teal didn't ask him how he was dealing with the height. If Niles hadn't been spooked by hanging suspended from a buttress face by one fist, he probably had everything under control. In the four years he had known Niles, he had never seen anything scare him. Teal had learned last year of Keagan's and Kelly's claustrophobia, though, and he had never seen anything scare either of them before they went into that mine. While their fear was rooted in reality, fear was more often irrational.

The wind had picked up now that the sun was high. Neither one of them relished the open-face climbing they'd need to do to keep up with Musaiyib. They changed their footwear. Teal had remembered what Keagan had said about Mount Cleveland when the team met in his shop to make last-minute plans, so he had brought his climbing shoes. Niles didn't have any, but he did bring his running shoes. They'd have to do.

"Let's go, Niles. Musaiyib is getting up there."

They both stood. "Ah, shit. I knew it was too good to be true," said Niles, more to himself than to Teal, but loud enough for Teal to hear him.

"What?" he said, although Teal had a good idea what initiated the expletive.

"The *villains* have finally made their appearance. They must have found their own cave on the cliff face and been following us, following Musaiyib. I wonder where Mick is in this queue?" said Niles.

Niles called Keagan.

"Mick, the *villains* have arrived."

"Where?" asked Keagan.

"We're near the top of a chimney that leads up to a big snowfield on the right. Musaiyib is three hundred feet above us, working his way up a crevice to the left of our position. He's wide open," said Niles.

"I see him. Where are the *villains*?" asked Keagan.

"About five hundred vertical feet below us."

"Have they seen you yet?" asked Keagan.

"Good question. I don't know. My guess is, they came in from our right, and figured they'd bisect Musaiyib's route, well away from the rescuers. But I've got to believe that they've spotted Musaiyib by now, whether they've seen us yet, is another matter."

"What do you want me to do?" asked Keagan.

"Depends. Where are you?"

"I'm about three hundred yards, distance not vertical, below the chimney they're in, if I'm reading you right. I can't see them from here," said Keagan.

"The way I read this is, we have three choices. We can wait here and either shoot them, or hold them off at gun point when they get closer, but I've got to believe they are armed as well...wait a second." Niles put down the sat phone and reached in his pack for his binoculars. "They don't seem to have any long guns. OK, we can wait here for them, but then nobody's following Musaiyib. Or I can send Teal ahead, or we both can follow Musaiyib and face off with the *villains* after we've gotten the cylinder seals from him. They shouldn't be too much of a threat if all they have are handguns, especially if you can cover us. Plus, I don't think they'll do anything until Musaiyib retrieves the seals," said Niles.

"Do what you think is safest. Whatever choice you make, I'll follow your play, but leave your phone on. Can you rig it so your hands are free?" asked Keagan.

"Yeah, I think so."

* * *

"Randy, ya have any idea where Musaiyib's headin'?" asked Barlow.

King put the field glasses on Musaiyib and scanned ahead of him.

"Well, there's a fracture to the left of him and about three hundred feet up. That would be my guess."

"Can he get off this mountain by continuin' on in the direction he's headin'?"

"I can't say, because I haven't seen that side of the cliff face. It could be a knife edge, which I don't think he could handle. Remember what Lévesque said about him; he's good because he works at it, but he hasn't been at it more than a couple of years. But, shit, he gotten this far on his own. What are you thinking, Joe Pete?"

"Howland, when do ya think we should take the two followin' Musaiyib?"

"Well, depends if they follow Musaiyib out onta the rock. If they don't go out there, they might just be some recreational climbers. If they do go out there, though, I think we've got no choice but ta follow them. Hearin' what Randy just said, I think we better follow them. Otherwise, they could just disappear over the far edge."

"Joe Pete, what if them fuckers got MP5s like the other two had? We're at a disadvantage. Maybe we shoulda taken 'em."

"Too late now fer *what ifs*. Kinda hard ta explain if we got stopped and searched. We're carrin' handguns because we're in bear and mountain lion country. Besides, all I saw on them were day packs.

Could be big enough fer MP5s. We'll just have ta see. Let's hold back behind that outcroppin' and see what they do. I'm guessin' they don't know what's on the other side of this cliff face, either, so they'll follow Musaiyib out there. We should have a better idea of armament, then. Hell, them guys don't know who we are. Maybe we should play dumb and act like we're just climbin' a mountain."

* * *

Musaiyib had gained another three hundred vertical feet, and was now traversing the cliff face to his left, inching along, crimping with his finger tips, and edging on the ledge. He still seemed unaware of any other presence on the mountain. Teal and Niles were doing their best to shorten the distance between them. They scrambled up the gully faster than they should have.

They were on the ledge now. The ledge was about two feet wide there, which was more than enough to accommodate a sober walker or one without impaired proprioception. However, raise that footpath just ten feet and curiously, the same path seemed much narrower. Raise it three thousand feet, and it became a knife edge. Curiously, too, the wind had picked up with the sun's rising, and, while they barely noticed it in the chimney, here on the open cliff face, it seemed to rage.

Niles wondered if he shouldn't have stayed behind in the chimney and held off the *villains* from there. There was nothing for it, now. He followed Teal out onto the ledge. They had decided that they couldn't take the chance that Musaiyib might retrieve the seals and then keep going over the far edge or over the summit. It didn't look like there was any other route down, except back the way he had come, but they couldn't take the chance that there was. Periodically, Niles looked down to locate the *villains*. They, too, seemed to be doing their best to cut their distance to Musaiyib. Keagan was out of sight.

The ledge narrowed to a point where Musaiyib didn't feel safe free climbing. He removed his pack and loosed the two straps that held his climbing rope. Next, he removed his rock hammer from its loop, and then, the ring of hardware from where he had lashed it to the vertical loops that daisy chained along his pack sides. He unclipped two stoppers from his rack, slotted the first in a constriction in the crack above and then wedged the second just below the first. Then he equalized them with a little sling trick so that when he fixed the rope with a clove hitch; the two metal wedges would share the load.

He ran the lead end of the rope through a figure eight that was attached to his climbing harness. He let the rope drop down the cliff face, allowing him to feed line through the figure eight as he needed it. Musaiyib made his way across the rock face, adding protection as he progressed – clipping his rope into stoppers he'd wedged into cracks. He continued in this fashion until he reached a distinctive fracture. This was where he had hidden the seals. He had placed them in canister, made out of PCV pipe, that he had painted a greenish-gray to blend with the lichen-colored rocks. The canister was at the bottom of the fracture, about twenty-five feet below the cliff face. He still had plenty of rope. He wedged in two more stoppers at the fracture's mouth, clipped carabiners onto them, and ran the rope through the carabiners. He tested the hold again, and, when he was satisfied, he dropped the remainder of the rope into the fracture, and disappeared from sight. Either he had no idea there were others on the cliff face, or he assumed that they were climbers like himself.

Teal and Niles had reached the point where Musaiyib had begun using the rope. Teal told Niles to stay there and hold off the *villains*. As strong and fearless as Niles was, he just didn't have the skill to move across this last stretch. Niles was relieved by Teal's reading of the situation. Gunfights were something Niles understood, but edging and crimping were not.

* * *

The *villains* had cleared the final erosion trench and were now out on the open rock, about fifty yards down the crevice that led up to the ledge. King was in the lead. Even though he left Nepal when he was two years old, he seemed to be genetically predisposed to rock climbing, not unlike the mountain goats that lived in Glacier. Barlow and Bosheers weren't far behind, though.

"Where are you, Mick?" said Niles into the sat phone strapped on his chest.

"I'm just coming around a narrow ridge. Ah, now I can see them. They're about two hundred yards above me," said Keagan.

"Well, get up as high as you can, but you need to set up soon. We're about to have a gunfight on open rock, and there's not much to hide behind here. Remember, these guys were combat soldiers, too. Musaiyib has gone down into a fracture, and Teal is making his way over there. I'm by myself here."

Keagan pushed himself as hard as he safely could. Finally, he realized he had to stop and set up. The *villains* were gaining on Niles, and he had to quickly lower his heart rate. He found a table rock that was reasonably level. He undid the sling that held the .460 Magnum to his back, telescoped the bi-pod legs, locked them into position, got his breathing under control, and looked through the Leopold scope, adjusting it to eight power. Just as the *villains* came into view, he heard shooting through his sat phone.

"You ready yet, Mick? I'm in a bit of a spot here."

"Fuck, I forget whether I'm supposed to aim higher or lower when shooting uphill."

"Lower."

Keagan sighted on King, who was in the lead, but then King wasn't there anymore. He moved over to Bosheers

"Any time now, Mick." said Niles into the sat phone.

Keagan squeezed off a shot. He was more than 250 yards away and shooting at a forty degree angle. The 200-grain ballistic tip SST bullet struck at Bosheers' feet.

"Too low, Mick."

Keagan adjusted his hold and squeezed off another shot. Bosheers disappeared.

"Much better."

While he re-adjusted, Keagan could see bullet strikes in front of and around Niles. He sighted on Barlow, and then he was gone from sight.

Musaiyib heard the shooting, especially the three big booms that sounded more like bomb explosions than gunshots, but he knew he couldn't stay in the fracture. The rope led right to him and if someone cut it, he'd probably be stuck there. After running through his possible choices, he realized there was only one. He climbed out. When he got to the fracture's mouth, Teal greeted him by name, pointing his Camp Perry Colt .45 at his face.

"You have some things that don't belong to you; we want them."

"Or, what?" said Musaiyib. "You'll torture me, then shoot me like you did my friend Awwal? Maybe I'll throw them down the cliff face."

"That wasn't us, Musaiyib," said Teal. "That was the three men that were following you that my friends just shot off this cliff face. They're also the same ones who killed Maloaf. I'm with a team that recovers stolen art and antiquities. We've been following you since May. You're not going to keep the cylinder seals. You better face that fact. And if you throw that canister off this cliff face, I'll cut the rope and let you drop to the bottom of the fracture, which looks deep enough to break your legs but not kill you. You will, however, die of thirst and starvation after a great deal of suffering. But, if you hand over the seals, you're free to go. Your choice."

"That's what you say, but why should I trust you?"

"Because, Musaiyib, you don't have any other smart choices" said Teal. "To get off this mountain, you've got to come passed me. And, in case you haven't noticed, I'm the one with the gun."

Musaiyib, mentally skimmed through all the events of the last eight years that were connected to the seals: stealing them, hiding them, patiently biding his time for a chance to sell them, Awwal's murder, fleeing to Canada, hiding them in this remote place, waiting another three years, the death of his neighbors, and all the people who must have been after him. Then, he started laughing. After some minutes, he calmed himself, handed the canister to Teal, and hoisted himself up onto the lip of the fracture. Teal edged back a few yards along the safety line, unscrewed the canister lid, and saw the seals inside.

"I got 'em," he yelled over to Niles, holding up the canister. Niles relayed the message to Keagan.

"Good, now let's get off this mountain," came back Keagan's directive.

"What about me?" Musaiyib asked Teal.

"Like I said, you're free to go."

"Free to go," Musaiyib repeated and again broke into uncontrollable peals of laughter over the humorous ways of Allah. Teal left him there, still gripped in laughter, clinging to his climbing rope on the lip of the fissure, and made his way over to Niles, who didn't seem displeased at all that he could get off this rock slab.

Thirty-Six

Teal and Niles made their way over to the chimney where Keagan was waiting for them. Niles showed them the seals. Keagan examined him. They were very old and, if not beautiful, had an allure of moment about them. Keagan handed the canister back to Niles and gave Teal the .460 XVR. He knew better than to try to get either item through customs. They had arranged to meet in two days just below the border at the Chief Mountain parking lot.

* * *

While not elite law enforcement officers or Special Forces, the rangers didn't entirely buy Lollard's story about the injuries his friends suffered. However, when Homeland Security called at the behest of the CIA, they dropped their inquiries.

* * *

Keagan and Kelly managed to make the last sailing at the Goat Haunt dock. The rangers asked them where they had been and if they had heard any shots. Keagan said he had heard something but thought it might have been boulders breaking away from a cliff.

Sound traveled far in the outdoors, especially across water and open spaces like cliff faces, but mountains rerouted sound waves, so the rangers hadn't heard the 9mms that the *villains* fired at Teal and Niles. Nor did they hear Niles' .357 Magnum. But they did hear three very loud booms. And so, they were asking everyone who came out of the woods about the noises.

What the rangers learned, was what police generally learned when they questioned witnesses to a crime scene or an accident. There were almost as many versions of what had happened as there were witnesses.

Keagan and Kelly stayed two nights in the Prince of Wales Hotel again. They felt guilty because Niles and Teal were bivouacking in the woods, but Kelly would make it up to them.

The next day, they cleared Customs after answering only a few routine questions about where they had been and what purchases they had made. Niles and Teal were waiting in the Chief Mountain parking lot. Keagan knew they would be, having called them just before the border crossing.

They drove together to the Loop parking lot, where Niles had left the rental. He gave Keagan the seals, and Teal gave him the .460 Magnum. Kelly told them to spend a few days in the Park on Sinn Féin.

Keagan and Kelly drove to Missoula and spent the night there. They visited a branch outlet of a national outdoor gear retailer, and Keagan bought Kelly a rain jacket, which he had shipped to her at the inn. The clerk told him it would go out with that afternoon's FedEx pickup. Keagan returned in an hour and told the clerk that his wife had changed her mind; she wanted to take the jacket with her. The clerk called the shipping room and Keagan left with the labeled package. Back in their hotel room, Kelly used the hotel's iron to steam open the package and substituted the cylinder seals for the Arc'teryx rain jacket. They left the seals with the hotel for their FedEx pickup and flew out of Missoula early the next morning, arriving in Albany at 9:25 p.m. They were back at *Beyond Good and Evil* by 12:30 a.m. They went directly to Keagan's lake lodge, where he locked the .460 Magnum in the gun vault. He had already cleaned it with a kit he had bought in a Missoula gun shop. He hadn't wanted TSA to find any evidence that the gun had been recently fired. Keagan made them two large drinks. They were both tired from the trip, but were also still wired.

"So what do we do now?" asked Keagan, after he had a long pull on his drink.

"Good question, Mick. I'll have to make some phone calls tomorrow. Then, we'll wait."

July 15th, 2011:

Keagan was at the inn at seven o'clock in the morning, checking on the dining room and the kitchen. Of course, everything was fine. Jimmy the Gimp made sure of that in the dining room, as did Cassie in the kitchen. However, when he was leaving the kitchen, Cassie asked him if she could talk with him after breakfast. Keagan didn't like the sound of that, nor did he like the look in her eyes.

"Everything all right, Cassie? The Gimp isn't getting to you, is he?" asked Keagan.

"No, Mr. Keagan, he's fine. We just need to talk."

Now Keagan knew something was very wrong. Cassie always referred to the Gimp as 'the bigot.'

This is not good, he thought. "Sure, Cassie, I'll either be in my office or in the bar."

Keagan poured himself a pot of coffee and went upstairs to deal with the paperwork that had accumulated in his absence.

Kelly showed up at nine o'clock. They had breakfast in the dining room at Keagan's table.

"Mick, something bothering you?" asked Kelly.

"Yeah, Cassie wants to talk with me after breakfast. I'm worried she's leaving."

"She may want to talk to you for any number of reasons: menu changes, new equipment, renovations, anything."

"When I asked her if the Gimp was getting to her, she said, 'No, he's fine.'"

"Uh, oh."

"Yeah. Did you make your calls?" asked Keagan.

"I did. We've got a wrinkle."

"What kind of wrinkle?" asked Keagan.

"The consensus at Sinn Féin seems to be that the public relations aspect of returning the seals to the Iraqis outweighs the financial benefits," said Kelly.

"So, we just give them back, *gratis*. Is that what you're saying?"

"That was their first position, but then I reminded them of the expenses I incurred and the risks we took. I told them, if they wanted to forego their remuneration that was their decision, but I had a verbal contract with my team, and I'm not reneging on it, nor am I prepared to personally absorb the front money for this project. I also reminded them that the Coalition Forces had set up a reward fund for Iraq's looted artifacts. I told them they needed to tap into that. The price tag on the seals was five million dollars, and that, if they didn't meet it, I was done. They're meeting now to discuss my terms," said Kelly.

"How about I pay your expenses and pay Niles' and Teal's fees, and we call it even?" offered Keagan.

Kelly wistfully smiled at him and sipped her tea.

Keagan met Cassie in the bar after breakfast. They sat at the big table in front of the river-stone fireplace. He asked her if she wanted coffee or a Ting, a Jamaican soft drink she liked that Keagan imported for her.

"No, thank you, Mr. Keagan, I'm fine." Keagan waited. "I'm afraid, Mr. Keagan that I'm going to be giving you notice. I'll be leaving the inn after the fall season." Keagan started to interrupt, but Cassie held him off.

"Please, Mr. Keagan, this is not easy for me, either. You have been very good to me and I love working at the inn. I think I've even gotten to like the Gimp, but I'm lonely and I want a family. There are very few black men in Lake Placid, and the white men don't seem to be open to being with a black woman. It got so bad that, for a time, I even considered Lester, the one they called 'the Molester', until the Gimp won me in a pool game."

"You knew about that?"

"Yes. I was very angry at first, but then I realized why he had done it. I also learned that getting rid of Lester cost the Gimp three thousand dollars. I fetched a pretty good price, don't you think?" Cassie smiled. Cassie had a beautiful smile and was a beautiful woman, but she was right about the pool of available men in the area.

"I'll stay through October 15th; that should give you plenty of time to find a suitable replacement, and I'll be more than happy to train my replacement in the way we do business here at the inn, but my mind is made up."

Cassie stood, and so did Keagan.

He opened his arms and she hugged him. "I'll miss you, Cassie O'Sullivan. You wouldn't consider marrying the Gimp, would you?"

Cassie broke into laughter. "I haven't grown that fond of him, Mr. Keagan."

* * *

The Sumerian cylinder seals arrived two days after Keagan and Kelly had. Niles and Teal returned the next day, and Sinn Féin's answer came the following day. Kelly's expenses had been covered and the team's fees had been paid. Kelly was to bring the seals with her when she flew into Dublin the next day. All arrangements had been made for her, including the border crossing into Canada and customs clearance.

July 20th, 2011:

Keagan drove her to the airport in Montreal, as he always did. It rained most of the way. They had little to say during the trip. Both knew how the other felt. There were only so many times one could say the same thing before it went stale or became palpably painful. They waited together as long as they dared, until Kelly had to leave to go through security and catch her flight. Keagan watched Kelly's flight take off as he always did, and then he drove home in the dark.

Epilogue

Saeed ibn Musaiyib: Musaiyib made his way off the summit of Mount Cleveland and over to West Flattop Mountain, where Niles and Teal had camped their first night in the adventure. He took the same trail down to the Loop parking lot, and from there, he got a ride to Missoula. Rides were easy to get if you were hitchhiking with a backpack in a national park, especially from other backpackers. From there, he made his way to California, where, with the money he had saved scrimping his whole time in Canada, he began to develop software. This time, however, he did it for himself, rather than working for someone else. Musaiyib knew there was a lot of money to be made from designing and writing computer games, and, while there were more than enough games that dealt with shooting down aliens or bad guys, or with saving the world from a cataclysmic event, there were few that dealt with finding lost treasure. Musaiyib, too, became rich doing, vicariously, what Kelly and the team did for real. Soon after he established himself as a very creative game writer, he moved to Orcas Island in the San Juans off the coast of Washington State, where he says his prayers at home and enjoys quiet walks in the rain.

Zare, Karimi, and Sharifi: With the exception of one instance from which he managed to extricate himself safely, Sean Byme held himself together long enough to get out of Waterton Lakes National Park. He delivered the three Takavaran to Lethbridge, where, very late that evening, O'Dea and Mulvahill deposited the three trussed up Takavaran on the lawn of the RCMP barracks. Shortly afterwards, O'Dea made an anonymous call to the Mounties, telling them that the men trussed up on their lawn might bear looking into for some of the murders that had occurred in Montreal earlier that month.

It took the Mounties a while to confirm the story because the H&K P30s that O'Dea reluctantly left with the three were not the guns used in Montreal, but the H&K knives were a good match, and all three had left their fingerprints at the Trailhead. Mac Dowell's report linked them to the murders of Musaiyib's two neighbors.

O'Dea, Mulvahill, and Byme: On their way back to Vancouver, near Stoney Squaw Mountain in Banff National Park, Byme grew impatient with a line a RVs, which he attempted to pass on a blind curve. However, as luck would have it, or, perhaps it was simply the consequence of stupidity, a 1,300 pound bull moose was posing for pictures in the other lane.

Byme totaled the rented van and landed the three of them in the hospital. O'Dea and Mulvahill were treated for multiple bruises and abrasions, and released. They were wearing seatbelts. Byme, of course, was not. He was thrown from the van, bounced off the rock face that lined the road in that section of road and was kicked in the head by the moose in its death throes. In addition to re-breaking his jaw, he suffered a fractured skull and had to remain in the hospital for ten days. When he was released, the Mounties arrested him, and he was awaiting the disposition of the Crown Court, where he faced a $10,000 fine for recklessly causing the death of wildlife.

Barlow, Bosheers, and King: Three weeks after their falls, some climbers found the bodies of Barlow and Bosheers. When the rangers came out to investigate the scene, they also found King's remains. He hadn't fallen quite as far as the others, perhaps because he was smaller. But even Barlow and Bosheers hadn't fallen all the way to the base of the cliff face. The human body had too many angles to it to bounce and roll so far down. Still, a fall of over fifteen hundred feet did a great deal of damage to the human body.

Moreover, the climbers weren't the first ones to find them. The first was a mountain lion and her cubs, followed by eagles, coyotes, foxes, and ants. There was, however, enough tissue and fabric left on their bones to tell the rangers that they hadn't died that long ago. The fall itself would have been enough to hide the actual cause of death, and the critters that had dined on them made identification impossible. There was no need for an autopsy, because they had obviously died of injuries sustained falling from a great height. Also, there weren't all that many remains to autopsy. Had there been some, however, the pathologist would not have been able to determine they had been shot. Niles took out King with a through-and-through neck shot, and while both Keagan's shots were body shots, a hit anywhere in the human body with a .460 S&W Magnum, unless the victim was a Jabba the hut lookalike, was almost always a through-and-through.

The three were, however, identified from dental records. When the rangers found the Khukuri still in its neck scabbard on King's remains, they grew suspicious. They might never have made the connection if Zare, Karimi, and Sharifi hadn't already been tied to three of the four Montreal murders. They forwarded details of the *villains'* deaths to the Mounties, who, when they learned that the three had died at approximately the same time as when they found the three Takavaran trussed up on their lawn, they – in turn – forwarded the file to Detective Inspector Duclos in Montreal, who had found Barlow's fingerprints on Maloaf's identification cards. Moreover, King's Khukuri bore out Esterbridge's theory that it was the weapon used to torture and murder Maloaf.

Akbari and Shaker-Doust: They did not go back to rescue their comrades. While Akbari was busy with the rangers, taking the rangers' uniform shirts, packs, sat phone, weapons, wallets, and boots, Shaker-Doust took the ranger's pistol that Akbari had placed in his waistband at the small of his back.

When Akbari asked him what he was doing, Shaker-Doust told him that he believed that the Colonel and the others had been captured, but even if they hadn't been, he was not going back for them. He told him that he was done.

When Akbari demanded to know how he could abandon his comrades, Shaker-Doust told him that, just before they boarded their plane in Montreal, he had seen a news report about three murders that took place near Musaiyib's neighborhood. The newswoman said that all three victims were linked to Salar Wusaivid. Shaker-Doust reminded Akbari that the victims were civilians, and that he didn't join Takavar to kill innocent people and hunt for treasure. The whole project was political, not military. In short, it was an insult to their training.

He gave Akbari the option of going back to look for the three others, but told him he would not be joining him, and if he tried to stop him, even though they had been friends, he'd kill him. It didn't take Akbari long to make his decision.

They made their way back to the Loop parking lot where, after carefully determining that their rental car hadn't been staked out, they drove to Los Angeles.

Shaker-Doust became a very successful security consultant for the movie industry. Akbari is his vice-president in charge of operations. Not only did they pose no threat to American security, but both were reveling in American materialism.

Major General Bandari: Major General Bandari died in an unexplained auto accident in Tehran.

Hap Larson: The Watch Commander of the Kalispell Ranger Station was correct in his assessment of screwing up the extraction and containment of two Takavaran. At first, it seemed that his superiors in the National Park Service were not going to discipline him. After all, he didn't let them escape. But just as things were winding down for the 2011 season at Glacier National Park, he received his transfer orders.

Larson was re-assigned to Gates of the Arctic National Park, where he was responsible for monitoring the park's Muskox herd. He didn't work out of any fixed base because Muskoxen migrated.

Gates of the Arctic was also a very protein-rich habitat because of the abundance of mosquitoes. The park was so rich in this protein source that the Arctic Tern traveled eleven thousand miles just to feed on them. Millions of other birds joined the terns in their feeding frenzy. As soon as summer broke, Larson reported that the supply side of the ecological equation far outstripped the demand side. Since the National Park Service had denied his request for transfer, he had requested more birds. So far, his superiors hadn't seen fit to honor that request either.

Claude C. Dodge: Dodge kept close tabs on Barlow. He knew Barlow's story was bullshit. After he looked into it, he knew about the looting, Awwal's murder, Maloaf's murder, Musaiyib's reservation on the *International*, and his reservation at Kootenai Lakes. He had even accurately guessed where Musaiyib had hidden the cylinder seals.

When he learned about Waterton Lakes National Park and Musaiyib's early departure from Montreal, he sent a team of five of his best operatives to relieve Barlow and his friends of the cylinder seals they took from Musaiyib when they found him. Dodge's team, however, had been unable to make the 10:00 a.m. sailing of the *International*, even though Dodge had gotten them tickets for it. As they were approaching Waterton, a van – for no apparent reason – swerved into their lane, forcing them off the road and down onto a wetland formed by the outflow of Waterton Lake.

The driver of the van seemed to think it was their fault that he had arrived in their lane, and flipped them the bird before getting back where he should have been.

Roth, Kennedy, and Wade: After surgeries and significant physical therapy, Roth and Kennedy made full recoveries, except for slight limps. However, their injuries were enough to qualify them for full pensions, which both opted for. Roth started a sailing school on Sanibel Island.

When Wade's hitch was up, he handed in his papers. He and Kennedy began to operate a very successful club that catered to yuppies in Hoboken, New Jersey.

Ian Lollard: Socko was reassigned to Unit 22 of the SAS. Every once in a while, when the unit got together for drinks and *Who Dares, Wins* stories, Socko sat back, smiled, enjoyed his pint, and remembered when he met an SAS legend whose name they were warned against ever mentioning. His mates often wondered what he was smiling about and why he didn't share his stories with them, especially since he was the best of their unit.